THE TIDES
OF SLIGO

THE TIDES
OF SLIGO

L. G. SHREVE

A
Joan
Kahn
BOOK

ST. MARTIN'S PRESS
NEW YORK

Other than well-known public figures, whose places in the games of nations bring them within the scope of the scenario of this novel, the characters are entirely fictional. While the story is imaginary, everything in this book was suggested by something that did occur, or could have, in the real-life arena of espionage or secret operations.

Design by Robert Bull Design

Library of Congress Cataloging-in-Publication Data

Shreve, L. G.
    The Tides of Sligo.

    "A Joan Kahn book."
    I. Title.
PS3569.H72T5   1989   813'.54   88-29882
ISBN 0-312-02655-2

First Edition

10 9 8 7 6 5 4 3 2 1

As flies to wanton boys are we to the gods;
They kill us for their sport.

—William Shakespeare, *King Lear*

THE PRINCIPAL PLAYERS

Mark Raven An Irish-American author living and writing in County Sligo, the Republic of Ireland

Deidre O'Brien A native-born Irish woman and political activist; winner of the Nobel Peace Prize

Brigadier Ian MacKenzie Head of Section IX, MI-5, British Intelligence

Major Peter Lindsay His principal deputy

Thomas Fereyes Detective Chief Superintendent, Metropolitan Police, Scotland Yard

Captain Evelyn Sinclair Wiggins Commanding HMS *Taurus*, a British submarine

Commander Geoffrey Castlewood His executive officer

Captain First Rank Anatoly Bereznoy Commanding the *Novosibirsk*, a Soviet submarine

Viktor Soroshkin Another Soviet naval officer

Nikolai Alexandr Burdin and

Sergei Petrovskiy Career officers in the KGB, the *Komitet Gosudarstvennoi Bezopasnosti*, the Soviet Committee for State Security

Hans Bettelmans A man of indeterminate origin and hidden purpose

Saul Ben-Udris Mission chief in London for the Mossad, the Israeli intelligence service

Michael Francis O'Farrell A member of the Provisional Wing of the Irish Republican Army

Renée Koulatsos An itinerant Gypsy

Tim Costello Keeper of the Corkscrew, a Belfast bar frequented by members of the IRA

Margaret Thatcher Prime Minister of Britain

Menachem Begin Prime Minister of Israel

Colonel Muammar el-Qaddafi Military dictator of Libya and linchpin in the world terrorist network

ACKNOWLEDGMENTS

The author gratefully acknowledges significant help from the following individuals in writing this book. While none of the information received was classified, some was technical and if not profound, well beyond the ken of this essentially land-locked person. If any of it has been misinterpreted in transit, the fault lies with me, not with the originators.

Mr. John Richmond-Gale-Braddyll, Engineering Manager, the Armstrong-Vickers Shipbuilding Group, Barrow-in-Furness, Cumbria, England, Retired;

the late Mr. F. E. Dodman, Deputy Director of Public Relations (Navy), British Ministry of Defence, London;

Commander T. J. K. Sloane, Royal Navy, and Lieutenant Jason Steinman, Royal Navy, of the same office;

Admiral Kinnaird R. McKee, United States Navy;

and last but of equal importance, to Catharine Carton Smith, who provided information on an isolated area of the Republic of Ireland not readily available. My thanks to all of them.

L. G. Shreve
Baltimore
October 1988

SLIGO BAY

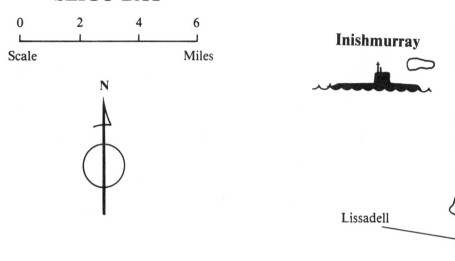

Scale — 0　2　4　6 — Miles

N

Inishmurray

Lissadell

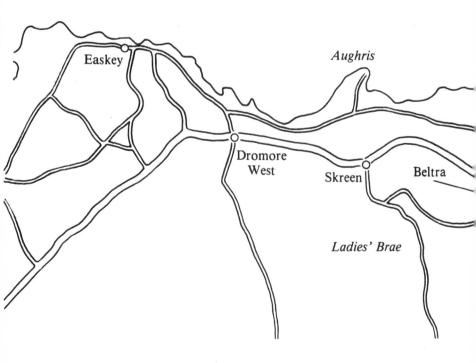

Easkey

Aughris

Dromore
West

Skreen

Beltra

Ladies' Brae

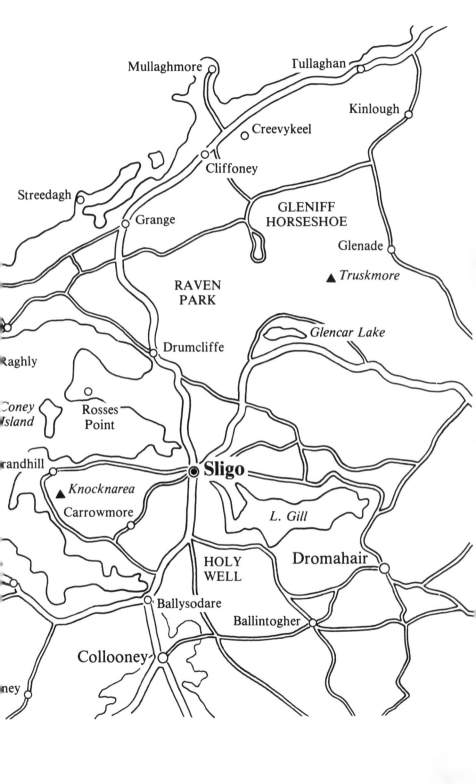

P R O L O G U E

NORTHERN IRELAND
THE SUMMER OF 1979

In the summer of 1979 Northern Ireland was a tinderbox. The soft Irish air tasted of violence and carried the scent of murder. A land that had heard the footsteps of Celts and Gaels and Vikings now listened for the footfall of the conspirators, who alone knew when and how the explosion would come. The ticking of the bomb began when the six northern counties that comprise Ulster, as Northern Ireland is called by its overwhelming Protestant majority, were carved out of Ireland in 1920 when the Republic of Ireland was created, these northern counties would remain under British rule. Ulster's southern border is an anomaly, wandering irregularly from Carlingford Lough on the Irish Sea to Lough Foyle on the north, leaving County Donegal as part of the Republic and all but stranded to the west. Along this border edginess has replaced serenity and there are few calm moments.

Patrolling British soldiers call the rolling green hills and stone hedgerows of South Armagh "Bandit Country," and the helicopter pad at Bessbrook the "Bessbrook International Heliport," with reason. There is a war going on. The sector is fifty-four miles long and includes forty-three border crossings. On any given day groups of guardsmen in camouflage uniforms with greasepaint on their faces will assemble at the pad, waiting for a helicopter to take them out. A Gazelle, the French helicopter used for reconnaissance, swoops low over the countryside to avoid being brought down by an Irish Republican Army rocket.

* * *

At Crossmaglen, a border town in the South Armagh district, a Saracen, the personnel carrier used extensively by the British, comes to a halt just before reaching a checkpoint. The Saracen's paint is blistered from numerous attacks by Molotov cocktails. Six guardsmen, the black tail ribbons of their Glengarry caps whipping in the wind, sit three abreast in the open port, weapons pointing up. They are the relief for the sentries manning the checkpoint around the clock. "Stop your vehicle, cut the motor, and dismount. Then stay exactly where you are." The voice, in crisp, public-school English, echoes from a loudhailer. The helmeted lieutenant, fresh out of Sandhurst and newly assigned to the Coldstream Guards, adjusts his flak-jacket, then approaches whatever car or truck has stopped at the checkpoint. He wants a closer look. Arms and personnel are the objects of his search, and suspicious car numbers are radioed to headquarters in Belfast for a computer check.

Most of the time the area is a quiet and peaceful one, where the small cottages of the Catholic inhabitants often fly the orange, white, and green tricolor of the Republic of Ireland. Yet this land of browsing cows and meadows fed by gurgling streams often erupts in violence, then swallows the bloody debris as effortlessly as the ocean engulfs a stricken ship. For it is here that the Provisionals of the Irish Republican Army—outlawed on both sides of the border—are prone to strike, determined to wrest Northern Ireland from British rule and reunite the Protestant-dominated province with the predominantly Catholic Republic of Ireland.

In Belfast, behind the barbed wire that held the city in its prickly embrace, life imposed a special burden on its inhabitants, a kind of depression induced by the ravaged environment. Burned-out buildings and bombed-out stores were everywhere, and the streets of Republican areas were virtually paved with broken glass. There was the indignity of the ritual frisk as one entered the center of town at Donegal Square, any large hotel, public building, or train station. British troops patrolled like the occupiers they were, in green battle kit, their weapons at the ready. "Remember 1690" the whitewashed gable-ends of the Shankill Road told the Protestants, and the Catholics of the neighboring Falls Road were exhorted to "Remember 1916." Worse than the physical evidence of the conflict was the dispiriting knowledge that Belfast was dying at its core. Like figures in a bad dream Belfastians moved through the littered landscape dragging their collapsed possibilities behind them.

Yet amidst Northern Ireland's turmoil, there were voices of moderation persistent and clear. Principally they were those of Jerry Fitt, a prominent Irish Catholic member of the British Parliament, and Deirdre O'Brien, an Irish Catholic widow and cofounder with another Irish widow, a Protestant, of Peaceful Means, an organization dedicated to putting an end to the violence. But explaining the Irish to the English or the English to the Irish has always been difficult and seems to be rooted in the same old cliche: The Irish never forget and the English never remember. The antagonists, while homicidally despising each other, are also suicidal blood brothers in an endless blood feud. Neither side can claim the moral high ground and it seems neither side can win.

In Westminster, Mrs. Thatcher and the British government watched and waited, at once determined to protect the lives of those who live in the North and work for a modus vivendi between the belligerent factions. A system of home rule agreed upon by Catholics and Protestants alike would deprive the IRA of much of its legitimacy among Northern Catholics, as well as alleviate the costly administrative burden imposed by it. Astute observers believed that it is not the British who prevent a united Ireland, but the Ulster Protestants, abetted by the Catholic majority in the Republic, which wants no part of them. Similarly the government of the Republic did not want to annex the Catholic sectors of Ulster, even if this could be done peacefully. The Catholics of Northern Ireland were largely unemployed and lived off England's welfare state. They would be an economic burden to the south.

In Dublin, where the Republican government supports the British initiative, home rule for Ulster is greatly desired for reasons paralleling those in Westminster: It could help undercut the IRA and reduce Dublin's high expenditure for security. But more important for the Republic, home rule—or more modestly, an agreement by Ulster's Catholics and Protestants to live together without bashing each other—would put the reconciliation of Northern Ireland with the south back on its historical course. The Dublin government adheres to this line despite knowledge that the long-term objectives of the "Provisionals" of the IRA include a coup d'état, its violent overthrow and the establishment of an all-Ireland socialist state.

And in that summer of 1979 Lord Mountbatten of Burma, with members of his family, came to Classiebawn Castle overlooking Sligo Bay in the Republic's County Sligo, a scant twenty miles from the troublesome border with Northern Ireland, for an accustomed annual holiday. Concerned friends had warned that the atmosphere was highly charged. The warnings went unheeded.

I am the resurrection and the life, saith the Lord; he that believeth in me, though he were dead, yet shall he live; and whosoever liveth and believeth in me shall never die.

It was no ordinary funeral. The words, intoned by the Archbishop of Canterbury, the Most Reverend F. Donald Coggan, were the first as the hour-long ecumenical service got under way. Ten days earlier the world had been shocked by the death of the man so many were now remembering, his boat blown up by the Irish Republican Army as it left the harbor at Mullaghmore, in Sligo Bay. Bareheaded young sailors had carried the heavy oak coffin into Westminster Abbey, where Queen Elizabeth and the rest of the royal family waited with two thousand others. Greeted by the fanfare "Supreme Commander," played by trumpeters of the Royal Marines, the coffin was carried slowly up the center aisle of the 900-year-old abbey and placed before the high altar on a blue-draped catafalque, an amber candle flickering gently at each corner.

Out of the deep have I called unto thee, O Lord; Lord, hear my voice.

Five princes, led by the Prince of Wales and Prince Philip, their faces plainly showing their sorrow, had followed the coffin—borne on the same gun carriage used for the earlier state funerals of Kings Edward VII, George V, and George VI, and now drawn by 118 sailors from the Royal Navy—through streets packed ten deep with Britons, most grieving but some simply curious, on the three-quarter-mile route of the procession from Saint James Palace to Westminster Abbey. Throughout the congregation there were flashes of army scarlet, but navy blue dominated. In a clear, composed voice Prince Charles, in naval full dress, read the lesson from Psalm 107, his last tribute to Albert Louis Victor Mountbatten, born Battenburg, Earl Mountbatten of Burma, for fifty-two of his seventy-nine years an officer in the Royal Navy, Admiral of the Fleet, and Queen Victoria's last surviving great-grandson, a man whom Prince Charles called "Uncle Dickie."

They that go down to the sea in ships . . . these men see the works of the Lord and his wonders in the deep . . . and so he bringeth them unto their desired haven.

Light years away in attitudes but only 327 miles to the northwest of London, four men sat in a locked, smoke-filled room in the rear of an Irish pub watching the procession on television. They were in Lisburn, a few miles south of Belfast. Two had participated in the planning when the *Shadow V*, Mountbatten's fishing boat, had been blown up, putting a violent end to his life and killing also the Dowager Lady Brabourne, mother of his son-in-law, Mountbatten's grandson, Nicholas Knatchbull, and Paul Maxwell, a local boy. For more than half an hour not a word had been spoken. All were drinking beer. No sound, other than that coming from the television, broke the pervasive silence.

As Prince Charles and the Duke of Edinburgh passed in front of the screen, Frank Fitzsimmons, assistant chief of brigade staff, 2nd Provisional Brigade, Irish Republican Army, spoke up.

"Fookin' Brits. You're next, Charley me boy."

"Shut up, Frank." Though spoken in hardly more than a whisper, the voice was hard. It belonged to Nolan O'Rourke, brigade commander. The others looked at him, but said nothing. In another ten minutes the procession was over. O'Rourke switched off the television and left by the back door, closing it behind him without another word. He got on a bicycle and pedaled away northward. The others followed at intervals of from two to five minutes, the next two also on bikes. The last—an American-born Irishman called Mike O'Farrell—rumbled off in an old Vauxhall with a faulty muffler.

As the poignant notes of "Last Post and Reveille" echoed through the galleries of the ancient abbey, the congregation stood to join in singing "Eternal Father Strong to Save," the international naval hymn. The abbey bells began to peal as the coffin, carried from the high altar by the naval honor guard, reached the door and the dazzling September sun where the army—the Life Guards, now mechanized for field service—took over. Placed on a Land Rover and escorted by six armored reconnaissance cars, the coffin was driven to Waterloo Station for a ninety-mile trip by rail.

The state funeral, rivaling in pomp and pageantry that of the Duke of Wellington in 1852 and that of Sir Winston Churchill in 1965, was over. Lord Mountbatten was going home to be buried at Romsey, the family estate in Hampshire where, in accordance with his expressed wish, his body would face the sea.

Outside the abbey, unnoticed by all but two detectives from Scotland Yard who never took their eyes off him, Mark Raven had watched the unfolding panoply with total absorption. Now he began the slow process of detaching himself from the mostly quiet multitude to make his way back to his club. No tears had dampened his eyes, but the inner compulsion that had brought him here still possessed him. From a vantage point in Parliament Square, close to the statue of Sir Winston, he had waited for hours before the slowly moving cortege reached the great west door of the abbey. All along the procession route the insistent booms of throbbing, pace-setting bass drums, draped in black, had punctuated the funeral marches. Raven had watched as the coffin was manuevered into the abbey, the almost unearthly silence broken only by the measured tread of the sailors' boots and the far-away cannonading of guns along the Thames embankment, fired in salute.

For part of each year he had been a neighbor of the man whose funeral he had just witnessed. He was little more than an acquaintance, having talked with Mountbatten only once, and that just three weeks ago, but the violent death had brought to a traumatic end a phase of Raven's life that he now looked back upon with bitter regret, feeling an almost personal responsibility for the carnage just off the harbor at Mullaghmore ten days ago.

That brief encounter had been as pleasant as it had been unexpected. En route to the village hardware store Mark had just pulled into the parking area above and behind Mullaghmore's walled harbor when he saw Lord Mountbatten, accompanied by two young boys, walking up the stone steps leading to the grassy plot adjacent to where he was parked. This was the first time he had seen him since the previous August, so, motivated by curiosity, he lingered for a better look. To his intense surprise Mountbatten caught his eye and waved to him. Although thinking he had been mistaken for someone else, Mark waved back. Then Mountbatten walked over to him and put out his hand.

"I'm Louis Mountbatten. You're Mark Raven, aren't you? Forgive me if I'm intruding, but I had dinner with David and Evangeline Bruce in London a fortnight ago and they told me that you were a friend of theirs and lived somewhere close to Classiebawn. David also told me that you were one of those Jedburgh fellows. Anybody who put his life on the line the way you chaps did, and willingly, has my unbounded admiration."

In the middle of the ensuing handshake, and before Mark had the opportunity to respond, Mountbatten continued. "These are my grandsons, Philip and Nicholas Knatchbull. Boys, this is Mr. Mark Raven, an American writer who lives near here. Moreover he's a genuine war hero who parachuted into France a number of times to work with the French Resistance in disrupting the German advance to the Normandy beaches."

"Hello, Philip. Hello, Nicholas," replied Mark, thrusting out a hand to each. "Lord Mountbatten, you flatter me. Yes, I'm Mark Raven, but I'm no war hero. I was lucky, that's all. I'm delighted and honored to meet you, sir, having been an admirer of yours for many years. The Bruces are indeed good friends of mine. In addition to them we have at least one other mutual friend, Joe Bryan, who visited me a month ago here at Raven Park. He told me then that he had had a long session with you at Broadlands."

"Ah, yes—Bryan. A very attractive and witty chap, and like you a writer. He's doing a book on the Windsors. That's why he came down to Hampshire to see me. I must say, Raven, you do look like your pictures. Evangeline sent me your last book. It has you on the dust jacket."

"That's a nasty habit I can't seem to get my publisher to abolish," parried Mark. "Despite that handicap it's selling well—enough to keep body and soul together."

Mountbatten chuckled. "I have that trouble myself. My mug gets smeared all over the place. Well, Raven, I'm glad we've met. We've got to trot along but I'll have one of my daughters, Patricia or Pamela, whoever's playing hostess at Classiebawn at the time, call you to invite you over for dinner."

"Nothing would give me greater pleasure, sir—and it would be a great honor."

"Come along, boys. We must be off. Cheerio."

An easy guy with a down-to-earth manner, thought Mark, as the tall, hatless figure with the tanned face and broad and ready smile moved away, grandsons in tow. *I haven't met many royals, but they ran out of stuffiness when they created that one.*

Now it was over. As Mark turned to lose himself in the fast-dispersing but silent crowd he felt his chest, almost subconsciously. Normally a cheerful, robust man whose muscle tone and vigor belied his age, he noticed again his shortness of breath. And there was a slight twinge of pain, no doubt about it. Was he ill? Something told him it would not go away.

PART ONE

THE
SCHEME

In County Sligo, a part of Ireland not noted for Georgian houses, Raven Park was a rare spectacle. A few miles from the village of Drumcliffe, it sat in the middle of a tract of some six hundred acres. An expansive green park surrounded the house, with not a tree to cast an unwanted shadow across the pebbled courtyard, raked daily to remove the last vestige of automobile tire, wheel of jaunting cart, or droppings of the horse that pulled it. For the first-time visitor, the view of the house came suddenly as an approach was made through an avenue of ancient oaks that stopped abruptly at the edge of woods on either side. Three hundred yards away, shallow steps led to a raised balustrade graced by figures chosen by Capability Brown himself as part of the landscaping scheme so painstakingly laid out in the last half of the eighteenth century. Over a hundred thousand cubic yards of earth had been moved by mule and scoop to create the flat, square plateau upon which Raven Park sat. To the left of the house, one looked down through another avenue to a sizable lake surrounded by a profusion of willows, rhododendron, azaleas, and other flowering shrubs to accent a stone pavilion designed by Henry Holland, the architect of the main house also. The entire project had been one upon which Brown and Holland, his equally talented architect son-in-law, had toiled in absentia, creating by their joint craftsmanship exactly the right touch of eighteenth century elegance so admired by those who had already arrived or whose upward mo-

3

bility, adequately supported by requisite wealth, made fotunes for Brown and Holland as well.

When Mark first saw Raven Park, its appearance was totally different. He was ten years old and stood at his father's side as the latter said, quietly, "There it is, my boy, Raven Park—my patrimony, and yours, except that we no longer own it."

"What's patrimony, pop?"

"Something that you inherit from your father, or should have. It doesn't look like much, does it?"

The forlorn look of neglect had settled in. The courtyard was overgrown with weeds and the rainspouting sagged precipitously, one section heavy with its own weeds—even a small sprouting tree. Plywood covered two of the upper story windows and the panes of another were missing, giving ready access to wind and rain. Pieces of broken statuary lay behind the balustrade. The once well-trimmed lawns surrounding the house were nothing more than overgrown fields. It was a depressing sight.

"I don't see anything here that money won't fix," said Mark. "Let's ask granddad to buy it for us. He seems to have plenty."

"Don't you dare," replied Michael Raven. "He's a kind old man, but not that kind. Besides, your mother wouldn't like living here."

"But I would. Think of all the fun we could have fishing in Lough Erne and the Black Gap. Who built this place, and why haven't you told me more about it?"

"Your great-great-great-grandfather, Josiah Tyndall Raven, built it over two hundred years ago. He made a fortune in the coal trade between Whitehaven, in England, and Irish ports, then lost it by his own extravagances."

"Yeah, I remember now. But I like the looks of this place. I'd love to live here. Who owns it now? Let's find out."

"I made some inquiries before we left home. It's owned

by an Irish lady, a widow who now spends most of her time in the south of France. I got a letter from her solicitors in Dublin the day before we left. It's under contract to be sold to a labor union for use as a nursing home."

That was thirty years ago. Now Raven Park was Mark's. It was inevitable that, free to choose his own way, he would end up in Ireland—not just for the fishing, of which he was passionately fond, but also to meet his needs, ceremonial and otherwise, as a writer. At every stage of his life he had found an appropriate frontier from which to move on to the next. Now it was Raven Park. He lived in a house that he had come to love, reconverting it from the nursing home it had become to the handsome house that it now was, appropriating it and making it his own. It capped his existence as Raven, the writer. In a sense, he invented his own life in Ireland. He had learned to omit many things to create his graceful style, but a salmon stream in Ireland or a Calcutta street came to belong to Raven alone. He seemed able to work out in advance just what he needed from any particular place. He himself was a better, more complex and interesting character than any he invented. All in all it was an unusual house, presided over by an unusual man.

A marriage of twelve years had ended with his move to Ireland, the coup de grace delivered by Mark's determination to occupy Raven Park, which he had already purchased. Attracted by Ireland's free and easy tax laws for those in the creative arts, and by the Irish Immigration Act of 1956, which grants Irish citizenship to anyone with one or both parents born in Ireland, he was sure that his ancestral home would become a spiritual one as well. He found the climate conducive to serious and uninterrupted writing, and removed himself as well from a social life in which he had become an unwilling participant and which he had grown to despise. An apartment in New

5

York and a house on Martha's Vineyard had gone to Allison, his ex-wife, as part of the divorce settlement. Another, in Palm Springs, occupied intermittently when they were not traveling to other fashionable places frequented by the Beautiful People—or those who thought they were—formed the background for a pattern of frenetic activity from which he simply had to remove himself. He had fled first to a remote ranch on the Snake River in Idaho, but Allison, of whom he was genuinely fond, had refused to budge from a life that to her seemed charming and satisfying. Divorce was the inevitable solution, and after the move to Ireland his literary output continued to the point where his novels were commanding advances of a half million dollars or more. He became a saner and better writer, jumping into this more private existence as if it were a lifeboat.

On the same afternoon that Mark first saw Raven Park his father gave him more of his family background. They were still looking at the boarded-up and broken windows.

"Have you ever wondered about your name, Mark—not your Christian name, but your family name?" he said.

"No, not really," replied the boy, "but I like it. I'd hate to be named Bluebird."

Michael Raven laughed. "So would I. I like our name, too—not a usual one in Ireland. Its origin is obscure, but I learned from my father that the earliest known Raven in Ireland was Raphael, whose death in 1654 in Bantry, on Bantry Bay in County Cork, is a matter of parish record. An unsubstantiated legend has this Raphael Raven as the son of a Spanish sailor named Ravel, washed up with scores of others on the south coast of Ireland after the defeat of the Spanish Armada in 1588. In the next generation the name became Raven, by design or otherwise. Ever heard the term *Black Irish?*"

"Sure, but I'm not certain what it means."

"Well, I'll tell you. The term *Black Irish* is often applied to descendants of those Spanish sailors who chose to stay in

Ireland. The black hair of generations of Raven men, as well as Raphael's Christian name, supports this theory. Look at yourself in the mirror sometime."

Mark touched his head, almost involuntarily, then slipped his hand into that of his father.

"Okay, pop. So we're Spaniards. But I wish you'd let me ask granddad to buy this place for us."

"Not for a minute, Mark. And our Spanish blood, if any, has long since disappeared. Now off we go, back to the inn, or we'll be late for dinner—and I'm hungry."

"Me too. I love you, pop, even if you won't let me put the squeeze on granddad. Let's go."

Possessed of an extraordinary mind, Mark Raven seemed to be the perfect representative of his class. He was graduated from Groton in 1939 and Yale in the accelerated, war-time class of 1942, having been deferred from the draft by ROTC enrollment. It is not enough to say simply that he was intelligent. His easy demeanor, instinctive courtesy, and wide acquaintance, accompanied by an awesome memory and a fortifying self-confidence, were already giving him a presence characterized by an early maturity. There were those, however, who felt that his sharp mind was fatally flawed, and that his enthusiasm for ambitious projects crossed the threshold of recklessness. Despite his East Coast schooling, he retained something of the flavor of the American West, particularly when taking his ease at Raven Park. In faded jeans, loafers, and navy blue pull-over sporting the owl emblem of the Bohemian Club—a happy reminder of life in San Francisco—he looked like a relaxed airline pilot on his day off.

It wasn't until after the death of Michael Raven, his actor father, when Mark was eighteen, that he realized how close had been their ties. Easygoing, charming, with dark good looks, Michael Raven had stumbled—quite literally—into the upper reaches of San Francisco society while appearing with the Abbey Players on one of their infrequent appearances in the United States. At an after-theater reception on Nob Hill he had met Grace Hutchinson, who took to him immediately, overlooking the fact that he already had had too much to drink, a state reinforced—smilingly but frequently—with more champagne throughout the evening. In months, he and Grace were married. Her father's early disapproval of her marriage was canceled by Michael's promise that he would quit the Irish stage and try to establish a name in America. Now no longer forced to take any role that came along, he soon did well enough in little theater projects in the San Francisco Bay area to attract the attention not only of New York producers, but those in Hollywood as well. The winter before Mark was sent off to school in New England, Grace and Michael Raven took an apartment on Park Avenue in New York while Michael appeared in Terence Rattigan's *The Winslow Boy.* Mark's younger sister Patricia went to day school in the city. Two years later she died of peritonitis, a blow from which Mark's mother never recovered. She retreated to a sumptuous house in Woodside, south of San Francisco, and never left California again. Michael gave up his acting career entirely to devote his life to his despondent wife and to Mark. An acceptable substitute came to be his performances in the annual extravaganzas staged by the Bohemian Club each July at its expansive grove in Marin County, events that he also helped to produce.

The grip that Roman Catholicism may have had at one time on Mark's Irish ancestors had started to slip in Mark's grandfather's lifetime. A scientist steeped in Darwinism, he viewed the fundamental teachings of the church on Creation, as interpreted in the Book of Genesis, as so much nonsense. The slippage continued in the religious practices of his childen, particularly those of his actor son, Michael. Consequently, when it was suggested that Mark be sent east to Groton, a school following closely the precepts of the Protestant Episcopal Church, there were no objections from his father, who wanted to get the boy away from an overly protective mother. Mark, baptized and reared in the Catholic Church, viewed the matter pragmatically, anxious to follow in the footsteps of a favorite uncle, his mother's brother, who had gone there.

In the years before his father's death, Mark grew very close to him, salmon fishing with him in Alaska, Ireland, and Scotland as well as going for trout in Montana and Idaho. From Michael he inherited a quick wit, a love of the theatrical, and an Irishman's bent for telling tales. Later in life, when Mark's name had become well known, he never hesitated to speak or act or write in accordance with his conscience.

Many who knew Mark, including those who saw him daily, believed his spirits to be always high. With the optimism of the well-adjusted, he saw the physical world as merely an arena, with death a chance misfortune. Despite his love of company, he was a private, self-sufficient person. He could deal with fears and anxieties alone, without demanding sympathy or understanding. Only madmen and robots are without fear, but with no need to be sustained by the approbation of others, his self-sufficiency produced a courage that stood him well in his three-plus years in the United States Army in World War II. Commissioned as a second lieutenant of artillery, he requested parachute training. Accepted, he went through jump school at Bragg, then to the army's language school at Monterey, where his already fluent French became accent-free. Clearly a leader with a noticeable aptitude for languages, he was a standout. No sooner had he been assigned to the 82nd Airborne's artillery brigade than the prowling recruiters from the Office of Strategic Services had him in their sights, and in mid-April 1943, he found himself standing in front of ex-Governor William Vanderbilt of Rhode Island, now a navy captain, in the Washington headquarters of the OSS. Vanderbilt was executive officer, Special Operations Division.

"Sit down, Lieutenant. Let's have a little talk. How much do you know about us?"

"Not much, sir, but I like what I hear."

"Good. Are you in love with the artillery?"

"Not necessarily. I want to serve where I can be of most use."

"Good again. Major Fleming, who talked with you last month at Bragg, reports that you speak idiomatic French. True?"

"So I'm told, sir. Others can judge that better than I."

The interview went well. Despite warnings that his assignment would be dangerous, Raven applied for a transfer to the elite organization. General "Wild Bill" Donovan's clout prevailed, and the transfer was made. Six months later, a week after his promotion to captain, Mark was parachuted into France on the first of four reconnaissance drops. Getting out was another matter—always by submarine and at night. Help from the French Resistance was sometimes lacking, twice because the French themselves got rolled up by the Germans. Evading enemy patrols and one concerted effort to capture him—a quisling French peasant had seen the drop—he learned early to carry a hidden second weapon for emergencies, and even a third, a knife. By the completion of his fourth mission he had killed six men, five German soldiers and one renegade Frenchman who was about to betray him, the latter with a twisted wire garrote. He had learned to shoot to kill and always twice, a painful leg wound having taught him that his targets had the nasty habit of getting one off as they went down. The deaths of faceless others came to mean little to him. The American captain became, in the French underground term, *un ancien,* a soldier not afraid to kill or be killed, one who could survive for a month with four hours' sleep in twenty-four and walk thirty miles toting as much gear as necessary, sometimes in inky darkness.

But it was when he was dropped into south central France in April 1944 for a clandestine mission of three months' duration that Mark gathered the experience that would propel him to almost instant success as a writer. With him was a FANY, an acronym for what the British called their First Aid Nurses Yeomanry, a cover name for Special Operations Executive's female agents, most of whom were drawn from the aristocracy or who had been educated, or had lived for long periods, in France. This one, Sergeant Winifred Lake, was his radio operator, to keep them in touch with Colonel David Bruce, OSS's man at SOE/SO headquarters in London. Mark had become a leader of one of ninety-three inter-Allied "Jedburgh" teams, dispatched to serve as commando officers in the field. Their arrival in uniform was intended to boost the morale of the maquis. His mission, called Operation Houndsworth, was to delay the movement to the Normandy beaches of the German High Command's most formidable division, the 2nd SS Panzer Division, *Das Reich,* held in reserve for a counterattack against the landings on the Channel coast that the Germans felt would surely come in later spring or early summer. It was now in position in and around Montauban, retooling, regrouping, and gathering strength. Raven's assignment was to coordinate the efforts of the *resistants,* the *maquisards,* and *cheminots,* all elements of the French Resistance, the latter specially trained saboteurs who could blow up a railroad bridge or disable a freight yard with minimum amounts of explosives, then disappear into the darkness.

Despite bitter rivalry between local factions motivated by opposing political ideologies, Mark and his crew were able to pull it all together. He embodied the exact spirit that SHAEF had intended to send in with the Jedburghs. He wore his uniform at all times and ordered his subordinates to do the same.

They had brought with them money belts laden with gold sovereigns, Sten guns, gammon bombs, explosives, and most important of all, cigarettes. A maquis with cigarettes retained some cohesion and morale. Without them, he often came close to collapse. Within a few hours of landing—chiefly to stiffen the morale of those he was sent to lead—Raven had mined and blown up an unguarded rail bridge on the Souillac-Brive railway line, where it crossed a canal. This was the first manifestation of a veritable epidemic of demolished bridges, road blocks covered by machine gun fire, and aerial bombardment of targets pinpointed by messages tapped to Baker Street by his FANY. Until the moment of liberation, Raven waged a campaign against the Germans all across the region, attacking trains and convoys, rail links and roads with remorseless energy. Houndsworth was an unqualified success. It took the 2nd SS Panzer Division three weeks to reach Normandy, where its disheartened commander, Brigadenführer Heinz Lammerding, was ordered to fight a rear guard action while retreating back into Germany.

The war over, and with an aptitude honed in college as an editor of the *Yale Daily News,* he wrote *Drop Zone B,* his first novel, in a little more than a year. He took it to Owen Newcombe, an old friend of his father's and now a literary agent with offices on both coasts. It was sold on a first submission. Mark was off and running.

More adept than most in his trade, Mark nevertheless came to realize that writing was a desperate business and that the wellspring of his creativity sometimes ran dry, an unfortunate circumstance that novelists would rather not explore. When this happened he suffered in silence, presenting to the world his usual cheerful demeanor despite the blackness of the mood that had overtaken him. To recover he sought sanity in the mists and rains of rural Ireland, walking or riding around

Raven Park or on the beaches at Rosses Point. At such times many creative persons turn to drink, but Raven found his solace in illusions. The gift of cloaking those illusions in the trappings of reality made him the writer that he was.

But perhaps the most singular aspect in the life of this otherwise law-abiding individual was the fact that he had become, unknowingly, the largest single financial contributor to the coffers of the Provos, the Provisional Wing of the Irish Republican Army. This fact did not long escape the attention of the Royal Ulster Constabulary. The very way in which he had made his last two contributions, substantial withdrawals from his royalties account in a Dublin bank, provided the telltale trail. Traced to a numbered Swiss account in the name of an IRA front, the transactions were duly reported to MI-5 and to Scotland Yard. Moreover the CIA also became aware of them, as ordinary protocol between enforcement agencies insured that such information got to the CIA and the FBI as well, both alert for any signs of the illegal transfer of funds to the IRA. By their own means the Americans were able to match up similar withdrawals by Raven from an account he still maintained in the Wells Fargo Bank in San Francisco—withdrawals made to reconstitute to acceptable levels monies kept in his Dublin account for running expenses.

Two later events pulled him up short, however, making him view the IRA through different eyes. First, he fell in love, completely and wholeheartedly. Second, IRA terrorists, senselessly and cold-bloodedly, murdered his neighbor, Earl Mountbatten of Burma.

DUBLIN
SAINT STEPHEN'S GREEN
JUNE 1979

The voice was what attracted him. Mark stopped to listen, fascinated by the sound and sight of the woman who was speaking to a crowd of people in Saint Stephen's Green. Dierdre O'Brien, of course! The cofounder of Peaceful Means. He recognized at once her much-publicized face and joined the outer fringes of her attentive audience. He was in Dublin on business, not the least of which was to reinforce his Irish bank account after a substantial withdrawal of cash to be turned over to COMMEND, and had taken a short cut through the park on his way back to the Royal Hibernian Hotel.

Indifferent to his own position as a well-known literary figure, he was unimpressed by prominence alone in others. But right away he could see that there was something unique about this O'Brien woman. The instant gloss of celebrity was there, but beyond that it was evident that her listeners felt irradiated by her, by being in her presence. Her voice carried clearly across the heads of those in front of him.

"There is," she was saying, "one particular shade of our feeling today that is unique to those of the Irish nationalist tradition. I refer to our deep anger at the arrogance of the Provisional IRA in committing acts of violence in the name of our tradition, in the name of our aspiration, in the name of our legitimacy. We know that what they are seeking is domination, domination won through the corruption of our nationalist heritage and self-esteem, and through the destruction of our democratic values. I know that Southern Irish who dream of a united

1 4

Ireland are as appalled by the prospect of an IRA victory as are Ulster Protestants. None of us expects Yeats's 'terrible beauty' to spring from the glass- and rubble-strewn streets of Belfast or from the blown-out walls of a London department store."

Deirdre had been born in Derry in 1944, the third of seven children. Her father was unemployed from the end of World War II until his death twenty years later. Crushed by his inability to meet the weight of family responsibilities and assigned by fate to the worst kind of anonymity, he had very little to say to anyone. Every night he sat with his pint or two of ale, staring out the window, down through the endless parade of slums, until he could stand it no longer. Then without a word he would leave the house to walk, sometimes for hours, through the deserted streets.

To augment the slim wages of her mother and the unemployment payments, Deirdre started to work at the age of twelve in the mills at Sion, having gone to Strabane to live with her widowed Aunt Deirdre, her mother's sister, for whom she was named. Fourteen miles to the south of Derry, the grim rowhouses of Strabane seemed to stretch for miles, one side of the cobblestoned street reflecting the other, monochromatic gray clones, their original colors lost under decades of industrial dust. Her memories of her early life were principally those of too many people living in a drab infinity of small houses, where the grit-caked paint seemed constantly to be peeling, like dead skin from a burned body. She remembered, too, lots of pork, including minced butcher's leavings, at once the staple and bane of the poor of that part of County Tyrone. After two years in the mills she returned to school at the urging of her aunt, who recognized her intelligence and natural aptitude for learning. Her aunt had remarried and was able to foster her education.

"It must be clear to all of you that I lay the blame on both sides equally. The Provisional IRA, although brazen and morally self-righteous about its law and order activities, such as they are, is doing nothing that the Ulster Defense Association isn't doing, but it is doing it more often. It is the nature of terrorism to be unappeasable. It is not because she is intransigent that the IRA is afraid of Mrs. Thatcher, but out of fear that she is not. The weakness of terrorism and its unrecoverable moral investment in the destruction of the innocent makes it impossible for those who practice it to deal other than in the absolutes of victory or death. Against such passion, and the movements it inspires, time and belief in one's own values have to be relied upon. If you want peace, work for justice. Join us, support us. There is no other way."

As she finished there was a crackle of applause, which grew to sustained proportions. Cries of "Erin Go Bragh!" and "O'Brien for Taoiseach!" interspersed with other shouts of "Peaceful Means!" came from several quarters. From the base of the statue of Parnell, Deirdre waved in acknowledgment before speaking earnestly to several of those who came forward to drop pound notes or coins into the cap of a young girl, part of the small Peaceful Means entourage. Mark watched as twenty or thirty people contributed. *Ten pounds? Fifteen? Not much for a morning's work,* he thought.

While at Dublin's Trinity College Deirdre decided to go into teaching. After earning degrees in French and modern history she returned to Derry, taught school for six years, became involved in social work, and researched a brilliant master's thesis on the social and economic history of County Tyrone. In November 1974 she was married to Gillian O'Brien, full of Irish charm but struggling to make a living as a chartered surveyor. A scant ten months later the first of two tragic events hit her. She had a troublesome miscarriage from which she had barely recovered when Gil, as everyone called him, was killed when an Aer Lingus flight went down between Dublin and Portugal. She was devastated by this double misfortune. She had loved Gil dearly, but the loss of her child unsettled her almost as much. A year later, as she struggled to rebuild a shattered life, her entrance into politics was almost inadvertent. A nonviolent woman troubled over the fate of her people, and realizing that politics offered the most direct path to social justice, she stood for Stormont and won. Witty, passionate, sometimes profane, and utterly fearless, she had become a nettle in the side of the extremists, Protestant and Catholic alike. Several years after the administration of Northern Ireland was shifted to the British Parliament she became, with Jerry Fitt, a Catholic member of the British Parliament from Catholic West Belfast. Deirdre, Paddy Devlin, and Austin Currie of the Social Democratic Party were voices of moderation in a place torn by bigotry and iconoclasm. Her road was that of negotiation and compromise. No friend of the IRA, she publicly expressed her doubts as to its motives and deplored its violence. Dedicated and unshakable, she was recognized as being beyond personal intimidation.

Three years earlier British soldiers had shot and killed an IRA man driving a getaway car in West Belfast. The dead man's auto, out of control and traveling at a high rate of speed, jumped a curb and smashed into a mother and her three children. Two of the children died instantly, the third the following day. Megan McKinnon, mother of the three, suffered a broken pelvis and two broken legs, fractures that eventually mended—but psychologically the damage was permanent. The deaths sparked a crusade that came to be known as *Modhanna Siochanta,* or Peaceful Means, led by Deirdre O'Brien and Martha Quinlan, the dead children's aunt and a Protestant. The two stood up together and became overnight sensations. Within a few weeks they were leading thousands of Catholics and Protestants in peace marches all over Ireland. By the spring of 1979 Deirdre O'Brien had become the movement's spearhead and chief spokeswoman. She traveled to America seeking funds to further the ends of peace, and there was widespread speculation that she and Martha Quinlan would share the Nobel Peace Prize. The crowds were smaller now, but her compelling voice continued to be raised in the cause of moderation.

The crowd was dispersing. A group of well-wishers surrounded Deirdre and then it too faded away. Mark recognized Martha Quinlan, who went off with a companion after an animated conversation and a warm embrace. The young girl with the cap, money accounted for, took off with a curly-headed youth. Suddenly, from being the center of attraction, Deirdre appeared lonely. She was opening a pack of cigarettes as Mark walked up to introduce himself.

"Mrs. O'Brien?" He couldn't bring himself to use "Ms." He considered it an abomination.

"Indeed. And you? You're a Yank—at least you look and sound like one." She was smiling.

"You're half right—or maybe one-third, considering the fact that I've lived in Ireland for years. I'm Mark Raven. I'm from California but my father was born here in Dublin."

"Aha! A quid says you're the son of Michael Raven, well known to any student of the Abbey Players. You live in County Sligo, do you not now?" There was a graceful lilt to her words. "And a rich one, too, you are. We need money, Mr. Raven. May we count on you?" Laughter lay just below the surface, as if no offense could be taken.

She was an impressive woman of thirty-five with expressive deep blue, almost violet, eyes set off by dark eyelashes. Black hair tied back with a velvet bow crowned an oval face with smooth pale skin and good bone structure—all very pleasing beneath the gleaming hair. He couldn't forget that face, nor the voice: well modulated, middle register, nothing hoarse or raucous, with a touch of something else in it besides Irish—French perhaps. Later, when he got to know her well and learned about her education, he discovered that he was right. The neat gray skirt, white silk blouse, dark stockings, and good shoes accentuated her undeniable attactiveness.

"Tell you what," said Mark. "Have lunch with me and we'll talk about it."

"Then people will talk about us, but if your generosity matches your charm it'll be worth it." This time she laughed openly, but with him, not at him.

As he lit her cigarette she cupped the flame in her hand with long, warm fingers. The sexual touch was such a ploy that he was disappointed until he saw in her eyes that she was welcoming his friendship. Such expressive eyes—enough to make the homeliest girl interesting. This first brief encounter gave him the sense of being momentarily illuminated.

They lunched at The Bailey, one of Dublin's elegant restaurants, just around the corner on Duke Street, over poached salmon and an excellent bottle of Moselle. From its beginning their conversation was charged with a certain magnetism, tender but inquisitive, as if each were trying to breach the wall of the other's inner self. Deirdre found herself recounting her early life with surprising candor, holding back little, priming Mark for equal answers as she talked. Then partly in response to his questions but also prompted by her own dedication to Peaceful Means, she began to talk about the movement and its efforts to neutralize Northern Ireland's bloody struggle.

"Outside of the Catholic ghettos in the north, Mark, there's no real support for the IRA, even in the wider Catholic community. The young Irishmen from the streets of Belfast who form the guts of the Provos feel left out, hurt by fate and nature. So the sense of belonging to an influential, powerful organization gives them a feeling of superiority over the more prosperous people around them. No one should object to the entry of Irish republican nationalism into politics—that's where it belongs. If Sinn Fein, the political branch of the IRA, could rid itself of terrorism and take wholeheartedly to politics, it would deserve the support of American sympathizers. Instead, it must be said, Americans in general don't have a great reputation among the Irish, the prevailing view being that they are extremely naive and dangerously meddlesome. They are seen as loud and insensitive, inquisitors who would rather talk than listen and who treat Ireland, on their high-speed visits, as an extension of Disneyland. You've seen this yourself, because you live here, but to most Irish-Americans the situation takes on its simplest form. They see two groups of people here—the British who don't belong and the Irish who do. Everything would be just fine, they say, if the British would just go back to their own country. But this view fails to take into consideration the Prods of the north who are both British *and* Irish and who have no intention of going anywhere. Their own ayatollah, the Reverend Ian Paisley, never lets them forget this, fomenting as much dissension as the IRA."

"I've heard Paisley speak," interjected Mark. "He's a virtuoso all right. He can play on the emotions of his audience as if he were stroking a Stradivarius."

The restaurant was filling up. Nearby tables were being occupied—people intruding on the privacy of their tête-à-tête. The editor of Dublin's leading daily waved a greeting. Deirdre returned it by a raised hand and nodded smile, without enthusiasm.

"Cheeky bastard. One day he calls us the answer to all of Ireland's problems and the next a bunch of fuzzy-minded intellectuals living in a dream world. If I weren't a good Catholic I'd hope he gets a bad oyster."

Turning back to Mark, she leaned forward in an attitude of intimacy masking the seriousness of her words.

"I'm sorry to denigrate your countrymen, Mark, but you must understand that most American dollars flowing to the IRA, through COMMEND or otherwise, are used to buy the bombs that go off in the garage of the House of Commons or to purchase the guns of Armagh."

It was a jarring note in an otherwise enchanting interlude. It shook him.

"I lead a somewhat isolated life," he replied, "and don't see as many American visitors as you. Sure, I've heard that funds given to COMMEND go for arms for the IRA, but have always brushed such statements aside, choosing not to believe them. Foolishly perhaps, I've considered them as so much propaganda, British or otherwise. Are you sure of this?"

"I know it for a fact, Mark—without the shadow of a doubt. If five percent of all funds raised goes for humanitarian purposes, then I'm the Duchess of Leinster. And how about that name? Did you ever hear such hypocrisy? What, pray tell, is commendable about COMMEND? I must say it's a public relations triumph, and I hate to think of how many well-meaning people of Irish ancestry in the United States have been hoodwinked by it."

Mark said nothing for a moment, then continued. "You know, if it came from anybody but you I still might not believe what you are telling me. Now I'm doubly disturbed, particularly since I've been a contributor to COMMEND—and a generous one. But in the light of what you've said, and since it looks like I've been duped, may I make amends—no play on words intended—by contributing to Peaceful Means?"

"Of course you may. We have so many needs. We're now down to only four paid staff members, working literally for fish and chips money, and our budget is rapidly reaching the vanishing point. All of us will be very grateful."

Mark looked at his watch. "The bank closed twenty minutes ago, but I'll send you a check for five thousand pounds the minute I get home. There'll be more when you want it."

She reached across the table to clasp his hand. "You're wonderfully generous, Mark. How can I possibly thank you? But I'll be even more grateful if you'll stop supporting COMMEND. Believe me, that way you'll be making an even greater contribution to putting an end to this madness than by giving to Peaceful Means."

He thought he saw the beginnings of tears in those expressive eyes. He returned the pressure of her hand.

"I promise. If what you say is true, it's a trade-off I'll gladly make. You're not only a beautiful woman, you're a persuasive one as well."

"That's what I like about you Americans—flattery will get you anywhere. You're not a bad looking lad yourself. Now—what about you? Have you shaken off the sunshine of California for good?"

"The part of California where I come from isn't necessarily all that balmy. But to answer your question, yes, I now consider Ireland—not California—my home. Nothing's easy about writing, but I find it easier here than there."

He talked on, freely, about San Francisco and Idaho, the insane days that he had spent in Hollywood, about Allison and his divorce, about the war and his drops into France. He didn't talk about the future because all of a sudden he thought he saw it differently.

They were lingering over coffee when Deirdre became aware that she had to leave. "Saints alive! Look at the time! I've got to meet Martha in twenty minutes. We're going back to Belfast. If I don't hurry we'll miss our train."

Phone numbers had been exchanged. Downstairs on the sidewalk the mutual reluctance to end this first meeting made it obvious that they wanted more from each other than conversation.

"Come to Raven Park," Mark said, clasping her hand.

"Bring a friend if you must. My intentions may be strictly dishonorable, but we'll mask them in respectability." He was laughing, but they both knew what he meant.

"I'll do that." Deirdre laughed with him. "Maybe a four-legged friend?"

She turned to go. Then in a characteristic gesture she wheeled and hugged him, topping off the embrace with a lingering kiss. Her violet eyes were more communicative but with her lips she said, "I like you, Mark. I'm glad we're no longer strangers. À *bientôt*."

She was gone. His heart pounded and he knew that a new life lay before him.

MARYLAND
FORT GEORGE G. MEADE
14 AUGUST 1979

The British called it Operation Pleiades. Some called it insane, but later changed their minds. The first indication of the deadly game that was to be played half a world away arrived unheralded in an office in a building halfway between Baltimore and Washington.

The trade called it an intercept. It emerged at the headquarters of the National Security Agency at Fort George G. Meade in Maryland on a summer morning that had the NSA staff whistling as they moved from the parking lot into the building.

Several floors above and to the rear of Gatehouse 3, behind a solid steel-gray door replete with warning signs and a cipher lock, lay the center of NSA's worldwide eavesdropping net, and the office of the DDO, chief of signals intelligence. The office was the quintessential black chamber; into it poured the whole spectrum of signals intelligence, from the profound to the merely provocative, from ultrasecret to useless. Here it was sifted and sorted, the electronic driftwood from friendly countries as well as foes, superpowers and micronations.

Among the millions of bits of data that morning, the intercept sprang full blown at exactly 9:23 A.M. on August 14, 1979. It was at that precise moment that Dr. Nate Abramson squinted at the printout and his normally gloomy countenance began to droop even further. Tall, bald, bespectacled, and dour, Abramson received each new message with a decided air of fatality. This one confirmed his own worst fears, and without really thinking about it or knowing why, he stood to read the message a second time. Labeled TOP SECRET/CHEROKEE, it contained data of the highest SIGNINT sensitivity. As he started over it yet again he seemed to feel the pages crackling in his fingers. It was, clearly, trouble.

The decoded intercept was less than an hour old, but for Abramson there was no turning back the clock. It was all spelled out in words that left no room for doubt, or compromise: RPG7 rocket launchers and infrared intensifiers for night fighting. Enough ammunition to supply a battalion and support it in a sustained combat situation. Grenades, of course, concussion, fragmentation, markers. Kalashnikovs, the AK47 Soviet semiautomatic assault rifles that had inflamed the Middle East; a listing of hundreds of them. Reluctantly, he read on. Twenty AM-180 rifles, a recoilless, laser-sighted supergun of Austrian origin that permitted targeting as easy as pointing a flashlight beam. Most alarming of all there were thirty Helvir 20-mm antitank guns with an armor-piercing capability. They were a Finnish product not used by any Western powers.

Abramson put the printout down on his desk and stared at it, no longer seeing it. Millions of dollars of sophisticated weaponry and all spelling out, unequivically, trouble and violence. Nobody could miss it. A key word on the printout was transshipment, and nobody could miss that, either. Abramson sat down again and rubbed his head, a gesture his subordinates had learned to dread, a sure sign of long hours and hard work.

He leaned back in the chair, his frame long enough to allow him to keep his feet flat on the floor. With one hand still on his head he tried to picture the route the intercept had taken. Scooped off the airwaves by an intercept station at Trabzon, a small coastal village in the shadow of the Turkish mountain range of Anadolu Daglari, the intercept had been made only seventy miles from the border of the Soviet Union. Abramson shut his eyes and seemed to see the message passing uncoded through the rhombic array at Vint Hill Farms, that hidden but huge estate ten miles out of Warrenton, Virginia. On that site sophisticated antennae had been sprouting like mushrooms for more than two decades. The message then was fed simultaneously into half a dozen of the banks of giant computers at Fort Meade. Now partially decoded, the intercept passed into the hands of the sorcerers in cryptanalysis. In a matter of hours the whole message, running to three full pages and including crate numbers, dimensions, and weights, was as clear as if it had been written in the next room as part of a training exercise. Which Abramson wished fervently had been the case. But— there were two essential pieces of information missing. To whom was the message directed? And since transshipment was involved, where were the arms going?

Abramson brought his chair forward with the quick, sharp squeak he had never been able to get rid of, and today ignored. He leaned over the message again and tried to remember if anything he had read recently had disturbed him more. He couldn't remember it, if it had. A twenty-year veteran at NSA, he had reached this desk by way of Northwestern University, the United States Navy, and MIT, where he had taken an advanced degree in mathematics. Now he tried to think in the simplest mathematical terms, as a starting point.

No solving an equation without all the elements. He reached for the telephone and punched up the CIA. He was still thinking about the missing data when Lamont came on the line.

"Jack?" He could hear the anxiety in his voice, and tried to lower the intensity level. "Jack, we have an intercept here this morning that's hot—so hot we'd better talk about it personally. My place or yours, and how are you fixed for time?"

There was a moment's hesitation while Lamont checked. Then the answer.

"Yours. I'll come right now. I'm due at the Pentagon for lunch at noon, so I'll hustle. I'm on my way."

Like Abramson, Lamont was a professional, one of the last survivors of the close group that had come into the agency straight from the OSS—a group that would ultimately include two directors, Dick Helms and Bill Colby, as well as three of Lamont's immediate predecessors as deputy director for plans, Frank Wisner, Desmond Fitzgerald, and Tom Karamessines. All three were now dead, two from heart attacks and one by his own hand, all victims of selfless, patriotic burnout.

As Abramson hung up, a subordinate came in and wordlessly placed on the chief's desk a folder carrying the same top secret classification. He flipped it open. Inside was the same intercept. He could tell from the pale blue paper and the boxed numbers in the upper left hand corner that it had come through from GCHQ, Britain's government communications headquarters located on Prior's Road, Cheltenham, in Gloucestershire, eighty-five miles west of London. There was close liaison between the two installations, including regular exchange of personnel. From the boxed numbers Abramson knew that the British had also successfully decoded the intercept.

"So the Brits have it, too," he said, half aloud. He replaced the message in the folder, sealed and initialed the interoffice transmission slip, marked it for the attention of Colonel Colin Ferguson, Royal Signal Corps, the British liaison officer at NSA headquarters, then handed it to the waiting aide, who departed promptly.

By 1979 any Soviet submarine designated by Western naval analysts as belonging to the so-called *Whiskey*-class could most charitably be called obsolete. Based on filched German designs, 240 of them had been built in the 1950s. More than forty had been sold to Moscow's least reliable clients. Too small for attack, when built they were ideal for patrol and reconnaissance missions. Since 1975 Jane's *Fighting Ships* had indicated that the *Whiskey*-class *Severyanka* had been converted to "oceanographic and fishery research." Nothing could be farther from the truth. Stripped and rebuilt, the *Severyanka* had become the principal means by which the Soviets made clandestine delivery of arms and ammunition to its client states and to dissident and terrorist groups around the world. With its crew cut from fifty-four to twenty-five, the extra living space had been bulkheaded to contain the cargoes of death-dealing weapons and ammo now top-loaded through watertight hatches installed on deck. Torpedo tubes had been removed and all other armaments eliminated. In short, it had been turned into an undersea delivery van, cramped and thoroughly uncomfortable. The only concession to creature comfort was an increase in the BTU capacity of the air-conditioning system, due solely to heightened expectations of warm weather deliveries. Its electronic gear had undergone a complete revamping with more emphasis on communications and less on radar, in keeping with its mission. In particular, its radio equipment was upgraded to include the capability for split-second "squirt" transmission or reception, super-compressed messages recorded on large tape drops, later to be slowed down, the signal demodulated and deciphered.

South Yemen had seen the *Severyanka* on more than one

occasion, as had Luanda in Angola. She had picked up arms in Havana and taken them to a rendezvous with dissidents in Nicaragua for further clandestine shipment into El Salvador. West African ports knew her well, as did the Syrians and the Ethiopians. Submerged, and cautiously, she made her way into the Strait of Hormuz to make a beachhead at Bandar ʻAbbās with a cargo of easily concealed handguns for a break-away group of Shiʼite Muslims. Weapons used by the Baader-Meinhof gang had come through her hatches as had grenades used by the Red Brigade of Japan. So successful had been her voyages that some senior Soviet naval officials were on the point of reconsidering the circumstances that had brought her commanding officer, Viktor Soroshkin, to the *Severyanka* in the first place.

Soroshkin was a man with a problem, a shadow over his past of compelling proportions—one that was to grow rather than decrease with the passage of time. Had his seniors, or the KGB, known about the deterioration in his outlook as a loyal Soviet naval officer he would have been summarily shot. The son of one of the Old Guard Bolsheviks who had served as a Red Army commissar in the civil war and who had later held a succession of important party posts, Viktor had been a gifted student and organizer of youth groups. His entry into the Soviet naval academy at Gorky was accomplished without a hitch, not remarkable in the light of the fact that his father's reputation for party loyalty and as a successful administrator had lived on after his death, which occurred when Viktor was just turning sixteen.

Commissioned as a sublieutenant shortly after his twenty-second birthday, Viktor, in accordance with his stated preference, was assigned to the submarine service. His first post was a junior officer aboard another *Whiskey*-class submarine, a sister ship of the *Severyanka*. A Great Russian, as testified by his internal passport, he served honorably and well, moving on to better assignments, and then—after returning to the naval academy for a six-months' course in nuclear propulsion—into nuclear submarines in the early 1970s. Continuing his upward mobility, his last promotion, in 1976, brought him to the rank of captain first rank. Steady, sobersided, and considered utterly reliable, he was given command of the new *Yankee*-class nuclear-propelled *Admiral Razhnikov* upon her launching at Komsomolsk. She was a missile-bearing submarine assigned to patrol the Atlantic coast of the United States, the missiles in her payload able to reach inland as far as the Mississippi River.

But as often happens in life, good fortune deserted him with stunning speed. Late in the afternoon of a rain-swept September day in the same year, off the South Carolina coast, disaster struck. The sub was cruising slowly at a depth of seventy fathoms, unaware of the surface menace of the *Eutaw Springs,* a United States Navy antisubmarine frigate equipped with the most advanced and sophisticated equipment developed at the Johns Hopkins Applied Physics Laboratory and at Cal Tech. The *Admiral Razhnikov*'s propeller became hopelessly entangled with a cable running between the surface vessel and a supersensitive BQR-15 towed-array sonar, designed especially to listen for and locate offshore Soviet submarines. The skipper of the U.S. vessel, guessing correctly what had happened and enjoying every minute of it, radioed fleet headquarters at Norfolk for instructions. As ordered, he activated the self-destruct mode in the listening device, called for aerial surveillance, and returned to his base at Charleston. Some sixteen hours later, as dawn was breaking, U.S. Navy reconnaissance planes took dozens of photographs—some of which appeared in newspapers in both the States and the United Kingdom—clearly showing the *Admiral Razhnikov* wallowing in increasingly heavy seas as a Cuban navy tug attached lines to the hapless sub to tow her to Havana.

Flown in disgrace to Moscow and then transferred to the naval base at Gorky, Captain Soroshkin was held incommunicado in the base prison compound for five months, during which time his mood and his outlook festered. None of his father's old comrades were around to help him. It was like a bad scene from Chekhov. Moreover, in the subsequent court-martial the *zampolit,* the political officer aboard, turned on him, delivering testimony which, while partially true, was so colored by jealousy that it came out black rather than a tattle-tale gray. Convicted of dereliction of duty, criminal negligence, and endangering the lives of his crew, Soroshkin was reduced in grade, denied promotion, and put on half pay for two years. Most observers felt that he was lucky to escape being sent to a gulag, as he would have been were not the Soviet navy in short supply of qualified submariners. It was clear from the tone of the trial that the most damaging evidence against him was the U.S. Navy's photographs, newspaper copies of which were introduced by the prosecution, since they clearly held up to the world's ridicule the Soviet navy's most advanced undersea weapons. Ex-Captain Soroshkin then suffered the further humiliation of being given command of the *Severyanka,* considered by his navy peers to be little more than a floating scrap heap. He had been away from sea duty for almost seven months.

Outwardly Soroshkin was a typical Russian, a little thick in the waist, a bit slow, a bit pedantic. When perturbed he had a habit of rubbing his chin. From beneath dark eyebrows his brown eyes looked askance at the world—they were windows for a mind tuned to science and mathematics but rather naive when it came to humanities. But his appearance was a shell, a carapace masking a soul that was sick with longing for something more, more than the vodka, the whores, and the bouts of incredibly long hours of work in which he immersed himself, to forget. It was Natalya, his captivating cousin Natalya, who had infected him with the virus of disillusionment, stirring him to curiosity about the world beyond the borders. Natalya who loved good wine and western music, decadent Western art and culture, and who had followed her husband into the gulag on a morning so cold he could hear her footsteps crunching in the crushed snow. Soroshkin had been half in love with her himself, and she was gone. But she had planted a seed of desire and a seed of doubt and it was these hidden thoughts that the *zampolit* had somehow sensed; it was the beginning of the growing antagonism between them.

Embittered and depressed, Soroshkin now moved in a world that appeared strangely opaque. Nothing followed logically the hopes and expectations of his early years in the Soviet navy, nothing was what it seemed, no one told quite all the truth, old friends revealed themselves as older enemies, ideology yielded up corruption, and pieties convoluted into blasphemies. He found himself in surroundings that tended toward abstraction, complex, baffling, painful to live in—full always of profound disappointment. Here the only certainty was loss. Moreover he was appalled—not at the mission of his boat, about which he was ambivalent—but at the Spartan, downright dangerous conditions under which he and his crew had to live and operate. And yet he saw no way out. Retirement was two years away, provided he and the *Severyanka* weren't depth-charged into oblivion in the interim. His retired pay, thin at best, would be reduced to reflect the lower rank meted out to him for fouling up on his last assignment. Letters from his wife revealed the widening gap between them. He brooded and waited. But not for long.

In the spring of 1978 there were two governments in Britain: Her Majesty's political government in Westminster, and the permanent government of bureaucrats, whose crucial organ of perception was the secret intelligence service. The recent creation of a supersecret Section IX in MI-5, the counterespionage arm of British intelligence, operating exclusively against the terrorist threat, was about to score an important coup. Through their own sources, the British knew of Soroshkin's punishment and of his assignment as CO of the Soviet's principal clandestine delivery vehicle. They picked up on the situation immediately, and mission chiefs everywhere were alerted to watch for the *Severyanka* and her commanding officer. The target was not the submarine, but Soroshkin himself. Disaffection, rightly judged, will take the opposition to a likely prospect for defection quicker than a killer shark will respond to the sight or smell of blood, human or not.

The payoff came in a small park off Istanbul's Kemal Ataturk Boulevard. The surrealistically azure sky, the sporadic Byzantine and sometimes savage urban landscape, the sudden, stinging colors that accompanied the confrontation of the ancient and the modern, plus the colorless, somewhat heavy sunlight provided the proper backdrop for the culmination of Section IX's efforts. A fragrant, voluptuous Hungarian girl (or so she had presented herself to Soroshkin, promising much but delivering little) introduced him to a self-confessed arms and ammunition merchant named Hans Bettelmans, who claimed to be Dutch. After some initial sparring, Bettelmans produced his passport in confirmation of his identity. It had been forged so skillfully that Bettelmans used it frequently, even when passing through the Netherlands. He wished to know, said Hans, and was willing to pay handsomely for such information, who was getting what and when—in detail. Object: to offer his own wares to fill whatever gaps might remain in the military arsenals of the recipients.

"What is handsome?" Soroshkin was thinking of his meager pension. The conversation was in Russian, which Bettelmans spoke fluently.

"Swiss francs to equal twenty-five hundred rubles a month, deposited regularly to an account that will be opened for you in the Bahnhofstrasse bank in Zurich. More with each delivery manifest turned over to me. To start us off on the friendliest of terms, here's a month's bonus right now." The brown manila envelope contained twenty-five hundred ruble banknotes.

Soroshkin hesitated momentarily, then took it.

"I will need a receipt," said Bettelmans quietly. "Without it I cannot be reimbursed by the manufacturers."

He got it.

"And what will I get for each manifest?"

"What do you need?"

Soroshkin had been doing some mental arithmetic. Ten deliveries, maybe twelve, in the next twenty-four months.

"The same amount—twenty-five hundred rubles for each manifest."

Bettelmans showed no reaction. Quickly, Soroshkin raised the ante. He was under no illusions about what would happen to him if he were caught. "Plus an additional fifteen thousand rubles each year if all goes well."

In a very businesslike manner Bettelmans took out a pocket computer and punched in some numbers. Soroshkin's mind raced ahead. Two years down the road and with luck, the equivalent of a hundred and fifty thousand rubles, maybe more, waiting for him in a Swiss bank. Enough. For that he could put up with the *Severyanka* and all of her attendant problems. Somewhere, somehow, he'd break out. Bettelmans nodded to himself, then looked up.

"No problem—agreed."

"How do we communicate?" Soroshkin's head was spinning.

"Here's a phone number in Amsterdam. Call at any hour, day or night, any day in the week. Identify yourself as Boris. At the other end you will be told that 'Oscar' is speaking. Then you will know that all is well. Leave whatever message you wish. Then mail a copy of the manifest to whatever name and address is given to you. As a precaution, the names and addresses will vary. Remember, dates, numbers, destination, types of weapons—the works."

Soroshkin took the penciled notation as Hans said, "I hardly need tell you to memorize, then destroy the number."

Soroshkin looked at him and smiled. "Don't worry, comrade." The Soviet greeting slipped out, partly from force of habit, partly because of the friendly feeling that Soroshkin was developing for Bettelmans. "I have a good memory."

"Now that we are in agreement," Bettelmans continued, "I will look forward to hearing from you often. The number of your account in the Bahnhofstrasse bank is 435-CCS-67. As a measure of our trust, and to quiet any concerns you may have over your balance there, call them anytime during normal banking hours. Say that Boris is speaking, then give them your account number and you'll be given the information."

Before they parted, Lyskya, the young Hungarian girl whom Soroshkin had found so enticing, embraced him warmly and kissed him with equal ardor on both cheeks, then lingeringly on the lips.

"Will I see you again?" he said.

"I hope so." She squeezed his hand, then turned away with Bettelmans, leaving behind the fragrance of springtime.

Out of sight, Bettelmans patted his breast pocket to see that the wallet containing the receipt signed by Soroshkin was there. It was. MI-5 had the ex-Soviet captain, to be known hereafter to British intelligence as Ashley, firmly in its grip.

Under the ultratight security measures in effect at the National Security Agency, Jack Lamont, deputy director for plans, CIA, the single most important officer responsible for all of the agency's clandestine operations, and to whom all chiefs of station everywhere reported, was stopped at the main entrance. He was known by sight and name to the guard, but nevertheless his ID card, without which he couldn't get into his own headquarters, was routinely inserted into an electronic computerized scanner. Cleared, and with a large plastic badge hung around his neck proclaiming him a visitor, he proceeded at once to Abramson's office. Colonel Ferguson was already there.

"Good morning, Nate. Good morning, Fergy."

"Good morning, O chief of the forces of darkness. You'll have your coffee black as usual, in keeping with your character?"

"Black, as usual, thank you. And all that crap doesn't make me any easier to get along with. Not your cheery greeting, but the article."

Abramson's greeting reflected a reference to Lamont in a recent issue of a left-wing, liberal monthly, castigating the mission and methods of CIA.

"Not to worry," replied Abramson. "Nobody reads all that bullshit except those with a mind-set that an earthquake couldn't change. But on a more interesting and important note, read this." He handed him the intercept.

Lamont read it in silence. "Hell's teeth," he said when finished. "Quite a laundry list."

"At this point, Jack, we know the following," continued Abramson. "The message originated with the Sovs, probably in the Ministry of Defense, and was probably intended for someone in the Arab world. You've undoubtedly noticed that it specifies transshipment. Transshipment to where? My God, did you ever see such stuff? Infrared intensifiers, rocket launchers, thousands of rounds of ammunition, Kalashnikovs of course—that's no surprise—but twenty AM-180 rifles? I thought the Austrians were forbidding their export. Whoever's getting this shipment is readying a big push—a big, big push."

"What comes next, Nate, and what's going to be the distribution on this?" Lamont asked.

3 5

"We can work with the externals of the message, grade of cipher system used, and check for frequency and volume of other follow-up messages. That way, maybe we can learn more. Distribution—State, National Security Agency, CIA, DIA, with requests for related input from any one of them. Could be Central America, you know, or Cuba. But if Cuba, why transshipment for some intermediate point? Makes no sense. What's your suggestion?"

"First of all, a signal to Chief of Station, Vienna, with an urgent request for anything he can tell us about the AM-180 rifles. Secondly a routine, smokehouse inquiry to all stations, Eastern as well as Western Europe, Central and South American, Mediterranean, Caribbean, Far East—across the board. Fergy, got any thoughts?"

Colonel Ferguson, a six-foot-two, mustachioed, motion picture facsimile of a Coldstream Guardsman, which he had once been, and who had served two tours in Northern Ireland in a lesser grade, shook his head.

"Cheltenham's got it, which means that it's been passed to Whitehall and to MI-5. It would be presumptuous for me even to suggest to them what to do."

"Okay, troops. For the moment that seems to be it." Abramson was making his wrap-up. "Thanks, Jack, for coming over. This could be something, or it could be nothing—but I don't think so. We'll soon know. Stay tuned."

LONDON
10 DOWNING STREET
17 AUGUST 1979

There is no security service in the West that does not have direct ties to the Mossad, the Israeli intelligence service. The Israelis worked with the Germans to crack the Baader-Meinhof gang. MI-5 got vital information from them, leading the way to members of the Angry Brigade responsible for the planting of bombs in London. They were helpful to the Italians in the rescue of Brigadier General James L. Dozier, held hostage by Italian terrorists. Which is why it was not surprising that when Eitan Kidron, the Israeli ambassador to Britain, pulled up in his limousine to Number 10 Downing Street for an eleven o'clock appointment with the Prime Minister he had with him Saul Ben-Udris, Mossad's chief of mission in London. In spite of a drizzling rain the usual small crowd of sightseers was gathered on the opposite side of the short street, mainly tourists kept in place by a couple of police constables. Another constable stood in his usual place by the door, but there were others, inconspicuously attired, ready to swarm in at the first sign of trouble. It was, after all, the best known address in all of England, the seat of political power as well as the Prime Minister's private residence.

The door was opened even before the ambassador reached for it. Inside he was greeted by a young man. "Ambassador Kidron? Mr. Ben-Udris? Right this way, please." The press room on the right was humming with activity as they crossed the entrance hall to enter the corridor leading to the rear of the house and the cabinet room.

Prime ministers since Sir Robert Walpole in 1732 have used the house as both residence and office. The main staircase leading to the first floor is lined with their portraits—Peel, Disraeli, Gladstone, Baldwin, Macmillan, and Churchill. At the end of the line is a color photo of Mrs. Thatcher's immediate predecessor, the avuncular and pink-cheeked James Callaghan. Kidron, a distinguished Israeli diplomat with a track record of virtuoso performances all over the world including Paris and Washington, as well as an earlier background in intelligence, always felt an acute sense of history as he mounted those stairs. The Prime Minister was a damn clever woman. He had learned this in his first meeting with her. He wondered about her reaction to what he and Ben-Udris were about to tell her. In the top corridor the young man knocked on a door, opened it, and ushered them in. "Ambassador Kidron, Prime Minister, and Mr. Ben-Udris," he said and left, closing the door behind him.

With no thought of protocol Mrs. Thatcher arose from her desk to greet them. She admired Kidron. He was bright, had an attractive wife, and played croquet with dash, as if it were polo. She liked that.

The study had undergone redecorating since Kidron's last visit. Now gold curtains and pale green brocaded walls set off the comfortable furniture with which the room abounded, all in perfect taste. A burst of spring flowers added to the general air of elegance. But nothing was more elegant than the woman who greeted them. The blue suit with the froth of white lace at the throat offset perfectly the blond hair. An elegant, handsome woman of the world, whose sharp, intelligent eyes could turn hard on those occasions when tough decisions were thrust upon her.

"Prime Minister, may I present Mr. Ben-Udris? He is well known to your people as an intelligence officer." The ambassador was smiling as he spoke. "So you see, all of our cards are face up."

After shaking hands with both and motioning them to sit down, she returned to her chair behind the desk. Her visitors were to one side.

"Prime Minister Begin called me late last evening to say that he considered your request to see me of the utmost urgency. So here we are. What is the problem?" She was crisp without being impolite.

"Prime Minister, I fear the problem is yours. We have learned from a source of proven reliability that a shipment of arms, of a size and sophistication hitherto unheard of in such channels, is being or has been assembled in Libya, awaiting pickup and delivery to the Provisional Wing of the Irish Republican Army. We know the makeup of the shipment, amounts, the nature and characteristics of the weapons, the means of delivery to the IRA, but not the point of delivery."

No change in the Prime Minister's expression, not the slightest flicker, indicated that much of the same information had reached her early that morning, that the highly classified dispatch was in the black box on her desk at this very moment. Less than five minutes before Kidron and Ben-Udris had entered the room she had had the last of a half-dozen conversations on the subject with Brigadier MacKenzie of MI-5, with the Secretary for Northern Ireland, and with Lord Carrington, the Foreign Secretary. Over her clasped hands, resting easily in front of her on her desk, she continued to look intently at the ambassador.

"There is more." Kidron reached down beside him and brought up his own dispatch case. "There is a price tag of four and a half million pounds sterling on the shipment, to be paid by the IRA in gold—I repeat, in gold—to the account of the Libyan government." He paused for emphasis. "The demand is for cash on the barrelhead, payable on delivery, in the Soviet Union's Wozchod Handelsbank in Zurich."

Kidron handed the prime minister a copy of the dispatch, typed on a plain piece of white paper, with no distinguishing or identifying marks on it. There was a moment of silent contemplation as she stared down at the paper, thinking as quickly as possible. The information about the IRA paying for the arms was new—and more than alarming. *Where did the Israelis get it? Not from us. We didn't have it, so no leak there. The Jews are bankers. It had to come from international banking circles. Probably an agent in Switzerland. Give them credit. By God, the Mossad is good—if the dispatch is accurate.* Finally she spoke. She couldn't help wondering about the payment. *Why in gold?* She looked up.

"Ambassador Kidron, it would be trite of me to say that I'm astonished, because I am not—except by the amount of arms and money involved. The list of weapons will get our close scrutiny. This has happened before and will probably be attempted again. We are truly grateful to you for bringing this information to us. Its importance cannot be overemphasized. You may be sure it will have our immediate attention. May I assume that this copy is for me?"

"It is, Prime Minister."

"And may I assume also that the presence here this morning of Mr. Ben-Udris means that he will be kept fully aware of any new developments?"

"You may, Prime Minister—absolutely."

"Good. Mr. Ben-Udris, we are all on friendly turf here. You know Brigadier MacKenzie, do you not?"

"I do, Prime Minister."

"Also good. I would have considered it odd had your answer been otherwise. And how to get in touch with him?"

"Yes ma'am, I do."

"Very good. I will instruct him to be on the lookout for you. Tell me, gentlemen, before you go, where does the IRA get four and a half million pounds sterling?"

"Bank robberies," said Ben-Udris, "bank robberies worldwide. Activities as middlemen in the trafficking of drugs. This is a relatively new departure with a minimum of risk. Also Soviet subsidies, and not forgetting contributions from well-meaning but totally misguided Irish-Americans. Open sources, such as *The New York Times,* report that last year such contributions, made through a front called the Committee to End Oppression in Northern Ireland, or COMMEND, ran into millions of dollars."

"All of these things we know about, and all are deplorable. I was simply wondering if you had any new thoughts on the matter. We have had excellent cooperation from the Federal Bureau of Investigation in the States with respect to gunrunners, but voluntary contributions of funds are hard to stop. Don't worry. We'll get to the bottom of it. Please tell Prime Minister Begin for me that the days of the King David Hotel are long since gone, that we know who our friends are and that we will not forget."

The interview was clearly over as she arose to bid her callers good-bye.

"My best regards to your charming wife, Mr. Kidron. And Mr. Ben-Udris, more from you, when you have it, through Brigadier MacKenzie."

As they departed, Kidron gallantly kissed her hand. Outside, as they pulled away in the ambassador's Daimler, Ben-Udris turned to Kidron with the remark, "She already knew. She didn't ask enough questions."

Inside, a worried Prime Minister was already back on the phone to Brigadier MacKenzie, the head of TESS, MI-5's Terrorist Search and Seizure Team, the special unit set up in Section IX to combat the ever-growing threat from everywhere.

GREATER NEW YORK
QUEENS
THE EARLY SEVENTIES

In the Queens neighborhood where Liam Francis McCarthy was born, outward signs of a pervasive Irishness abound. In an area of shabby circumstances and limited anticipation the saloon on the corner, if not actually called the Shamrock, will certainly sport a neon sign in the shape of one and the Harp of Erin, two blocks down the street, will have another painted in vivid green on its glassed brick window. On Saint Patrick's Day the streets will be strangely empty as everyone takes off for Manhattan and the parade on Fifth Avenue. The Roman Catholic churches are well attended on Sundays, but for the most part Ireland ends right there. In New York the mystique of being Irish is more attitude than reality, stemming from an almost hysterical pride in ancestry, manifested by the obligatory trip—more often than not undertaken under the sponsorship of the Hibernian Society, the Friendly Sons of Saint Patrick, or a parish priest—back to Shannon Airport and thence to County Cork or County Down or wherever one's antecedents are. Most New Yorkers with an Irish name had to go back at least two generations to come face to face with their Irish heritage, but for Liam it was much closer. His father had been born in Belfast and his mother in Armagh.

For Liam, Queens was now only a memory. He had not been seen in his old neighborhood for some time, for he was a man on the run. He started running on his own passport, genuine but now invalidated by the U.S. Department of State.

However, the lack of such a document was not a problem, for he now had two others, both forgeries provided by the Provisional Wing of the Irish Republican Army.

Often irascible, always irreverent, McCarthy was a stocky 190-pounder with icy blue eyes, a short-fused temper, and forearms as thick as most men's biceps. He had sandy-colored hair and a mustache. Strong from his early teens, he had a natural aptitude for athletics and emerged as a running back of more than normal talent on the Woodside High School football team. His parish priest, a loyal alumnus of Notre Dame, lost little time in letting his old school know that he had a hot prospect for recruitment, the end result being a full athletic scholarship for McCarthy at one of the nation's best centers for shaping football greatness. Bright enough, he had no trouble academically but made the fatal error of getting hooked on drugs—first marijuana and later cocaine. Dismissed with four others after a promising start in his freshman year, disheartened and disillusioned, he enlisted in the United States Marines. Although he was able to rid himself of his dependency on drugs—all the more remarkable since he ended up in Vietnam—his military service set him on a path that took control of his life.

He was assigned to the 4th Marine Regiment, 1st Marine Division, an outfit noted for its toughness, where his training could not have been more pertinent to his future role as a member of the IRA. After six weeks of basic, McCarthy had six months of intensive training in such areas as explosives, interrogation, survival behind enemy lines, riot control, unarmed hand-to-hand combat, and the use of a wide range of modern military weapons. More importantly he received concentrated training in village and rural guerrilla warfare, at times playing the part of the guerrilla and at others that of the trooper seeking to destroy him. That training took place in a whole mock complex set up at Camp Lejeune, in North Carolina, with Vietnam in mind. If the IRA had planned the whole training cycle itself, it could not have come up with a better facility or one better suited to its purposes.

The termination of his three-year hitch found him in the jungles around Bien-Hua—twice wounded, combat hardened and with a casual disregard for death born of long exposure to it. Bloodied and fed up after fourteen months of off and on frontline duty, he opted out and returned to New York, honorable discharge in hand and drug free. He was careful to have with him a statement from navy doctors to that effect. Vietnam had changed him as it had few others. He yearned for the better things of life, in particular a career in professional football. That goal, and his belief that he could make it happen, is what carried him through. While in the Marines, if he thought about it at all, which wasn't often, he viewed the thousands of miles that separated him from the New York Police Department as insurance that the John Doe warrants issued against perpetrators of a half-dozen automobile thefts that he and two other money-hungry teenagers had committed would not catch up with him.

Back in Queens he sought out Father Laughlin, who had given him the start that he botched.

"More than anything else, Father, I want to play football. I'll do anything to do so. You think you can get me back into Notre Dame?"

The old priest, nearing seventy and retirement, listened sympathetically, paying special attention to the navy doctor's statement that no traces or symptoms of drug addiction could be found in the rigid exit physical examination given Sergeant McCarthy.

"You're a good lad, Lee," he said, using the shortened nickname that McCarthy preferred and used himself. "You've paid heavily for your transgression. I'll see what I can do."

Meanwhile the well-informed IRA network, which included two old friends of his father's, was waiting for him.

Operating under the umbrella of COMMEND, the front set up ostensibly to aid the families of persons jailed in Northern Ireland and the Republic for their political beliefs, one of its purposes—despite steadfast denial—was the clandestine purchase of arms to be smuggled into Northern Ireland. It was early June and while waiting for some word from Father Laughlin, through IRA influence McCarthy got a job as doorman-bouncer in a midtown Manhattan nightclub. He was good at it; he liked the work and the hours, and in particular his associates—all of whom were Irishmen, native-born or otherwise. He was good-looking in a rugged sort of way and popular with the patrons. It was a job and a life that almost made him forget his goal of playing professional football.

Not surprisingly, Notre Dame flatly turned down Father Laughlin's request for readmission for McCarthy. But three weeks later, at about ten on a hot summer's night, the priest arrived at the Maybelle Bar and Nightclub with a stranger in tow.

"Lee, this is Terry Robertson, backfield coach for the Los Angeles Rams. Get us a table and a drink. He wants a word with you."

"You the same Lee McCarthy that played at Notre Dame four years ago?" Robertson inquired. It was early and few patrons had arrived. They were seated at a side table away from the single musician at the piano.

"Yes sir."

"I scouted you a couple of times, when I was with the Baltimore Colts. You've got some stuff—at least you had it then—we might be able to use."

McCarthy's heart leaped within him.

"I know you got thrown out on a drug bust, but Father Laughlin here tells me you're clean and off the stuff. Is that right?"

"Absolutely. I swear it."

"How old are you? What kind of shape are you in?"

4 5

"I'm twenty-two. You pick out any three guys in this joint and I'll throw 'em out singlehandedly. That's the kind of shape I'm in."

"That won't be necessary—I believe you. Okay, we'll give you a tryout as a free agent. You'll have to get yourself to the coast, but we'll pay you a hundred and fifty bucks a week in training camp, until we either sign you or turn you loose. Want to give it a try?"

That was it. Robertson downed his bourbon, as did Father Laughlin, and with handshakes all round, the two left. McCarthy quit his job that night. He had two weeks to get ready. The next day he started a rigorous program of weight lifting, jogging and working out at the local YMCA. He was a happy man.

Dedicated football fans will remember that McCarthy not only became a starter for the Rams but also that he was named NFL Rookie of the Year, rushing for more than a thousand yards. The secret of his success stemmed not only from the fact that he loved the game but also because he played it with an inner joy born in the nightmare of Vietnam, coming out of every huddle in the sure knowledge that while he might accidentally break his leg, nobody would be shooting at him and that the field wasn't laced with land mines. Frank Deford, senior writer at *Sports Illustrated,* described his running style as "combining the grace of a gazelle with the power of a locomotive." It was also the year that he met and married Elsie Caruthers, a sultry, ambitious young actress, and with her moved into the inner circles of Hollywood's glittering movie society. Ensconced in a house on the fringe of Beverly Hills, the pair of them—young, handsome and talented, although in separate ways—found themselves wallowing in success, surrounded on every side by anxious studio executives, ad agency types, gossip columnists, assorted swamis, lawn specialists, professional party-goers, spiritual consultants, hairdressers, and most damaging of all, too much alcohol—at least for Elsie.

The same football fans who remember McCarthy's spectacular rookie year will also remember that in the last game of the following season, played in the heat of Miami's Orange Bowl against the Dolphins, when the Rams were making a last-ditch bid for a trip to the Super Bowl, McCarthy's Achilles tendon snapped loudly enough, some swear, to be heard on the sidelines. Elsie had vanished from the scene, a victim of too much too soon, and McCarthy never played again. The dream was not only over, it was shattered.

Once more Lee went back to Queens, and this time all the way back to drugs. He needed work and considered himself lucky to get his old job back at the Maybelle Bar. IRA men straight out of Ireland and in the United States illegally, spotted him and saw in him that air of almost manic desperation worn by men who know they are losers but hope to hide that fact from the world. He was perfect material for their purposes. His mind had been scored by adversity like a wall once raked by machine-gun fire. He was in the middle of a costly divorce, he had had military training and experience, and had an easy claim on Irish citizenship. Carefully nurtured, he went in a matter of weeks over the ideological hill and became in reality an agent of the Provos, the Provisional Wing of the IRA.

In his new role as a Provo agent in the States McCarthy became a security and technical procurement officer for arms to be smuggled into Northern Ireland. At first his operations were small time, buying weapons offered him individually—shotguns, submachine guns, rifles, Lugers, Beretta and Smith & Wesson pistols, anything of use. Among his purchases was a Smith & Wesson .357 Magnum, which he appropriated as

4 7

his own. One of his biggest worries was evading undercover agents from the FBI and the BATF, the U.S. Treasury's Bureau of Alcohol, Tobacco and Firearms. In six months' time he had procured over a thousand assorted weapons, all paid for from donations made in countless bars in New York and Boston and other centers of Irish-American populations or by funds stemming from bank heists in Ireland—north and south—by the IRA itself.

But big trouble was on the way, the result of an ill-advised raid on a National Guard armory in Kingston, Rhode Island. At a time when the demand for small arms was large and the coffers of the IRA small, a tip from a sympathizer in Providence led McCarthy and three other IRA men to plan and execute a raid on the armory to steal 170 M-16s, still in their original packing cases and bathed in Cosmoline. Based on close observation from well-disguised positions over a period of three days, the raid went well and had it not been for the chance arrival on the scene of an inquisitive state trooper, would have been a total success. Instead, the trooper—blinded by one flashlight while firing at another—died from the second shot from Liam's Smith & Wesson. The four burglars got away with all the encased guns but realized to their horror that in their haste they had left behind a tire iron, used to jimmy a lock. McCarthy made it to the little-used Whirlpool Bridge, linking the U.S. and Canadian cities of Niagara Falls, a scant twenty minutes before an all points alert put an effective screen on it that would have resulted in his arrest. His fingerprints had been identified. Moreover an alert detective on the auto theft squad of the NYPD successfully linked the prints on the tire iron to the auto thefts committed in Manhattan years earlier. McCarthy never made it back to the United States.

TEL AVIV
PICKPOCKET SIX
22 AUGUST 1979

On receipt of Ambassador Kidron's report of the meeting between himself, Saul Ben-Udris and Prime Minister Thatcher,
Begin had sent for Ben-Udris. Begin admired the big, rangy
former tank commander as did General Hofi, Mossad's chief.
In the middle sixties, while stationed in Vienna, Ben-Udris
had played a significant part in the rescue from neo-Nazi terrorists of a ranking CIA official, prompting a personal letter of
commendation from the U.S. director of Central Intelligence
to Golda Meir. Begin was aware of this, and realizing the importance of maintaining close ties between the Mossad and the
CIA, was doing what he could to advance Ben-Udris's career—sometimes openly. In time this became known to Ben-
Udris, giving him not only confidence but also added determination to serve Israel to the limit of his abilities.

Tel Aviv was oppressively hot and sticky when Ben-
Udris, accompanied by Chaim Shalev, Mossad's UK and
North American desk chief, arrived at the Prime Minister's
office in response to Begin's summons. The air-conditioning
offered a welcome haven from the humid streets. In a session
that lasted more than an hour, Ben-Udris reported not only on
Mrs. Thatcher's reaction to the news of the arms shipment—
including his considered opinion that she already knew about
it—but also on his subsequent conversations with Brigadier
MacKenzie. Moreover he was also able to brief the Prime
Minister in depth on his several hours' conversation with a
highly placed Israeli agent in Zurich. In that Zurich meeting,

undertaken with Shalev's full knowledge of the anticipated scenario, plans were formulated to hijack the gold bound for Libya and turn it over to the British. Working drawings were laid out for Begin's inspection by Shalev. As the meeting progressed, it was obvious that Begin was warming to the subject, especially in anticipation of getting prototypes of the Helvir antitank guns and the AM-180 rifles. But what particularly intrigued him was the possibility of getting the entire cache of arms essentially cost-free.

When Ben-Udris and Shalev were finished, Begin took off his thick glasses, wiped them clean, turned his chair toward the window, and looked out in the direction of Judea and the west. He remained deep in thought for a moment, then turned back.

"Will this work?" he asked.

"This will work," answered Ben-Udris.

"And our man in Zurich?"

"He will not be compromised," said Shalev. "But we will reassign him in any event."

Begin nodded his head several times, slowly, then smiled.

"That Qaddafi," he said. "It'll serve him right. Go to it."

The next morning at seven, a high-level meeting, called on Begin's instructions, convened in an obscure but heavily guarded building close to 85 Ben Yehuda Street, where the Mossad was born in 1952. Presiding was the chief of Mossad, Major General Yitzhak Hofi, called Hacka by his contemporaries. Others present were Major General Shlomo Gazit, chief of military intelligence, Shimon Peres, the Defense Minister, Chaim Shalev, Ben-Udris, and the shadowy Efraim Teveth, a sort of *chef du cabinet* to Begin, who had left that very morning for Washington and a state visit to President Jimmy Carter.

Operating on the level of a minister without portfolio, Teveth had not only the ear but also the confidence of the Prime Minister, a unique figure in an administration where the Prime Minister played his cards close to his vest and delegated authority only with the greatest of reluctance, a hangover perhaps from his days in the Irgun. In Israel in 1979, where the machinery of government was unencumbered by numbers, high-level meetings, with participants coatless and tieless, were often held in an atmosphere reminiscent of a poker game at the Elks Club in Dubuque, Iowa.

Again the formulated plans were gone over in detail. Much was made of Begin's approval, as confirmed by Teveth. General Gazit was dubious.

"Suppose the Brits don't intercept the arms?"

"In that case, the gold will be returned to us," said Shalev. "That is, if the lift goes as planned. If it doesn't Libya gets the gold, the IRA gets the arms, and the Brits are in for big trouble. And I'll add that Saul and I—to steal an Americanism—will have egg all over our faces and will undoubtedly be replaced. If we had the courage and know-how to get our own people out of Entebbe—with a minimum of casualties where many were expected—why shouldn't we again seize the initiative and make this attempt to get a shipment of gold out of Switzerland where we foresee little chance of any casualties?"

There were nods and murmurs of approval. Shalev, born in Israel but raised in Lebanon Springs, a little town in upstate New York, was a persuasive speaker. Encouraged, he continued.

"This bar of gold was bought for us the day before yesterday at the Soviet-owned Wozchod Handelsbank, in Zurich." He placed it on the table in front of him. "It weighs two hundred and forty troy ounces and is, in keeping with Soviet practice, of a standard weight, size, and assay with other bullion used or exchanged by them in large transactions

5 1

through Switzerland. Gold was fixed yesterday in London at four hundred and eighty dollars per ounce, so that bar is worth one hundred fifteen thousand two hundred dollars. The pound sterling was quoted on yesterday's exchange at two dollars and thirty-eight cents, so in pounds the bar is worth roughly forty-eight thousand four hundred. For the sake of the transaction and to facilitate shipping we know the bars will be valued at just that, forty-eight thousand four hundred pounds, with an exchange of bank drafts to even out any differences. That means that the shipment will be made up of ninety-three bars, the weight, shape, and size of each conforming to this one."

"What's the backup plan?" Hacka Hofi wanted to know.

"If the switch fails, the original bars will be delivered— on schedule, at the designated point of delivery. We could be out four and a half million pounds, but this is a matter I think the Brits will negotiate. In any event, we'll have the arms—or ninety-eight percent of them. In money, a high price for what we're getting, but we stand to gain much more."

Shalev sat back in his chair to await reaction. As he did so, Defense Minister Peres picked up the bar to examine it. Eight inches long, two inches high and two and a half inches wide, only its width set it apart from the dimensions of an ordinary brick used worldwide in construction. Then he asked, "Where's the money coming from? Don't hit my budget for it. We're starving to death already."

"We have a contingent liability only, Shimon," answered Teveth. "In any event, the defense budget won't be touched. Any sum that we come up owing the Brits will be handled through the Prime Minister's office. You have his word for it."

"Subject to General Hofi's approval, Lieutenant Colonel Ben-Udris will have full responsibility for the successful completion of the mission, including instructions to and liaison with our agent in Zurich." Shalev was again speaking. "I point out to you gentlemen that while this is a daring concept, nothing is involved here but deception. In the event of failure, blame can be shifted to others with a minimum of effort and a maximum of credibility. Even when we are in possession of the arms, the hand of Israel will have been hidden. What questions are there?"

"How shall we refer to this operation? What will it be called?" The questions were posed by General Gazit.

Shalev looked around the table. "We are six," he said, ignoring the male secretary sitting off to one side, taking notes. "We are just about to pick the pocket of our Arab friends. So why not Operation Pickpocket Six? Okay by you, general?"

General Hofi nodded his assent.

The meeting broke up with the customary handshakes and several well-directed "Shaloms." Six hours later Ben-Udris was back in Zurich.

ZURICH
THE BAHNHOFSTRASSE
23 AUGUST 1979

On an irregular basis, but averaging once a fortnight, a noisy Russian Ilyushin air freighter lands at Zurich's Kloten Airport. Under the watchful eye of a Swiss army tank commander, the Ilyushin taxis to a waiting armored truck where security men unload heavy wooden crates full of gleaming Russian gold ingots. Most of the cargo is then whisked down to the banks on the Paradeplatz, to be quietly entered on the numbered accounts of those banks' clients. What's left goes to Russia's state-owned Wozchod Handelsbank, just off the Bahnhofstrasse. The Russians like Swiss secrecy and security; consequently they use Zurich for virtually all foreign exchange transactions involving gold.

Gold, termed by many the Holy Grail of greed, to a proper citizen of Zurich has a very special quality. It is taken on faith that all the good things of life depend on it, whether as an elaborate ornamentation forming part of a Fabergé Easter egg made for a Romanoff Czar or appearing as a bar, of uniform shape and size, for transportation out of Switzerland to settle a trade deficit of some Third World country. The Swiss monetary system, backed by gold, is paramount, and Zurich is the city most particularly devoted to that end. Securely Swiss in its values, it does not attract rich Arabs the way Geneva does, or retired American army colonels, as does Lugano. It is a beautiful city, congenial, and in its way, a welcoming one. From the Café Kronenhalle, in the old town, cobbled medieval streets go in all directions, and from the heights near Zwingli's Grossmunster one looks down over the Limmat and the flags of the guildhalls on its quais to the gilded stretch of the Bahnhofstrasse, where one in every seven buildings is a bank.

There is no mistaking the feeling about midtown Zurich. It is a feeling that close by, just around the next corner, a British heist artist is entering a bank, his pockets figuratively bulging with the swag taken from a train ambush. Or perhaps a Mexican with a cardboard suitcase jammed with American dollars, the fruits of smuggling countless illegals across the Texas border. It is similarly easy to conjure up the image of a drug-and-numbers racketeer from Philadelphia walking boldly in to launder the money his son, at Princeton, or his daughter, at Smith, will need for the next semester. Or maybe for alimony for his third wife.

The Swiss take their interest and service charges on foreign scams without batting an eye. They keep a jaundiced eye cocked on the mess that the world continues to churn up, but an inner voice tells them that if they happen to help finance that mess—and in so doing add to the lining of their own pockets—it's no one's business but their own. What humiliates them is when their own financial wizards go overboard and get caught with their hands in the cookie jars of their valued clients, such as the scandal that erupted in the spring of 1979 with the disclosure that bankers from the Schweizerische Kreditanstalt, or Credit Suisse, had embezzled from depositors some eight hundred and forty million dollars.

From his elevated perch at the Bahnhofstrasse Bank Jacques Freiburg had watched all of this unfold with calm detachment. Totally uninvolved, he nevertheless had tucked away in his compartmentalized mind the fact that a great deal of flight money—imported illegally across the Italian border, only two city blocks south of his own bank's Chiasso branch—was involved. Zurichers tend to look upon Italian Switzerland as the poor relative at the banquet table, or last among equals, so when the scandal surfaced, in a manner best described as Italian baroque, little was done to tighten the existing security gap. Noting the ease with which illegal funds had entered the country, Freiburg had every reason to believe that the surreptitious exit of funds by the same route could be as easily managed.

Freiburg, Jewish and a native of France, but of Swiss extraction, fit comfortably into his role as a principal Israeli agent in Switzerland. He was first noticed by the Mossad during a summer visit to relatives in Tel Aviv, and his competence, quick turn of mind, and personable qualities made him a natural choice for subsequent recruitment. Approach and cultivation are the first phases in recruitment and here the Israeli service has a built-in advantage, having ready access in nearly every country in the world to persons prominent in political, scientific, and economic areas. Brought into being in 1952, shortly after Israel's controversial birth, the Mossad was smart enough, shrewd enough, and its leaders experienced enough to know that in order to survive in a hostile world—outnumbered twenty to one and surrounded on every side by Arabs totally dedicated to the destruction, by force or otherwise, of their tiny state—they had to be accurately informed not only of the capabilities of their enemies, but also of their intentions. To accomplish this meant the penetration not only of the forces of their principal enemies but also of the industrial, financial, and technical complexes of the West, a ground floor investment of talent and funds that was to prove highly beneficial. Freiburg was among the earliest recruits to become such a long-term, hidden asset.

He was well embarked on his career as a low profile, in-place agent before the scholarships that came his way, an opening in one of the great Jewish banking houses of Europe, and other manifestations of the largesse of his invisible bene-factors made him aware of just how directed his life had become and would continue to be. A graduate of the prestigious L'Académie Nationale d'Economie Politique in Paris and with a further degree from the London School of Economics, he was ultimately assigned to the Zurich branch of a Rothschild subsidiary. He slid into his designated role with ease, was never called upon to report upon or act on matters detrimental to Switzerland, and in a short while was accepted as one of the "gnomes of Zurich," the title accorded some members of the Swiss banking fraternity more out of jealousy than derision. Consequently, when a consortium of banks, among them the Bahnhofstrasse, decided to establish a trucking firm equipped with the latest in armored vehicles, to transfer specie, currency, and other valuables among themselves and to and fro from the airport, it was almost a certainty that Freiburg, who spoke fluent Italian and German as well as French and He-brew, would be asked to take an active part in its management. He accepted, and in so doing both he and Tel Aviv knew that their long-term strategy and infinite patience had added yet one more significant weapon to a well-oiled manipulative complex.

The armorers of a secret service agency are among the most skilled employees on the staff. They are experts on every imaginable form of gun or explosive, but are as well men of great technical skill and—the best of them—imaginative inventors. The three men who followed Ben-Udris to Zurich were the best that the Mossad had to offer. Hours later and on different flights they entered Switzerland on temporary work visas. At Chiasso, where they went separately, each put up at a different *pensione*.

Shortly after nine o'clock the following morning Freiburg paid a visit to the garage and central dispatching point of Associated Transfer, Ltd. He had noticed from the daily manifests, he told the dispatcher, that armored truck number TF87 needed a new transmission. Had it been fixed? It had not, replied the dispatcher, who was also in charge of maintenance. Freiburg, whom the dispatcher recognized as the company director who took the greatest interest in such matters, then suggested to him that since the Chiasso branch of the Bahnhofstrasse Bank would need to return within the next several days a sizable amount of cash to its main office in Zurich, and since the Castiglione garage in Chiasso had established a good reputation with Associated Transfer, Ltd. as transmission experts—as the dispatcher no doubt remembered—it would seem logical to send number TF87 to Chiasso forthwith to have the necessary repairs made before the pickup required at the Chiasso Bahnhofstrasse. Furthermore, said Freiburg, this conformed to the wishes of Dr. Ernst Schmeisser, the managing director of Associated Transfer, with whom he had discussed the matter several days ago.

Within an hour TF87, empty of cargo, was on its cautious way to Chiasso, its driver under instructions to return to Zurich by train, ready to go back to Chiasso when the work was completed. By three o'clock that afternoon, behind the locked doors of the Castiglione garage, Mossad's armorers went to work.

LONDON
BELGRAVIA
25 AUGUST 1979

It was 4:00 A.M. in Belgravia. The early morning hours had turned in upon themselves like a sleeping cat, the tail of the previous day hiding the beginning of the new one. Ben-Udris drove his small sedan slowly as it entered the unfamiliar territory of Sloane Mews, searching for number six and Mac-Kenzie's flat. In his headlights the streets were still shiny-damp from a still earlier shower. Swissair had brought him into Heathrow three hours earlier from Zurich, where he had had a long session with Jacques Freiburg and the two armorers from Mossad. He had also had a firsthand look at what they had been working on in the isolation of the Castiglione garage in Chiasso. Moreover, Ambassador Kidron had been briefed and would ask to see Mrs. Thatcher at the first opportunity.

Ben-Udris was ready to play the Israeli card, the early morning hour to the contrary. MacKenzie had emphasized that he wanted to be kept informed when anything of importance came up, day or night. And this couldn't wait.

He found the building. The beam from his pocket flashlight was scanning the names of the six tenants when a soft, confident voice behind him delivered the message.

"Easy, laddie. Don't move—not an inch." Something hard pressing into the small of his back told him he'd better obey. Instinctively he dropped his hands to his sides, closer to the holster strapped to his lower right leg and its small Walther PPK automatic. He should have known. While in London MacKenzie was guarded around the clock.

"And who might you be?" The voice had backed away, far enough so that Ben-Udris couldn't suddenly swing on his yet unseen adversary. "Turn around, chum. Easy now." The plainclothesman from Scotland Yard looked at him quizzically. "A strange time for a social call, or a business one for that matter. You'd better tell me who you are and what you're up to."

"I know it's an odd hour, but I'm looking for Brigadier MacKenzie. I know too that he lives in this complex. I have urgent business with him. I'm an Israeli diplomat attached to our embassy here. I can identify myself—but I'll have to reach for my inside pocket."

Collie recognized the ingredients of the situation. Mac-Kenzie did business with a lot of people. "Let's see what you've got," he said. "Then we'll ring him up. But if he explodes all over us, you'll jolly well take the blame."

Collie looked at the offered diplomatic passport, then rang the buzzer to MacKenzie's flat. In a moment, over the intercom, MacKenzie answered.

"Begging your pardon, Brigadier," said Collie, "but there's a bloke here who says he's from the Israeli embassy. Name of Ben-Udris. His passport looks kosher. Says he has important business with you." He stopped to listen, then "Yes, sir. Right away, sir." He turned to Ben-Udris.

"Okay, but I'm going up with you. Strange hours you chaps keep. I warn you—if you're bogus, I'll have your scalp."

Five minutes later Collie had rejoined his backup man outside and a tousled but alert MacKenzie had poured a scotch for Ben-Udris and one for himself and settled down to listen.

"Brigadier MacKenzie, I'm here to talk about the arms

shipment from Libya to the IRA. My government has every confidence that your government will, one way or another, intercept it. We're sure of that."

I wish I were, thought MacKenzie.

"Here's a list of the whole lot," continued Ben-Udris, pulling it from his inside pocket, "one with which you're familiar. The capacity for mischief represented by these weapons is great, but the range, quality, and type of the weapons themselves are not all that exotic—with two noteworthy exceptions. I'm talking about the Helvir antitank cannon and the Austrian AM-180 rifles. Both are lethal—almost to the extent of being doomsday weapons. As far as we know, Britain doesn't have them. Neither does Israel, but Israel covets them. We want to get our hands on both. For a consideration, of course."

"Young man, at this point we don't have any of these weapons ourselves, but what are you proposing?"

Ben-Udris didn't answer directly. "The IRA is going to have to pay for the shipment—in gold. I wish I could tell you why, but I can't. It may be that Qaddafi needs the gold—specie to stir up more trouble where arms won't do the trick. That's where we come in. You seize the arms, we'll seize the gold—bullion worth four and a half million pounds sterling. Then Israel will turn the gold over to Britain in return for the arms, even up."

"And how, pray tell, do you intend to lay your hands on such a sizable shipment?"

"We have our own plans on that," replied Ben-Udris. "We're not going to ask Britain how it intends to seize the shipment, but we are confident that you will. So let us worry about the gold. None of your people will be involved, except to effect the exchange at a place and time mutually agreed upon."

MacKenzie was thinking about Entebbe. "Let me see that list," he said.

Wordlessly Ben-Udris handed it over. Almost at once MacKenzie found what he was hunting for. Both items he sought had been circled in red.

"Twenty AM-180 rifles. Thirty Helvir 20-mm antitank guns." He looked up. "Assuming that we do intercept this shipment, why should we turn over to Israel, staunch ally that you are, the two most sought-after weapons on the list?"

"A good question, Brigadier, but we're not greedy. Give us two each for our further study and development. That will suffice. You keep the rest. The remainder of the shipment consists of arms and material that we all know about and that Israel can use. A nice little twist, don't you think? Arms supplied to Qaddafi by the Sovs, destined for the IRA, ending up in Israel? And the IRA's coffers stripped clean, to end up in the vaults of the Bank of England? I find it a very pleasing scenario."

For a moment MacKenzie said nothing. It suddenly occurred to him that somewhere down the line, if all went as planned, the Israelis might be held responsible. He wondered if they'd thought of that.

"Is this a firm offer? And is this the whole message? Where in your government did this originate?"

"The answers are simple, Brigadier. I speak for Prime Minister Begin. And as our American friends would say, that's the whole enchilada. And it's firm. The deal *and* the enchilada. I'll add that as soon as the hour is respectable, Ambassador Kidron will ask to see Prime Minister Thatcher to tell her the same thing. If she can't see him on such short notice, he'll try Deputy Prime Minister Whitelaw. One way or another, he'll confirm the validity of what I'm telling you."

It was an unconscionable hour for anyone's phone to ring, much less that of the First Sea Lord and Chief of Defence Staff. Sir Roderick Kendall, instantly awake although sound

6 1

asleep seconds earlier, rolled over to lift the receiver: 6:10 A.M. showed on the digital clock. These days he was sleeping in a separate bedroom, as Lady Kendall, older than he by five years and suffering from a debilitating neurological disease, needed all the rest she could get—more than allowed by the red phone on his bedside table that had the nasty habit of ringing at god-awful hours. *A bloody nuisance,* thought Sir Roderick. *What now?*

"Kendall here."

"Sir Roderick, my apologies for this early morning call, but I think it's frightfully important that I see you at the first opportunity." It was MacKenzie. "A most unusual development—a proposal, I might say—with respect to the operation that has our immediate attention." Knowledge of Pleiades and the planning for it was so closely held that even its designated code name was classified. "Protocol and channels aside I'd like to see you at once."

"Morning, Ian." Sir Roderick was a courteous man, even when routed out of bed by an unruly telephone. "As a matter of fact, I've wanted to see you since last evening, and was going to call you at a more civilized hour. Are you in London?"

"I am indeed."

"Good." Sir Roderick glanced again at the clock. "Eight o'clock soon enough? If so, I'll be at Whitehall and we'll take it from there. Is this something you want others to know about? Anybody else you want there?"

"For the moment, no," replied MacKenzie, "but this is something I'm sure we're going to have to take to the PM."

As early as he thought he could reach him, MacKenzie called the Prime Minister's appointment secretary, throwing his considerable weight around to break through what was always a tight schedule for Mrs. Thatcher.

"Impossible for you to see Mrs. Thatcher today, Brigadier. We've even had to shunt the Israeli Ambassador off on to Deputy Prime Minister Whitelaw."

"I'll remind you, young man, that I have been instructed personally by the Prime Minister to bring to her immediate attention developments in a situation of the gravest importance. Now if you want to take it upon yourself to delay my seeing her, you'll have to answer to that yourself—because I intend to tell her."

That was enough. After a few minutes' delay, and a lot of grumbling that he couldn't hear, MacKenzie was instructed to be at 10 Downing Street that afternoon at two-thirty.

The delay was fortuitous. In mid-morning, following an urgent call from Amsterdam, MacKenzie received a Portuguese merchant, recently arrived from Angola, going under the name of Manuel Segura. A long conversation followed, in MacKenzie's flat. Segura's information fit right in with the Israeli proposal. So when MacKenzie showed up at 10 Downing Street he had considerably more to report to the Prime Minister than earlier.

"Back so soon, Brigadier?" said Mrs. Thatcher. "I hope that whatever it is you have to say will brighten the situation."

6 3

"I think it will, madam, provided I can persuade you to authorize an operation which, if successful, should give us peace and quiet for a very long time."

"I'm all ears, Brigadier. What's on your mind?"

"Prime Minister, the matter has taken a new and ominous twist. Yesterday morning early, word came through from Luanda to our Amsterdam station that one of our assets, a Soviet naval officer, code name Ashley, wanted to talk with us. A meeting was arranged and took place on schedule. Our man who met with Ashley reached London this morning with a full report. The Soviet submarine *Severyanka,* commanded by Ashley and originally scheduled to make the pickup in the Libyan port of Benghazi, will not now do so, due to space limitations. The *Novosibirsk,* an early Soviet *Yankee*-class submarine, will go in instead—plenty of room in her, especially if her missile tubes are empty. She is to anchor in deep water off the outer mole and the cargo will be lightered out. Ashley is being flown in early, to see that the cargo gets on the lighter and then to the submarine. The *Novosibirsk* is scheduled for a refitting job at Sevastopol, where the Sovs have built a new naval base to accommodate the growing number of their submarines operating in the Mediterranean."

"The *Novosibirsk*? Nuclear-powered, no doubt. I assume from what you've told me that her draft is such that she can make it in and out with no difficulty."

"She can, Prime Minister. Plenty of water, with perhaps ten feet to spare."

"So we track the submarine to see where it goes?" asked Mrs. Thatcher.

"No, Prime Minister, that is not the answer. Once the Sovs discover, as they surely will, that they are under observation, you can bet your last shilling that they will abort delivery. And don't forget that we ourselves don't yet know where that delivery point is. The arms will still belong to the IRA. The Sovs will simply stash them somewhere, figure out new ways to get them into Northern Ireland—or the Republic for that matter—and smuggle them in piecemeal. The threat remains, and we'll be stuck with big trouble for months, if not years."

"Then how would you deal with this, Brigadier?"

MacKenzie looked at the Prime Minister, meeting her blue-eyed quizzical gaze squarely on.

"Don't think me daft, madam, but we should take a leaf from the Russian book. We should go into Benghazi and pick up the cargo ourselves."

The Prime Minister was so startled by what MacKenzie had said that she made no reply for a moment, then blurted out, "Great heavens, man, are you mad? Do you want to start World War Three?"

"Not mad, Prime Minister. Determined, yes, and very concerned—but mad, no. I've been up half the night on this. I don't want the threat of those arms hanging over me, or over you and your government. Here's how we'll do it—and we won't start World War Three or any other war if we're successful. In fact, we'll stop one."

"I can't imagine what you're going to say, but you have an attentive audience. Get on with it, Brigadier."

"Ashley, once a captain first rank in the Soviet navy, was demoted as a result of disciplinary action. His name, for what it's worth, is Viktor Soroshkin and his disaffection is complete. We got to him just at the right time. We pay him well and he's served us well. Consequently we trust him. Furthermore, in the operation that I'm about to lay out for you, Ashley will see an opportunity to get out—all the way out. If we fail, he'll die. That alone makes him trustworthy. And should he attempt to double-cross us, he's equally dead."

"So?" The Prime Minister was listening intently. She nodded her head, half in agreement, half in question.

"He will be in charge of the loading process. He will also be in communication with the *Novosibirsk*." MacKenzie was warming to his subject. "Under normal circumstances, he can therefore delay her arrival. Any number of factors—the tide, weather, dockside delays—could supply sufficient reasons to do so. Meanwhile we go in, pick up the cargo, and are out in a matter of hours. And we bring Soroshkin with us."

"Stop right there," Mrs. Thatcher said. "Am I hearing you correctly? What sort of vessel are you talking about? The Libyans will be expecting a Russian submarine. Are you suggesting that a British submarine go in, take the cargo by force, and get out? By the saints, Brigadier MacKenzie, you *are* daft."

"Bear with me, madam. Not by force, but by deception." MacKenzie reached for the chart that he had brought with him. "With your permission," he said, as he unrolled it on her desk. "This is the admiralty's most recent chart of the Gulf of Sidra. Notice Benghazi and the outer mole. When anchored a quarter mile off the mole, one is in deep water and well away from land. The chance of a surprise attack, other than by air, is virtually nil. By coincidence, HMS *Taurus* is now in Scotland, at Faslane, being readied for refitting with trident missiles. *Her* missile docks are empty. With the exception of a lack of sail planes off her sail, to all but expert eyes she is a carbon copy of the *Novosibirsk*, both designs being closely related to U.S. subs of the *Yankee*-class. I say use her. And before you ask, MI-5 can supply a crew of totally trustworthy, physically qualified men—all Russian-speaking—to appear as a loading detail."

"Brigadier MacKenzie, do you know what a nuclear submarine such as the *Taurus* costs? Suppose we lose her? The risk is totally out of proportion to the gains. And what about the crew? Suppose they were to die—or be captured?"

"I've thought about this, Prime Minister. We are at war, and war is a risky business. But how about the cost of maintaining British troops in Northern Ireland? How long have they been there? Seven years now. And how much longer? I see no end to it. Look at this." He handed over a handwritten note

6 6

from Ben-Udris. "The Israelis know what's in the shipment. If we give them the arms, they'll give us the four and a half million pounds in gold. A tidy sum, madam. They haven't told us how they're going to do so, but they're planning to take the gold—to kidnap it. And if they're unsuccessful, they'll give us four and a half million pounds anyway—that is, if we're successful in seizing the arms."

"Four and a half million pounds for a shipment of arms, and from the Israelis? They have a thriving arms manufacturing capability of their own. Why go out on a limb for this particular shipment?"

"Included are two weapons, Prime Minister, that they—and we—want very much indeed. More to the point we cannot, under any circumstances, allow them to fall into hands unfriendly to us. I'm referring to the Helvir antitank guns, made in Finland, and the Austrian laser-sighted automatic rifle, neither of which have been seen before in NATO countries. Both are real doomsday weapons. The Sovs undoubtedly stole them. In the case of these two weapons, the Israelis want access only, but physical possession of everything else."

Mrs. Thatcher was careful to keep her ministers at arm's length, seldom if ever calling them by their first names, and never in the presence of others. But she and MacKenzie were old friends, so this afternoon the rules were relaxed.

"Ian," she said, "I still think you're slightly mad. Not all the way mad, because I've known you well enough and long enough to know that your judgment is very often sound. I've seen you patch up broken egg shells, find the irretrievably lost, and solve the unsolvable. So maybe you're just a little bit mad. What, pray tell, does the Royal Navy think about this? What about the Home Secretary? Have you broached this to either Mr. Whitelaw or to the Chief of Defence Staff?"

"To some extent, Prime Minister, but not fully. I thought I'd let you have a go at it first. Some of what I've just told you I've known only for a matter of hours."

"Well, you've got a lot of ground to cover, Ian. Talk with them both. Get their reactions, then come back to me. That is, if they don't do you bodily harm in throwing you out of their offices." She was smiling, but inwardly thinking that such a bold and daring operation would die a-borning.

MacKenzie nodded and also smiled, but his smile was one of confidence.

"Thank you, Prime Minister. I had hoped that your instructions to me would be as they have been. I'll see Mr. Whitelaw and then Sir Roderick. You'll have a full and complete report."

He rolled up his chart and made a respectful and cheery departure. But he took with him the gut feeling that the wild and daring venture was going to prevail.

When conditions in an untidy world permitted, MacKenzie preferred to work at home. In London home was a flat in Belgravia, small by comparison with others in that fashionable area, but centrally located. Weekends, subject to the same limitations, he retreated to Corscombe Hall, a comfortable if somewhat drafty cut stone house on the outskirts of Abbotswood, a village in Hampshire. In London a secure telephone in his book-lined study was his principal tool, reinforced by the physical presence, when summoned, of his principal assistant Peter Lindsay, ex-major, Scots Guards, middle thirties, indefatigable, and a bachelor. Lindsay's left femur and pelvic bone had been shattered by a bomb while on duty in Belfast two years before and he walked with a pronounced limp, a disability that in no way affected his capacity as an intuitive operator in the murky waters in which he and his chief swam daily. He had been with MacKenzie a little more than a year.

But it was not Lindsay who greeted MacKenzie when he returned to his flat in Sloane Mews after leaving the Prime

Minister's office in Whitehall. He had called for Lindsay on his car radio and told his driver to stand by. The coat on the chair in the hall told him he had a welcome visitor.

"Barbara darling, where are you?" She was out of sight, but rarely out of mind.

"Here, love, brewing a pot of tea," she answered from the kitchen. A moment later she emerged, tray in hand. Putting it down on the tea table, she embraced him, then on tiptoes to reach his commanding height of six feet plus, kissed him warmly.

Barbara Romney was thirteen years younger than the sixty-two-year-old brigadier. A taskmaster who demanded much of his subordinates—some said he ate junior officers for breakfast—MacKenzie was, under a gruff exterior, a reasoning and gentle man whose neighborly kindnesses made him a favorite in Hampshire—and with Barbara Romney.

MacKenzie first met the Romneys after his return from India, where he had been aide-de-camp to Lord Mountbatten in the latter's term as last viceroy. MacKenzie's wife had died in India of dysentery complicated by a weak heart. Back in England MacKenzie, an expert on the Arab world, had been posted to Sandhurst, as had Alan Romney, a lieutenant colonel in the Royal Electrical and Mechanical Engineers, following duty in Germany. Despite the disparity in their ages, the widowed brigadier and the compatible married Romneys had been drawn together by their mutual fondness for low-stakes bridge and shooting. Unexpectedly, Alan had died from peritonitis following a ruptured appendix while the three of them, with other friends, were shooting in Yorkshire, near the border of Scotland. As time went on, it seemed to follow naturally that marriage between the widower and the widow would take place, and the wedding was now scheduled for November in a little church in Saint Ives where Barbara's parents had been married and were now buried.

Not all of MacKenzie's service had been in the Middle

East. He had had his share of combat, beginning with long service under Wavell in the desert campaign in World War II, followed by an assignment in Korea from which he was lucky to come out alive.

It was November 1950. North Korea, where the formidable ranges of the Changpai Mountains reach out for the Yalu River, was a hell of a place to fight a war. Winter storms that make up in the distant Manchurian wastes scream down unheralded and lay ten-foot drifts. The terrain is so divided that it is impossible for an army to maintain a solid front or even liaison across the trackless and impassable summit ridges.

It happened along a road near Mupyong-ni, west of the Chosin Reservoir. All day long the 2nd Battalion, Duke of Wellington's Regiment, had fought a rearguard action, trying desperately to fall back in some sort of order. All along the line the men were dead weary, half frozen, every line and sag of their bodies bespeaking their inhuman exhaustion. Their faces were black and unshaven. They were young men, but the grime and whiskers made them look middle-aged. In their eyes was no hatred, no excitement—just the simple awareness of being there, as if they had been there forever marching, fighting, regrouping, retreating,and nothing else. They were withdrawing, together with elements of the U.S. Eighth Army, to which the battalion had been attached, after hordes of screaming Chinese troops had smashed forward on all fronts, turning the UN offensive into a full-scale retreat. Superbly disciplined and thoroughly trained, without armor and with little artillery, unencumbered by complex communications, the Chinese seemed unnaturally accustomed to extremes of weather and meager rations.

Captain Ian MacKenzie, six weeks to the day away from his last assignment in the searing heat of the Persian Gulf, lay prone in a foot of the still falling snow. A northwest wind blew it in swirls to give him better cover but also to cut his visibility to no more than ten feet. He knew that the wounded man he was trying to reach was no more than twenty feet in front of him, just short of the ridge that they had been defending for the past two hours. He knew, too, that he had to keep moving; otherwise he'd freeze to death in the subzero temperature. But he couldn't stand or even crouch, for to do so would bring a hail of Chinese small arms fire that would cut him down as surely as it had the wounded man he was inching forward to rescue.

In the deep purple, snow-laden dusk of 4:00 P.M.—it seemed idiotic but when the gathering darkness was temporarily illuminated by mortar flares fired by the Chinese he found the scene quite beautiful—he had seen his man fall. He had been attempting to retreat by a few yards and when hit, fell like a stone. It looked to MacKenzie as if he had caught it in the shoulder.

"Cover me, Corporal. I'm going after him. Better for us all if he walks out of here."

The corporal raised a frost-bitten hand to brush aside a woolen scarf wrapped around his chin and mouth.

"Righty-o, Captain. Them fookin' yellow bastards never seem to get cold." His voice was war-weary and strained.

An Irishman, thought MacKenzie. *I don't know the company roster yet, but I'll bloody well know every last man on it if we get out of here alive.* During World War II there had been no conscription in Ulster. Catholic men, largely unemployed, joined the British Army in large numbers. It was a pattern that carried over into the postwar years.

He inched forward again. Suddenly a staccato burst from a semiautomatic rifle made the snow dance like splattered whipped cream, so close he could feel an impact under his leg. They had seen him. But he had spotted the muzzle flash, on the left. It was the first Chinese automatic weapon fire he had seen or heard that afternoon. *Can't have that!* He rolled to his right.

He shouted to the corporal. No answer. Again—no response. MacKenzie reached for a grenade. Another burst, this time equally close but to the right of him. The fire was coming from the protection of a mound ten yards away. He pulled the pin. Two seconds later he hurled it, over his head, to clear the mound. His aim and his timing were perfect. The grenade exploded on impact, killing two of the three Chinese riflemen who had started to zero in on him. The third, wounded and dazed, could still move but the automatic weapon was useless. The firing from the mound ceased.

In minutes he had reached the wounded man. His collarbone had been shattered and he had taken a second bullet through his right leg. He was in shock, but able to move with help.

"All right, laddie, let's get the hell out of here. A bit drafty, don't you think?"

"Cold as hell, Captain. I think one of me fingers caught it too."

Another Irishman, from his accent. "Put your arm around my neck, push with your good leg, and we'll be on our way. You'll be back in Ireland before you know it. Easy now. Roll over on top of me."

"May the saints be praised if that happens." The words were mumbled and weak, but the man saw life regained.

With the wounded man's rifle in his hand, MacKenzie started to crawl. The man was heavy, but with help from the man's good leg, progress was possible. It was downhill to the point where he had left the corporal. When they got there, he was gone.

Behind the semblance of a line that passed as a company front, they stopped to rest.

"God bless you, Captain. I won't forget this." The man offered his hand to MacKenzie. It was covered with blood and one finger was broken, grazed by a bullet.

"Piece of cake, laddie. You'd do the same for me. What's your name?"

His answer was lost as four riflemen opened fire simultaneously on a single Chinese soldier who had suddenly appeared in front of them, yelling obscenities and lunging forward in a suicidal bayonet charge. He was stopped in his tracks. A half-dozen more bullets, one through the face, killed him. He had been the survivor of MacKenzie's grenade attack.

I won't forget it either, thought MacKenzie, *particularly that lance corporal whom I told to hold his position and to cover me. The bloody bastard mucked up. I'll have his hide for this.* That night he did. MacKenzie put him on report and demoted him back to private.

The next morning they reached Hagaru-ri, on the southern tip of the Chosin Reservoir, where the battalion regrouped. Forty-five miles away, down icy mountain trails, lay the sea. Fighting all the way, the battalion made it in three hellish days and nights—burying its dead, carrying out its wounded, and retaining its equipment.

The consummate leader, Captain MacKenzie was everywhere in that nightmarish interlude. Tireless, hungry, cheerful in the face of exhaustion, the integrity of the command had been thrust upon him—his battalion commander had been killed a week earlier—and the welfare of his men was uppermost in his mind. Somehow he got them down the mountain, to the sea, and to evacuation. His performance didn't go unnoticed. The day after reaching the coast he was promoted to major and given the Military Cross "for extraordinary heroism in rescuing the wounded and rallying his men under heavy enemy fire and extremely adverse circumstances."

Shunned by his fellow soldiers, the ex-lance corporal marched out in disgrace. The incident and the retreat cemented a lot of memories.

DUBLIN
THE GRESHAM BAR
28 AUGUST 1979

The hydrofoil from Liverpool to Dublin was crowded, but then it usually was. The well-dressed, athletic-looking young man was traveling light, having with him nothing but a briefcase. He spoke with an American accent, was of medium build, and had on a glen plaid suit. He favored glen plaids and pinstripes, which in some instances he ordered from Brooks Brothers, but only because he couldn't afford to buy all of his clothes from the best London tailors in the Burlington Arcade or Regent Street. Moving quickly to get ahead of the crowd, he took an aisle seat, opened his briefcase, took out the day's *Manchester Guardian*, and remained absorbed in reading it throughout the trip, slightly less than two hours.

He came to Dublin frequently, sometimes as often as once a month. Recently it had been more like weekly. He much preferred to fly, but in keeping with his calling he varied his route, using the hydrofoil, the available car ferries, and all of the airlines that flew between England and Ireland, regardless of takeoff or landing point. He was traveling on a forged United States passport issued in the name of Nicholas G. Moran, a document for which he had a particular fondness. He used it exclusively on this run, ever mindful that a sharp-eyed English or Irish immigration official might remember his face. His real name was Nikolai Aleksandr Burdin and he was a career officer in the KGB.

* * *

Born into the Soviet Union's new elite, Nikolai's father Valentin Burdin had been the possessor of a distinguished career dating from World War II, when he was stationed at the Soviet Embassy in Berlin and acted as interpreter for Vyacheslav M. Molotov, the Soviet Foreign Minister. He later translated for Josef Stalin and still later became editor-in-chief of a magazine published by the Institute for the USA and Canada, the Soviet think tank on North American affairs. When Nikolai was a teenager his father became First Secretary at the Soviet Embassy in Washington.

Most youngsters of parents who are Soviet diplomats in Washington are schooled where they live—inside the sprawling Soviet compound on Tunlaw Road, a virtual city within a city that includes apartments, offices, a gymmasium, commissary, theater, and a swimming pool. But for Nikky, as he was called, life was different. His family was among the few allowed to live outside the compound. Their home was a luxury apartment near Wisconsin Avenue, adjacent to Chevy Chase where people felt safe strolling alone in the early evening. Nikky swam in the building rooftop pool, which drew numerous young Americans and children of diplomats from other nations. He could walk to nearby movie theaters, the Neiman-Marcus department store, and to the Booeymonger, a restaurant popular with teenagers. He affected the dress of his well-to-do American friends—jeans and a T-shirt or a casual sweater over a button-down shirt, and always loafers. In a remarkable display of tolerance, Nikky's parents were allowed to enroll him in the Sidwell Friends School, where he became a bright and popular student, even playing on its football team.

More was to come. The KGB recruits from the upper strata of the Soviet Union's managerial and professional classes by means of an Old Boychik network. Promising candidates are picked for loyalty, intelligence, presence, and family connections to the party, and every effort is made to spot them early on. Sensing an already developed talent in Nikky for ready assimilation into the Western landscape, the Russians extended his father's assignment in Washington to twice its normal length of three years, thus allowing young Burdin to enter the University of Maryland at nearby College Park, well within the prescribed limits on travel imposed at the time on members of the Soviet Embassy staff. He was there for two years, until just after his twentieth birthday, which fell in May.

A daily commuter, he was in a Monday morning physics class when abruptly summoned by phone to the Embassy. There he learned that both his father and his mother had been killed in an auto crash in Queen Annes County, on Maryland's Eastern Shore, while on their way back to Washington from a weekend spent at the large estate, formerly the home of a General Motors magnate, which the Soviets had bought two decades earlier and were permitted to maintain as a rest and vacation center for their own people.

Nikky's minor league indoctrination was over. Possessed of all the necessary attributes—language, looks, a natural affinity for things Western, including an intimate knowledge of American football—Nikolai Burdin was sent back to Moscow and enrolled in the prestigious Institute for International Studies for further intensive instruction. The *Otdel Kadrov*, personnel directorate of the KGB, felt they had a winner. After lesser assignments elsewhere he ended up in London, ostensibly a bureau chief of the Novosty Press Agency.

Possibly the most un-Russian institution in all of the Soviet Union, the Novosty Press attracted some of the brightest young men and women from the universities, the exceptional linguists and writers. Brainchild of the KGB and housed in a modern glass-fronted building on Moscow's Pushkin Square, it had employed Galina Brezhnev, daughter of Leonid, and Julia Patrova, Khrushchev's granddaughter. In 1959 senior KGB officials began an inquiry in depth into the secret of western, and particularly American, communications; why glossy American magazines flood the world, and would flood the Soviet Union, too, if the ban on them was lifted; why the western wire services like AP, UPI, and Reuters enjoy world-wide prestige while Tass, an extremely tough and efficient or-ganization, has almost no influence outside the USSR, and why Soviet diplomats in the UN and Washington read *The New York Times* before *Pravda* if they think no one is watching. The Novosty Press Agency became the answer—a news, fea-ture, and photographic service designed not only to resemble a western agency in style and operation but also to instill into its editors, writers, photographers, and even secretaries some-thing of the same sense of collective morale as one finds in *Paris-Match*, the London *Daily Mirror*, and the big U.S. mag-azines. Beyond that, a primary objective of the new agency was the spreading of disinformation, a function that it per-forms with unusual sophistication and credibility. With its ser-vices extending to over 700 Soviet newspapers and magazines, Novosty has correspondents in all the major capitals of the world, including three in London. Significantly Novosty does not maintain separate bureaus, but has its correspondents oper-ating out of Soviet embassies, presumably to give the KGB better control over its freewheeling operatives.

It did not bother Burdin at all that his office was small and inconveniently located in the Embassy compound, as he had not spent much time there since taking on the job eighteen months earlier. By western standards he was a singularly un-productive reporter; his byline had appeared on fewer than twenty stories, no more than once a month, since his arrival. But it was most unlikely that he would be called into account for his performance. As a senior KGB official visiting from Moscow ruefully observed during a discussion of Burdin's as-signment, he could pass as an American anywhere in the world—which was probably true. If ever a Russian appeared to be the antithesis of someone engaged in the esoteric business of espionage, it was well-groomed, clean-cut, scotch-drinking Nikolai Burdin with his idiomatically correct, American-accented English, a man who could readily be believed to have more in common with the intelligence chiefs among his nominal enemies than he had with many of his colleagues. But just the opposite was true; he had developed into a tough-minded, disciplined, and pragmatic operator, now entrusted by his bosses in the Western European department of the KGB's first chief directorate with the sensitive matter of liaison with certain members of the Provisional Wing of the Irish Republican Army and, to an increasing degree, the funding of its operations.

When Burdin left the hydrofoil terminal located on City Quay, well up the River Liffey, he went by taxi to the Gresham Hotel on O'Connell Street, then walked the short distance across Parnell Street to Parnell Square. In the small park north of the Rotunda Hospital a familiar figure was sitting on a bench. As Burdin approached, the man folded his newspaper and raised it slightly in recognition. Burdin spoke to him in Russian, then sat down next to him.

"Greetings, Sergei. How goes it?"

"Well enough, Nikky. And you?" Sergei Petrovskiy, also a KGB officer, served under diplomatic cover at the Soviet Embassy in Dublin.

"*Nichevo*, comrade. What have you got for me today?"

"You are seeing O'Farrell?"

Burdin looked at his watch. "In twenty minutes."

"Good. He will want to know if the shipment will be ready, and you can tell him yes. But he will not be happy to know that more money is needed. A lot more—within ten days. I hope he can deliver."

"Who knows? How much more money?"

"In terms of U.S. dollars, a hundred and seventy-eight

thousand, or roughly a hundred thousand pounds sterling. If he objects, remind him that we are providing five times that amount. If he's going back to Raven for the additional funds, he's to get a bank draft payable to Nicholas G. Moran. You'll be responsible for its delivery in Switzerland."

In his assumed role as an American, Burdin sometimes thought like one. O'Farrell wouldn't like this news, but screw him. He knew him to be an Irishman with a smouldering temper that often flared into flame. A hundred thousand pounds in ten days? A lot of money and not much time, unless Raven turned out to be a soft touch, which he doubted. Privately he often wondered at the effectiveness of the IRA's methods.

"That's it?"

"That's it."

"What if O'Farrell or the people he supports can't come up with the money?"

"Then as far as I know, the deal is off."

"Does O'Farrell know the particulars, what's in the shipment?"

"That I can't say, but if not, obviously there are others that do. And they're counting on it—heavily."

Burdin thought for a moment. "Okay." In Russian, the universal word came out as *hokey*, with a first syllable accent. "Anything else?"

"Yes. O'Farrell is to let you know immediately. Then you let me know. At that point you'll have further instructions."

The meeting was over. Petrovskiy went off in one direction; in several minutes Burdin left in another.

Burdin's rendezvous with O'Farrell was set for the basement bar of the Gresham at 4:00 P.M., an hour when it shouldn't be crowded. When Burdin arrived the only occupants, other than the bartender, were three American tourists, two men and a woman. The men had on Boston Red Sox base-ball caps and unlikely Hawaiian shirts and the woman, over-weight and noisy, a purple polyester short-sleeved blouse and too tight slacks that made her rear end bulges seem even more grotesque.

Burdin viewed them with distaste, ordered a Bushmill's, and retreated to a quiet corner to wait for O'Farrell. To his relief the trio, which had been discussing the Irish sweepstakes while trying to order Budweiser, departed, almost bumping head on with O'Farrell, who was coming down the steps.

"Watch it, mate," said O'Farrell, pushing one of them aside.

"Lovely people, those Americans. Friends of yours?" queried Burdin as O'Farrell sat down.

"Not bloody likely. And we won't be seeing many more like them for a while, thank God. The tourist season's almost over. But wait until next March and Saint Patrick's Day. Battalions of 'em—the Friendly Sons of Saint Patrick and the Ancient Order of Hibernians will descend on Dublin either to watch the parade or be in it. There won't be a hotel room in town without a letter from your parish priest. I hope I'm not around."

"Don't you like Americans?"

"Sure I like Americans. I was born there. But I like Americans in America." O'Farrell looked at Burdin quizzically. "I sometimes think *you're* an American. Are you? You've got an American name."

"I've been there. But let's get down to business. Mike, more money is needed—a lot more. The ante hasn't gone up, but the pot is short."

O'Farrell looked at him uneasily. "How much more?"

"A hundred thousand pounds sterling, or roughly a hundred and seventy-five thousand dollars."

"How soon do you need the money?"

"Within ten days."

O'Farrell had ordered a drink. When it arrived he ordered another, neat, and combined the two. The voice of Linda Ronstadt—unmistakable, international, and sexy—pleaded from the stereo.

Uncharacteristically O'Farrell didn't explode. When word had come through that Moran sought a meeting with O'Farrell or another emissary, O'Rourke, the point man on the shipment, had warned O'Farrell not to rock the boat, to stall, to play for time. Why, reasoned O'Rourke, would Moran ask for another meeting unless to ask for more money?

"My God, Nick, where's the money coming from? I know little about the money picture and care less, but it strikes me somebody's awfully greedy. O'Rourke is pissed off at the Mountbatten scene—as God is my witness, we knew nothing about that until it was over—and this news isn't going to make him any happier."

Burdin nodded, knowing less himself. This was Petrovskiy's show, on orders from Moscow, but Petrovskiy couldn't surface. He thought it a little odd that a self-confessed terrorist would call on God to witness anything, but let it pass. He was trying to be sympathetic, not because he liked O'Farrell, but because he wanted things to go smoothly. The bottom line was that he liked London and wanted to stay there.

"It's up to you, or your group," replied Burdin. "If I read about a bank robbery next week I won't be surprised. Get in touch with me in the usual way—and at once."

He got up to go, leaving O'Farrell staring at his glass, wondering if he wanted another drink before heading north to break the news to O'Rourke. Ronstadt had finished her pleading and was now singing a song of satisfaction.

Burdin didn't get back to London until 1:00 A.M. the next morning, via air to Manchester and then by train to Euston Station.

8 1

An early morning mist lay over the fields around Raven Park, but the promise of a sparkling early fall day was evident from the total lack of clouds in the rose-colored eastern sky. Atlantic winds were blowing but had been cut down to no more than gentle breezes by the time they reached Mark's bedroom window.

Normally a sound sleeper, Mark had gotten up at dawn. The night had been a troubled one, brought about by his recurring remorse over the Mountbatten assassination. Worst of all, he felt totally out of touch with Deirdre. She was campaigning all over Ireland, in Ulster as well as in the Republic, for support for Peaceful Means, trying to capitalize on the general attitude of anguish to bolster the movement's sagging bank balance. She had accepted ten thousand pounds from Mark but would take no more, making a strong case for broadening the base of the movement's support.

What Mark did not know, because she hadn't told him, was that she was spending every spare hour at Strabane visiting her aunt, now widowed for the second time and in the last throes of a lingering illness. Mark had left messages for her at every conceivable place and was now genuinely concerned for her safety.

Having talked with Lord Mountbatten only once, and that by accident in Mullaghmore, where the *Shadow V* was docked, Mark nevertheless realized that this British peer of almost pure German ancestry had character flaws like everybody else. But along with the vast majority of people in Britain and Ireland Mark had been intrigued with Mountbatten's larger-than-life figure and was an admirer of his military and public service record. Moreover he sensed that Mountbatten had been a genuine friend of the Irish, north and south, wanting nothing more than to see the intransigence of the Protestants of Northern Ireland give way concurrently with the religious animosity of the Catholic minority to bring about a lasting and just solution to an age-old problem.

Of one thing Mark was certain. He'd never again contribute to COMMEND. He wanted to tell Mike O'Farrell just that, and as speedily as possible. He would soon get the opportunity.

The reverberations of the violence at Mullaghmore that had shocked the world had other results, hidden from ordinary eyes. The splinter groups within the terrorist movement in Ireland were thrown into even more disarray, with charges and countercharges thrown around indiscriminately. The Irish National Liberation Army, which normally lives in the shadow of the Provisional IRA, while publicly applauding the Mountbatten attack disagreed with its timing. One significant result was the delaying of negotiations for the arms to be smuggled into Northern Ireland from Libya, as Provo leaders played for time and a lessening of the public outcry. They would have waited longer had it not been for pressure from the other end, originating with Qaddafi himself, then funneled back to the Chief of Staff of the Provos through Moscow by way of Soviet agents in London and Dublin.

Which is why it was a week before O'Farrell was dispatched to see Mark Raven to ask for the still indispensable hundred thousand pounds. Security had been tightened to such an extent, north as well as south, that a bank heist was judged to be out of the question.

After an earlier than usual breakfast Mark sat down to rid himself of his guilt complex. He was determined to extricate himself from this mental morass by getting in a good morning's work, a catharsis that he had found highly effective in the past. It was while showering that he had the first indication that the morass might be more than mental. He had dropped the soap, and when he stooped to pick it up he was hit by a dizzying spell that was severe enough to make him lean against the side of the shower for perhaps ten seconds before he could straighten up. And for the first time he noticed particularly that he was short of breath. *No matter*, he thought. *That's happened before. Nothing that a good night's sleep won't take care of.*

He had sharpened his last pencil, stoked up his instant coffee machine, and could find no more excuses to postpone the compulsory, always painful self-amputation. A passage written yesterday and considered imaginative was a fuzzy mess to today's more reflective eye—an unfortunate wallowing in intellectual ooze. He began crossing out unnecessary sentences, obliterating phrases, making rewrite notes in the margins. He worked on, forgetting about the glorious day unfolding outside, forgetting about time.

After retyping his last two days' output he wrote on, seizing the inspiration of the moment. His novels ran to a pattern: first the soft sell and easy beginning, followed by a surprising but never-failing twist running right down the middle, crescendo, gathering momentum as the story progressed. The entrance of his characters, sometimes unobtrusively, sometimes with the subtlety of a hammer blow to a Chinese gong, was always accomplished with enough credibility to maintain that sense of authenticity so admired by his readers. Then the tapered ending, with the hidden twist so skillfully camouflaged that the true solution to the tale was never revealed until the last paragraph—sometimes the last sentence—of the book. It was a rare gift, often imitated but seldom equaled.

The persistent ringing of the phone interrupted him. It was a cardinal rule that he wouldn't take calls, even those from New York, London, or California until after lunch, time differentials to the contrary. Normally his secretary Mrs. Wilkins, a witty, efficient little woman, the wife of the local postmaster, answered, but she was in the kitchen brewing a pot of tea. Mark answered, hoping that it was Deirdre.

"Mike O'Farrell, Mr. Raven. How be you this fine day?"

Pretty good until you called. But he mustered sufficient politeness to say, "Well enough, Mike. What's on your mind?"

"Well, Mr. Raven, the boys are needing some more help. They've asked me to come to see you."

Now he was glad he had answered the phone, even glad it wasn't Deirdre. Gladder still that it was O'Farrell. He could sign off right now.

"Mike, you are no longer talking to the right man. I don't like what happened at Mullaghmore. In fact, I'm appalled." Mark was trying to keep the anger out of his voice. "The well has run dry. There will be no more."

"There will be no more? Just like that? Don't you want to hear what I've got to say? And I think the lads would like to hear what you've got to say. I'd like to see you tonight, Mr. Raven. Believe me, it's important."

Against his better judgment Mark found himself saying, "All right. But if it's important to you, it's just as important to me. But you should be aware that I'm going to tell you face-to-face what I'm telling you now."

Throughout lunch and a long afternoon there was no call back from Deirdre. Mark was worried. He dined alone, unhungrily, between concern over Deirdre's silence and uncertainty over how and what he was going to tell O'Farrell, other than that the free ride was over.

O'Farrell showed up just before nine. He had waited for the last remnants of daylight, but in the dusk of a long Irish day he pulled up in front of Raven Park without benefit of headlights.

"I drove down, coming through the Belcoo-Blacklion crossing, then N16 into Sligo," he said, in greeting Mark. "Normally nice and quiet that way, but the bloody Brits have doubled their forces all along the border. The cheeky bastards now want to know everything but your blood pressure and your mother's maiden name. I told them I was coming back that way tonight, and so I will. With your permission, Mr. Raven, let me state my business and I'll be on my way. I hope you can see us through this one last time. You've been very generous."

Then he told Mark what he wanted.

Raven was aghast.

"A hundred thousand pounds? That's a hell of a lot of money. I'm not made of the stuff, you know. The most I've ever contributed at one time was ten thousand U.S. dollars, and if my memory's correct, not more than thirty-five thousand all told. Moreover, I've done enough. I've been led to believe, particularly by your friend Moran, that the funds would be spent to support the families of IRA men killed or jailed. The bombing and the terror has got to stop. I can't support that. I'm beginning to wonder if any cause is worth the loss of a single human life."

"You've been a good friend, Mr. Raven. Don't let us down now. Think what you please, but you know what we say in the IRA—once in, never out."

"What is this, blackmail?"

The conversation had started in a rather relaxed and casual manner. Now slow waves of anger were rising in O'Farrell and Raven sensed that his remark had suddenly switched the atmosphere to another plane. Carefully he arranged his face and eyes and mind so that nothing else he might say could be considered provocative. He felt that his jugular was under inspection. O'Farrell too was struggling. He knew that he had to offer something that Mark needed, otherwise he would lose him—and a chance at the money. With a skill born of a life in the shadows he buried the visible evidence of his emotions while probing for an advantage.

"No, it's not blackmail, Mr. Raven. Let me say something about the bombing. I've heard about you and your record in World War II. You remember the wholesale havoc and destruction the RAF and the Eighth Air Force caused in Cologne and Hamburg. The fire storms in those cities killed more people, including women and children, than were killed in Hiroshima or Nagasaki by atom bombs. The only difference between high altitude bombing and an explosive left in a department store cafeteria is that the airman can't see what he's doing."

"And where does it all end, Mike, all the violence, all the killing?"

"A united Ireland."

"I'm for that—you know that as well as I. But a week ago the IRA murdered Lord Mountbatten, an innocent man and a friend of all Irishmen, Catholic and Protestant alike. You also killed two children and a helpless old woman. There are those who say that Mountbatten had his dark side, but don't we all? I'm outraged—angry, cold, and numb. Why I'm even talking to you amazes me. I'm not sure but what I'm liable for prosecution as an accessory. My help has been for compassionate reasons, not violence or terrorism."

"Whatever else it does, Mr. Raven, Mountbatten's death will bring the message home. Until the British presence is gone forever from Ireland, the IRA won't be silenced. Ulster is a bloody police state, made up of masters and slaves. How else to overcome oppression except by violence? We're told to keep our mouths shut about British crimes in Ireland, that Jack Lynch and Margaret Thatcher will somehow solve the problem with power sharing. It sounds good and reads well, but it's a shameful fraud. It's like saying you could have had an agreement between the guards and victims at Auschwitz. We're going to do here what the Vietcong did to American attitudes. We will so shock British public opinion that a kind of war-weariness will set in. The ball's on the five yard line. An end run or two plays down the middle and we'll score—and win it all. You're a good Irishman, Mr. Raven. Help us. We'll never ask you again."

Inwardly Raven knew he had made his last contribution to COMMEND, but he was thinking about Deirdre. He would have to tell her about this latest confrontation. He went over to the window and looked out with determined interest. After a moment he turned to make his reply.

"I think you've got your psychology all wrong. In my view the Mountbatten killing will simply stiffen British backs. There may be something to what you say, but I'll have to think about the money. Moreover, if I give it to you, I'll want absolute assurances that it will be spent only for nonviolent ends. Political action, if you want to call it that, relief for families, food, medical supplies, whatever—but not for arms."

O'Farrell sat back in his chair, brooding, his eyes giving nothing away.

"The Brits have already lifted the alleged killers. Francis McGirl and Thomas McMahon were picked up at a road block last Wednesday. You don't think I'd be here talking with you if I were guilty, do you? It's well to remember, Mr. Raven, that the IRA, like the British army or any other institution, consists of a wide variety of human beings. Some want to follow one path, others another. Beyond the fact that we need money— and fast—that's all I know myself."

"For the moment, I'll accept that. I'll tell you what. You

find out what the money's for, and tell me. If I like what I hear, I'll come up with the cash. If not, then no dice."

Sensing a turndown, O'Farrell needed advice. "I'll take your message to the central committee," he replied, "and let you know. This is Monday. Suppose I come back Wednesday night?"

Raven looked at his calendar. Monday, September third. Wednesday would be the fifth.

"I'm afraid not. I'm going to London tomorrow, and then to California. I'm not sure when I'll be back. It'll have to wait."

"We'll know when you get back." A caged animal looked out through O'Farrell's eyes, caged by O'Farrell's frame and skin, eyes that indicated power under restraint, eyes that showed no fear at all. O'Farrell's anger was flowing again. He did not take kindly to refusal, but he knew instantly that his remark gave something away, something that it was just as well that Raven be unaware of. To make amends he said, "We'd appreciate an answer as soon as possible."

"You'll get it," replied Raven.

The transparent fakery of the affability that accompanied O'Farrell's departure did little to lighten the blackness of the mood on both sides.

"We like your style, Mr. Raven," O'Farrell had said. "God save the good work. And may you die in Ireland." It was the most ancient of Irish toasts. *Yes,* thought Mark, *but not too soon.*

As the sound of O'Farrell's tires crunching on the gravel receded, Raven stood and watched until the red of the taillights on the car disappeared into the woods. *We'll know when you get back.* The words had an ominous ring. This time he knew his jugular was under inspection.

LONDON
BUCK'S CLUB
5 SEPTEMBER 1979

MI-5, the counterintelligence arm of British Secret Intelligence, does not officially exist. No law established it nor sanctifies its actions. It is seldom mentioned in the British press. Nevertheless it does have a headquarters, plus a body of often sleepless personnel who spends their time in a never-ending battle of wits aimed at controlling the activities of agents of foreign powers operating in the British Isles. Increasingly, however, MI-5 has had to concern itself with what has become an even more serious problem: the movements of European terrorists in London, including those who plant bombs for the Provisional Wing of the Irish Republican Army. Like the United States CIA, a counterpart with which it often cooperates, MI-5 has no powers of arrest. For its effectiveness it must depend on the Special Branch of the Metropolitan Police at Scotland Yard. It is they who make the arrests to preserve the anonymity of MI-5 personnel by keeping them out of court.

Which is why, on the morning of the Mountbatten funeral, Detective Chief Superintendent Thomas Fereyes hurried into the large building in Knightsbridge, close to Harrod's and the Basil Street Hotel, harboring the faceless men and women who do MI-5's work. It is a nondescript place with a marble facade, a roosting place for pigeons and starlings, uncooperative birds that have been known to single out those who labor within as recipients for their droppings. Unmarked, unpretentious, and unloved, its only outward connection with officialdom is the occasional presence of one or more black staff cars parked in front.

Today a target had been spotted, a man wanted for questioning, if not arrest. Fereyes himself would handle.

As Mark Raven left the plot of grass where he had been standing, heading for Pall Mall, Scotland Yard followed—a plainclothesman on foot, two more in a small sedan. He walked for perhaps twenty minutes, slowly, into Saint James's, past Boodle's and White's Club, into Piccadilly, and through the half empty Burlington Arcade, unaware that he was being followed. Inside him, the reasons for his disturbed state were crowding in. He had pulled no triggers, had set no charge, had had no direct contact with the killers, and did not know their identities until their names appeared in the press. And yet he felt guilty of murder—guilty of the death of a national figure, one for whom a million and a half people had stood shoulder to shoulder for hours on end as a mark of almost universal respect.

Back at Buck's Club he inserted the key in the lock of his bedroom door, turned it, and was just about to push it open before becoming conscious of the figure behind him. A hand reached over his shoulder to give the door a not so gentle shove.

"Go right in, Mr. Raven. We've been expecting you."

At that moment Raven's emotions were hard to define. Beyond his surprise at being called by name, Mark knew instinctively that the stranger was a policeman. His mind flashed at once to the half-finished note addressed to Scotland Yard, now in his inside coat pocket. Would it be a silent witness for the defense? When he had started it this morning it had sounded too dramatic, too unreal. Unreal—that was the word. Whatever was coming next, he knew nothing would ever be the same again.

He looked closely at the controlled, impassive man standing next to him. Under a felt hat that had seen better days a weathered, not unhandsome face with sky blue, searching eyes and a firm mouth presented the world with an unmistakable air of authority. He held an unlit pipe in his free hand.

"Detective Chief Superintendent Thomas Fereyes, Special Branch, Metropolitan Police." To Raven's surprise he held out his hand. The handshake was reassuring.

"Obviously you know me. Am I under arrest?"

"No—not yet." To Raven Metropolitan Police meant Scotland Yard. If he was not under arrest, they were at least on to him. Somehow the knowledge came as a relief, followed immediately by the ludicrous recollection of an American television commercial. Raven saw himself repeating the word *relief* and then spelling out the words *Scotland Yard* in the air with his finger.

There was a knock on the door. Fereyes opened it to let in Detective James Collie. Another introduction and another handshake. *How many more?* Raven wondered. *Should I offer them a drink?*

"You don't seem surprised, Mr. Raven, at our presence here." Fereyes held up his pipe. "Do you mind?"

"Not at all," replied Raven. "And no, I'm not surprised. May I offer you gentlemen a drink—a cup of tea, perhaps?"

"Thank you, no. Don't be misled by the tenor of this conversation. We know enough about you and your support of the IRA to lock you up forthwith—and maybe we will. Why don't you sit down?" Fereyes motioned to the bed. Collie stood with his back to the closed door, silently. The hostility factor was dormant but the atmosphere was decidedly cool.

"When did you last see Michael Francis O'Farrell, Mr. Raven?" The directness of the question was disconcerting. No preliminaries, no lead-in questions, just straight to the point.

"The day before yesterday—Monday. In Ireland."

"At your house in County Sligo?"

"Yes. It was Monday night, actually."

"How much do you know about him?"

"I know that he's an American, that he's a pipeline to COMMEND, on whose behalf he has asked me for contributions and to which I have responded, and I know that he is sometimes rude and overbearing."

"Who else do you know that's connected with COMMEND?"

Raven thought for a moment. "There's a man in the background named Nick Moran. O'Farrell talks about him as being connected with COMMEND. Whether he's from Belfast or not I have no way of knowing. He too appears to be an American."

From behind a cloud of smoke Fereyes wrote something in his notebook.

"Why did O'Farrell come to see you this last time?"

"To ask for money—a lot of it."

"How much?"

"A hundred thousand pounds." Fereyes did not react, but to himself he thought, *Bloody hell! They're going for broke this time.*

"Did you give it to him?"

"No. I told him I'd have to think it over. But I have no intention of giving him anything more—now or in the future."

"Why the change of heart, Mr. Raven?"

"Mountbatten's death. I know you'll find that hard to understand, but all at once the violence and its senseless criminality got to me. I live fairly close to Classiebawn, where Lord Mountbatten and his family spent every August, but we were acquaintances only, so this has no personal angle. My father was an Irishman, Dublin born, and—"

The phone rang. Fereyes nodded to Mark to answer it. It was the club's operator, saying that the overseas call that Mark had asked be put through at this hour was now ready. A familiar voice said, "Hello?"

"Charlie? Mark here. How the hell are you?" Almost six thousand miles away Dr. Charles Sanner, a leading cardiologist in San Francisco, was on the line.

"Mark! How the hell are you? You in Ireland?"

"No, London. I'm okay, I guess, but I'd like to see you. I've been planning a trip over." Mark looked inquiringly at Chief Inspector Fereyes. There was no change in his expression. "Maybe I still am."

"My God, you sound like you're in the next room. When you coming?"

Mark plunged right in. "As soon as possible. I'll be at the Bohemian Club. I'll call you as soon as I get there. I really called you now to see if you'd be around. The last time I showed up you were in New Zealand."

"Yeah, lecturing—and trying to catch a trout or two. Why do you say you *guess* you're all right? What's the problem?"

"I wish I knew. Occasional shortness of breath is what I notice."

There was a moment's hesitation before Sanner replied, "That could be a lot of things. Look, old friend, since you're in London I can put you in touch with one or more Harley Street types and you won't have to come all the way to San Francisco."

"No thanks. I want to see you." Raven and Charlie Sanner had roomed together at Yale and had remained close. In fact Mark had picked up, anonymously with his mother, a portion of the considerable tab that it took to put Charlie through Harvard Medical School.

"Okay, call me at the Presbyterian Hospital when you get here, or at home. You sure you feel up to the trip?"

"Absolutely. You'll hear from me in two or three days. Love to Sally and the kids."

"Thanks, chum, and mine to your girlfriend of the moment. So long."

Raven turned away from the phone. The slight squint around Fereyes's eyes foretold the question.

"What was that all about? Under the circumstances, Mr. Raven, you will understand why we must know."

Fereyes was by birth a Cumbrian, where his parents had been innkeepers at Ambleside. Taciturn in the manner of some Englishmen from the north, he was much given to the use of the Scottish "aye" for an affirmative answer, a vernacularism that had crept into the speech of the border country where he was born. He had been a policeman for twenty-one years, devoting himself so assiduously to his job and putting in so much overtime that he was seldom home—a fact that his wife found sufficiently irritating to cause her simply to pack her bags and move out. That had been five years ago.

He had a face made of cut glass and a thin mouth to match. People felt as much chastened by his thorny sincerity as by his prodding, twitching honesty that was like an incurable itch. Without charm, without ease, without conceit or vanity, nevertheless his capacity to grapple with, and solve, some of the Yard's most baffling mysteries put him high on the roster of Britain's legendary detectives. He was one of those indispensable policemen with a memory as reliable as a computerized data bank. Furthermore, he had another quality for which no computer could substitute: the ability to smell out the hidden connections between seemingly unrelated facts. He was particular about the pronunciation of his name, which was "Ferris" and no mistake about it.

"I was talking with Charlie Sanner, a doctor in San Francisco and a close friend with whom I went to college. I want to see him."

"You're not well? What seems to be the problem?"

Raven shrugged. "I suspect something's the matter with my heart. There's no pain, or at least very little, and then only spasmodically. Shortness of breath, however, every now and then. More than normal, I think."

"I see." Intuitively Fereyes felt no reason to question Raven further on that score. *God knows he looks healthy enough. This man owes me something. Let's get along with it and pray that the Almighty doesn't interfere.*

"Before that call came through I was about to tell you about my father."

Fereyes cut him short. "I think I know enough about your father—and about your grandfather, too, for that matter. What I don't know is why a seemingly sensible American, even if half Irish, should contribute to Irish murder. Sensible Irishmen, north as well as south, half American or otherwise, have long since abandoned violence and turned their backs on the IRA." He was about to add *Your friend Mrs. O'Brien should have persuaded you of that,* but thought better of it.

Seeing that Raven was about to make a rebuttal, Fereyes raised his hand. "Not to be abrupt," he said, "but I've really heard all the answers on that score." He got up, retrieved his hat and coat in silence, then turned to look again at Mark, sitting on the edge of the bed, engrossed in his own thoughts. "I'll say this, Mr. Raven, you're honest enough. Jamie here is going to keep you company for a little while." He pulled an old-fashioned hunting case watch from a vest pocket. "It's five after five. I'll leave you in his company for maybe an hour, then I'll be back. Then I'll have that cup of tea—or maybe a wee drop of whiskey. Be a good lad, now."

Detective Collie stepped aside and Fereyes was gone.

Forty-five minutes later he was back. He hadn't gone far, having spent most of that time cruising in the car of Brigadier MacKenzie, in earnest conversation with him and Peter Lindsay. Both men were with Fereyes when he returned. MacKenzie introduced himself.

"Brigadier MacKenzie, of the Home Office, Mr. Raven, and this is my associate, Major Lindsay. We're interested in

9 6

your traffic with the man called O'Farrell. Tell me, do you know how to reach him?"

"There's a pub in Belfast where I can leave a message," Mark replied. "I don't have the number with me, but the pub is called the Corkscrew, run by a man called Costello."

MacKenzie knew it well. British Intelligence had long since tapped its telephone lines, both Costello's own and the one in the telephone box, and transcripts of calls, replete with spurious names of people and places, regularly reached his desk.

"Nothing will undo the mischief that's been done, Mr. Raven, nor bring your titled neighbor in Ireland back to life, but if you're sincere in what you've told Inspector Fereyes, you can help us." Collie was back at the door, Lindsay standing next to him. Fereyes was lighting his pipe with a great show of deliberation. The tone was friendly, but the hostility level decidedly higher.

"God knows I'll do what I can. It's hard for me to understand how I got so enmeshed in circumstances that I now deplore."

"I'm privy to the whole extent of your conversation with Inspector Fereyes," continued MacKenzie, "including the fact that you wish to go to the United States for medical reasons. Do you feel that you must?"

"*Must* is a pretty strong word, Brigadier, but I'll certainly feel more comfortble after getting advice from someone in whom I have complete confidence."

"Then by all means go. But first get word to O'Farrell that he can have his hundred thousand pounds. We think the promise of it may be enough to satisfy him."

Raven was stunned. "You mean you want me to give it to him—in face of all that's happened? That's a hell of a lot of money."

"Precisely, but not out of your own pocket. The Crown will provide the funds."

There was a long pause before Raven said, "I'm not sure I can do that, Brigadier. And I'm not concerned about the money, or its source. That's secondary."

"Then what's the problem?"

"My word is the problem. The truth of the matter is that I've given my word to someone that I will no longer contribute to COMMEND."

MacKenzie eyed him quizzically. "Would you care to tell me who that someone is?"

"No, I would not. It's a private matter."

"Privacy, Mr. Raven, has gone out the window, I'm afraid. In the light of your reluctance to tell me, I hope you'll not be offended if I tell *you* who that someone is."

Raven shrugged. "Anyone can play."

"Mrs. O'Brien, of Peaceful Means."

My God! How did he know? Raven made no reply, but a shrewd guess had found its mark.

"If I am right, Mr. Raven, as I have every reason to believe, I want you to know that despite the fact that her name has come into this, we have had no traffic with her or with Martha Quinlan. I assure you that this is true. We applaud and admire the goals of Peaceful Means, but both of these estimable ladies would be repulsed by any approach by British authorities. So forget them as a source of this information. Moreover, if we turn you loose, as now seems likely, what is said here today stays here. I trust that you understand that—fully."

"Yes, I do. But why not some other means of passing the Crown's money to O'Farrell? Why me? And neither you nor Inspector Fereyes has yet told me why the money is so important."

"Mr. Raven, you are not exactly in what in your country is sometimes called the catbird seat. We're asking for your cooperation, whereas in fact we're in a position to demand it. But we're not going to do that. You've established yourself in

9 8

the eyes of the IRA as a reliable friend. Did it ever occur to you that if you break that friendship, or try to, they may kill you?"

"You think O'Farrell's a killer?" asked Raven.

"Without a doubt—certainly in the past, and he'll kill again in the future unless we can stop him. His remarks to you follow the Provo line to the letter."

"Why don't you arrest him?'

"With your help, we will, but we've got nothing on him now."

"How about other Provos? You certainly know who they are."

"That we do, laddie, that we do." MacKenzie was a tall man, erect, with an angular, lined face. His once blond, now graying hair and mustache, coupled with dark brown eyes that seemed to have X-ray qualities, gave him an air of authority that often led him to address equals and others even higher in authority in the familiar terms of his native Highlands. Nobody seemed to mind. The only person who made him feel the least bit uncomfortable was Mrs. Thatcher. "In fact some of them brag about it," he continued, "but to catch them with the goods is another matter. Provo leaders like to be photographed with the aging leaders, now long in the tooth, of the 'old' IRA—the men who led the Easter Uprising in 1916. They are heroes to the Provos because that uprising led to just the kind of public outcry in Britain that the Provos are trying to generate now. 'Get out of Ireland!' is a cry that would be music to their ears."

"I used to think it was going to happen, but I don't anymore."

"You're right. There's no overwhelming support for the IRA in the Irish Republic. Even with proportional representation, the Sinn Fein—the IRA's political arm—has been unable to elect a single member to the current parliament. Moreover, in the minority Catholic community in the North, a new public-opinion survey found that only a third of those questioned supported the Provos' goal of driving the British troops out."

"Is there a Soviet connection? I keep hearing about this."

"Yes, without a doubt, and the evidence is more than circumstantial. But Mr. Raven, you're an educated, intelligent man, well read, with all sources of information available to you. You must know all this."

Raven nodded. "Granted, but I need to hear this from you. Remember, you're talking to someone with a new perspective, someone who's viewing the problems of Ireland from a different point of view. Maybe, like Jimmy Carter, I'm a born-again Christian."

MacKenzie chuckled at the comparison. "I certainly hope your point of view is different, as you've been dead wrong so far. But more about the Russian connection. In 1973, in an operation funded entirely by the Russians, a trawler loaded with arms and explosives from Libya was intercepted off the Irish coast. Last year Belgian officials stopped a shipment of automatic weapons from Lebanon. Now we have reason to believe that the Sovs, at least by indirection, are at it again. That's why we need your help. Cash on the barrelhead is demanded for a big shipment of arms to the IRA, the largest ever, and the IRA is short of cash. We believe we can interdict that shipment—if it's made. It it isn't, the arms will be smuggled in piecemeal, giving us trouble for years. So pass the funds to O'Farrell, or at least pass the word that you'll come up with the hundred thousand pounds. That amount will close the gap for them, and they'll be in a position to pay. Then as far as we can determine, their coffers will be exhausted and they'll be flat broke, at least temporarily. And as I've told you, we'll come up with the funds. Moreover, if word of this gets out, we'll get to Mrs. O'Brien. You have my word she'll be made to understand that at our urging you acted in an effort to put an end to the killing that we all deplore and are trying to stop." MacKenzie stopped talking for a moment, then laid his hand on Mark's arm. "And you can count on that," he said.

Mark made no reply, thinking of O'Farrell's statement, *We'll know when you get back.* Then he said, "In light of what you've told me, I must say that COMMEND and O'Farrell—or both—seem to know a lot about what I'm doing."

"Precisely, and don't think for a moment that I'm exaggerating. It's important for us to keep you alive—important for our sake as well as yours. So give him the money. If you can't get it to him personally, arrange to leave it with Costello at the Corkscrew. Time is everything. The passage of this money has to be expedited. You are our best and most logical means of accomplishing this. Any other way is too risky, too prone to public exposure. Can you imagine what the public reaction would be if it were known that the British government was financing arms shipments to the IRA?"

Brigadier MacKenzie felt that he had made his point. When he spoke again, his voice was soft and the tone gentle, almost as if he were a headmaster reasoning with a wayward student in an effort to straighten him out after an infraction of the rules. The message, however, was clear. "So go to San Francisco if you must, but get back here as soon as possible. And don't entertain any crazy notions about staying there, because we'll have our friends in the FBI ship you back as an accessory to murder." MacKenzie knew the charge wouldn't stick but he threw it in anyhow.

At 6:00 A.M. Mark woke again after a fitful night's sleep. London was beginning to stir. Trucks and lorries were rumbling through nearly silent streets, bound for early morning deliveries. He got up and closed the window, noticing that a light rain was falling. He had agreed to advance the money to O'Farrell and in his wallet had a number where he could reach MacKenzie or Lindsay at any time. *Brigadier* MacKenzie and *Major* Lindsay, of the Home Office. That didn't add up, as Home Office personnel don't carry military titles. Somewhere he had read that the Home Office has supervision over MI-5 and MI-6, so MacKenzie and Lindsay were undoubtedly from British Intelligence, which did add up.

Earlier, around three-thirty, lying in bed and going over in his mind his conversation with O'Farrell four days earlier, he had a sudden flash of intuition. A Freudian slip on O'Farrell's part, a simple reference to football, brought old images to mind. He was on the verge of calling New York in pursuit of that hunch when he realized that the time differential was wrong and that the man whom he wished to reach wouldn't be in his office until much later. So he'd call him this afternoon from Ireland.

Twelve hours after that early morning thought he was back at Raven Park. At 10:30 A.M., New York time, he dialed the New York number. The call went through immediately to the office of Frank Deford, senior writer for *Sports Illustrated*. He was in.

"Frank, Mark Raven here. How the hell are you?"

"Never better. Good to hear from you. How are you and where are you?"

"I'm fine, and I'm in Ireland, but flying to California tomorrow. Listen, Frank, you remember that red-hot running back named Lee McCarthy who played for the Los Angeles Rams a few years back?"

"Hell yes. NFL Rookie of the Year in 1973. Saw him play a number of times. As a matter of fact, had dinner with him and his wife one night at Chasen's in Hollywood. She was gorgeous, but booze got her."

"Where is he now?"

"God knows. After an injury that took him out permanently he disappeared off the radar screen in a hurry. In trouble with the law, I think. Maybe a drug bust."

"Your files must have dozens of pictures of him."

"Hundreds, I'd say."

"Good. Frank, I need a favor. Will you ask your people to sift through those pictures and pick out any that show McCarthy without his helmet on? Full face, if possible, and close up. I'd like very much to see them."

Deford was puzzled. "Sure. We can do that. What's this all about?"

Mark hedged. "I'll tell you later, but they'll be for my personal use only, not for publication or public display in any way. Is that a good enough answer?"

"I guess it's going to have to be. You writing a book about this guy?"

"Maybe I will, although I hadn't thought about it up to this moment. But the pix are for me alone."

"Okay, if we can find what you want, where shall I send them?"

"Send them to me at the Bohemian Club, Taylor and Sutter streets, San Francisco. What'll I owe you?"

"Nothing—not a cent. Just speak kindly of me in front of friends."

"You know I'll do that. Thanks a million, Frank. Keep the faith."

At eight the next morning Mark called the Corkscrew to tell O'Farrell he could have the hundred thousand pounds. God damn life's complications! How could he ever explain all this to Deirdre? He felt like a traitor, but MacKenzie's message had gotten to him. Moreover he felt that he was on to something with O'Farrell, whom he knew he'd have to face again. He had nobody to blame but himself, and this seemed the most honorable way out. McKenzie would have to back him up.

No answer at the Corkscrew. That annoyed him, but two calls later, at a little after nine, a gruff Irish voice answered. It was Costello.

"Mark Raven here. I'm trying to reach a man called Mike O'Farrell. I don't suppose he's there? If not, may I leave a message for him?"

"No, he's not here and yes, you may leave a message. Begging your pardon, squire, but who did you say this was?"

"Mark Raven." Mark spelled out his name. "Got it? The message is extremely important. I'd like for you to tell him that the item he requested can be picked up at my house in County Sligo. He's been here before and knows the way. To whom am I speaking?"

"Tim Costello, Mr. Raven. I've heard Mike speak of you. I'll be sure to give him the message."

"Good. I was going to leave an envelope there at the Corkscrew for him, but I've got to fly out of Shannon later today for California. You'll tell him it's here for him, won't you?"

At that moment Costello felt a hand on his shoulder. Surprised, he turned to see Nolan O'Rourke standing behind him, a finger to his lips to indicate silence. Costello nodded, then continued.

1 0 4

"That I shall, Mr. Raven. You can count on it."

"Thank you very much. You won't forget, now?"

"I won't forget—I promise. A good day to you, Mr. Raven."

"Good day, and thank you very much."

"What did he say, Tim?" An anxious O'Rourke could hardly wait for the answer.

"He said the item O'Farrell requested could be picked up at his house in Sligo, and to please tell O'Farrell. As he said that, I was thinking that if O'Farrell didn't come in today, or if I couldn't locate him, I'd tell you."

"And you'd have been absolutely right, Timmy boy. O'Farrell's off somewhere in one of his moods. Consider the message delivered. I'll handle the matter from now on. Now—since this is a great day for the Irish, let's have a pint to keep the good luck rolling."

Immediately following his conversation with Costello Raven placed another call, this one to Fereyes at Scotland Yard. He got through to him right away.

"Inspector, I'm on my way to San Francisco. I'm not sure I can reach Brigadier MacKenzie, so will you please tell him that the matter has been taken care of?"

"Well, now, Mr. Raven, that's very good of you," replied Fereyes, his voice not revealing the way he really felt. "In the full amount—and to O'Farrell directly?"

"In the full amount, yes, but not to O'Farrell directly. I've drawn a draft on the Midland Bank, payable to Nicholas G. Moran, in accordance with the last instructions I had. I've tried to reach O'Farrell and couldn't, so I've left a message at the Corkscrew in Belfast saying that he can pick it up here at Raven Park."

"That's a little loose, Mr. Raven, but if that's the way it has to be, then so be it. We're obliged to you for your cooperation. Have a safe journey. We'll be looking for you on your return."

I have no doubt, thought Mark. "Thank you. I'll let you know how things turn out." As he spoke he was aware that his breathing seemed a little more difficult, a little more exerting—or was it his imagination? "Forgive me if I seem to be in a hurry, but I've a plane to catch and Shannon's a long way off."

When he left the Corkscrew, O'Rourke went to a phone box to call a London number acquired only the night before from O'Farrell. He had long suspected that the Corkscrew's phones were tapped, and Costello shouldn't know too much anyhow. He was glad things were turning out this way. Maybe O'Farrell had served his purpose.

Burdin was in and answered the phone, a private line with limited access. It had a lock on it, so when Burdin wasn't in to answer, it simply rang.

"Nolan O'Rourke here, Mr. Moran." *Who the hell is Moran, anyway?* Speculation was rife, but nobody seemed to know for sure except the rumored Chief of Staff of the Provos, a shadowy Belfast lawyer named Tiernan whom O'Rourke had never seen. "I'm calling for Mike O'Farrell. I want you to know the package is complete. I'm leaving now to pick up the goods—you understand?—at Raven's place in County Sligo. Then, if you can meet me, I'll continue on to Dublin. I know the matter is urgent."

"That's very good news for all of us," replied Burdin. "Hold on for a second." He looked at his watch, then reached for a notebook in which he had tabulated all his London-Dublin travel information. After a moment he was back on the line.

"What time will you get to Dublin?"

"I should be there by five o'clock."

1 0 6

"That's good. Meet me at the south end of the Liffey bridge over O'Connell Street. Do you wear a hat?"

"A cap."

"Better still. Take it off and carry it in your hand. I'm an American and I think I look like one. We'll find each other. If I'm not there go to the Shelbourne bar and wait."

So now Nolan O'Rourke was going to pick up Raven's last and most significant contribution. As the full panoply of Raven Park came into view he stopped the rental car he was driving to have a more meaningful look. He was even happier now that it was he who was making the pickup rather than O'Farrell. They had had a flaming argument the night before and O'Farrell had stormed out of the bar where they had been drinking after telling O'Rourke he was fucking fair fed up with the whole deal, and that what he wanted was action. Screw 'em all, he had said. Handle it your way. They had been drinking whiskey from tumblers that got darker, and O'Farrell had moved rapidly from high to drunk. In his last gesture that made any sense O'Farrell had literally thrown at O'Rourke the telephone number in London where Moran could be reached, then abruptly stumbled out. *Good riddance,* thought O'Rourke. *He's not to be trusted. The IRA has ways of dealing with malcontents. I hope I never see him again.*

O'Rourke had seen big Irish estates before, bigger and more grandiose than Raven Park, but Raven lived in style, he'd have to admit. What's a hundred thousand pounds to a bloke who lives in a spread like this one? He was sorry they hadn't asked for more. Even the gravel sounded rich as he moved slowly along to the shallow steps leading up to the balustraded front and to the Georgian doorway.

Five minutes later he had been handed a sealed envelope by a somewhat reluctant housekeeper who insisted upon a receipt. He signed it in Moran's name. In leaving, he cleared the driveway, then stopped again in the woods out of sight of the house to slit open the envelope. It was there, all right. Pay to the order of Nicholas G. Moran, one hundred thousand pounds, drawn on the Midland Bank in London. He put it in his inside pocket and headed for Dublin.

He made it on time and so did Burdin. The envelope changed hands and O'Rourke turned back for the four-hour drive to the little used Blacklion-Belcoo crossing between Northern Ireland and the Republic. Burdin, as Moran, flew directly to Zurich, where he turned over the draft to a waiting KGB officer from the *rezidentura* at Bern. He was back in London the next afternoon in time to report to the London *rezident* that the funding of the IRA shipment was now complete.

O'Farrell had confided in no one. Quite on his own he had decided that what was needed to boost the flagging fortunes—as he saw them—of the Provos was another act of violence by someone who would remain unapprehended to raise again in the minds of the public the perception of the IRA as an invisible and all-powerful force. Moreover he was tired of being treated as little more than a messenger boy, used for no understandable purpose. Last night was the last straw. Talking and drinking with Nolan O'Rourke—whom he considered a washed-out has-been with no guts, one who made it plain that he expected a certain amount of deference from his "boys," such as not being called by his first name—he made up his mind that the time to act was now, and screw the consequences.

Three weeks earlier he had seen a reference to a Brigadier MacKenzie, of the British Home Office, in the London *Times*. Later that same day he heard O'Rourke speak about MacKenzie in a guarded sort of way that suggested that without him the Provisional Wing would have an easier time of it.

The conversation had been in the Corkscrew, where O'Rourke had been drinking with two other IRA men. After they left, O'Farrell found on the floor under the table in the booth where they had been sitting a sketch, crude but revealing, of an area near a village clearly identified as Abbotswood. It seemed to indicate a path of some kind, with a telltale X marking a point along its meandering way. It puzzled him at first and he was on the point of returning it to O'Rourke or throwing it away but then, with the cunning of a true conspirator, he tucked it in his pocket for further consideration.

The next day, after a call at the library, he drove down to Dublin. In the main office of the telephone company he located a telephone directory for the English county of Hampshire and in it a listing for Brigadier Ian MacKenzie, at Corscombe Hall, Abbotswood. It was enough.

C-4, a variety of plastique, is the superbang of explosives. Easy and cheap to make, an eight-ounce can of it can obliterate a small house. Cyclotrimethylene trinitramene, its active ingredient, when mixed with isomethylene and ordinary motor oil forms a substance with the physical characteristics of putty or soft plastic. A high-impact explosive, it is tailor-made for anyone who must work with a concealed bomb. O'Farrell knew all about it.

He entered England the unobtrusive way, flying from Dublin to Paris and then by train to Saint-Malo, traveling on his forged U.S. passport, a tourist on holiday. From there he took the ferry to Jersey in the Channel Islands, putting him firmly on British territory. From Jersey he knew he could take any one of a number of internal flights to cities on the British mainland where the immigration and customs people were considerably less strict than those handling incoming passengers from overseas at London Heathrow or Gatwick. Under any circumstances he had little to fear, as he was carrying

1 0 9

nothing to brand him as a terrorist except a small package of flat, miniaturized batteries, no bigger than a dime, such as one finds in the latest cameras or hearing aids.

From Jersey, O'Farrell's choice was a British Airways flight into Birmingham's West Midlands Airport, then train to London. It had been ridiculously simple. By 4:00 P.M. on the day of his departure from Dublin he had completed his round-about journey and had put up at a small hotel on Half Moon Street close to Shepherd's Market, that quaint but crowded area where inexpensive breakfasts and lunches were available, as well as a random selection of expensive prostitutes. By noon the next day, from shops in London's West End and from the industrial and electrical houses in the area around the southside docks, he had all the necessary ingredients. He was ready.

SLIGO BAY
INISHMURRAY
JULY 1979

Western Ireland is Europe's western wall, erected by time against the press of the sea. It is at once the country's most primitive and beautiful part. It has a jarring, wild beauty, far removed from the gentle hills and sculptured gardens of County Wicklow in the east, or the soft sandy beaches of the south. Close to the top of western Ireland the rock-studded headlands of County Sligo stick out like fingers into the Atlantic, rebuffing the sea, breaking its force before it reaches the county's few sheltered harbors. Salt-scented winds breathe in from Sligo Bay in the morning, the kind that encourage walking and make a man think he can beat the devil himself. But in another mood the wind can rise to a destructive force and howl like a banshee to drive boats to protective harbors.

Off this coast there is an island, so treeless that the word for tree, when people lived there, was the word for bush on the mainland. It is a stark place, and small, a mile long and a scant half mile wide. Nine miles by boat from Mullaghmore, in Sligo Bay, it is uninhabited except for rabbits, snipe, and other birds and it is called Inishmurray.

If one looks west from the island toward the distant lands of Iceland and Greenland, the Norsemen come to mind, invaders who raided Inishmurray in A.D. 802, butchering almost the entire population. If the winds are calm and the day clear, one can watch the whitebirds in flight, the waves crash, and the foam slither over black and slime-green rocks. It is nature in its most Gothic form.

The site of an ancient monastery now in ruins, Inishmurray would be an archeologist's dream were it not so difficult to reach. Few places in the world are so isolated. The remains of a walled cashel and half a dozen houses are all that is left from the days when it supported a population of its own. In 1947, however, the last of the islanders, perhaps a hundred souls, moved to the mainland. For generations they had lived off poteen, an illicit liquor that was smuggled to and sold on the mainland or to fishermen who came to fetch it in their boats. But the peat had run out and they had no more fuel. Moreover the rising generation was no longer prepared to endure the rigors of life on the island.

Two small inlets come off the harbor at Clashymore on Inishmurray's southern shore, one leading into a miniharbor protected on all sides by perpendicular rock walls, some almost twelve feet high. The water inside is deep and its opening into the main harbor is not more than twenty feet wide. Any boat lying in this protected pool is invisible from the sea. If effectively camouflaged, and with nobody in sight to raise other questions, such a boat would be equally difficult to spot from the air by any but extremely low-flying aircraft. More to the point, Inishmurray is Republic of Ireland territory and not subject to search by the British.

An hour and fifteen minutes after departure from Mullaghmore a small cabin cruiser badly in need of paint entered this hidden harbor, the insistent growl of its engine cut to a low purr. The intermittent rain had been heavy, and a steady northwest wind at fifteen knots had kicked up choppy seas, extending the normal cruising time from the mainland by fifteen minutes. Despite a night as black as pitch the boat, once out from behind Mullaghmore's protective quay and far enough at sea to escape observation, had run without lights. Of the three men on board two had been seasick, but not Eddie McKenna, the twenty-three-year-old skipper. Wee Eddie they called him, on account of his baby face. Unlike most Provos he was a man of the sea, supporting himself from the fish and lobsters the sea reluctantly surrendered to him.

Using a heavy-duty electric torch, Eddie had brought his boat into the harbor and alongside the century-old stone quay with consummate skill. It was the fourth time in as many weeks he had made this run, always at night and always with two passengers, one of whom made every trip. He didn't know who they were or why they would want to come to such a God-forsaken place in the middle of the night, although one didn't have to be a genius to know that it was to escape detection. Word simply came through from brigade headquarters to expect them, and to do their bidding. He asked no further questions. He knew that other boats and other men must be coming here, as on one occasion he had seen some lumber piled on the quay and when he came back it was gone. He figured it was going to be a hideout for other IRA lads the Brits or the Garda were hot after, or even a place to stash hostages. Word had come through, too, that no tourists were to be landed at Inishmurray. "Give 'em a ride, boys, or take them fishing, but stay off the island." Everyone knew that a scuttled boat, or worse, would be the penalty for disregarding such a warning, a warning reinforced by the periodic presence on the docks or in the village of strangers, determined-looking Irishmen that common sense told you were enforcers for the IRA. So Wee Eddie, who was always paid promptly, kept his own counsel and his mouth shut.

Nolan O'Rourke, commander, 2nd Provisional Brigade, Irish Republican Army, scrambled ashore and after him Frank Fitzsimmons, second in command. *Christ, but I am glad to get off that fookin' boat!* The wind and rain in O'Rourke's face had helped some but not much and he had lost the remnants of his supper over the side an hour ago. He had tried stretching out on one of the two bunks in the small cabin but the smell of the diesel engine and the constant thumping of the seas against the bow made his nausea even worse, driving him once more to the partially shielded deck. Fitzsimmons—sick, miserable, and uncharacteristically silent—was hanging over the side. Once on the quay O'Rourke tried to throw up again, but his empty stomach rebelled. A nip of Bushmill's made him feel better. He handed the bottle to Fitzsimmons, who couldn't move. He could only shake his head in disgust.

"I'll go it alone, Frank," said O'Rourke. "I'm leaving the bottle for the both of you. Have a wee drap when you're able. It'll make you a new man. Mind now, don't drink it all. The captain got us here. Fuel him up so he can get us back."

"Don't be longer than a half hour, Mr. O'Rourke," said Eddie. "If the clouds break up, it'll be getting light by four-thirty."

O'Rourke nodded in assent and was off.

It was still raining but the foul-weather poncho that covered him from the neck down kept him dry. He left his cap on the boat, as the rain on his face made him feel better. A grass-covered road led east, and he took it, flashlight in hand. A minute later he turned north up a grassy lane between capped stone walls. In another fifty yards he was at the cashel. Turning west again, he passed through its thick stone wall by a wide opening, put there more than a century ago by well-meaning but misguided preservationists. Inside, the open ground was firm, made so by the layering over the centuries of repeated applications of crushed rock and pitch. Striding quickly to the west side of the cashel, he reached his goal, a half-hidden entrance to an underground tunnel in a labyrinth of low stone buildings. Heavy timbers laid lengthwise down the slight incline formed the floor of a passageway leading to an underground chamber. Where it leveled off a heavy iron door blocked his way. This was what he had made this last rain-soaked, miserable trip to see, to check out for himself.

It had once been the door to a secondary vault in a country bank in County Tyrone, but months earlier had been blown off its hinges in a daring midnight break-in by four of his masked boys, who had got away with not only seventy thousand Irish pounds but with the door as well, manhandling it out of the bank to eliminate all possibility of fingerprint detection. He had thought it stupid at the time and had raised merry hell, but later, when the Inishmurray cache had been conceived and the island cased, it was decided—*he decided*—to put the door to good use. Brought all the way around the northern tip of Ireland on a trawler, hidden under fishnets, it had been put in place the same way it had been taken from the bank—by main strength and awkwardness, punctuated by plenty of Irish obscenity.

Never mind. The door was now in place and would do what it was intended to do—withstand any but a direct assault with explosives. It was not locked and would stay that way until later, when booby traps would be added. He pushed it open. Inside there were more planks and boards stacked next to one wall. It was easy to imagine what the place would look like when put to the use that he and others had so carefully planned. A high-risk undertaking, but well worth the down side chances of stashing so many weapons in such a remote place. If they were discovered before deployment, who could say with certainty who put them there? For this was to be the wellspring of the IRA's own Tet Offensive, the arsenal from which the Provos would draw their weapons for the all-out assault on the British to force them out of Northern Ireland.

It was just before 4:00 A.M. when Wee Eddie's *Ballintra Lassie* crept back into the harbor at Mullaghmore. The rain had ceased even before departure from Inishmurray. Running with the wind rather than against it, they found the seas mercifully calmer and no one was sick.

Minutes after docking, O'Rourke and Fitzsimmons disappeared into the darkness to bed down for what was left of the night. At midday, a less chancy hour, they would go back across the border into Northern Ireland, giving a wide berth to Armagh and its concentration of British troops.

O'Rourke would have been comforted to know that less than thirty-six hours earlier Flight Lieutenant Geoffrey Farnham, Royal Air Force, with Sergeant Pilot Kenneth Willett as copilot and photographer, had lifted a British helicopter off the pad at Bessborough on a reconnaissance flight, looking for any signs of smuggling or illegal border crossings. High altitude infrared photographs of Inishmurray—taken at an oblique angle out of deference to Republic of Ireland air space—failed to show anything of a suspicious nature.

THE ROYAL NAVY'S SUBMARINE BASE ON THE IRISH SEA
HMS *NEPTUNE*
8 SEPTEMBER 1979

An RAF helicopter had ferried Peter Lindsay to Britain's primary submarine base in mid-afternoon. He was accompanied by a TESS staffer carrying two attaché cases bulging with files. In short order they were picked up and driven to a secure building where the unusual procedure of identifying the Russian-speaking auxiliary loading crew for Operation Pleiades would begin. To avoid any possible leak, Brigadier MacKenzie wanted no Royal Navy submariners, in uniform or out, seen in or around MI-5 headquarters.

"How many spaces do you chaps want the Royal Navy to give up in this harebrained scheme?" Capain Jeremy Lewis was flipping through the dossiers handed him by Lindsay.

Lewis was in naval intelligence. The potential of Operation Pleiades, despite Lewis's personal opinion, had been judged to be of such strategic importance, with sufficient urgency attached to it, to lead the First Sea Lord and the Home Secretary to give permission to TESS to begin the screening, on a preliminary basis, of candidates for the loading detail for HMS *Taurus* prior to the operation's approval. Consequently Commander Evelyn Sinclair Wiggins, her commanding officer, had been cut in for full briefing. Wiggins was an exuberant Yorkshireman who had followed in the footsteps of his father in choosing a naval career. Of medium build, he tipped the scales at 160 pounds—a nice design for the accompanying confinement of the submarine service. His rosy complexion, which long periods submerged at sea didn't seem to alter, brown hair, and a clipped mustache set off by blue eyes gave his rigidly Anglo-Saxon face a look well suited to his role as a man marked for steady promotion in the Royal Navy. Because of the dangers of the mission, he had been asked to volunteer, which he did readily, speaking with a single voice for his crew as well.

"Eight's the magic number, Captain. It seems to me that where they come from is up to Captain Wiggins." Lindsay nodded in the direction of the Yorkshireman.

"Well," replied Wiggins, "under normal circumstances the crew of a *Resolution*-class submarine includes ten missile men. With no missiles aboard the *Taurus* we can cough up that number handily. You can have all ten spaces if you want them."

"We can't raise the number," said Lindsay. "The Chief of Defence Staff says eight. Sir Roderick is a stubborn man, so the number stands. Two SAS men will be available from Q Squadron, Twenty-second Regiment, Bradbury Line Barracks, Hereford—a real departure for an organization that always wants to run its own show. These two lads, however, speak not only fluent Russian but Arabic as well, so obviously we're taking them, subject to concurrences all around. That reduces to six the number we're looking for here."

"You know, I'm going to enjoy this." Wiggins leaned back in his chair, hands clasped across the barest trace of a stomach and a wry smile on his face. "The golf courses near Faslane are all holy horrors and my game is beyond repair under any circumstances."

"Better you than me, Evelyn," said Captain Lewis. "I say it's too bloody risky. But who am I to buck Whitehall?"

"Don't let it spook you, Jeremy." Wiggins again, lightheartedly. "If everybody does their bit as planned, I'll be in and out of there before that ex-goatherd from Sandhurst is the wiser. Britannia rules the waves and all that. Remember?"

"I remember and so do you, but will Qaddafi? He's a right bastard and a certified loony as well." Lewis shook his head in disapproval.

"Believe me, he'll never know. My boys can drive that submarine like you drive a car—probably better." Wiggins knew Lewis well enough to be irreverent. "Now let's get along with it."

"Okay," said Lindsay. "We need six men—fluent in Russian and in top physical condition. The initial approach will be on a standby basis only. All must volunteer for this mission, the details—and the dangers—of which won't be revealed to them until the chances of a leak are nil. *After* the *Taurus* has cleared Gibraltar going in."

"In other words," said Lewis, "you're not going to tell them how far it is to the bottom until just before they jump off the precipice?"

"That's as good a way of putting it as any I can think of."

"Will they jump?"

"We think so." He motioned to the files. "These are profiles—psychological as well as biographical—of Russian-speaking men and women, including defectors, whom we trust and who we feel will be responsive."

"Women? We need women for this operation?"

"Certainly not, but the files contain both sexes, as there are some obvious pairs here. But no contact to be made to anyone without the Joint Intelligence Committee's—which in this case means Brigadier MacKenzie's—expressed approval."

"And the Royal Navy's." Captain Lewis had raised a finger in protest. "Let's not forget that."

Lindsay nodded. "Absolutely, Captain. We're all in agreement on that score. All right, gentlemen. There are fifty-two files here. Let's have a go at them."

The preliminary screening eliminated all but eighteen. The number soon became twelve, then ten, then nine, and finally six, with two alternates. All were men. It was dawn before the job was finished.

A weary Captain Wiggins ran through the files of the six finalists again. The occupational cross section was one to fascinate anybody. A horse trainer, a Cuban guitar player, a former Olympic ice hockey player, a Cambridge physicist, a British nuclear engineer—*there's a bright spot!*—and a Canadian-born oceanographer. What a crew! Whatever the outcome, this cruise of HMS *Taurus* would be one to remember.

Hundreds of miles to the southeast, in the Swiss town of Chiasso, there had been frenetic activity in the Castiglione garage. In the area given over to body work, lights had burned continuously, day and night. When Associated Transfer's truck number TF87 was brought in to have its transmission fixed it had been backed into that part of the garage, segregated from the main repair area, and its body removed from the chassis by overhead lifting gear. The bodyless truck was then wheeled away to be turned over to the transmission men, who did in fact replace the old transmission, noting as they did so that what they were replacing did not seem to be in as bad shape as had been reported. But the Swiss, being Swiss, made no comment, simply completing the repair job in their usual competent manner. After all, francs were not all that easy to come by, even by the industrious Swiss.

In the segregated area, behind heavy canvas curtains hung there to keep molecules of sprayed paint from contaminating other personnel or vehicles they might be working on—not unusual in a paint and body shop—the men from the Mossad set out to accomplish their highly irregular assignment.

They had brought with them a set of preliminary sketches based on accurate measurements given by Freiburg to Ben-Udris. Within hours of their arrival they had finalized the intended modifications, including the placement of hidden ducts to be connected to the air-conditioning system in the cab. On the morning of the second day after their arrival, working around the clock, they had finished.

That same morning Jacques Freiburg came to the garage to check on the transmission job, bringing with him one of the wooden crates, all of a uniform size, used by the Zurich consortium for the shipment of bullion. Twenty-six-year-old Youssef Shuhan, a graduate of Cal Tech and the wizard of the lot, then gave him a carefully detailed look at the newly renovated body—a job bound to please the guards who from time to time accompany shipments of value in and around Zurich. For the first time there were solid benches, running the length of either side of the interior of the truck, on which to sit. The tops were hinged and could be securely locked. What was not apparent was that a second front interior wall of the body of the truck had been erected fifteen inches to the rear of the original one, creating a space in which one or more men of average size could stand with ease, braced against the movement of the truck by the proximity of the two walls. Access was provided by two perfectly concealed spring doors, one on either side of the heavy plate glass window, eighteen inches square, between the cab of the truck and its interior, its sill slanted away on the driver's side so that the width of the now double-sided front wall was not immediately apparent to someone looking at or through the window from the truck's interior.

Freiburg viewed it all with professional satisfaction. He

would, of course, report the improvements to the truck's interior to Dr. Schmeisser, with a recommendation that the other five carriers belonging to Associated Transfer, Ltd. be similarly modified. He would make no mention of the foreshortened front wall nor of the fact that he had left at the garage a wooden crate that he would, by his own means, make sure was used in the Wozchod Handelsbank's shipment of bullion to Libya.

SAN FRANCISCO
THE BOHEMIAN CLUB
9 SEPTEMBER 1979

The purple magic of a Pacific sunset was waning as the wheels of the 747, with a reassuringly gentle bump, hit the runway of the San Francisco Airport. The aircraft's approach had been from the southeast and as the city came into view its emerging lights penetrated the soft mauve to bestow upon it a measure of the mystique that so many associate with that hilly and often fog-bound sprawl. To Mark it was a welcome sight, old but ever-changing. With a sense of relief and belonging he picked out familiar landmarks—the Golden Gate Bridge, Russian and Nob hills, Candlestick Park, the pyramidal, needle-topped Transamerica Insurance Building, and johnny-come-latelies in his life, the Presidio and the San Jose Freeway. From New York, where he had holed up at the Plaza for a night, he had made a call to Charlie Sanner to tell him he was on his way, then one to Belfast and Deirdre. Her reassuring Irish voice, tender and concerned, had lifted his spirits. He had to see her—and soon. He missed her more than he would have thought possible.

1 2 1

A combination of jet lag and the two first-class meals he had consumed, the second preceded by a pair of straight up gin martinis, had taken its toll and he was bushed. Despite Sanner's advice to ease back on food and drink in anticipation of his forthcoming medical tests, he hadn't spared the horses, mostly out of boredom. But two thoughts kept running through his mind. The first stemmed from O'Farrell's words, "We'll know when you get back," and the second from Brigadier MacKenzie's admonition, "Go to San Francisco if you must, but get back here as soon as possible. And don't entertain any crazy notions about staying there, because we'll have our friends in the FBI ship you back as an accessory to murder." Hobson's choice either way.

A twenty-dollar taxi ride took him to the Bohemian Club and to a good night's sleep. The next morning at nine he checked into the Presbyterian Hospital. Twenty-four hours later he was out, after Sanner and other assorted medical sorcerers had probed with exotic instruments, taken X-rays, extracted blood, thumped, pumped, given him a stress test, and otherwise made his stay thoroughly uncomfortable.

"I don't yet know what the angiographs are going to reveal, and there are some blood studies I want to look at. We'll know in a couple of hours," said Sanner, releasing him. "But I'll say this. You've got the muscle tone, lungs, and the physique of a man twenty years younger. The hospital board meets today at noon at the Bohemian Club and they want me there to discuss a new cardiovascular lab. That shouldn't take long, so let's you and me have lunch afterward." He hesistated a moment. "But if I were you, I wouldn't count on going back to Ireland for a while. Save that until later."

"**W**eaving Spiders, Come Not Here." As one enters the Bohemian Club from Taylor Street the club's motto and its owl emblem are prominently displayed in the marble entrance hall. The motto always amused Mark. Meant to admonish members not to pitch to customers or clients, but simply to enjoy the club, its sumptuous food and superb library, and to revel in its strong artistic and theatrical traditions, its spirit was often overlooked. Among its members are a number of ex-presidents of the United States, cabinet members, European royalty, industrialists and educators, luminaries from the stage, screen, radio, and television, as well as representatives of the innermost bastions of San Franciscanism. Mark was no cynic and loved the club, but knew for a fact that a great deal of business, including the preliminaries of gigantic corporate mergers, had been consummated behind its ivy-covered facade.

Its Cartoon Room, decorated in red with a strong oriental motif, is possibly the handsomest bar in the world. It was filling up fast as Mark strolled in, just before twelve-thirty. Choosing a table on the left, where Charlie could spot him easily, he ordered a Bloody Mary and sat down to wait. Minutes later Sanner appeared. In the manner of an old friend he sat down wordlessly, took an envelope out of his inside pocket, and placed its contents, a single piece of paper, in front of Mark. It was a sketch of a human heart and its arterial connections, done by medical technicians at the hospital. A cardiologist with a reputation extending well beyond California, Charlie Sanner had taken a long and lingering look and now—gently but no less firmly—was about to tell his long-time friend that his life was at risk.

"This, my dear boy, is a map of the roadways to and from your heart. You've got some blockage here," Charlie said, pointing to a depiction of Mark's right coronary artery, "and here," indicating his left circumflex artery. "In the first instance the blockage is perhaps fifty percent, and in the latter, maybe forty. That's good, because the best indicator of long-term survival is good left ventrical function before surgery, and you've got it. In some instances, Mark, conditions no more threatening than these can be managed with medication, but I've discovered that this does not give you the same recovery qualities as a bypass. So in my opinion, which your trip from Ireland indicates to me that you value, you should let me operate. Your chances of a full recovery are very good. What the hell, Mark? You're a writer, not a long distance runner. Your life expectancy can be equal to mine—maybe more. Better still, come back to California to live where I can keep an eye on you. Give up that Irish squire bit. Pay your taxes like all the rest of us American peasants. I'll guarantee to keep you alive long enough for you to find another wife. God knows she won't be as charming as Allison, but life is good here, despite the crazies. And you can write a show for our resident thespians and we can all have a helluva time up at the Grove when they put it on."

It was an uncomfortable moment. Charlie looking at Mark as if he expected him to say "yes" or "okay," as if he had asked him to play golf or drive out to Woodside for dinner, and Mark looking at Charlie as if he wasn't the friendly executioner he suddenly appeared to be. Mark had suspected that bypass surgery might be indicated, but had tried to put it out of his mind. Now that he was confronted with it he almost felt betrayed. Charlie was acting from conviction, of course, but knew nothing of the IRA connection, nothing of the developing situation between himself and the British authorities, particularly Brigadier MacKenzie, nothing of the recent demands put upon him by O'Farrell, and nothing of Deirdre. Suddenly it occurred to him that he might never see her again. That thought, above all, brought him up short. He needed time to think it through. For almost a full minute he was silent, toying with his glass.

"It's a big decision, Charlie. There's no other way?"

"Yes, there's another way, but I can't see you in that role. Reduced activity. Constant rest. Rigidly controlled exercise. A strict diet. Sustained medication. Little or no alcohol. But more to the point, dubious results."

"I see." He didn't see at all, but he knew that he would have to delay an answer until after he had talked with Deirdre. If a telephone call wouldn't fill the bill he'd go to her or get her to come to him. "I can't give you an answer right now, Charlie. I need some time." He glanced at his watch. Nine in the evening in Ireland. "I'll call you in the morning."

"Okay. If we're going to proceed, and I hope to God you'll consent to this, I'll need some lead time for scheduling—possibly two days. So don't let's put it off."

"Charlie, I trust you implicitly, you know that. But a lot's at stake. Bear with me. I'll call you tomorrow—maybe tonight. I have to talk to Ireland."

He spent all of that afternoon and into the evening trying to reach Deirdre, maddeningly without success. She was in Dublin and couldn't be reached. Disconsolate and troubled, he walked for a change of scenery over to a once favorite Chinese restaurant on Grant Street for dinner. He'd always heard that the Chinese were notably free from heart problems, mainly on account of their diet. Why not test the theory? After a great meal built around rice and crispy duck he was back at the club and in bed by ten.

Mark awoke around seven and ordered a light breakfast of fruit, toast, and tea and a copy of the *Chronicle*. He was shaving when a knock on the door signaled the arrival of his order, pushed in unobtrusively on a wheeled table. He finished shaving, showered, then settled down to enjoy a delicious-looking half cantaloupe. After one look at the paper's headline and a quick scan of the lead story all thoughts of breakfast vanished.

IRA TERRORISTS ASSASSINATE
ANOTHER BRITISH OFFICIAL

London (UPI)—In another daring attack, the IRA claims to have taken the life of another British official, Brigadier Ian MacKenzie, a retired army officer on assignment to the Home Office. MacKenzie was killed by an explosion that he presumably triggered while walking near his home, Corscombe Hall in Hampshire. Further details are not yet available, but police officials, in attempting to reconstruct the event, have indicated that those responsible must have known of MacKenzie's habit of walking through the woods and fields adjacent to Corscombe Hall, as well as the route that he normally took. Fragments of a detonating device have been recovered. The blast was of sufficient force to clear a circle around the impact area of some twenty-five feet in diameter. Medical authorities say that MacKenzie, whose legs were blown off, must have died instantly. An autopsy, however, will be performed for any remaining clues.

Why MacKenzie should have been singled out by the IRA as a victim of its violence is not immediately known. There are indications, however, that he was associated with British Intelligence in its efforts to unravel the labyrinthian conspiracy that culminated in the assassination of Lord Mountbatten a fortnight ago.

A Mrs. Barbara Romney, a visitor at Corscombe Hall, is in a state of shock and refused to be interviewed, other than to say that only the fact that she stayed behind to prepare tea kept her from accompanying Brigadier MacKenzie and almost certainly sharing his fate.

An anonymous phone call received at the *Times* several hours after the explosion, which occurred at approximately 4:45 P.M., claimed that the IRA was responsible.

Villagers in Abbotswood, the closest community to Corscombe Hall and the spot where the murder took place, report seeing no strangers in the area. Police theorize that the explosive device was set at night and that the perpetrators left the area at the same time, trusting that it would snare its intended victim. Immigration authorities and special details from Scotland Yard have been alerted to watch all airports and surface transportation departures. A government spokesman said that Prime Minister Margaret Thatcher is convening an extraordinary meeting of the Cabinet to deal with this latest crisis.

As Mark read the last of the dispatch, he leaned back in his chair, numbed by shock. He hardly knew MacKenzie, but as the meaning of the atrocity became clearer, frustration and anger took over. For the first time he realized that the victim could have been himself—or, God forbid, Deirdre. Rumblings against her were not unknown. The contemplation of this hideous possibility gave him back some measure of self-control. He was deep in thought when there was another knock at the door. The same waiter was back.

"Express mail for you, Mr. Raven. I told the office you were up and about, so they sent me back with this."

He quickly opened the heavy red, white, and blue envelope with its distinctive postal logo. A short hand-written note from Frank Deford was ignored as Mark examined the enclosed pictures, all glossy eight-by-ten prints. He didn't count them until later—nineteen. Some served no purpose, but six showed Lee McCarthy, full face and helmet off. Smiling or scowling, the identity was there—unmistakably. Lee McCarthy and Mike O'Farrell were one and the same.

By God, I thought so, said Raven to himself. *Wait'll MacKenzie sees these.* Then he caught himself. MacKenzie was dead. *Well, somebody's going to see them!* In that moment of revelation he felt renewed—even whole. With the back of his hand he slapped the pictures hard. *O'Farrell, my friend, if nobody's looking for you now, they sure'n hell are going to be when I get there! I've got a lot of questions to ask.* He would prove to the world, and more importantly to himself, that past mistakes need not feed future ones. Out of humiliation and shameful regret would arise a new and more potent pride. Forget the bypass surgery. He would return to Ireland and do his best.

He called Charlie Sanner, who at first was puzzled, then angry, taking the news as any responsible physician should.

"I don't undersand, Mark. You come all the way from Ireland for a thorough examination, you get it from competent people, I give you my honest professional opinion, and you reject it. Now you're telling me you don't want a second opinion, that you're just going to live with it. Well, let me tell you something, friend. You ain't going to live with it very long. If I were recommending an operation for a hernia or adenoids, that would be one thing, but Mark, you're putting your life at risk. Then you come up with a big portion of cockamamie about going back to finish a job. What job? Something I must do, you say, something nobody else can do. Mark, I kid you not. You're going to go downhill fast, inviting a serious, possibly fatal heart attack. I was easy on you yesterday, as I didn't want to alarm you, but you're sicker than you think."

"Maybe so, Charlie, but I've gotta go back to Ireland— right now. But this I promise. I'll be back here soon, maybe in six weeks. Then you can slice and patch as much as you wish."

"You mean this?"

"I mean it."

"All right." Sanner's anger was subsiding. "You always were stubborn. But I'm going to send you a hell of a bill for this, because I'm afraid I'll never see you again. When you get back to Ireland, see your local doctor and follow his advice. And I'll add no smoking, moderate drinking only—it'll do you good—no tennis, golf, or riding, lots of sleep and rest, and cut way back on fatty foods. This is not your surgeon speaking, but a devoted friend. Promise me this."

"So long, Charlie."

"Promise me this?"

"So long, Charlie."

"God dammit, tell me you'll do what I say." The phone went dead. "Son of a bitch," said Sanner in disgust. "Damn if I don't send him a big bill." Somehow it never got done.

As soon as he hung up on Sanner, Mark placed two overseas calls—the first to Deirdre, whom he reached immediately, to say that he was returning at once and would call her again from New York to let her know when he would be arriving in Dublin. She was concerned, but he assured her that he was okay. The second was to Peter Lindsay. To his surprise he got through to him also.

"Major Lindsay, Mark Raven here. I'm in San Francisco and have just learned of Brigadier MacKenzie's death. Godawful news. I'm returning to Ireland today."

"As a result of what happened to MacKenzie?" Lindsay had been numbed by MacKenzie's death and was now operating out of a cold fury. "What did your doctors tell you? I hope your condition's all right."

"Hardly," replied Mark, "but I now consider that secondary. And yes, I'm returning on account of MacKenzie's death. I want you to know I'm available."

"Good show. There are important developments at this end. But stay out of England. If you're seen here you'll be the subject of unwanted attention. We'll meet you in Ireland. Don't call us; we'll call you—and soon."

Raven hung up with a sense of disquiet. It had never really occurred to him that he was going to die, either in San Francisco or back in Ireland, peacefully or violently. Dying is something that happens to your rival's screenplay or your ex-wife's second husband. It is acceptable as metaphor but totally inconvenient as reality—something to be viewed as a last in-

1 2 9

comprehensible failure by an overachiever, or to be ignored like the woolly taste in one's mouth accompanying a hangover, an ephemeral condition that vanishes with a slosh of the proper mouthwash. But now it seemed to be for real. He hoped he hadn't been too short with Charlie Sanner. He had the feeling, however, that the longer he talked with Charlie the better Charlie's chances were of talking him into staying. And that would not have been good.

It was mid-afternoon when his flight arrived at Kennedy International Airport. He had fretted throughout the flight to New York, looking again at the pictures sent him by Frank Deford and wondering what events had turned a running back for the Los Angeles Rams into an active member of the IRA, complete with new identity. By great good fortune there was space on an Aer Lingus flight leaving at 10:00 P.M. He hated night flights, especially eastward across the Atlantic, but since this one should get him back to Raven Park by early afternoon the next day, he took it. He felt entirely well, but as a sop to Sanner's advice he checked in at an airport motel to rest until flight time.

After a hot shower he called Deirdre, then settled down to read *The New York Times*. Suddenly it occurred to him that there should be a considerable sum of money, all royalties, in the hands of his agent, Owen Newcombe. Better have them. When the phone rang in his office, Newcombe was on the point of leaving to catch an early train back to Greenwich. Impatient to get away, he was in the process of telling his secretary that he had left for the day when she recognized Mark's voice and spoke to him by name. *My principal meal ticket,* thought Newcombe, *I'll talk with him anytime.* Moreover he was genuinely fond of Mark. He listened with surprise as Mark told him he had been in San Francisco for a medical checkup, that bypass surgery had been recommended, but that he wasn't buying it—at least not for now. Instead he was returning to Ireland to help out some friends.

"What kind of help?" said Owen.

"I'm really not in a position to say," replied Mark, "but I've got myself embroiled in Irish politics. I'm going back to try to straighten matters out."

"You're not a politician, Mark. What the hell are you up to? And from what I know of bypass surgery, that's something that's not recommended unless the guy who's going to get it is almost around the bend. You're not in that shape, are you? My God, Mark, why haven't you told me this before? I don't want to sound selfish, but we've got book contracts out. And another picture offer brewing on the coast. I got a call yesterday from Sid Weisman at Paramount. If you're going to be out of commission for a while that one won't be affected, but the book contracts will."

"There may be another kind of contract out on me. I'm going home to try to cancel it."

"What the hell are you talking about, Mark? Are you serious? Jesus, what gives?"

"It's a long story, Owen—one that I don't want to get into right now. Suffice it to say that I've been a dead-wrong idealist in supporting elements in Irish society that want a change."

"Mother of God, you're not talking about the IRA?"

"I'm talking about the IRA. But that information is for you alone; otherwise you've lost a client. Maybe you've lost one anyway."

"I can't believe what I'm hearing."

"Believe it—but look at the bright side. If I get out of this one, I can see another novel looming up—maybe called *The Tides of Sligo*. I dreamed that one up this morning, on the plane from California. How does that grab you?"

"Nothing's going to take much of a hold on me until I know you're all right. Come clean with me, Mark. You and I have come a long way together. We're business partners, whether you like it or not."

"Owen, I've done a lot of harm, which I bitterly regret. I'm no longer sure which side is right, but in my own way, maybe I can help make amends. If you're holding any royalties for me, put them in the Wells Fargo Bank. I'm going to need all the money I can get."

He paused, then added, "So long, Owen. In fact, maybe good-bye. You've been a good friend."

He hung up on his puzzled agent, then lay back on the bed, staring at the ceiling and thinking about Deirdre. He knew that she was deeply troubled by his views of the problems between the two Irelands and by his support for the Provos. Moreover he was convinced that had she known—or even guessed at the extent of it—the love that now engulfed them both could not have blossomed, much less survived. Enshrined in her own peculiar brand of Irishness, she was for him both tender and tough, flexible and immovable, saintly but a creature of worldly flesh. She had shaken him to his roots, expressively and incisively understanding much of what he had revealed about himself—and in the process revealing an equal amount about herself.

But now, all of a sudden, MacKenzie's assassination rears its ugly head to further complicate his latest contribution of £100,000! *Mother of God, what have I done!*

PART TWO

THE HEIST

NEW ORLEANS
MARDI GRAS
13 FEBRUARY 1979

Shrove Tuesday in New Orleans. It was approaching midnight and Bourbon Street was alive with the falloff of Mardi Gras, revelers in enough shapes and sizes and varying degrees of respectability to tax the imagination of a Pulitzer Prize novelist. Shoulder to shoulder they mingled—clowns, clones, tramps, Queens of Sheba, queens of the night (both sexes plus some in between), ringmasters and lion tamers, Arab sheiks, seventeenth-century swashbucklers, pirates, male and female half-naked dancers, fully clothed nuns (a favorite ploy for streetwalkers looking for johns interested in kinky sex), ladies with painted faces in long gowns and short, witches, a sprinkling of Jimmy Carter masks to more effectively hide the identity of their wearers, Mickey Mouses by the dozen, cowboys and Indians—all caught up in the four-day frenzy preceding Ash Wednesday and beginning of Lent and all having, or giving the appearance of having, a hell of a good time.

If jazz is a religion then Bourbon Street is its cathedral, a strip four blocks long where "The Star Spangled Banner" has been replaced as the national anthem by "The Saints Go Marching In." Where memories of Al Hirt invoking the angels to sing can bring all the smiles that the song says accompany that phenomenon. Where Dizzy Gillespie, Louis "Satch-mo" Armstrong, and Ray Charles have sung, played, and blown their hearts out for cheering and appreciative aficionados. On this night, however, the music of the high priests of jazz was notably lacking, lost in a cacophony of sound from kazoos, rattles, and every other sort of noisemakers fighting for recognition in a snowstorm of confetti and paper streamers. And in this bedlam drug pushers, pickpockets, and prostitutes found the rewards of their calling highly satisfactory despite the best efforts of the New Orleans vice squad to sort them out and keep the situation under control.

At the corner of Bourbon and Terrebonne streets a thirty-year-old man in a Louisiana State University sweatshirt and faded blue jeans lolled disarmingly against the waist-high but somewhat elaborate wrought iron fence in front of Louie's Bar, as announced by a blue neon sign over the entrance. His only concession to the scene and to the players around him was a pair of fake black plastic eyeglass rims, complete with a large flesh-colored nose and black mustache, making him look for all the world like Groucho Marx. It also made him unrecognizable, even to his close associates. As he looked around, taking in more than he appeared to, he seemed lonely. On the other side of the street a girl dressed as a Gypsy had been watching him intently. *He looks lost,* she thought. *A good mark.* She moved in his direction.

As she made her way across the crowded street, a tiny bell tied to one ankle tinkled with each step, its sound lost in the confusion of a hundred competing noises. In forty feet she rebuffed that many whistles and cheery greetings, including one or two hands injudiciously reaching out to touch her. She was just coming off a marijuana high.

LSU Sweatshirt saw her coming, his antenna tuned. She stopped, smiled, and took one of his hands in hers, pushing the sleeve of the sweatshirt back to rub his forearm gently.

"You nice-lookin' mon," she said, raising a bracelet-heavy wrist to touch him lightly on the cheek. "I tell your fortune. Real nice."

Then without asking, she removed his false nose and glasses. She leaned back to look at him more closely. "You *are*

1 3 6

a nice-lookin' mon. I tell you all about future—girls, money, anyt'ing you want to know."

"You're going to tell my fortune? Right here? For how much?"

"For you, nice mon, twenty doll-aires."

As she spoke, a clown in a battered hat, with a face painted like Emmett Kelly's, moved closer from his position ten yards away to see what was going on.

"Right here, on the street, you're going to tell my fortune?" said Sweatshirt.

"Sure. We sit down there." Gypsy Girl started to tug him in the direction of a bench just inside the wrought iron fence. *I'm sure as hell not going to get screwed there,* thought Sweatshirt. *But this looks like a bust. We'll go for it.*

"Okay," he said.

She sat down. "Pay me first. Then I bless money. Then I tell your fortune—real nice."

He reached for his wallet. Outside the fence the clown was watching. Sweatshirt took out two marked ten dollar bills, which she took, stuffing them into her bag. As she did so Sweatshirt's attitude took a new turn.

"Sweetheart," he said, "I got news for you. I'm going to tell *your* fortune. And it ain't going to be real nice." He flipped his wallet open to display a police badge. "Detective Stack, New Orleans Vice Squad. You're under arrest." He grabbed her wrist in an iron grip.

"Shit," said Gypsy Girl, half under her breath. *I'm losing my touch.* Then she started to cry. Wordlessly the clown produced a pair of handcuffs, passing them over the top of the fence. Ten minutes later they were on their way to night court in a squad car.

Judge Walter Bailey presided over Section II of the New Orleans Night Court. "Old Bailey himself," as he was often called, rheumy-eyed and bulbous-nosed. His face was a road map of small red capillary veins, the result of a steady diet of rich Cajun food lubricated by numerous infusions of bourbon whiskey. He'd been dispensing his own particular brand of justice in these honorable chambers for the better part of ten years and in a perverse way had developed a certain fondness for some of the street people who came before him, a fondness not extending to those accused of crimes of violence or abuse; but for the unfortunates who dealt in flimflammery, minor fraud, or even prostitution he had in fact developed a certain empathy that often manifested itself in lighter sentences or jocular words.

Winnowed out from a dozen other defendants including two pickpockets and an assortment of prostitutes, among them a stunningly dressed black transvestite brought in moments behind her, the Gypsy girl now stood before the judge, the vice squad man at her side.

"The charge is fortune-telling, Your Honor. For money."

"A fortune-teller? What's your name, honey?"

"Desdemona, dazzling, loyal and pure, daughter of the moon and the stars, born under Aquarius the water-bearer, with Pisces and Uranus in close collaboration to bless my nature with sweetness and light and the occult powers of the east." It was a description she spoke by rote, a spiel delivered a hundred times in carnivals and side shows. The effects of the marijuana had left her but her voice was clear and strong, with an accent not often heard in Judge Bailey's sordid world.

He listened with amused tolerance, noting as he did so the girl's erect carriage and the utter lack of subservience as she spoke. It was a welcome break in an otherwise monotonously repetitious session. He noted too the way in which she was dressed—a costume straight out of the book. Jet black hair held in tow by a red bandanna, circular gold earrings, a blouse of coarse white cotton worn with a half dozen cheap, variety store necklaces nestling naturally in the cleavage of her bosom—firm without benefit of bra—and a red flowered skirt, no stockings, and open sandals on her feet.

"Say that again, Fortune-teller. I know it ain't so, but it's sech a pretty speech."

She smiled, then complied, with no further intimation that she shared his amusement.

That was enough for the judge. Moreover others in the crowded chamber were getting restive.

"Okay, honey. Now tell me your name. Never mind the malarkey. Where do you live? How old are you?" A civil rights lawyer would have had a field day in Judge Bailey's court, but they are not usually found in such low-level legal proceedings except by prearrangement.

"Aha! You say malarkey. Good Irish word. You Irish mon, Your Honor? You good mon. You no hurt me. My name? Renée Koulatsos is my name. Born in Ireland. Father and mother born in Rumania but get out before Hitler kill all Jews and Gypsies. I'm good Irish Gypsy. Born in Cork."

She reached into a voluminous crocheted handbag slung over one shoulder and got out a well-worn brown manila envelope, taking from it a document that she laid in front of the judge.

"Renée Koulatsos," she said again, as if for emphasis. "I'm twenty-four. Where do I live? Where all Gypsies live—in Romany." She nudged the document that she had laid on the judge's bench, as if to prove something.

"Romany? Where's Romany?" Judge Bailey picked up the document. It was a valid Republic of Ireland passport, her most treasured possession, which she had obtained with great difficulty, an accomplishment impossible without the concerned help of several Catholic nuns.

"Romany is everywhere. All Gypsies live in Romany. Here, where we are now, is Romany. All of United States is Romany. So is Canada and Australia. England, Europe—everywhere. All is Romany."

"So you're an honest-to-God Gypsy and that's not just a costume you're wearing?"

"I speak truth, Your Honor. Yes, I'm Gypsy. But born in Ireland. Look at passport."

The judge looked, then read out loud. "Born 13 February 1955, Sacred Heart of Jesus Hospital, Cork, Ireland. Well, I'll be damned. And today's your birthday. How'd you get here?"

"Win Irish Sweepstakes, Your Honor. Five t'ousand doll-aires." She seemed eager to tell all about it.

"Okay—New Orleans is Romany. And you're a Gypsy. And you've been picked up for fortune-telling—maybe a better charge would be soliciting for prostitution. Both are against the law here, honey. Both are offenses."

"No, Your Honor," she replied quickly. "No prostitute. Gypsy women virtuous. Tell your fortune, yes. We good at that. Steal a little, maybe, but no prostitute. If I like someone I love him. You know what I mean, Judge? But no do it for money. Gypsy women virtuous. Have to be. Gypsy men beat the hell out of you if they find you with goy. Ask this mon here, he tell you."

"How about it, Tom. What did she say to you?"

"She's right, Your Honor," replied Stack. "All she asked me was if I wanted my fortune told."

"Then what?"

"I said 'How much?' She said 'Twenty bucks,' and I gave it to her. Then I arrested her. City code, section four-twenty-two, prohibits fortune-telling in New Orleans. Maybe she's a hooker too, but I figured get 'em off the streets one way or another."

"Renée, you heard what the man said. Twenty bucks to tell his fortune is too much. I think maybe you make your living between your legs and were going to take him somewhere, or try to, for a roll in the hay or maybe just a roll, relieving him of all of his money in the process. In any event you're in violation of the city code and I'm going to have to fine you or send you to jail. You got money for a fine? Money you didn't steal?"

Renée reached once more into the brown manila envelope. This time she brought out a plane ticket. This too she put in front of the judge.

"Your Honor, you nice mon. Good Irish mon. I can tell. No malarkey. Tomorrow I go back to Ireland. Plane ticket New Orleans to London. That's why I came here. Last May I win Irish Sweepstakes. Five t'ousand doll-aires. First I buy nice secondhand caravan—shower, hot water, stove, everyt'ing. Then I come to U.S. to see relatives. My brother runs welding shop in Mobile. I also like to make a little money. You know, state fairs, carnivals, resort towns—some nice but mostly chickenshit places. Sorry, Your Honor, but that just slip out. You nice mon, you no hurt me. You let me go, I leave here, go to Greyhound bus station, pick up suitcase and vamoose. Got plenty money left. Seven hundred ten doll-aire."

Judge Bailey looked at Detective Tom Stack. It was his charge and the arrest would be part of his charted record. The vice squad man shrugged, then nodded, ready to go back on the streets. Two more nights of Mardi Gras madness and things would return to normal.

The judge switched his gaze back to the girl. Beyond a general air of easily corrected dishevelment she was good-looking, no doubt about that. Moreover she had pretty teeth. Judge Bailey was a sucker for pretty teeth, probably because his own were false.

"Renée," he said, "I'll tell you what I'm going to do. I'm going to give you a birthday present. When's your plane leave?"

"Eight o'clock, Your Honor."

"Is it a through flight—no stops in the U.S.?"

"Yes, Your Honor."

"Okay." Judge Bailey glanced at a wall clock. "It's two-twenty. Renée, honey, you're going to have to spend a few

1 4 1

hours in the station lockup. Then around six in the morning I'll get Sergeant Loiseaux to run you by the bus station so you can pick up your bag. And I'm gonna instruct the sergeant to see that you get on that flight. Get out of the U.S. Go back to Ireland. And don't ever let me catch you around here again, because if you do I'm gonna send you straight to jail. You understand?"

"Judge, you nice mon, just like I told you." Renée's relief was palpable. "Sure I understand. And I go straight back to Ireland."

"One more thing," said Judge Bailey. "There'll be some others with you in the detention cell. Don't try to hustle 'em or the deal's off."

"No way, judge," said Renée, moving off with Detective Stack. "I behave real nice." She looked back and smiled. "You sure you don't want your fortune told?"

As Renée and Stack went off to the lockup the black transvestite, his thinning face already showing the first traces of an as yet unrecognized case of AIDS, came forward to face the judge, accompanied by a uniformed police officer. One look at him and Judge Bailey exploded.

"Alvin! Goddammit, you back here again? What am I gonna do with you? My patience is at an end. This time you're gonna leave the streets for good."

The judge was right. Alvin, once a singer with a high falsetto voice well known on Bourbon Street, died four months later in the infirmary of the Orleans Parish jail.

On TWA's morning flight from New Orleans to London Renée slept most of the way. After a timely connection at Heathrow she found herself on the flight to Shannon sitting next to an American who introduced himself as Mike O'Farrell, frequent business traveler to Ireland. She didn't try to sell him a bill of goods or tell him her name was Desdemona,

1 4 2

dazzling or otherwise. She played it straight. The conversation became very friendly, if not intimate, punctuated by much hand-holding and subtle pressures in both her lap and his.

When they deplaned there was a more than friendly good-bye kiss and for O'Farrell a general delivery address, care of postmaster, Swinford, County Mayo, through which Renée Koulatsos, self-confessed Gypsy, fortune-teller, and spiritual adviser, could be reached—on an irregular basis. And Renée had the number of a bar in Belfast called the Corkscrew where she could leave a message for her newfound friend. He had hit a responsive chord in the itinerant Gypsy and she very much wanted to see him again.

OPERATION PLEIADES—THE ROUNDUP

TESS STRIKES CLOSE TO HOME FOR NUMBER ONE

The finals of the Midlands Invitation Squash Racquets Tournament at the Telford Center were being played before an appreciative group of spectators. Space limitations kept the group to less than a hundred, but they were seeing the game played at state-of-the-art form, with Suleh Banjih, a Pakistani, pitted against Roger Delafield, ranked third in all of Britain. The game score stood at two each, the advantage having alternated back and forth between the opponents for the first four games. In the rubber game the score stood at eight to five, in favor of Delafield, but it was hard fought all the way. For the last ten minutes of play Delafield had been watched with consuming interest by a latecomer who had squeezed into the last available space in the small tiered gallery. In doing so he stood close to where Fiona Gascoyne, a violet-eyed Irish girl with jet black hair, was sitting. She was Delafield's fiancée, and they were planning to be married as soon as Delafield could get away from his job for a proper honeymoon in the States, as he was anxious to show his new bride the places where he had both worked and studied.

Delafield served, a carom shot off the front and side wall. Banjih waited, took it off the back wall, and drove a hard, straight shot down the side. The instant he had returned

1 4 3

it he knew it would be high enough above the telltale for De-
lafield to shift over behind him and recover. He was right. De-
spite a monumental effort he lost the match when Delafield
eased his return to the far corner of the court, a drop shot
impossible for Suleh to reach. It was over. A standing ovation
and noisy acclaim for both players followed as the several re-
porters present scrambled for the telephones.

The following is a transcript of the summary—updated
periodically—appearing on the inside cover of the personnel
file of a consultant to British naval intelligence at its Whitehall
headquarters. The existence of this file, with indications of its
contents, is known to both MI-5 and MI-6.

FEODOR ROGUCHIN aka ROGER CHINN DELAFIELD—
British subject; born 17 October 1946, Shanghai. Father was
Viktor Andreovich Roguchin, an expatriate White Russian;
mother Elizabeth Kerne, native-born Englishwoman, former
saleslady, Shanghai bookstore. Speaks fluent idiomatic Rus-
sian, several Chinese dialects as well as English. Brought up
in Hong Kong, where his parents moved in 1950. Father died
in 1957, after which mother remarried to Robert Delafield, an
Englishman with the Hong Kong and Shanghai Banking Corp.
Roguchin sent to England 1958 to Eton College, after adoption
by stepfather with legal change of name to Roger Chinn
Delafield.

Graduate mechanical engineer, from Balliol College,
Oxford. Armstrong Vickers Shipbuilding Group, Barrow-in-
Furness, 1968–; graduate studies Massachusetts Institute of
Technology 1972–74; U.S. Atomic Energy Commission, Ma-
rine Design Group, 1974–75; an acknowledged expert on sub-
marine design. Unmarried; lives at Newby Bridge, Cumbria,
commuting to A-V Yards at Barrow. Hobbies: squash racquets,
hiking, and sailing.

CLEARANCES: BRITISH/COSMIC:US/TOP SECRET

Forty minutes after the match was over the latecomer
was waiting for Delafield as he left the locker room. He intro-
duced himself, showed Delafield a black leather-encased cred-
ential, and handed him a sealed envelope. Delafield tore it
open, read the contents through hurriedly, then once more—
carefully. When finished he nodded, returned the communica-

1 4 4

tion to its envelope and handed it back to the stranger. The latter put it back in his pocket, shook hands with Delafield, and departed.

Two hours later Delafield was back at Newby Bridge, an interim stop before returning to his office at the yards in Barrow. Fiona, normally a bubbly girl, was not only disappointed but positively testy. She had counted on having a lovely dinner and spending an even lovelier night with Roger at the Sparrow, an inn at Telford. And she certainly couldn't understand why he couldn't tell her where he was going or for how long.

"I suppose the next thing you're going to tell me is that this will delay our marriage even more?" she had asked, tartly.

"Darling, I don't think so, but if it turns out that way, there's nothing I can do about it." He had hugged her reassuringly.

"Roger, you can be very annoying at times," she replied, pushing him away. "It must be the Russian in you. But don't press your luck too far." She turned and stormed away, heading for her car.

Delafield looked after her in dismay, sighed, and went back into the locker room to retrieve his bag.

"Bloody hell!" he exclaimed, to nobody in particular. But he knew he'd have to go.

MI-5 was moving fast. The roundup for Pleiades had started, and the first of the intended auxiliary crewmen was on notice.

HAMPSHIRE
CORSCOMBE HALL
11 SEPTEMBER 1979

The memory of that awful moment would haunt her for the rest of her life. Barbara Romney had put down the needlepoint on which she was working, gotten up off the sofa, turned off the telly, and was on her way to the kitchen to brew a pot of tea when she heard—no, felt—the explosion. It was not the sound so much as the rattling of the window that frightened her. Instinctively she knew that something terrible had happened. She stopped, all senses alert for a clue to what it was. Suddenly Corscombe Hall seemed to be in the grip of a death-like silence. In panic she ran back through the dining room to the hall and to the garden door.

Throwing it open, she shouted, "Ian, Ian! Where are you?"

In the late afternoon of a windless day she felt as if she were shouting into the teeth of a hurricane. Her words were lost in the pervasive silence. In the distance she could hear the honking of several automobile horns, blown as if in anger, and persistent. Tearfully she ran back to the pantry and to the telephone, frantically jiggling the hook for the attention of the operator. When she got through to the local constabulary, Mr. Comstock could tell her only that there was an emergency of some sort.

With mounting apprehension she heard the sounding of the fire alarm, then twenty minutes later Mrs. Hawthorne, the village seamstress, with tears streaming down her cheeks, reached Corscombe Hall with the shattering news.

The path through the trees skirted a meadow on the left, then broke out into the open as the woods gave way to open fields divided by low stone walls, a rare sight in southern England but always an added attraction for Brigadier MacKenzie as he took one of his favorite walks. Rick, his Irish setter, nose to ground, frolicked playfully in wide-ranging arcs as he ran from and returned to the striding Scot in response to the whistle slung around the neck of his master.

MacKenzie turned and looked in the direction of Corscombe Hall, nestled in the valley below. He was perhaps three-quarters of a mile away. Abbotswood lay just beyond, its one church with its ancient square stone tower, built in the fifteenth century, giving the village at once its identity and its name. It was a view he had savored for years, from childhood on, one that he remembered and carried with him through tours of duty in the Middle East, in Korea, in Belize, and in West Germany—wherever his soldier's life had taken him.

Fifty yards away, on the opposite side of a pasture where horses normally grazed, and over a stile, the path reentered another wooded area to dip down gently to a stream. As a boy MacKenzie and his chums had dammed it to make a pool in which to swim, but all evidence of that early building project had long since vanished. Now wild gooseberry bushes grew in profusion on both sides and the path leading down to the now easily fordable stream was blanketed with leaves, twigs, and other refuse of the forest.

MacKenzie was halfway to the stream, pushing aside the few low branches of overhanging trees, when Rick, trotting contentedly by his side, stopped. He raised his nose in the air, sniffed, then uncharacteristically growled.

"What is it, Rick boy? What do you see?" said Mac-Kenzie, patting the dog.

The dog had seen nothing unusual, but his keen nose had picked up the scent of a stranger, together with an acrid smell that he could not identify, upwind and to one side.

From his concealed position O'Farrell—a safe distance away and his face covered by a ski mask—had watched with apprehension as MacKenzie had crossed the stile and started into the woods. He had not expected the dog, an unknown and therefore a dangerous factor. He was sweating and now cursed softly under his breath.

As the dog left MacKenzie's side and started in his direction O'Farrell, irrationally but in a gesture of self-defense, reached for his revolver and cocked it.

Seconds later MacKenzie continued toward the stream. He could hear Rick, now barking continuously, splashing through the water. Unsure of his footing, MacKenzie looked down, then recoiled as if he had seen a puff adder.

It was too late. His instep had hit the nearly invisible piece of black wire stretched across and inches above the path, triggering the explosive device set by O'Farrell. In that infinitesimal part of a second before consciousness ceased he was aware of a blinding flash. His eardrums were punctured by the force of the blast but not before he heard it. There was a searing stab of pain at the base of his spine as one part of his brain upbraided another for a lack of caution. Then oblivion.

The charge, cannily constructed by O'Farrell at a third of the potential force contained in a can of C-4, temporarily stunned the Irish setter but also had the effect of enraging him, as if taunted by another animal. The hair on his spine was standing straight up as he started up the hill after the still unseen scent, alternating barking and coursing, seeking the offensive odor. By animal instinct alone he knew that the odor and his master were enemies.

As Rick burst out of a thicket O'Farrell fired at the charging animal. He missed. Before he could fire again Rick had sunk his teeth firmly into the ankle of the still hooded figure. Howling with pain, O'Farrell tried to kick the dog loose but succeeded only in making Rick—growling in rage through clenched teeth—clamp down harder. Afraid to fire again for fear of shooting himself in the foot, O'Farrell, with all of his strength, hit the dog in the head with the butt of the heavy Magnum pistol. The blow hit the still battling Rick just over one eye. Rick went limp, the growling stopped, the jaws relaxed, and he collapsed on his side. His eyes were ablaze with hate as he bared his teeth to growl one last time at the strange-looking figure who stood over him, gun in hand.

A second shot opened up the dog's skull and killed him

instantly. As O'Farrell retrieved the soft moccasin he had been wearing and inspected his bleeding ankle, he cursed aloud.

"Shit! God damn dog! What the fuck were you doing here?"

Then he heard the village fire alarm. *Christ! Gotta get outa here!* The pain was considerable but as fast as he could he took off in the direction of his rented car a quarter of a mile away.

Halfway there both the pain and the swelling had increased to the point where it was difficult for him to get through a barbed wire fence he had easily negotiated on the way in. In his anxiety to make good his getaway he was at the point of panic, so much so that when he put his pistol on the ground to make it possible to slip through the barbed wire, he forgot to pick it up. Driving like the wind, he was on the outskirts of Dover before he missed it.

A frantic search of his car turned up empty. Not until then did he remember his blunder and recognize the dilemma that he had created for himself. The sight of his badly inflamed ankle, however, kept him from the risky business of going back for the missing weapon. Not only panic but now fear possessed him, but his only option was to press on, hoping that a clinic he knew about at Outreau, sixteen kilometers beyond Calais on the road to Paris, would be open to treat his wound.

Approaching the Irish coast, the plane dropped through the overcast as the gray, rain-laden clouds dissolved into thin mist. From his window seat Mark could see the beaches and the rocky shoreline of County Clare holding back the ocean's foam from the green fields that lay behind. The plane would land at Shannon, where he had left his car. The prospect of a three-hour drive—easy on N17 highway—did little to dampen his enthusiasm nor his consuming desire—physical as well as emotional—for a reunion with Deirdre. It would be good to be home. All thoughts of San Francisco and Charlie Sanner's unmistakable warnings had vanished. As if to reassure himself he felt his chest, inhaling and exhaling several times. All seemed to be okay.

In his last phone call to Deirdre from New York Mark had told her what flight he was taking, but hadn't asked her to meet him. Yet as the flaps came down for the approach to Shannon his hopes arose that she might be on hand.

The big 747 with its bulging brow taxied up to the terminal and cut its motors. Next came the motor-driven passenger ports, fore and aft, to snuggle up to the side of the aircraft. Mark hurried to get off. Just inside the terminal, behind the rope barriers giving exiting passengers a clear way to baggage claim, there she was, looking radiant. *Wunderbar!* Mark's heart leaped within him, and he rushed to hold her in his arms. For a moment neither spoke, but Deirdre hugged him until she was afraid she was going to crush his ribs. She wanted to stay like this forever, never letting him go.

Finally Mark, who had been kissing her on the nape of her neck and cheek, backed away enough to kiss her on the lips. He saw that she was crying.

"What is it, darling? What's the matter?"

"Oh, Mark, I'm *so* glad to see you. That's one reason I'm crying. Are you all right? I want to know everything your doctors told you in San Francisco. Let's go over here and sit down." The words came tumbling out and she was dabbing at her eyes with a handkerchief. Arms about one another, they walked to the nearest chairs.

"*One* reason you're crying?" countered Mark. "Is there another? I'm going to be all right. Don't worry about me."

"I can't let anything happen to you, Mark. Please don't die. Yes, there's another reason, but first, kiss me again and hold my hand. I just want to look at you."

She looked and tried to smile, but the tears came again. She leaned on his shoulder, with his arm around her, holding her tightly. In a moment she had regained her composure.

"My Aunt Deirdre died, my mother's sister. The funeral's tomorrow, in Strabane, and I must go. You never knew her, Mark, but I owe her everything. I was devoted to her, and I'm so grateful. If it hadn't been for her and her generosity I'd still be working in the mills at Sion. I'll tell you all about her later, but she's the one who made it possible for me to have a decent education. I flew down from Belfast on the shuttle to see you but I must go right back. I needed to see you, Mark, so here I am."

"Thank God for that," said Mark. "I'll go to the funeral with you."

"No! You mustn't. I forbid it." Suddenly she seemed upset. "This latest atrocity, Brigadier MacKenzie's death, has pumped even more poison into the atmosphere. I don't even think you should move around too freely—and you certainly shouldn't be seen with me in Strabane. People wouldn't understand."

1 5 1

Mark was silent for a moment, thinking about the hundred thousand pounds he had left for O'Farrell to pass to COMMEND. He knew that this was not the time to try to explain.

"Very well," he said, "but I don't like it. You know I'm here to help in any way I can—and I expect you to call on me. Will you come down to Raven Park as soon as you can?"

"Of course, right after the funeral. But now tell me—what about the bypass? Are you going to have that operation?"

"Not now. Maybe later. And if so, in San Francisco. And I'll want you there with me."

"And I'll go too." Deirdre was smiling again. "Maybe I can touch a few generous California hearts for support for Peaceful Means. Now I've got to be off or I'll miss my plane. When are we going to talk?"

"At Raven Park, when you come down."

"Promise?"

"Promise."

The Belfast flight was being called as they walked, hand in hand, to Gate 6. Deirdre drew admiring glances and some wondered if romance was catching up to a woman generally regarded throughout Ireland, north and south, as one with a single admirable aim in life—to bring peace between the warring factions in strife-torn Ulster.

"Good-bye, my darling. Now that you're back in Ireland I won't worry so." Deirdre kissed him again.

"Good-bye, Deirdre. How wonderful that you were here to meet me. I love you." One more kiss and she was off.

Less than five minutes after Mark had driven away from the airport parking lot an inbound flight from Paris arrived at Shannon. Among its disembarking passengers was a sturdily built, athletic-looking American, identified by his passport as

Francis X. Ambrose, of Boston, Massachusetts. He was on crutches and wore a shoe on his right foot only, his left ankle being heavily bandaged and covered only with a sock. For baggage he had only an Air France flight bag, half empty, which a stewardess had thoughtfully tied to the hand grip on one crutch.

He made his way slowly to immigration where, after a few perfunctory questions and an inspection of his basically genuine but skillfully doctored U.S. passport, he was allowed to proceed. Minutes later O'Farrell had struck a deal with a cab driver and was on his way to Dublin.

OPERATION PLEIADES—THE ROUNDUP

TESS AND NUMBER TWO—A WINTER OF DISCONTENT

The results of the Winter Olympics at Innsbruck in 1976 didn't give the British much to cheer about, but Lady Daphne Fortesque, the third child and only daughter of the Earl of Falkenhurst, Secretary of State for Commonwealth Affairs, scored high not only in the women's giant slalom but also in the hearts of the British public. Twenty-three years old, the divorced mother of a two-year-old son whom she had on skis shortly after his first birthday, she beat the best that the Scandinavians, the Americans, the Austrians, the East Germans, and the other countries of Central Europe could come up with. And that's not all she won. She walked off with the heart of a Russian hockey player, a twenty-six-year-old Red Army officer named Vladimir Igorovich Pontriagyn, although the enduring love affair between them was not to surface until almost a year later.

At that time the Russian hockey team, still playing the game in world-class fashion, was on tour as a piece of high-style Soviet propaganda. It had come to Montreal to play the Canadiens of the National Hockey League, beating them six to five in overtime. At 2:00 A.M. the following morning, after knocking out his political bodyguard, Pontriagyn walked into police headquarters to ask for political asylum. He almost didn't get it, as the Soviets—still smarting over the earlier de-fection in the same city of Igor Gouzenko, who brought to the West exceptional information on the KGB's infiltration of the intelligence networks of the free world—made such an issue over the circumstances that the Canadians almost caved in to Soviet demands for the return of Pontriagyn. What many ob-servers think was the crucial move that made such action un-thinkable was the much publicized flight to Montreal of the Lady Daphne, still the darling of the London tabloids, accom-panied by no less a person than her father.

Pontriagyn got his asylum and a wife as well. He and Daphne moved into a cottage on the Yorkshire estate of his father-in-law, where he transferred his athletic ability to tennis and to skiing, at which he was more than adept to begin with. A crack shot, he pleased Lord Falkenhurst mightily when the latter introduced him to grouse shooting, and his brother-in-law, Viscount Aylesworth, liked his earthy sense of humor. Handsome in a Slavic sort of way, Vladimir had a broad face, dark searching eyes, and a ready smile. One gold tooth, a replacement for an upper molar knocked out by a hockey puck, could sometimes be seen if his smile were broad enough. Daphne and Sandy Aylesworth made him realize that it really had to go.

While seeking his place in the scheme of things and grap-pling with the English language, Vladimir undertook to deliver a series of lectures at Wellington, the British public school most often thought of as a preparatory school for Sandhurst, Britain's equivalent of West Point. The Falkenhursts, father and son, had gone there and made the arrangements. At Well-ington, Vladimir was called the Russkie, but the boys liked him, laughing with him and at him as he sometimes tripped over his heavily accented but fast-improving English. He was supposed to talk about the Red Army, its size, deployment, and mission, but often strayed, at the urging of his appreciative audience, into his days as a hockey player.

As Vladimir was a skilled mechanic and knew something about agriculture as well, it seemed logical to make him the manager of Lord Falkenhurst's Yorkshire holdings, some three thousand acres largely devoted to the raising of sheep. On an unseasonably warm September afternoon he had been working on a tractor when a dark gray sedan drew up. As the driver got

1 5 4

out Vladimir recognized him at once as one of several inter-
rogators who had questioned him so extensively at the safe
house in Norfolk when he had first arrived in England.

The MI-5 man had hardly had a chance to open up the
conversation before Lord Falkenhurst himself drove up. Vladimir was surprised, as he had heard Daphne talking on the
phone with her father in London earlier in the day. Lord
Falkenhurst greeted Vladimir warmly, then stepped inside a
nearby shed for several moments of private conversation with
Wallace Comerford, as the man called himself. What Vladimir
did not know was that Deputy Prime Minister Whitelaw, the
Home Secretary, had that very morning briefed Lord
Falkenhurst in very general terms on the operation and told
him that Vladimir would be a target for recruitment by MI-5's
Terrorist Search and Seizure Team, emphasizing that the Russian would be needed. By plane and car the Yorkshire peer had
hastened to Falkenhurst Hall to insure that Vladimir understood the importance of what he might be asked to do and that
it had his blessing.

All of which came out in the three-cornered conversation
that followed. And yes, said Lord Falkenhurst, he personally
would straighten out the matter of Vladimir's unexplained absence with Daphne.

Score two for Pleiades roundup.

LONDON
10 DOWNING STREET
12 SEPTEMBER 1979

Sir Roderick Kendall was the first to arrive, accompanied by
two aides—a captain, Royal Navy, and a group captain, Royal
Air Force, both intelligence officers. As they went up the stairs
to the conference room Lord Carrington, the Foreign Secretary, was close behind. It was 8:45 on the morning following

the death of Brigadier MacKenzie, and Prime Minister Thatcher had summoned her ministers for an urgent meeting at 10 Downing Street to deal with this latest crisis.

"Shocking business, MacKenzie's death," said Lord Carrington. "We can't put up with this sort of thing any longer."

"Easier said than done, Peter," replied Sir Roderick, "but unless I miss my guess some drastic measures will come out of this meeting." Just how drastic no one yet knew, but Sir Roderick was in a better position to guess than anyone else. Major Lindsay, who had gone at once to Corscombe Hall with Fereyes the night before, had arrived back in London after midnight to find a message from the home secretary's office to be present. By 8:55 A.M. all those summoned had assembled in the conference room.

At the stroke of nine o'clock Mrs. Thatcher entered the room. All stood. The cheery greetings that normally attended the opening of any cabinet session were dispensed with as out of place. She looked around the room. Her gaze was attentive and incisive, her gestures neat and small. Sensibly dressed in a navy suit and pearls, she commanded attention. Motioning the somber men who faced her to be seated, she lost no time in making her feelings known.

Flanked by his two aides, Sir Roderick Kendall sat to her left at the head of the conference table. Then came Lord Hailsham, Lord Carrington, Francis Pimm, the Defence Minister, and Lord Soames. On her right was William Whitelaw, Deputy Prime Minister and Home Secretary, Sir Francis Gilmour, Sir Geoffrey Howe, chancellor of the exchequer, Humphrey Atkins, Secretary of State for Northern Ireland, and Norman St. John Stevas, leader of the House of Commons. Beyond him sat "C," the Director General of MI-6, British Secret Intelligence, never referred to in any other way. Away from the table, seated along the far wall, was Peter Lindsay.

"Many of you," began the Prime Minister, "I daresay

all, knew Ian MacKenzie, a man whom I trusted and relied upon. He was a soldier with a distinguished record. He served this country well and effectively, so effectively in fact that the Home Secretary and I recently put him in charge of MI-5's Section IX, the Terrorist Search and Seizure Team, referred to as TESS. Today he's dead, cruelly assassinated, a victim of the very people he was zeroing in on. We all know of the anonymous call to the *Times* by which the IRA claims responsibility. Such calls in the past have been proven accurate. I can only speculate that he was getting close to some target, and that the target responsible reacted, hoping to put an end to the search. I can assure you, my lords and gentlemen, that that search will not only be continued but will be accelerated as well."

No one spoke. The Home Secretary nodded silently in agreement. Francis Pimm looked around the table. Never had he seen a more attentive group.

"Terrorism moves in waves. One incident leads to another. This is not the heavy load the camel is carrying; this is the last straw that breaks his back. These are not normal circumstances. Unless the situation is dealt with boldly, harshly, it will happen again. And this we cannot tolerate." The voice was steely, yet silky smooth, ladylike but hardly gentle. "In addition to finding the murderers responsible for Brigadier MacKenzie's death—a search in which every available police and intelligence resource will be used—we see an opportunity to cut off, at the source, a very sizable arms shipment to terrorists with whom we are all too familiar. The risks will be great, but the rewards will be greater. I have called you together because I need your advice on an operation the ramifications of which far transcend the limited perspective that could be brought to it by the Joint Intelligence Committee.

"In mid-August, through our intelligence sources, we learned that a shipment of arms, of a size and sophistication hitherto unknown, is being assembled in Libya, earmarked for the IRA. With several notable exceptions the arms are of Soviet origin. U.S. and Israeli intelligence, the CIA and the Mossad, are all privy to the same information. The latter has come forward with an offer of assistance in connection with the interception of the shipment."

Mrs. Thatcher let that sink in for a moment, then went on. "Shortly after we learned of this Brigadier MacKenzie came to me, with the Home Secretary's consent, and the subsequent consent of the Chief of Defence Staff, with a bold plan to seize that shipment. It was—and is—imaginative, daring and, like most such operations, risky. I considered it carefully. It had many pluses and certain minuses. Forty-eight hours ago I told a very disappointed Brigadier MacKenzie that the risks were too great, and that other means of seizing the shipment would have to be found.

"Today Brigadier MacKenzie is dead, and I view our problems—and my decision—in a very different light. We have been pursuing the wrong course. We must stop the violence before it starts. Dublin is acting forcefully against the IRA, which has deluged it with bank robberies. Prime Minister Lynch, who was in Portugal on holiday but who returned at once after Lord Mountbatten's assassination, has assured me of his government's full and continuing cooperation. But that's not enough. Terrorists don't come from just anywhere. They are highly trained and well equipped with weapons. They bear false passports and other forms of identity not readily available. Dwelling in a strange, half-lit realm far less well known to the police than to the underworld, they depend on established groups for support. They are dedicated to the point of fanaticism, and rarely turn informer. They work out of countries that make no secret of their enthusiasm for terrorist activities, so it is unusual for them to be caught before they strike. In the Middle East, South Yemen and Libya fit this bill precisely."

The silence was broken only by the clock on the mantel as it struck the quarter hour. "That is my preamble. I've spoken my mind." She looked in the direction of the Chief of Defence Staff. "Sir Roderick, lay the plan out for us." Her confidence had seemed diminished only when she spoke of MacKenzie's death.

All eyes were on him as Sir Roderick looked around the table. He hadn't known that the Prime Minister had vetoed Operation Pleiades. Now, in the light of her implied change of heart, he felt an even stronger compulsion to make a case for its approval. As he began to speak his naval aide discreetly placed a file on the table in front of him.

"My lords and gentlemen, we know that the Soviet navy, acting on instructions from the defence ministry, plans to send one of its missile submarines, the *Novosibirsk,* to the Libyan port of Benghazi to transport the shipment of which the Prime Minister has spoken to a point as yet unknown—probably but not necessarily off the coast of Ulster—for delivery to the IRA. We have every reason to believe that we can delay that submarine, then send in one of our own submersibles, pick up the shipment, and depart. As the Prime Minister has said, this is a bold and daring concept, and any contemplation of it would be totally out of the question were it not for the presence in Benghazi of a British agent, code name Ashley. The key to our success lies in the fact that Ashley will be in charge of the loading."

"This man is a Libyan?" broke in Francis Pimm.

"No, Francis, he is not." William Whitelaw answered the question. "Please excuse the interruption, Sir Roderick, but since intelligence is a function of the Home Office, I'd like to say something about this man. And I'm telling you this only because of the singular importance of the proposed action. Ashley is a Soviet naval officer. He's been on our payroll for months. Moreover we tracked him for months prior to that. He knows that if he double-crosses us, or even tries to, his chances of ending up in Lubyanka prison, or dead, or both, are overwhelming."

"And you trust this man?" asked Pimm.

"Yes," answered the Home Secretary. "He's proven himself to us on a number of occasions. More to the point, he trusts us. Sir Roderick, sorry for the interruption. Perhaps you'd like to continue."

Sir Roderick raised his hand in assent.

"We have a vessel available—HMS *Taurus,* temporarily off patrol for missile modification," he said. "She can be ready on short notice. With the exception of a lack of sail planes, her profile resembles that of the *Novosibirsk,* the Soviet submarine in question, to a remarkable degree. Unless examined closely, the two would be indistinguishable. We intend to correct that difference. Moreover her commanding officer, Captain Evelyn Wiggins, is just the man for the job—able, eager, and fearless. The TESS men, Brigadier MacKenzie and his principal assistant, Peter Lindsay—" he waved his hand in Lindsay's direction—"have already identified and are ready to put on notice six of MI-5's assets from its extensive personnel bank, a group of Russian-speaking, able-bodied men, all with firm records of cooperation with British Intelligence, who can appear as Russian seamen. Among them is a lieutenant commander in the Royal Navy Reserve, born in Canada of Russian parents. Obviously he is a British subject. Without him this would be strictly 'no show.'"

"A question, Sir Roderick." Sir Geoffrey Howe, chancellor of the exchequer, had the floor. "The Prime Minister has told us of an offer of assistance from the Israelis. Aside from the risk, which appears to me to be considerable, can you tell us what part they will play in this operation?"

Sir Roderick looked in Mrs. Thatcher's direction. Her nodded assent was a signal for him to continue.

"In the actual seizure of the shipment, they will play no

part. But Qaddafi is demanding that the IRA, through their political front, pay for these arms, cash on the barrelhead. Furthermore he wants to be paid in gold, at the Soviets' own bank in Zurich. The amount is considerable—four and a half million pounds. But we know that the IRA is prepared to come up with it. Here's where the Israelis come in. They've offered us a quid quo pro. Without telling us how they intend to do it, they say they can hijack the gold. If they're successful—and even if they aren't—they'll give us the gold, or its equivalent, in return for the arms."

"They must want them awfully badly," said St. John Stevas.

"In two categories, yes," replied Sir Roderick. "The rest is pretty much run-of-the-mill stuff. Nevertheless the total represents a sizable arsenal capable of creating a firestorm from which it would be diffiuclt to recover."

"Why not get rid of Qaddafi?" Humphrey Atkins, Secretary of State for Northern Ireland, seemed querulous. "God knows he gives us enough trouble." Lord Carrington, shifting in his chair, shook his head in silence.

"May I speak to that, Prime Minister?" Lindsay had risen to his feet.

"Please do," replied Mrs. Thatcher.

Lindsay turned to Atkins. "Sir, we think our main concern should be to keep him alive. Men like Qaddafi, dictators and other disruptives, are expendable. Remove one and another, perhaps even more extreme, will spring up in his place. It is to our advantage to maintain in office our political adversaries, while directing our efforts to neutralize their deadliest efforts against us. This makes room for possible successors whose friendliness, if not guaranteed, is certainly more likely than that of the deposed. In Qaddafi's case everything that we know about him and his methods—which is considerable—becomes meaningless the day he dies. 'Better the devil you know than the devil you don't know.' "

That's a capable young man, thought Mrs. Thatcher. *Bright and impressive. I'll have to keep an eye on him.* She turned to the Foreign Secretary.

"Lord Carrington, do you agree with this?"

"I do, Prime Minister."

Then to Sir Roderick Kendall: "You've been fully briefed on this, Sir Roderick. Tell us more about the complement of Russian-speaking men this operation will require."

"The normal complement of the *Taurus* is one hundred and twenty-two," replied the first sea lord. "Without the missile men aboard, eight Russian-speaking men, whose only role is to visibly load the cargo, can be easily assimilated. Security will be high, as they will be held in isolation until the *Taurus* clears the A-V yards at Barrow. No inkling of the mission nor its nature has been explained to them, but all understand that what they will be asked to do is risky. Once aboard the *Taurus,* which they will join away from dockside, they will not know their destination nor exactly what is expected of them until the *Taurus* clears the Strait of Gilbraltar. She will not stop going in, as the risk of surveillance is too high. Coming out, the *Taurus* will go into the dockyard there, the contraband will be unloaded and held under tight security, and six of the extracurricular crewmen will be quarantined until the mission is completed."

"Another question, Sir Roderick." Norman St. John Stevas, Chancellor of the Duchy of Lancaster and leader of the House of Commons, leaned forward on the table to ask, "Who are these men? And why six and not eight?"

"MI-5 knows them best," said Whitelaw, the Home Secretary. "Major Lindsay can brief us on that."

"The youngest is twenty-three," said Lindsay, "and the oldest forty-seven—and strong as an ox. Two, including the twenty-three-year-old, are noncommissioned officers from the Twenty-second SAS Regiment, Bradbury Lines, Hereford. Of them, no further word should be necessary."

"And the other six?" asked Lord Hailsham, the Lord Chancellor.

Lindsay looked back to the Home Secretary for guidance. The latter nodded. "Very well—but no names."

"Men of Russian background, including defectors from the Soviet Union," replied Lindsay. "All ideologically motivated and all—except one whose papers are in the works—are now British subjects. All have a genuine sense of gratitude to Britain and are anxious to show it."

"You know these men?" Lord Hailsham, Britain's ranking legal officer, pressed his point.

"Sir, one I know personally. However, all are men with whom British intelligence has had a continuing relationship. TESS feels comfortable with all of them. Were Brigadier MacKenzie here I'm sure he'd say the same thing."

"Where does the forty-seven-year-old chap come in?" Hailsham again. "How can we be sure the Soviets haven't slipped us a bad apple?"

"The forty-seven-year-old chap is the one I know best," answered Lindsay. "If the Sovs have indeed slipped us a bad apple, I'll vow he's not the one. But we haven't the slightest reason to doubt any one of them."

"Let me get this straight," Lord Hailsham continued. "We are proposing to send a British nuclear submarine, stripped of its missiles, into Libyan waters to literally hijack a shipment of arms—admittedly a big one—destined for the IRA?"

"That is correct, Lord Hailsham," said Lindsay, "but please keep in mind that this will be done by deception and not by force. I refer you back to the Chief of Defence Staff and the Royal Navy for their views on the feasibility of the operation. I think you will find them in agreement—and willing to go for it."

"This submarine will go into the harbor at Benghazi?"

"Into the harbor at Benghazi."

1 6 3

"At dockside?"

"No. The shipment will be off-loaded from a barge brought to deep water off the outer mole."

"Mother of God! It's madness." Sir Francis Gilmour, Lord Privy Seal, had been listening intently. "Sir Roderick, won't the lack of sail planes on the *Taurus* give away the fact that she's British?"

"As I have said, Sir Francis, that difference in configuration will be corrected. At this moment HMS *Taurus* is under way from Faslane to the Armstrong-Vickers yard at Barrow," replied the First Sea Lord. "Mr. John Richmond, engineering manager at Barrow, and a Mr. Delafield, his principal assistant, were with us into the early hours this morning. The *Taurus* was built there, consequently construction prints for every section of the vessel are in their hands. Within twenty-four hours after arrival nonfunctional sail planes, removable at will, can be fitted to her sail. Made of heavy sheet metal, they will be relatively light, disposable, and can be attached or removed by crewmen with about the same amount of effort that it takes to change several tires on a lorry. Painted black, they will be indistinguishable from the real thing."

"You know, I can almost believe this." Lord Soames, Winston Churchill's son-in-law, Lord President of the Council and leader of the House of Lords, spoke with enthusiasm. "It's so unthinkable that neither the Libyans nor anyone else could possibly suspect what's up. That's exactly why it's going to work. Prime Minister, I vote aye."

"Sir Roderick, this is the second time in this discussion you've mentioned 'the sail' on a submarine. Please enlighten this nonseafaring man as to exactly what the sail on a submarine is." Lord Privy Seal was not finished.

"Certainly," replied Sir Roderick. "It's what used to be called the conning tower. On the newer submersibles that area is now a free-flooding zone, with its interior fittings restricted to a ladder or ladders, and an upper deck from which commands can be transmitted to the engine room. The periscope, which is retractable, rises through it from below."

William Whitelaw again: "I recognize the risks, and have since this matter was first laid out for my permission to move it forward. I'm gratified to have my initial reaction reinforced by the more informed opinion of Sir Roderick and his staff. I say go for it. But I have discussed this with C. Let's hear from him."

From behind glasses thick enough to resemble framed ice cubes, C, the director of MI-6, looked around the table. His remarks would reflect his calling. He knew more, but gave only what he considered essential. He had weighed all the risks and found the operation feasible. He would endorse it.

"I'll be brief. A squadron of Foxbats, advance models of the Soviet MIG 25, must be considered. They fly from the main Libyan air base at Okfa-Ben-Na'afi, the former American base called Wheelus. A new base, Banbah, is now operational and supports two squadrons of an earlier Soviet attack plane, the MIG 23, known as the Flogger and flown by North Koreans. If this operation is to proceed, it will be on the assumption that no one will be the wiser, and thus there will be no interruption. However, as an extra added attraction we can, if the Royal Navy wishes it, engage their attention by a diversion."

"How about ground troops?" someone asked.

"Hardly a factor in what will be essentially a seaborne scam. Let me add that there's much confusion in this country. Repeated coup attempts over the years are eloquent testimony to the fact that opposition to Qaddafi in the armed forces is strong. Disaffection is widespread. This is one reason—perhaps the prime reason—why the Libyan internal security apparatus is under the effective control of East Germans. Moreover there's an American named Wilson now based in Libya, a man of nasty reputation and greedy appetite. He's a former CIA official, fired for good reason and now operating, illegally, as an arms merchant all over the Middle East. He's a continuing factor in Libya's turmoil. I do not overlook the possibility that he may have engineered this entire deal between the IRA and the Soviets, interjecting into it Qaddafi's demand for payment in gold as the source of his profit."

"Do I understand then," asked the Prime Minister, "that you approve of this operation?"

"It is not for me to approve or disapprove, Prime Minister," replied C. "That is your prerogative. But with the U.S. Sixth Fleet never far from the Gulf of Sidra, I suggest to you that any reaction from the Libyan Air Force will be restricted to aerial observation, even at night. Flares, you know."

"You're ducking the issue," responded the Prime Minister tartly. "Give me an answer."

"Ashley will be on site to supervise the loading. He will also be in direct contact with the Soviet submarine, delaying her arrival sufficiently to allow the *Taurus* to come in, load, and leave. So much for that side of Operation Pleiades.

"But let me call your attention to another extremely significant factor. While it has been mentioned here, not enough importance has been attached to it. I refer to the gold. If the Israelis seize the gold—and predicated on their past performances against the Arabs I daresay they'll be successful—we will see that the coffers of the IRA are essentially bare. We seize the arms. The Israelis seize the gold. Everybody comes up short but us. It is a pleasing prospect. Consequently, Prime Minister, barring unforeseen circumstances and subject to the defence staff's approval, I look upon it with favor."

"Thank you," said Mrs. Thatcher. "Major Lindsay, what's next? Any more from you?"

"Only this, Prime Minister," replied Lindsay. "We have a man whom we call by many names, a man of many faces. He is at once the recruiter of and the control for Ashley. Once we have your final approval for Pleiades, we will send him into Benghazi to see Ashley and to tighten up any last details."

*   *   *

It was ten minutes after eleven when Mrs. Thatcher asked for a vote. Regardless of the outcome it had been decided that a squad of eight Royal Marines, armed with automatic weapons and under the command of a commissioned officer, would also be aboard the *Taurus* in the event of trouble.

"Retaliation is normally a spasm, but this one can be a paralytic stroke. There's no sense in keeping a watchdog if you don't let it bark," she said. "In my view, we must not be intimidated. We must take the risks. How say you, my lords and gentlemen?"

With two dissenting votes, Operation Pleiades was approved. Sir Roderick and his aides went back to Whitehall and Lindsay called Fereyes.

"Peter," said the Chief Inspector, "I've been waiting to hear from you. We've got a break—a big one. Get over here as fast as you can. Then it's back to Corscombe Hall for both of us. Hurry now. That's a good lad."

"I'm on my way." In minutes he was in a cab, bound for Knightsbridge.

OPERATION PLEIADES—THE ROUNDUP

ALL THE WAY TO THE PACIFIC FOR NUMBER THREE

The morning rush hour traffic on Honolulu's Lunalilo Freeway was moving briskly along as Dr. Alexei Gennadi Bochenkev passed under Koko Head Avenue in his Triumph roadster on his way to exit 24-B. In the distance, unobstructed this morning by the smog that sometimes gets trapped between Oahu's two mountain ranges, thus blanketing downtown Honolulu, he could see the Waianae Mountains beyond the smokestacks of the sugar mill at Ewa Plantation. He would miss Hawaii, no doubt about it.

Born of Russian Doukhobor parents in Manitoba, in

1 6 7

south central Canada, Bochenkev was a ruggedly handsome man of thirty-eight, bearded, with a cheerful outlook on life in marked contrast with his dour, restricted background. Almost entirely due to his own efforts he had somehow escaped the strange religious practices—including occasional public nudity—of the sect to which his parents belonged to emerge as a scientist of notable achievement, a fellow of the Royal Oceanography Society, now completing a two-year stint at the Tsunami Research Center of the United States National Oceanic and Atmospheric Administration on the Manoa campus of the University of Hawaii.

Brought up in a Russian-speaking household hundreds of miles from either of Canada's coasts, he had nevertheless been fascinated by the sea since boyhood. As a teenager he had hitchhiked his way to Alaska for three successive summers to work in bloody and smelly surroundings in a fish cannery, earning almost enough to put himself through McGill University. The deficit he made up by washing dishes in a Montreal restaurant. After graduating with a major in the geography of the sea he opted for British citizenship, a simple matter for native-born Canadians in those days, and a commission in the Royal Navy volunteer reserve, the "Wavy Navy," after learning that the British Admiralty was actively looking for oceanographers. As a civilian employee of the Admiralty he obtained a graduate degree in oceanography from the University of Edinburgh. He also managed a doctorate in the same discipline from the Scripps Institute in California, sandwiched between tours of active duty, spent mostly in frigates making soundings and studying currents in the Mediterranean, particularly in the Gulf of Sidra. He had married a Scottish nurse, met while he was a patient at Saint Mary's Hospital in Edinburgh.

As Dr. Bochenkev finished climbing the outside stairs to the third level of Hamilton Hall, a man was waiting for him, sitting on the bench outside the still locked door of his map-encrusted office. Even before the waiting figure spoke, his manner and dress betrayed him as an Englishman.

"Dr. Bochenkev?" Waiting Figure rose and thrust out a hand.

"Indeed. You wish to see me?"

"More than you know." The ruddy-faced man, immaculate in shirt and tie and a two-piece lightweight suit, seemed

strangely out of place in an area given over to aloha shirts and informal dress. "Called you at home a half-hour ago, but no answer." That sounded right, as Nellie had left before him to keep an early dental appointment. "I would like to speak to you privately."

"Of course. Let me get this bloody door unlocked—it sticks, you know—and we can sit down and have a proper cup of tea. And you are—?"

"Sorry, Dr. Bochenkev. Rude of me. I'm Cyril Hastie, Her Majesty's consul general, Honolulu."

Consul general, Honolulu, *thought Bochenkev.* What's this?

"I'm consumed with curiosity, Dr. Bochenkev. Are you British?"

"Yes. Canadian by birth, but a naturalized British subject by choice."

"I thought so, but your name threw me off. This came to me at home this morning at four by courier from San Francisco. It has Queen's messenger priority, and my instructions were to deliver it to you, personally, without delay." Hastie cleared his throat. "I'm terribly afraid I'm going to have to ask you for some identification." The brown manila envelope in his hand bore the Admiralty seal in four different places, pressed into red wax.

Puzzled, Bochenkev reached for his wallet. "How about a state of Hawaii driver's license? If that's not enough, I'm afraid my passport is at home."

"That'll do." Hastie gave careful study to the photograph on the driver's license, then handed Bochenkev the envelope. He seemed relieved to be rid of it. "You must be a very important fellow, Dr. Bochenkev. First time I've seen one of these in the consular service. I must ask you to sign here."

Receipt in hand, Hastie noted the time of delivery as he refused Bochenkev's offer of tea. With a wave of the hand and a "Cheerio" he was off.

Behind a locked door and at his desk, Bochenkev opened the envelope. Inside was another sealed envelope bearing his name, his naval reserve rank, and serial number. Inside that were Priority One orders to active duty, reporting at once to Room 218-SM, Ministry of Defence, Main Building, Whitehall, London SW1A 2HB, for a period not in excess of thirty

1 6 9

days, Reference D/DVR/133/1, vouchers for air travel, and an authorization for the normal daily travel allowance. The orders themselves were prominently stamped in several places Destination Secret. Another unusual aspect was the cachet "Uniform requirements—none." He put the documents down to ponder what it all meant. He had no clue, but his adrenaline was flowing as he took off to tell Nellie what he could.

Through Air New Zealand he made a connection with British Airways Flight 405, transpolar out of Seattle direct to London. Eighteen hours later a weary Lieutenant Commander Alexei Bochenkev had reported to Whitehall and was en route—by ministry staff car to HMS Neptune, *the Royal Navy's submarine base on the Irish Sea above Liverpool. Pleiades roundup now had number three.*

HAMPSHIRE
CORSCOMBE HALL
12 SEPTEMBER 1979

Peter Lindsay and Chief Inspector Fereyes, pipe in hand, sat uncomfortably in the small library at Corscombe Hall. It was a cozy room normally, radiating warmth and charm. One wall was completely given over to bookshelves; elsewhere there were fresh-cut flowers in profusion. A dozen framed photographs sat on the two tables in the room, including one of then Colonel MacKenzie shooting in India with Lord Mountbatten, another with Alan and Barbara Romney shooting in Yorkshire. Augustus John's portrait of MacKenzie's mother hung over the fireplace, and in one corner was the inevitable television set. Several flower-patterned needlepoint pillows, lovingly done by Barbara Romney, were on the sofa that faced the bay window overlooking the terrace and the garden beyond.

Today, however, although the sense of intimacy was there, the room radiated tragedy, not warmth. Inspector Fereyes would have given his teeth to have lit his pipe but didn't do so out of deference to the pale and subdued woman who sat facing them. Barbara Romney had been answering questions for the past half-hour and was visibly tired.

"You will have to forgive me, Inspector, but Ian's murder has nearly done me in. I didn't close my eyes last night. My daughter arrived from Cambridge about midnight to be with me and Ian's remaining son is on his way from New York. He's with Barclay's Bank there. The neighbors have been simply marvelous. Yes, I think I was the last person to see him alive—unless someone comes forth who saw him out walking before—" she stopped for a moment, her eyes glistening with tears—"before it happened."

"Mrs. Romney," said Lindsay, "tell us again, if you will, what transpired after Brigadier MacKenzie arrived yesterday afternoon. I'm sorry to ask you to repeat this, but in so doing, try to remember everything that he said or did."

"Well, I had come down on the two o'clock train from Victoria Station. Ian was driving down, as we were going to drive on to Brighton, today as a matter of fact. I got here about three and Ian an hour later. He seemed his usual self, composed and cheerful. We talked about a number of things, all very prosaic—the grocery list, who would be invited for dinner, Rick, his Irish setter—who would want to kill a gentle, loving dog like Rick?—my daughter's double first in philosophy at Cambridge, and new tires for his Vauxhall. Then he said he was going to take Rick for a walk, as he often does, but would be back for tea."

"What about his job, Mrs. Romney?" said Inspector Fereyes. "You're aware of his position? Did he ever talk with you about his job? Did he say anything yesterday that might indicate that he was in any kind of danger?"

"No," was her quick reply. "He never talked with me about such matters." The sharpness of her retort indicated a certain amount of irritation. "Of course I knew what he did. We planned to marry this coming November, so it would be only natural that I knew of his assignment to our intelligence services. But he never breathed a word of what his day-to-day responsibilities entailed. You should know that, Peter, even if Inspector Fereyes doesn't."

"Granted, Mrs. Romney, and I'm sure we regret the question." Lindsay seemed embarrassed. "But did he tell you that he had been in recent and direct touch with Mrs. Thatcher?"

"Yes, he did, but that's all. I have no idea what their discussion was about. Not many people have direct access to the Prime Minister. If one sees her, and admires her, as Ian did, I think that's a legitimate topic of conversation between two people as close as Ian and me. He did tell me that he had had a telephone call from her just yesterday and that she had told him that she couldn't agree with his proposal. I have no idea what that proposal was."

"I see." Lindsay looked at Inspector Fereyes, who seemed to nod slightly in answer to the unspoken question.

"Does the word TESS mean anything to you?" continued Lindsay.

"Well, yes. It's part of a title of a novel by Thomas Hardy. *Tess of the D'Urbervilles* it's called."

"I'm familiar with it. Anything else?"

"I have a Scottish friend named Tess. Outside of that— nothing. Why do you ask?"

"TESS, Mrs. Romney," replied Lindsay, "is the short name given MI-5's Terrorist Search and Seizure Team, its proper designation being Section IX, MI-5. Brigadier Mac-Kenzie was its head. Very recently he had suggested to the Chief of Defence Staff and to Mrs. Thatcher a bold and pre-emptive strike against a source of arms being smuggled to the IRA. We don't know yet what to make of this latest outrage, but one group has claimed responsibility. We can only surmise that its motives are to put a stop to TESS's activities. Now I can tell you that just the opposite is going to happen. I've just come from an extraordinary session of the cabinet, called as a result of Brigadier MacKenzie's murder. I attended as his representative. The Prime Minister made it clear to all of us that not only will every effort be made to find those responsible—equating his death to that of Lord Mountbatten—but also that the strike that Brigadier MacKenzie had anticipated will go forward, at once and with the highest priority attached to it. Beyond that I can say no more."

"With Ian gone, I don't know whether I'm glad or sorry about that," replied Mrs. Romney. "Anything to stop the killing. I think often of those two Irish women, one a Protestant and the other a Catholic, who are trying so hard to bring about a reconciliation between the two sides. They seem so far apart."

"Mrs. Romney," said Chief Inspector Fereyes, "I'm going to tell you something that I want you to keep to yourself until it's publicly announced—which may be as soon as tomorrow. We now have a very significant piece of evidence. On our way here we stopped at police headquarters in Abbotswood. A gun was found yesterday afternoon by one of the local constables while searching the area. In all likelihood it is the same weapon used by the person who killed Brigadier MacKenzie to shoot his Irish setter. The size of the dog's fatal wounds leads us to this conclusion. It's an American-made revolver, a Smith and Wesson .357 Magnum—very heavy. Only a strong man, one used to handling such a weapon, would carry and use it. We're going to have it tested for further clues. This may be just the break we need."

"What do you think, Major? Will you agree with me that the gun belongs to O'Farrell?" Fereyes and Lindsay were on their way back to London in Fereyes's staff car. The Smith & Wesson Magnum, sealed in a plastic bag, was locked in the trunk of the car.

1 7 3

"That's a new question, Inspector," replied Lindsay, "one I haven't given much thought to. Of course it could belong to O'Farrell, but why—at this point—single out him as the culprit? There are a dozen IRA men who are capable of having killed MacKenzie, men who might seem to have greater reasons to do so than O'Farrell. We don't know whether O'Farrell's ever killed anybody."

"Aye, laddie, but we do know that O'Farrell's an American. He carries an American passport. The Smith and Wesson is an American weapon—one hard to come by in England or Ireland. And Raven couldn't locate him before going to San Francisco. That means to me that he was here, skulking around Hampshire, setting his trap. It's not much to go on, but my guess is that we'll be looking for the right man if we go after O'Farrell. We'll fire the gun again, then send the expended bullet to our friends in the FBI ballistics lab in Washington for further identification. That should tell us something. And if we don't catch the bloke who did this it's Katy bar the door because we'll all be in for big trouble, laddie, big trouble. There's an old axiom that says 'Where the vanguard camps today the rear guard camps tomorrow.' One violent act breeds another. You know what I think? I think we can get Raven to smoke him out for us."

"How, Inspector?"

"Well, it goes like this. Raven gave O'Farrell, or gave to COMMEND, a hundred thousand pounds—at their request. At least that's what O'Farrell thinks. And that makes Raven culpable. Before Raven left for San Francisco Brigadier MacKenzie let it be known that he could be faced with arrest as an accessory to murder—Lord Mountbatten's. Now there's another—Brigadier MacKenzie's. We'll create an atmosphere that will make Raven and O'Farrell gravitate to one another. Honor among thieves? Why not honor among murderers? I don't know where O'Farrell is now, but if he's not already there, every instinct tells me he'll head for the Irish Republic. I

1 7 4

know that's what I would do. He'll at least be among some of his own, and even if caught will face doubtful extradition. Who better to finger him for us than Raven, particularly since Raven won't know what we know? The more I think about this the better I like it."

He lapsed into silence, then with a pat on the knee to Lindsay pushed the car to the speed limit and beyond to get back to London and to set more wheels in motion.

OPERATION PLEIADES—THE ROUNDUP

A CAMBRIDGE DON—DO NEWTON'S PRINCIPLES STILL OBTAIN?

Churchill College, Cambridge, 11:55 A.M., September 8th. A call had come through at 9:30 alerting Dr. Stefan Nagy to expect a certain Mr. Wallace Comerford at noon. In anticipation of his arrival the Hungarian-born theoretical physicist had gone to one of the windows in his rooms overlooking King's Parade to watch for the identifiable but to him unknown visitor. After years of cooperation with British intelligence Nagy was uneasy—a state of mind causing him unusual anguish.

As he watched from behind a half-drawn curtain he saw a middle-aged man, hatless and in a raincoat, stop a passing student in front of the porter's lodge at the gate. Dr. Nagy correctly surmised that the man was asking directions, as the student pointed across the street to the entrance to East Court, then up to the tower window from which he was watching, unseen. The man in the raincoat nodded, then crossed the street, on his way up. He had known precisely where to find Nagy but on the chance that he was being watched, he acted as if he did not. Two minutes later he was at the door, knocking.

Stefan Nagy had left Hungary in 1972, by which time some privileged Hungarians were being allowed to travel in the West. Nagy got out with less difficulty than others. While in Paris attending the Tenth International Symposium on Combustion in company with other scientists drawn from every country in the world, he had walked into the British Embassy

1 7 5

and asked for political asylum. *After careful investigation, and since his academic credentials seemed to be in order, including an advanced degree in physics from Charles University in Prague, he got it. His credentials had in fact been doctored, but not to a point that would have led to discovery, as borne out by subsequent inquiry from England. Multilingual, he spoke not only Hungarian, but also Russian, Czech and English, having been brought up in a household composed of a Hungarian father who was a medical doctor, a Czech schoolteacher mother, and a Russian grandmother who had left Russia in 1912, bringing with her some of the culture of Czarist days. Stefan had learned English on his own while a university student in order to read English texts in his chosen discipline.*

In 1975, at twenty-nine, he had married an American girl of mixed Central European ancestry similar to his own. From Cleveland, she had come to Cambridge on a scholarship to study European history. Two years later she was dead, and her unborn child as well, the result of an icy pileup on the M6 highway. It was a loss that affected Stefan deeply. He gave serious consideration to returning to Hungary, but in the light of his recently acquired British citizenship and the academic life at Cambridge, of which he had grown inordinately fond, he thought better of it. Two other factors affected his decision: He was being paid handsomely for two lucrative consultancies to several British defense industries, and he had grave misgivings as to what his reception would be back in Budapest.

Nagy listened attentively as the man called Comerford stated his business. When he had finished Stefan said, "I understand. I'll be ready whenever I hear from you again." A handshake and the session was over.

Pleiades roundup had collared number four.

It was way past his normal lunchtime before Dr. Nagy stirred from the chair where he had settled after the MI-5 man left. Lost in thought, he finally got up, poured himself a neat scotch, downed it, and went to his desk. From a lower drawer he took out a blue three-by-five card, compared it with another that he kept separately, then punched three holes in it at specified areas with a hand punch, put it in his wallet, and departed.

1 7 6

At the college library, where he was a familiar figure, he went to a certain corridor in the physics stacks and took down from the top shelf a well-worn copy of Newton's Principles. *He thumbed through it for a few minutes, made a note or two, then inserted the blue card and returned the book to its place. The card, blank with the exception of the three holes, had meaning only for those having a card to match the one that Nagy had retained. Nagy's KGB control had such a card.*

Before leaving his rooms Nagy had been careful to arrange the shades at the two windows overlooking King's Parade so that they were obviously uneven, thus informing the KGB that the drop was loaded.

LONDON
WHITEHALL—REFLECTIONS
12 SEPTEMBER 1979

When C got back to his Whitehall office from the extraordinary session at 10 Downing Street he went to his desk, picked up a random piece of paper and in his calligraphic hand carefully wrote the following:

ORION IS TO PLEIADES
AS PLEIADES IS TO TAURUS

Then he sat introspectively absorbed in thought while looking at the equation. He wondered if its hidden meaning, which only he and a very limited few could understand, had been ordained—or was it sheer happenstance?

Those engaged in espionage come in all shapes and sizes, cutting across all sociological and economic classes, all age groups, all shades of morality, and both genders. Some are motivated by patriotism, others by venality, and still others seek high adventure. Not unreasonably one finds a high percentage of academics in the trade, particularly in the top slots. The fields of science and mathematics have spewed up generous portions of qualified personnel, but so have the humanities. The enigmatic C, Britain's ultraspy, fell into the latter mold, but with a background peppered with enough other experiences to give him unique qualifications for the high position he occupied as head of MI-6, British Secret Intelligence.

When World War II opened he was teaching at Charterhouse, his alma mater, after graduating from Oxford with firsts in English literature and philosophy. Bad eyesight kept him out of the armed services, but within a year, introduced into the inner circles of Britain's cryptoanalysts by Sir William Samuel Stephenson, he found himself in ULTRA country, a complex of bases in some of the loveliest of England's rural retreats, linked to the secret armies, the spies, saboteurs, and partisans of Nazi-held Europe. Working at Bletchley Park, a Gothic-Victorian mansion near High Wycombe, the recruited dons and scientists, who called themselves "boffins," would eventually break and decipher the most sophisticated of the German codes, and by their efforts hasten the end of the war as much and as effectively as several victorious army groups.

Then came more teaching, this time back at Oxford, but the Bletchley Park experience had given him an appetite for something more than the sedentary life of a university don. An application for a post in the Foreign Office was expedited by wartime companions who had preceded him into Britain's diplomatic corps, leading to a life out of England for almost twenty years—in Hong Kong, Singapore, Mozambique, Argentina, and in the United States as consul general in Baltimore, a post that he and his wife Madge thoroughly enjoyed. Then into the Home Office and MI-6, and finally to the top.

He looked again at the equation. He was enough of a poet to appreciate the symbolism. Orion, the mythological Greek hunter transformed by Diana into a heavenly constellation near Taurus, the second sign of the zodiac and, like Orion, a constellation visible in the northern skies containing the Seven Sisters, the Pleiades. Could it be all chance that had coupled such closely held knowledge with the operation which now had the attention of not only MI-5 and MI-6 but of the Chief of Defence Staff as well? HMS *Taurus,* the submarine, epitomizing John Bull, the figure used for more than a century to represent the English nation to the world and—like the constellation from which it drew its name—a soon-to-be container of the Libyan arms shipment, even as its heavenly counterpart contains the Pleiades, one of whom was in fact lost in limitless space.

Then Orion. This was the part that shook him up. For if one read O'Ryan for Orion, one would be privy to the code name of a deep cover agent whom only the most trusted few knew about and fewer still acknowledged, not only for the sake of O'Ryan's own life but also to protect the security of the most carefully orchestrated effort to infiltrate the Provisional Wing of the Irish Republican Army. If one read O'Ryan for Orion, one would be targeted straight at the heart of the most closely held source that MI-6 had to the increasingly xenophobic operations of those leading the Irish rebellion. The coincidence—if that's what it was—was startling. True enough, the agent known as O'Ryan wasn't privy to every move that the IRA planned or made, but his trustworthiness had been proven and his placement was such that he was close to an even deeper penetration into the target area.

But MacKenzie's murder made C think twice, even as it had affected the prime minister. Had O'Ryan's identity been too tightly held? Could O'Ryan have delivered advance information that might have saved MacKenzie's life? How about Lindsay? Should he know? A very bright young man, with an exemplary record. But C was ever mindful of the Coventry Syndrome—sacrifice some for the many—and O'Ryan and his potential had to be protected at all costs. The thought was disturbing. Perhaps he should take this one to Whitelaw, even to the PM.

To shake off any doubts and to seek a new direction he left his office to go once more to the privy vault for another look at O'Ryan's file, a top secret document with restricted access, one where extracts or copies of any kind were strictly forbidden. He studied it more thoroughly than he ever had before.

When finished he was careful to leave in the file the equation that he had written earlier in his own office. For C came away from this most recent look with a new discovery, one that made him wonder even more.

CAMBRIDGE
THE BUNCH OF GRAPES
12 SEPTEMBER 1979

When Nagy left the library and started to walk back to his rooms a chill was in the September air and a light rain had begun to fall. Soon he quickened his pace and before he got back he had extended it into a dogtrot. He was grateful for the rain, a good excuse for hurrying. The distance was no more than half a mile, but by the time he reached his quarters he felt as if he had made a journey of a thousand miles.

Had he been a monk, what had transpired might have been called a revelation. Revelation or not, once inside he did a strange thing. He went immediately to the windows facing King's Parade and evened the two window shades. Then he did another strange thing. He ran back to the library through the now steady rain, went to the same stacks and took down the same book where he had put the blue perforated card less than an hour ago. He was too late. It was gone. The KGB had picked it up.

Once more Nagy hurried back to his rooms. In a world

where conspiracies are supposed to be tidy, some turn out to have ragged edges. The flaw in this analysis is that the world is not tidy. Something had happened. Of great importance to spies is that no one really knows them. They like that. It is part of their nature. In this case the British didn't know that the KGB had facilitated Nagy's departure from Hungary. Nor did the KGB know that the death of his wife and unborn child had focused him anew, in a totally different direction. He went again to the phone, but this time Dr. Nagy called Scotland Yard.

That night he set out for a hurried rendezvous at a pub on the far side of Cambridge. He took with him a picture of his dead but far from forgotten wife, his naturalization papers, and an exact duplicate of the blue card he had left in *Newton's Principles*. Inwardly he took with him also a new resolve.

It was just shy of midnight when Nagy pulled into the parking area next to the Bunch of Grapes, a working class pub far enough removed from town and gown to be a discreet meeting place. On more than one occasion he had met there with his KGB control, a man whom he knew only as Dmitri. Only three cars were in the lot. He pulled in, cut his lights, and got out.

Fereyes and Detective Smithson had arrived ten minutes earlier. Stopped on the M11 Motorway for speeding, Fereyes had commandeered the motorcycling policeman as an escort, following him through Sawbridgeworth and Bishop's Stortford at accelerated speeds behind flashing lights and a wailing siren before slipping into Cambridge relatively unnoticed.

Although Fereyes had never seen Nagy before, he was easily recognizable. Hatless, with an unruly shock of hair, Nagy had about him the rumpled, inquisitive air of an intellectual. The rain had stopped, but he had his raincoat on, zipped only halfway up, with a plaid muffler on the outside. An angular face, eyes deep set under bushy brows. *He looks the part,* thought Fereyes. *Why doesn't he put the muffler inside his coat, where it bloody well belongs?*

1 8 1

"Inspector Fereyes, Scotland Yard." He stuck out his hand.

"Stefan Nagy. Thank you for coming." He sounded like a host greeting a welcome guest.

"Under the circumstances it would be difficult to imagine that we wouldn't. Smithson, see if he's carrying anything, then get in the car."

"Sorry, professor, but we must," said Smithson. "Hands on the top, please."

Nagy complied. An expert frisk revealed only a wallet and some papers, which Smithson showed to a nodding Fereyes.

"Now, professor, tell us your story. If the smoke bothers you, say so." Fereyes was lighting up. "Or put your window down."

Nagy, in the back seat next to Fereyes, rolled down the window on his side, slumped back, and began.

An hour later he had finished. Fereyes had looked carefully at everything he had been shown, noting the emotion with which Nagy spoke of his love for his wife and of the trauma inflicted by her death.

"I love England, too, more than I realized until recently. I don't know what I'm about to be asked to do, but I don't want to do anything—I *won't* do anything—to further compromise my position here. I don't want to go back to Hungary, and I certainly don't want to end up in the Soviet Union. If jail in England is the answer, so be it. It'll be a small price to pay."

Fereyes nodded. "Maybe you're telling the truth. Maybe you're lying in your teeth. We'll soon know." He held up the blue perforated card. Its coding and its use had been explained to him. "I'm taking this with me."

"By all means. But shouldn't I have it back?"

"You'll get it back. Now go home and go about your business—normally. Do nothing out of the ordinary. Here's a number to call. Your line may be bugged, so call from a box.

Keep me informed of *any* further contact with Dmitri or anybody else on the other side—and no mention of this meeting. You're in a peck of trouble, professor. One step out of line and we'll blow the whistle on you. Then you'll find that those whom you considered your friends will turn out to be your enemies—unforgiving and vicious. I don't want to find you the victim of a well-staged automobile accident or a fire in your quarters. Do you follow what I'm saying?"

"Precisely. I expected you to arrest me immediately. To say that I'm remorseful is the understatement of the year, but I'm prepared to make amends."

"You'll no doubt have that opportunity, professor, but only if you damn well do what you're told. If you don't we might indeed arrest you, but I somehow think we'd choose another course. We'll just tell the Sovs what you've been up to, that you've spilled the beans to us, and let them handle matters to their own satisfaction. And that, my dear professor, would be something more than just a pity."

Inspector Fereyes took another long draw on his pipe. "Remember, you've never heard of me, and this meeting never took place. Now back to your lodgings with you before you're missed."

A chastened Nagy took off, emotionally drained, unbelievably grateful, and wondering what the future held for him.

"**Y**ou've got a sour one, laddie. Nagy's on the wrong team—or was." Fereyes called Lindsay the next morning to let him know that Nagy had voluntarily revealed not only his contacts with the KGB but also that he had been feeding the Soviets information from the two consultancies which he enjoyed with British firms. "If my understanding is correct, and God knows it's sketchy at best, he has been working with sonar buoys, electrically activated, not exactly the hottest items at the Ministry of Defence. You chaps would know the firms

1 8 3

he's been working with and can readily appraise the extent of the damage. My advice to you is to keep him in place, turn him around, and alter his diet—a seductive playback to really confound the scenario. The Sovs have been buggering our affections through this tousled bird for a long time. Let's break their bloody red hearts. But first you've got to get him out of town for a week or so, as he's already told the KGB that he might have to be away on some business for you—nature unknown—for that length of time."

The nature and direction of the resulting ploy surfaced with surprising speed. Sir Alistair Widener, a veteran of long service in British intelligence and the man chosen as Mac-Kenzie's successor to head up TESS, called a high-level conference at which all interested parties were represented. An arrest warrant charging Nagy with violations of Britain's Official Secrets Act was issued and Nagy was actually taken into custody and arraigned, all quietly and without public notice. Released on his own recognizance, he emerged from the experience a shaken but utterly subservient man.

Ten days after his confession to Fereyes in the parking lot at the Bunch of Grapes, Professor Nagy, consultant, left England for an important visit to the United States.

OPERATION PLEIADES—THE ROUNDUP

FOR TESS LONDON'S NIGHTLIFE YIELDS UP NUMBER FIVE

Heraldo Sanchez was a lover. He loved music, he loved girls, he loved good food and wine, and he loved the good life in England. He loved the good life in England almost as much as he hated the Russians—but not quite. An unlikely Russian-speaking Cuban, an even more unlikely former student at Moscow's Patrice Lumumba University, the Soviet Union's focal point for training Third World students in general and revolutionaries in particular, he had found his way to London after deserting the Cuban army in Angola. He had arrived at his present station in life, a featured guitar player at a posh London nightclub, loaded with information of significant value to British secret intelligence and to the analysts of the CIA, courtesy of their British counterparts.

Born Miguel Rodriguez to peasant parents on a sugar plantation in Cuba's central plains, he had come a long way by a circuitous route. When he thought about it at all, it was principally to rejoice at his good fortune. As a gangling boy of twelve, illiterate but with a natural affinity for music and no worldly goods but a matched and somewhat worse-for-wear pair of rhumba drums won in a dice game, he found himself in the Youth Corps for Peace and Freedom in the early days of Castro's revolution. Here for the first time he was exposed to the elements of reading and writing. Then into the army at sixteen, and an assignment to work as a laborer with Russian technicians building the airfield at Santiago de Cuba, later to become the base from which Soviet TU-4s, Tupelov reconnaissance planes, regularly scanned the Atlantic coast of the United States, venturing as close as possible without inviting interception and flying as far north as the easternmost tip of Maine.

By this time he could not only read and write, but had taught himself to read music as well, and how to play the guitar. Moreover he had attracted the roving eye of a certain Major Bednarzik, a Soviet engineer and a closet homosexual. Rodriguez, streetwise in a rural sense, lost no time in rebuffing his not so subtle advances, serving only to whet Bednarzik's appetite for the handsome, happy-go-lucky Cuban boy.

But then with no prior warning, to the astonishment of his fellow soldiers as well as of Miguel himself, he was packed off to Moscow to fulfill the Soviet Union's need for young Cubans to train in Marxist ideology. Several weeks later Major Bednarzik showed up. He had maneuvered the move as a means to further his intended seduction. But things changed rapidly. In a scene witnessed by two other Soviet officers, one of whom was in the GRU, the Red Army's counterpart to the KGB and equally powerful, Miguel put an end once and for all to Bednarzik's unwanted attention by slashing him severely in the face with the jagged edge of the upper half of a broken vodka bottle, a self-defense mechanism learned in the rural barrios of Cuba. Seizing the opportunity, the GRU had Bednarzik jailed and all charges against Miguel dropped, keeping him enrolled at Patrice Lumumba University for the next eighteen months. Finally they sent him to Angola to join the Cubans fighting there, with a prearranged liaison with the local GRU man. They were confident they had a winner.

Miguel, however, had other plans. With two other Cubans he was sent on a roving recruiting mission. Three weeks later he had shot one, taken a pistol away from the other, and had made his way through the lines to surrender to a South African unit fighting to maintain control of Namibian territory. Recognizing that this rare Cuban defector was a source of valuable information, and anxious to strengthen ties to the government in Whitehall, the South Africans—after their own needs had been satisfied—acceded to Miguel's request that he be turned over to the British. A GRU defector, even a low-level one, was rare indeed.

What happened next was straight out of the book. He was flown to London, debriefed by MI-6 over a period of two months, given a work permit and a new name. It was even suggested to him where he might look for employment as a musician. Before he knew it his knowledge of the English language, first tackled in Moscow, had progressed to the point where his grammar and accent were something more than simply quaint, he had a job and was making the unbelievable sum of £250 a week. Moreover, women seemed to find him attractive. He was in his own particular paradise, and he was genuinely grateful to his newfound friends.

Which is why when a man who called himself Wallace Comerford (in reality Peter Lindsay) asked Sanchez, as he was now known, to stand by for a further contact from those same newfound friends, he was only too happy to oblige. Pleiades roundup now had number five.

LIBYA
TRIPOLI AND BENGHAZI
11-12 SEPTEMBER 1979

For Western Europeans a visa for Libya is not difficult to obtain. This is particularly true for citizens of West Germany, Italy, and France, countries that not only buy quantities of Libyan oil but also supply hundreds of skilled workers for the Libyan oil fields. So when the British wanted to send in the man whom Soroshkin knew as Hans Bettelmans, he went in as a West German. In reality a British subject with long service in both MI-5 and MI-6, Bettelmans had an array of forged passports for any occasion.

Bettelmans arrived in Tripoli on an early morning flight direct from Rome. He went at once to see Dr. Wali Muhayshi, the Finance Minister. He was greeted warmly, having been partners with Muhayshi in an arms deal made possible by Muhayshi skimming off surplus weapons received from the Soviet Union, arms that ended up ultimately in Afghanistan in the hands of the *mujahideen,* turned against the Soviets themselves. In the course of time some of these weapons were retaken by the Soviets and recognized, but their clandestine journey through MI-6 to the CIA and then through Pakistan to the Afghan rebels could never be traced.

"Hans! Delighted to see you." Muhayshi smelled another deal. "What brings you to our tropical paradise?"

"Arms, my friend, arms. Weapons of all sorts. Used or new, it matters not, provided they are modern and in working order. Nothing too big, you understand. No tanks, no personnel carriers—and no aircraft."

1 8 7

"What specifically? Surely one who seems to have clients everywhere can make a suggestion or two."

"Our needs are very flexible, friend Wali. Favored items include the ever-lovable AK47, Uzis in any quantity, rocket launchers, grenades, anything of Czech manufacture. Simplicity of transportation always sweetens the deal." For obvious reasons he made no mention of the AM-180 rifles or the Helvir antitank guns, centerpieces of the coup in the making.

Muhayshi was silent for a moment, rubbing and squeezing his lower lip as he frequently did when deep in thought.

"Can you deal with the Soviets?" he asked.

"If the numbers are right, I can deal with the devil himself. Why do you ask?" Bettelmans sensed that he was on target.

Muhayshi reached into a desk drawer and pulled out a typewritten list, then handed it to Bettelmans. Though some of it was written in Arabic, a majority of the items did not lend themselves to transliteration and consequently appeared in English. Bettelmans recognized it immediately. Pay dirt. Now—where to find Soroshkin?

"This is a list of weapons being exported by our leader, His Excellency Muammar el-Qaddafi, for the liberation of oppressed peoples—in this case the Irish. And before you ask me, I don't know where the shipment is to be landed—only that it is to be loaded at Benghazi, three hundred miles east of here, aboard a Soviet vessel sometime within the next week. A Soviet naval officer is in charge, having come in early to insure that the loading goes well. His name is Viktor Soroshkin. I know that the shipment contains a number of the weapons in which you have expressed an interest."

"So?" said Bettelmans.

"So go and deal with Soroshkin. You said you could deal with the devil himself. Try Soroshkin instead. If he's like you and me, he'll listen to reason. So reason with him. Reason and money can accomplish a great deal, my friend."

"And where do I find this Viktor Soroshkin?"

"In Benghazi, at the Hotel Metropole. Middle East Air flies there twice a day. Good luck."

The Metropole, for all of its classy name, was rapidly approaching the status of a fleabag. Benghazi attracts few tourists, so its clientele was made up largely of Arab traders, sailors, adventuresome students from Europe and America, and oil company employees—both male and female, often together in pairs—escaping the structured life of the compounds in Tripoli. Occasionally an archaeologist from Oxford or Cambridge would show up, intent on exploring the outermost reaches of the Libyan desert for traces of an earlier civilization. There was no central air-conditioning and the window units in the bedrooms were unreliable. The Metropole's dining facilities were so-so and its bar—once a haven for Europeans and Arabs alike—had been reduced to serving nonalcoholic beverages since Qaddafi's takeover of Libya. But it still had an east-of-Suez atmosphere and its ceiling fans were kept in working order to entice the thirsty and hot in for whatever else was available.

Bettelmans found Soroshkin sitting on a bar stool, trying to nurse some consolation from a bottle of nonalcoholic beer, the latest import from Holland. It was vile stuff, but he couldn't stand the thought of another cup of coffee. He'd be glad to be aboard the *Novosibirsk* and gladder still to be back in Luanda where vodka was readily available and where he was sharing the bed of a tasty dish called Bella, a half-Portuguese, half-black bar hostess.

As Bettelmans approached, Soroshkin had thrown back his head to drain his glass and there was eye contact. At first the casually dressed stranger looked only vaguely familiar, then suddenly—recognition. It had been months since that azure day in Istanbul, but the events of that day had become the central core of his life, especially the fragrant re-membrance of Lyskya, the young Hungarian girl whom he longed to see again. Moreover his Swiss bank balance was growing in direct proportion to the submission of the reports that he regularly dispatched to the addresses given. He had little reason to doubt Bettelmans's word, and he thought he knew his motives, but why was he here? He felt a strange uneasiness.

"Viktor! It has been too long." Bettelmans thrust out a hand. "So good to see you, my friend. We must talk."

Soroshkin swung around and stood up. He was several inches taller than Bettelmans, which in a primitive way was reassuring.

"Greetings, comrade. I'm surprised to see you, and of course glad. But is it well for you to be here—for us to be seen together?"

"Viktor, I've never been here before in my life. No one knows me and tomorrow I'll be gone. Don't worry. I'm in room six thirty-seven. I'm going up there now. Come up in five minutes. We have a lot to talk about."

Upon checking in several hours earlier Bettelmans had passed an electronic sensor, small as a pocket camera and very similar in appearance, over every foot of wall space in his room, in and around all the furniture and the lighting fixtures, to detect any listening devices. The red light on the sensor had stayed off, so when Soroshkin knocked Bettelmans was ready to talk with him in a somewhat different manner. He was still the impeccable, soft-spoken international arms merchant with the veneer of a world traveler, but this time he would speak like a man with an urgent message.

Soroshkin himself noticed the difference. He led off with a question, the answer to which had long puzzled him.

"You speak Russian very well, Hans. How come?"

"I'll answer that later, but for now there are more important things to discuss. I assume that you're satisfied with our business arrangements? I know you've checked your balance on a number of occasions, and I can promise you that the funds are there, in the amounts passed on to you. You have been very cooperative with us, and we are pleased."

"Who is 'us'? Who is 'we'?" Soroshkin felt he ought to know.

"Myself and my associates. But never mind that. In the course of time you'll know. Let's get down to business. Now—you are familiar with the AM-180 rifles? There should be five packing boxes of four rifles each."

"That is correct."

"And the Helvir antitank guns? Thirty of those, with their component parts broken down and packed separately."

"Also true. The crates holding the wheel assemblies are the largest of the entire shipment—very cumbersome."

"Good. Now listen carefully. Mark the AM-180 crates by putting a red stripe around them. You have access to paint?"

Soroshkin nodded.

"Just the stripes, no words, no lettering. When you load the lighter, stack them all in one spot. The same for the barrel and cradle assemblies of the antitank guns. I want you to stripe those crates also. You can do this? This is very important."

"*Da.*" Soroshkin nodded again. "I can do this."

"Here," said Bettelmans. "You'd better make some notes." He tore a sheet of paper from a notebook and handed it, with a pencil, to Soroshkin.

"Okay. Now we come to the wheel assemblies' crates. Mark all six sides of each crate with a black X. Load them on the lighter in one location also."

Inwardly Soroshkin began to back off. What was going on here? He was about to blurt out a revealing question when caution told him to keep his mouth shut. His earlier sense of uneasiness returned. He wondered why Bettelmans would be interested in the loading details. And how did he know he was staying at the Metropole? Just as suddenly he thought of his conversation in Luanda ten days ago with a Portuguese who seemed to know a hell of a lot about him. That prompted a question he could no longer contain.

"Look, Hans. There are some things I think I should know. Recently, in Luanda, I talked with a man named Manuel Segura. You know him?"

"Of course. He works for me."

"Do you know what vessel is going to pick up these arms—and when?"

The ball was in Bettelmans's court. Without hesitation he replied, "Yes, the Soviet submarine *Novosibirsk*. On the night of the sixteenth at twenty-two hundred hours."

Soroshkin had gotten up from his chair and stood over Bettelmans, who was sitting on the side of the bed. "What's going on, Hans? Whatever it is, I neither understand nor like it. Now tell me—why are you so interested in the details of the loading of this shipment onto a Soviet submarine? When we made our initial deal, nothing like this was mentioned. Now here you are, in this God-forsaken place, nosing into details. Why?"

"I'll tell you why." Bettelmans had known that the question would be asked and he had a ready answer. "Among my customers are the Provisional Wing of the Irish Republican Army, and their counterpart, the Committee to End Oppression in Northern Ireland. These arms are being bought and paid for by that committee at vast cost. They have sent me here to see that they are not cheated." As he answered he was looking Soroshkin squarely in the eye. "Fair enough?"

For the first time since seeing Bettelmans again Soroshkin felt relieved. Bettelmans's answer seemed genuine. He knew the shipment was being sent to the IRA—he had known that much before the *Novosibirsk* had been substituted for the *Severyanka*. He also knew that as the acknowledged expert on the clandestine delivery of smuggled arms he was going to have to board the *Novosibirsk* and go on her to the unloading point, the location of which had been given him by Sergei Petrovskiy, the commercial attaché at the Soviet Embassy in Dublin. Petrovskiy had been in Benghazi but had returned to Tripoli that afternoon. Soroshkin returned to his chair and sat down.

"*Nichevo!* If we had some vodka I'd drink to that."

In reply Bettelmans opened his briefcase. Inside, neatly bound, were two bundles of high denomination Russian rubles.

"I'll give you something better to drink to. There are ten thousand rubles here with your name on them. If all goes well, if the loading is done quickly and efficiently, I'll see that this amount is deposited to your account in the Bahnhofstrasse bank for a job well done. You'll trust me to do that?"

Now Soroshkin was smiling. Things were looking better all the time. "I'll trust you, comrade. It seems I have no other choice. You can count on me to see that things go well here."

"Good enough. We'll continue to work closely together. Now a few more facts. The arms, once loaded, must be unloaded at destination. How many stevedores in your loading crew? For comparative purposes my people want to know."

"Normally six to ten show up every day to work in the warehouse. But you can't count on these bastards. They are very unreliable."

"What are their daily wages?"

"Three dinars—tops."

"Okay, I'll tell you what we'll do." Bettelmans went again to his briefcase. Meanwhile Soroshkin was mentally calculating his bank balance. He wondered if he'd live to break away from a life that he now found forlorn, without meaning or hope. He wondered too if he'd ever find Lyskya, Lyskya who had reminded him so much of his beloved Natalya, lost forever in the gulag. For better or worse he had to trust Bettelmans. There was no other way.

Bettelmans turned to the bundled rubles, extracting five one-hundred-ruble notes. "Here—pocket money. There'll still be a ten-thousand-ruble deposit to your account." Then he handed Soroshkin more bank notes.

"Here are five hundred dinars. Pick your ten best men and guarantee them a bonus of fifty dinars each if the cargo is transferred to the submarine quickly and efficiently. That should make for a fast load. Under best conditions, how long should the loading take?"

"Three hours—maybe less."

"Excellent. Now another question. Will there be a crane on the lighter? If not, can you arrange for one? I can't believe that this amount of cargo could be handled entirely by hand."

"You're right. There is one—an integral part of the lighter."

"Lifting capacity?"

"Five hundred kilos, or eleven hundred pounds. No single crate weighs that much. Some weigh only a hundred pounds."

Bettelmans was nodding in satisfaction. Everything was falling into place.

"You can communicate with the *Novosibirsk?*"

"Not directly. The *Naporisty,* a Soviet corvette, is within shortwave radio range and relays any messages I wish to send. I reach the *Naporisty* with a Q–21 shortwave transmitter. It has squirt transmission capability. I transmit at a quarter before any even hour on even days of the month and at a quarter after any odd hour on odd days."

Bettelmans got up and looked out the window. The palm trees on the Alciera Boulevard, once called the Avenue Marseilles, had taken on a yellowish tinge with the lighting of the street lamps. In the distance he could see the harbor and the outer mole beyond which, in deep water, the cargo would be transferred. He came back and sat down again on the bed.

"Who will be with you on the lighter, other than the stevedores?"

"For one," replied Soroshkin, "Sergei Petrovskiy, from the Soviet Embassy in Dublin. I guess he's been the point man in the transaction. You should know."

"I do know. Anybody else?"

"Well, there'll be a boss stevedore, an Arab named Selim who speaks enough Russian to understand what I tell him. Then there'll be the tugboat crew—probably three men. Nobody else that I know of."

Petrovskiy? thought Bettelmans, *I wonder where he fits in?* He had never heard of Petrovskiy, and he was sure that Petrovskiy had never heard of him. An unforeseen complication that needed attention. *How much clout did this man have? It would be better if he were out of the picture.*

"Viktor," he said, "it looks to me like we're going to have a very successful operation. We've worked well together and I'm going to see to it that you continue to be well taken care of. The extra ten thousand rubles you'll get for this job should prove that. Now I want you to do something for me."

"And what might that be?" asked Soroshkin.

"Twelve hours before she's due off the outer mole I want you to send a signal to the *Novosibirsk* to delay her arrival by six hours, until oh-four-hundred hours on the morning of seventeen September."

Soroshkin thought a moment.

"Why not? That'll give me just that much more time to load and bring the shipment out. No problem."

"No, Viktor, it won't give you any more time. I want you—and the cargo, ready for unloading—to be on station at the time originally scheduled, which is twenty-two hundred hours on the night of the sixteenth."

"What sense does that make?" demanded Soroshkin. "The seas may be rough and the weather terrible."

"To you," countered Bettelmans, "it makes no sense. To me it's essential. Let me explain. The men that I'm dealing with don't trust Petrovskiy. They're laying out a fortune for this shipment and they want to be sure that everything goes on that submarine that they've bargained for. I'm going to ask the Libyan Finance Minister to arrange a final inventory, on the lighter, after it has cleared dockside and in Petrovskiy's presence, to insure the validity of the shipment. The extra six hours will allow for that. The fact that the lighter will be away from dockside precludes any late mischief."

"Hans, you mystify me. How could Petrovskiy possibly swindle the IRA? That's why I'm here, remember? To see that the shipment is loaded properly."

"Viktor, humor me. Do as I ask. Send the message. As insurance that your position is the right one, that you're not being compromised, give me a code word, one that you choose yourself. That word will be repeated to you after the *Novosibirsk* comes in, by one of her officers. That should say something about me, about this shipment, and that I have your best interests at heart." Bettelmans laid his hand gently on Soroshkin's forearm. "What do you say?"

Soroshkin hesitated. Running through his mind was the hideous possibility that Bettelmans was a counterintelligence agent for the KGB, or worse, the GRU, the Red Army's intelligence service that was often in bitter conflict with the KGB. He abandoned that idea, however, in the certain knowledge that he would have been pilloried long since were that the case.

"Okay. I'll do as you say. I'll send the message. And I'll give you a code word."

"Good man. You won't be sorry. Now what's the code word?"

"The code word is *Lyskya*. Spelled L-Y-S-K-Y-A. Lyskya."

Bettelmans smiled. "So you haven't forgotten?"

"No," replied Soroshkin, "I haven't forgotten—and I never will."

The first plane back to Tripoli left the next morning at 7:05. Bettelmans was on it. Upon arrival he booked himself to Rome on a mid-afternoon plane, then sent a coded cable to the chief of mission at the British Embassy, asking for pickup at Leonardo da Vinci International Airport. Then he went again to the Finance Ministry. It was 10:30 when he walked into Dr. Muhayshi's office. He learned to his dismay that the Finance Minister was in a meeting. His secretary and receptionist, a German girl whose husband was a pipe technician for a West German drilling company with long-term contractual obligations in the oil fields, was happy to have someone talk to her in her native tongue and took it upon herself to say she was sure Dr. Muhayshi would see Herr Bettelmans as soon as the meeting was over, at eleven o'clock.

Bettelmans decided to wait. If forced to return to Benghazi he could still get back there before the day was over. But it was imperative that he get to Rome for unobserved access to the MI-5 network without further delay. What was needed now was an assessment of Petrovoskiy—and maybe to neutralize him. One last move to win the game.

There had been no meeting. Muhayshi, suffering from a not unusual hangover, had called his secretary to say he would be in at eleven o'clock. Then he had given himself an intravenous shot of vitamin B-twelve, which he had discovered was a sure cure for too much scotch whiskey, and had arrived at his office, entering through a side door, almost on time.

Bettelmans again. What the devil is he doing back here? He was curious to know how he made out with Soroshkin. He had Bettelmans shown in.

He was pouring coffee when Bettelmans entered. "How

did you get along with Soroshkin?" he asked. "Sit down and tell me about it."

"Thank you, I will," replied Bettelmans, taking the offered cup. "As you said, Wali, he's a reasonable man. We reasoned together."

"With satisfactory results?"

"With satisfactory results."

"And I suppose you've come here to give me my commission?" said Muhayshi, half jokingly.

"Now how did you know that, Wali?" replied a smiling Bettelmans. "You're a very bright man. Could you use this?" He placed the two bundles of Russian rubles on the desk in front of Muhayshi.

Muhayshi looked at them silently. He recognized the currency as Russian, but had no way of judging the amount. He did not touch the packaged currency.

"How much is there?" he said, looking over his glasses at Bettelmans.

"Ten thousand rubles."

"And Soroshkin has no need for ten thousand rubles?"

"He's gotten his," replied Bettelmans. "This is for you."

"Hans, I doubt if you've ever given away anything in your life. Maybe you're just a generous man, but I doubt it. You want something. What is it?"

"Well, to start with, who arranged for the Soviets to pick up and deliver the arms shipment?"

"A number of people," replied Muhayshi, "but the point man in Moscow, for us, was our naval attaché there, Captain Mustapha Hindoyan. He's been here, coordinating the movement with Sergei Petrovskiy, but left this morning to return to Moscow. Petrovskiy has been to Benghazi several times to talk with Soroshkin. As a matter of fact he was there yesterday."

"Tell me about Petrovskiy. What sort of a man is he? How important is he in this deal?"

1 9 8

"How important is he? I can't tell you that, but considering the nature of the shipment, I suspect that Petrovskiy is a KGB agent under diplomatic cover. Regardless of that, I consider Soroshkin the more able. Incidentally, when you were here yesterday I told you I didn't know where the shipment was going to be unloaded. Last night Petrovskiy told me. You want to know?"

"Of course. I want to know everything."

"The cargo is to be off-loaded in the same way it's being loaded, onto a lighter off the coast of Ireland, under cover of darkness."

"Where off the coast of Ireland?"

Muhayshi reached into a coat pocket. "I wrote this down for you, on the off chance I might see you again." He handed Bettelmans a slip of paper. "I do not spell in English as well as I should, but I think this is correct."

Bettelmans looked at the slip of paper. No change of expression betrayed his feelings as he folded the slip and put it in his wallet.

"Thank you, Wali. I assume that Petrovskiy is still here?"

"Yes, he is. I don't think he's impatient to return to Dublin. I believe he's found some company, if you know what I mean."

"Yes, I know what you mean. And who can blame him? So many Russian women seem to have two dimensions only, height and girth, short and broad." Bettelmans nudged the bundled rubles, still on the desk, in Muhayshi's direction. "As I said earlier, this money is for you—if you want it."

"And I repeat my earlier question," replied Muhayshi. "What do you want from me?"

"I'll tell you. It's simple. Stay in communication with Petrovskiy, and Soroshkin. Persuade Petrovskiy to stay here to see that the shipment gets off properly. Soroshkin is leaving on the submarine, so it is logical that Petrovskiy should do that.

When Soroshkin tells you when he's going to load the cargo on the lighter, send Petrovskiy to Benghazi to make a last inventory. And this is the important part: Tell Soroshkin at that time that you've learned through diplomatic channels that the *Novosibirsk* is coming in at the time originally scheduled and that the arrangements are not subject to further change."

"That's all you want?"

"That's all I want."

Muhayshi was clearly puzzled. "Hans, you amaze me. I would have thought that you would have wanted just the opposite—for Petrovskiy to stay away from Benghazi."

"There is more than one way of skinning a cat, my friend, believe me. You'll do this for me—and for yourself?"

For an answer Muhayshi simply pulled open a desk drawer and, in a single motion, swept the bundled currency into it. Then he thrust out his hand. "It'll be done."

By the time Bettelmans reached Rome's Leonardo da Vinci Airport he had transcribed into a full report notes coming out of his conversations with Soroshkin and Muhayshi. MI-6's mission chief in Rome delayed a late-departing pouch headed for Whitehall until the report could be picked up from Bettelmans at the airport. It reached London just at the opening of the business day. In block letters Muhayshi had spelled it IN-NISHMURY, but the destination was clear and the choice logical.

That same day at least three groups of tourists were on the docks in Mullaghmore, inquiring about charter trips to Inishmurray. All got polite but firm answers that made it apparent that access to the island was not to be had.

"Sorry, governor, but the seas are a wee bit heavy. The

wind is wrong and we'd never make it into Clashymore, its one wee harbor."

"Nothing would give me greater pleasure, mate, and the saints above know I could use some of your money, but me motor's down," was another reply. "Gone in the gaskets, she is, and won't be running again until McSweeney gets here from Ballyshannon with replacements."

To one pair, who had left Dublin at ten that morning, driving as if pursued by demons, the answer was, "I'd like to do this for you and your ladyfriend, laddie, but I've got to wait out a new caulking job. You see, it's got to set, and I dare not take her into open water for at least another three days."

The pair went away with an obvious display of disappointment, but with reinforced knowledge that the word coming out of Tripoli that Inishmurray was slated as the unloading point for the Libyan arms shipment was almost certainly correct. Confirmation of this reached MI-6's mission chief in Dublin as soon as Archie Bentinck, the deputy chief, left the dock and could get to what he considered a safe public phone box for a short, cautious and coded conversation.

Moreover, two hours later the cameras of the same British helicopter that had done an earlier aerial reconnaissance of Inishmurray—and again using infrared film from an oblique angle—were able to pick up clearly defined pictures of construction material, including several jerry-built wheeled vehicles, in Clashymore's secluded harbor.

That same afternoon Peter Lindsay headed away from Whitehall on a different mission. Hard-pressed to beat the closing hour, he got to the London branch of the Wells Fargo Bank, deep in the heart of the City, close to the stock exchange, with just minutes to spare.

"The absence of a deposit slip is a bit irregular, sir, but

since you wish to make this deposit to the account of one of our well-known customers, with a wire transfer to our main office in San Francisco, we'll accept it."

MacKenzie's death had disturbed the normal functioning of the financial machinery of MI-5, but Sir Alistair, acting to keep TESS's momentum from slacking, had moved quickly to make good MacKenzie's word that £100,000 would be returned to Raven to make up for the solicited contribution to COMMEND. The check deposited by Lindsay was drawn on a bank in Freeport, in the Bahamas, transferring funds sufficiently laundered to make them virtually untraceable.

With a polite "Thank you," Lindsay pocketed the receipt and left. He was anxious to get back to Sir Alistair's office for a readout on what was turning up as a result of the Inishmurray lead.

OPERATION PLEIADES—THE ROUNDUP

ERIC MAKES A PHONE CALL—
TESS INVADES THE BRITISH TURF

"He's going well, Stan. Any truth to the rumor that Mrs. Poole is going to race him in the States?" Freddie Morrison, trainer for the Dowager Viscountess Gilfinnan, put the question to Konstantin Voroshilov, Stan for short. Aide-de-camp, a four-year-old bay gelding and a consistent winner on the turf in Ireland, England, and France was just coming off a workout.

"We don't know yet, but it looks that way. Maybe after Cheltenham." Voroshilov put his stopwatch away and called to the exercise boy. "Cool him out, Tom, then go with Plus Tax." His heavily accented English was at odds with the scene, made even more spectacular by the iridescent reflections of the early morning sun bouncing off blades of grass in the seemingly endless acres of greenery.

It was 6:30 A.M. on the Newmarket Heath, that wondrous stretch of grassland in Suffolk, world-famous as a center for the training and racing of thoroughbred horses. As Voroshilov continued with his instructions, Steve Cauthen, the young

American jockey who was burning up the English tracks with a record-breaking string of wins, waved as he trotted by on an untested yearling fresh from the Saratoga sales.

Konstantin Stepanovich Voroshilov was a well-known figure in the world of English racing. Born in the Soviet Union, he had been educated at the University of Moscow and the Kharkov School of Veterinary Medicine. Sent to the Krasnodar Agricultural and Horse Breeding Collective, he had defected at Laurel, Maryland, where he had accompanied Zaryad, a horse shipped to the United States by the Soviet Ministry of Agriculture to run in the Washington International Race. When Konstantin was a teenage boy his father had disappeared, later to die in a Siberian gulag, convicted of a minor infraction in the work rules of the sawmill where he worked. Before his death he had lost an arm under conditions known to be unsafe, surviving only by calling on his willpower and an inner strength hitherto unknown. Konstantin had loved him, and remembered. From the moment of his father's death he had lived for one thing only—escape, and freedom.

Making his way to England, he became in time a horse trainer, highly respected in the racing and hunting milieu of the wealthy English gentry. MI-5 knew him also, and trusted him. Working with British intelligence and Scotland Yard, he had been a key factor in breaking up a KGB-inspired effort to cripple the British bloodstock industry by the surreptitious introduction of a virus intended to spread hoof-and-mouth disease.

Just after eight o'clock he was getting ready to go back for breakfast to the comfortable house in Newmarket where he lived with Catherine Thompson, the divorced wife of a prominent British insurance underwriter. To his surprise he saw her drive up.

"Stan, there was a call for you from a man named Eric. He wants you to meet him at the Cat and the Fiddle as soon as you can get there. He said it was important and that you'd understand."

He understood, clearly. "Eric" was the code that identified any call from MI-5. Telling Catherine he'd get breakfast when and where he could, he took off. Pleiades roundup was moving on schedule. Provisional crewman number six was on notice.

2 0 3

At mid-morning Yuri Andropov, chairman of the KGB, summoned two of his principal subordinates to an unscheduled meeting in his third floor office at 2 Dzerzhinskiy Square, named for the first head of the Cheka, the first secret police agency established after the revolution. Fittingly enough, the KGB is the Cheka's lineal descendant. Two blocks from the Kremlin, KGB headquarters are located in a complex of unmarked buildings separated from the Lubyanka prison only by an open courtyard. The principal building in this complex is an ugly gray stone pile that in Czarist days housed the All-Russian Insurance Company. Over its main entrance a series of columns extends upward for seven of its nine floors. Known as "Building 2" to KGB employees, it is more frequently referred to as the "Center" by some ninety thousand staff officers around the world. It is the most important building in an area saturated with anonymous KGB offices, residences, laboratories, schools, and administrative installations, all north of Dzerzhinskiy Square on both sides of Dzerzhinskiy Street.

As befit his station, Andropov ran his empire from a plush office overlooking Marx Prospekt Square, on the same floor level with the offices of his six deputies. In stark contrast, however, to the bilious green and functional furniture that characterized theirs, his office was rich with mahogany-paneled walls, oriental rugs, and an ornate chandelier appropriated from the dacha of a Russian nobleman. Adjoining it was a secluded bedroom with a shower. From behind a bank of telephones connecting him to the Kremlin, the Defense Ministry, and the Politburo, Andropov would gaze across an immense desk at visitors with a cold and penetrating stare that most found wholly disconcerting.

This morning that gaze was directed at the two functionaries who entered his office. One was Georgi Mikhailovich Kozlov, head of the third department of the First Chief Directorate, and the other Vassily Kuzmen Chebrikov, head of the eighth department. The First Chief Directorate, the most important of the KGB's divisions, is responsible for all Soviet clandestine activities abroad, but its greatest striking power lies in its ten geographic departments. The third, under Kozlov, was targeted against Britain and the eighth, under Chebrikov, against Arab nations.

This morning Andropov wanted to talk with them both about Captain Soroshkin, now on detail to the KGB from the Soviet navy, the *Severyanka,* and the arms shipment to be delivered to the Irish Republican Army. He didn't know why, but there was something about Soroshkin that made him feel uneasy. The man seemed too pliable, too ready to accept what came his way. Then there was this business about the *Novosibirsk* going into Benghazi in lieu of the *Severyanka.* And what about the report, the one that had reached his desk only this morning, that the agent identified only as Feodor, operating in England, had been approached by British intelligence to stand by for further orders? Who, he wanted to know, is Agent Feodor?

For all of its numbers and all of its ruthlessness, the KGB has some conspicuous weaknesses. Political interference from the Politburo contributes heavily to this, as does the Soviet obsession with secrecy. The KGB keeps such sketchy records with its foreign *rezidents* that a sudden illness, accident, or expulsion can temporarily paralyze an operation, as the lost officer may well be the only one familiar with all its details. This passion for secrecy has also resulted in rigid and extreme compartmentalization. Officers are locked in niches in a vertical chain of command, dependent upon what their superiors choose to tell them.

Andropov, with twelve years of service in the KGB and case-hardened, was aware of these deficiencies. A stooping, bespectacled man of sixty-eight, fluent in English, one who habitually wore shirts a collar size too big for him, he dealt with them in his own particular way. His seemingly uncanny knowledge of the minutiae of the operations of his vast empire was no accident, resulting instead from his firm orders that all reports on what he considered to be significant operations, or those with a high degree of risk attached, were to come directly to him. Consequently he knew about Soroshkin and he knew about the movements of the *Severyanka*. Furthermore he considered the assignment of the nuclear submarine *Novosibirsk* as the surreptitious carrier of arms for the IRA from Benghazi to some as yet unspecified point to be foolhardy in the extreme. He had learned long ago that the U.S. Sixth Fleet played hardball and might well react to the presence of a Soviet North Fleet submarine, not usually found in the Mediterranean, by harassing it with depth charges. Eyes do not meet in this Strangelovian tactic, and governments remain silent. So in a memorandum to the secretary of the secretariat of the Politburo Andropov, cannily, had covered himself by objecting to the mission. He knew it wouldn't change anything, but it put him in the clear.

There were no preliminaries as Kozlov and Chebrikov entered.

"So Comrade Soroshkin will be in Benghazi to see that the shipment gets out in good order." Andropov put down the report he had been reading. "But what about delivery? 'To be transferred to an Irish vessel on the high seas.' Is that what you're going to tell me? Certainly not in the Mediterranean, and certainly not off the coast of Spain or France. Vessels of every nation run up and down that stretch of ocean like beetles on a bean stalk. What's the answer, Comrade Kozlov?"

Kozlov had the answer. He also had a report, received just minutes ago. If Andropov didn't have the same report, in conformity with strict instructions, he could be in trouble. His answer demonstrated his capacity to wiggle out of a potentially tense situation.

"I'm hand-delivering this latest report to you, Comrade Chairman," he said, laying the report on Andropov's desk. "There will be no at-sea transfer. That was never planned. Instead the *Novosibirsk* will rendezvous just off the uninhabited island of Inishmurray, well off the coast of Ireland. The offshore waters there, a hundred yards out, are seventy fathoms deep. Our trawlers have been operating in that area for years. Soroshkin has been in Benghazi for the last ten days. He has completed an inventory of the entire shipment and has supervised the repacking of some of it. No crate now weighs more than a hundred and eighty pounds, with the exception of the sighting and barrel assemblies of some antitank weapons. These will go to two hundred and forty pounds, in crates that are thirty-four centimeters square and two hundred and forty centimeters long—the longest, if not the largest, to be contended with. Soroshkin recommends that the wheel assemblies, of standard manufacture and uncomplicated, be left behind. I agree with this. Less the gun carriages there will be two hundred and nineteen crates."

It was a good recitation and Kozlov felt pleased with himself. He would have liked to have wiped the perspiration from his brow, but he didn't dare.

The chairman looked at Chebrikov over the top of his steel-rimmed glasses. "And you, Vassily, what can you add to this?"

"I can add, Comrade Chairman," said Chebrikov, pleased that Andropov had called him by his first name, a sign frequently signifying favor, "that Comrade Captain Soroshkin has, with his usual vigor, completed a dry run on the loading aspects. In the warehouse where the shipment is stored he laid out an area conforming to the dimensions of the barge that will lighter the shipment to open water beyond the outer mole to await the arrival of the *Novosibirsk*. Then, with lights out in the warehouse and working with ten men and secondary lights only, he was able to stack them in simulated order for transport in two hours. With ten crew members working, Captain Be-reznoy of the *Novosibirsk* should be able to transfer and load in just about the same time—at night, of course. The same holds true for the Irishmen who will have to unload in darkness and lighter in."

"And the *Severyanka*? Where is she?" Andropov seemed satisfied.

"In Angola, Comrade Chairman, docked at Luanda. She will stay there until Captain Soroshkin rejoins her. He will leave Libya on the *Novosibirsk*. Petrovskiy, who with Burdin from London has been most concerned with the details of this operation, will fly in from Dublin to wrap up any unfinished business. Turalin, *rezident* in Tripoli, has just been assigned. Moreover Petrovskiy has dealt with Qaddafi before and I'd like him on the scene." Chebrikov was rising to the occasion. Maybe when this was over he might be promoted to more and better things.

"I don't trust Qaddafi," said Andropov. "I'll be glad when we can stop dealing with him. But he serves a useful purpose. So much for that. Now, Kozlov, who is Feodor?"

"Feodor, comrade chairman, is our code name for Stefan Nagy, a Cambridge don and professor of physics. He is a distant cousin of Imre Nagy, the ex-premier of Hungary, whom you have good reason to remember. We got Feodor out of Hungary and into England in 1972 with a minimum of trouble and only slightly altered credentials. He has been useful to us ever since. He has become a naturalized British subject, and regularly reports to us on developments in two areas critical to navigational aids for the British navy." *Did I made a mistake, wondered Kozlov, in mentioning Imre Nagy?* Nagy had been an oldtime Communist but a rather gentle, philosophical man who enjoyed a solid measure of popularity with the Hungarian people. Andropov had been the Soviet ambassador in Budapest at the time of Nagy's execution.

"A double agent, obviously, if he's been in touch with the British. You've been aware of this?"

"Yes, Comrade Chairman. The British accepted him initially as a walk-in defector at their Paris Embassy. We arranged that, and we have always dealt with him accordingly. Our analysts here at the Center as well as Professor Breytigam at Moscow University have consistently evaluated his take as exceptionally useful."

"I see. What do the British want of him now?"

"He does not yet know, Comrade Chairman. They have told him only to stand by for further instructions."

"All right. See that he's followed. His control is to report at once on what the British want from him. If it looks like he's going to turn sour, we'll make other plans for him—maybe department V. Keep me informed."

"Yes, Comrade Chairman," said Kozlov, nodding in assent. "You may be sure I will."

"That will be all, comrades." Andropov picked up another report and started reading.

As he left with Chebrikov, Kozlov's mood turned grim. *If it looks like he's going to turn sour, we'll make other plans for him—maybe department V—for Viktor.* Mokrie dela. *Wet affairs!* Was the KGB about to extend to a distant cousin the death sentence carried out on Imre Nagy, a cousin who, by his own admission, had never met the more distinguished but hapless Imre? He hoped it wouldn't come to this. He'd never met Stefan Nagy, but the idea of assassination, and in Britain of all places, didn't appeal to him.

"So now what's the situation?" asked Detective Chief Superintendent Fereyes. He and Peter Lindsay sat next to each other at the conference table, the pictures of Lee McCarthy spread out in front of them. The question was rhetorical, one that Fereyes would answer himself. Sir Alistair Widener and Jeremy Lewis sat opposite. Lewis, at the First Sea Lord's direction, was now the point man for the Royal Navy.

"Our friend Raven has served us well," said Fereyes. "Detective Collie picked these up from him late yesterday at Raven Park. So now we know a whole lot more about the man who has been calling himself Michael Francis O'Farrell. He is in fact Liam Francis McCarthy, a renegade American. Liam Francis, Michael Francis—at least he kept his own middle name. And that's not all we know. The FBI in Washington has answered our ballistics inquiry. The gun that dispatched Brigadier MacKenzie's dog is the same one used in the fatal shooting of a Rhode Island state trooper in 1974. So McCarthy is wanted in the States to answer to a charge of murder—and now we want him on the same charge. The legal attaché at the U.S. Embassy, probably an FBI man on diplomatic assignment, is serving us with an extradition warrant, which we can honor or not, as we see fit. For my part I'm sure we want him much too badly to surrender him to the Yanks—despite the fact that they've reconstituted the death penalty. One thing's certain. If he's caught in the Irish Republic—and that's where I think he is—we'll never get our hands on him, and neither will the Yanks. So we've got to apprehend him ourselves."

"By what means, Mr. Fereyes?" asked Sir Alistair.

"A good question, Sir Alistair, but I think it's possible. First of all we must locate him. I think he's hiding out in Dublin where he has access to his own kind—and more importantly, to money. Assume for a moment that I'm right. Locate him? Dublin's not that big, and I'll wager that our friends in MI-6 have a pretty good notion of what goes on there. Major Lindsay here tells me that the means exist, once we know where he is, to let him know that one way out—*his only way out*—is via the Soviet submarine that will deliver the arms."

"But we're working to abort that."

"Quite true, Sir Alistair, but let's make another assumption. Let's assume that the abortion is successful and the contraband arms seized. Captain Lewis, tell us what happens then."

"The arms will be off-loaded at Gibraltar, along with the auxiliary crewmen recruited for the operation." Lewis spoke as if with finality.

"And then?" queried Fereyes.

"I would assume that the game's over," replied Lewis. "The *Taurus* returns to Faslane and her refitting continues."

"Precisely," said the detective, "but let's not be too hasty. What's to prevent *our* submarine, empty of its cargo and the laddies who put it aboard, from keeping the prescribed rendezvous? Then O'Farrell shows up, happy as a lark, thinking he's got a ticket out of his troubles. And if you gentlemen will allow this old copper to be aboard, I'll bloody well welcome him myself."

The silence of the contemplation was like that of a group

of theoretical mathematicians suddenly confronted with a new equation. Finally Sir Alistair spoke up. As he did so the faintest of smiles was emerging on Lindsay's face.

"But O'Farrell, or McCarthy, or whatever his name is, is bound to know that the shipment has been seized. Is this not so?"

"That's a possibility, Sir Alistair, no doubt about it. But who's to tell him? The Sovs will make no public announcement—the ridicule factor will take care of that—nor will Qaddafi, for the same reason. Certainly Her Majesty's government will not, at least until O'Farrell—let's call him that for the time being—is in custody. That leaves one source only—the IRA pipeline. And when will they know? When we jolly well choose to tell them, especially if we send the *Taurus* to keep the rendezvous. What have we got to lose? Only O'Farrell."

Sir Alistair said nothing for a moment, then, "Why not? It's worth a try. I've discussed with Major Lindsay what you said about spreading the word in certain quarters that Raven might be apprehended as an accessory to murder. It won't hold water but it might make O'Farrell view him in an even more favorable light. If you're going to do this we'll have Raven go to Dublin, inquiring in directed areas for O'Farrell, with the message that he wants to help him get away. If O'Farrell buys it, he will do so because he will think Raven's trying to save his own skin by getting O'Farrell out of Ireland. Is that what you're saying?"

"Sir Alistair, I couldn't have put it better myself. We'll make O'Farrell think Raven is helping him escape, not hunting him down. We'll put him right in the middle of O'Farrell's rearview mirror, except O'Farrell won't know the real reason why Raven is there."

"Mr. Fereyes, I have a lot of confidence in you. Can I have the same confidence in Raven? Why is he doing this? For all of his feelings of guilt, for all of his repentance, he may be a slim reed."

"Why is he doing this? I can tell you, Sir Alistair. Since Raven's commanding so much of our attention these days I've read a couple of his books for a better understanding of the man. Why is he doing this? I'll tell you why—he has to. He will be no slim reed. Mikhail Baryshnikov, the great Russian ballet dancer, *has* to dance. It has been his life, ever since he was a child. So with our friend Raven. World War Two, his first venture into maturity, into reality, and in which he served with great distinction, conditioned him to violence. All of his books deal with it, having as their core a violent struggle or conflict between two forces, often represented by good and evil. His experiences as a paracommando in occupied France have held him in a viselike grip ever since. There is a need of risk, of the ultimate challenge. In his latest book, the one I finished just last night, the protagonist, whom Raven calls Scott Clinton, welcomes going into combat for 'its clarity.' Illusion and reality are all too often synonymous in Raven's mind. Just before D-Day he and about a hundred French irregulars in the Corrèze area of France damn near stopped a whole German division from reaching Normandy. Every time he writes a book he relives those days. All writers are sensitive to some degree, I suppose, but his sensitivity surfaces most easily when stimulated by life's most extreme experiences."

"It sounds to me like he's trying to make peace with his own death," interjected Sir Alistair.

"That may be," continued Fereyes. "Whatever the case, I think such a compulsion led him to his liaison with and support for the Provos. It was a Dungeons and Dragons existence, one that he played to the hilt—even subconsciously. And he's continuing to play it, but this time on our side. We can count on that. I think he's bored to death rattling around in that attitudinal squirearchy he lives in. I'm quite aware that his father was born in Dublin and that he has, or can have it if he wishes it, Irish citizenship. That no doubt has a romantic appeal for him, but it doesn't account for his present actions. His own contributions to COMMEND, coupled with Mountbatten's death, have brought him back to a level of his life that he finds irresistible. He's been like a pudding without a theme. Now he's got one. Utterly seduced by an image of himself that he alone created, he's now going to play that part—a combination of James Bond, John Wayne, Hemingway, and Mark Raven all rolled into one. Furthermore what he's doing now may well kill him, and he knows it. At least that's what Dr. Charles Sanner, the cardiologist whom he recently consulted in San Francisco, told me last night on the phone. I called him to get the facts. Sanner was frank with me out of concern for a close friend."

The phone rang. Sir Alistair paid no attention, knowing that it would be answered in an outer office. A moment later his secretary opened the door.

"Sorry for the interruption, Sir Alistair, but the Home Secretary's on line one."

The new chief of TESS picked up the phone. "Good morning, Mr. Whitelaw." As he listened he nodded his head, silently several times. "Yes, sir," he said. "Right away— we'll leave immediately."

As he hung up he turned to Lindsay. "Peter, the Home Secretary wants to see us at once. He says it's important."

Getting up from his desk, Sir Alistair turned to Fereyes and Lewis.

"Sorry for the abrupt departure, gentlemen, but this appears to be a Red Ball Special. I'll call you, inspector, as soon as Whitelaw turns us loose. We'll want to move quickly on Raven and O'Farrell. Captain Lewis, you'll report all of this to the First Sea Lord? Chief Inspector Fereyes may have given us something to chew on."

"Right away, sir."

"Good. Come on, Peter, let's get cracking."

Striding down the hall, Sir Alistair said to Lindsay, "This meeting's going to be with C also—about a man called O'Ryan. Mean anything to you?"

"Not a thing."

"Nor to me. But we'll soon know."

COUNTY SLIGO
RAVEN PARK
15 SEPTEMBER 1979

The one luxury that Deirdre allowed herself was a decent automobile. Gil had left her a Triumph roadster, but she got rid of it when she entered politics. After all, the image she wanted to present to the world should be of a more settled woman than one who drove around Northern Ireland in a sports car with the top down and the wind and the rain in her hair. As a replacement she had chosen a Ford sedan with a right-hand drive, built in Ireland at the Ford factory in Cork.

As she came away from Strabane following her Aunt Deirdre's funeral, Mark was uppermost in her mind. She had stayed an extra day, helping to wind up the few details involved in her aunt's modest estate. Now she needed Mark. She had never met anyone like him. He was—for all of his initial reserve—a spendthrift with himself. He was open and warm and alive, sharing himself, enjoying life, making sure that the person with whom he was with at any particular moment was enjoying it also. He had the capacity to pull into his own orbit those people to whom he was attracted.

After four years as a widow, she found that any thought of Mark evoked in her an emotion as startling as that which first accompanied the realization that she was in love with him. No one had ever touched her as he had, nor—she was sure—

anyone ever would again. Often she was able to think of nothing else but his strength, his humor, his compassion. It is said that a man has to be strong before he can be gentle. Mark Raven was very strong. The one aspect of his life that frightened her, which she now had every reason to believe she had convinced him to abandon, was his past support of COMMEND. But she knew she could not afford to overplay her hand; she would not allow that to happen.

On her first visit to Raven Park she was surprised by its size and beauty. The well-kept grounds were lovely and the vistas, so artfully designed, emphasized the sweep and the serenity of the hills and meadows surrounding the house.

"But Mark," she had said, "why do you need three sitting rooms, a huge dining room, a library, seven bedrooms and six baths? Not to mention the galleria and all those lovely paintings? I take it back about the paintings; I can understand why anybody would want those."

"I don't need any of this, Deirdre, but it's conducive to my sort of life, plus the fact that I like to think that my great-great-great-grandpappy, who went broke building this place, would like the fact that I'm living here. I'm sure he knows it. I'm Irish enough to believe in ghosts. I think he's around. And I'm as happy here as I've ever been anywhere."

They had come in from a long walk and were having tea in the little sitting room off the library where Mark retreated to watch television. He was sprawled in an easy chair, legs out in front of him on an ottoman. Deirdre, on the sofa opposite, looked up from stirring her tea to ask: "What happened to your Catholicism, Mark? With your background, you must have been born into our church."

"True enough, and early on I guess I was a pretty good Catholic. But when Allison and I were divorced, I think that put the cap on it."

"And what are you now?"

2 1 6

"I guess you could say that I'm a pro forma Christian—one without portfolio."

"Better that way than not at all," replied Deirdre, nodding in agreement. "But tell me, what led you to support the IRA? I didn't think that truck with terrorists was quite your style. Why are you mixed up in this eternal, infernal war?"

Mark looked intently at Deirdre. Sometimes her candor surprised him, as it did now. But her question deserved a proper answer, and he chose his words carefully.

"I suppose my support is a hangover from my childhood. My mother was a Protestant and a lot of that washed off on me. But my father, an Irishman if ever there was one—and a Catholic, although not devout—made me aware of the painful injustices inflicted on the millions of Irish immigrants who swarmed into the United States in the years immediately following the great potato famine of the eighteen-forties. I know it wasn't their fault but there was established for them a stereotype of rude manners, boisterous humor, alcoholic belligerence, and political chicanery to which all Irish were assumed to conform. That was discrimination, pure and simple, a view foisted on them by the Protestant upper middle class who viewed them as belonging by nature to the servant and laboring classes and treated them accordingly. Maybe I'm wrong, but that's the view I think the Prods of Ulster take of the Catholic minority."

"Well, you're right on that score, but that doesn't excuse Irish murder of other Irishmen, or of Englishmen, for that matter."

"My father was an actor and for the most part escaped such discrimination—but it was there, a sort of behind-the-hand whisper," Mark continued. "His father was a biologist at Trinity College and an intellectual. Those circumstances plus my mother's Protestantism, plus the added fact that she was well off—a San Francisco euphemism for rich—spared me completely. But I was painfully aware that in California Irish laborers built the railroads, dug ditches, worked in the steel mills, or became firemen or policemen, and with an extra pinch of ambition, saloonkeepers. When I was very young it was not uncommon to see in help-wanted ads in newspapers the phrase 'No Irish need apply.' If they were not to be welcomed, even as employees, you know damn well they would never be welcomed in WASP houses or clubs or other self-perpetuating organizations. There's only one way to achieve such a reversal of fate—the oldest way in the world—a way no WASP has ever scoffed at. That way is simply to get more money than other people. For money always talks, sometimes it even shouts, and even when it whispers, the deafest of the deaf can hear it and make obeisance to it."

The earnestness with which Mark was speaking was having its effect on Deirdre. There was a quality in his voice that brought her to his side to lean over and kiss him. As she did so she took his hand in hers to press it to her breast. It was a gesture of love that she knew moved and excited him.

"And this is what has led you to give financial backing to the IRA?"

"To COMMEND—yes. I had a headstart and I've done well. That's why I've been as open-handed as I have."

"My lovely Mark, for all of your wisdom you're such a child. As I told you the first day we met, COMMEND is little more than a thinly disguised front for direct aid to the Provos. You certainly must recognize that by now."

"Yes, I do. I once believed otherwise simply because I wanted to. But Mountbatten's senseless death, more than anything else, has changed all that. In the past my reaction to bad news has been one of mild depression in a familiar, unfocused way. Reaction becomes dulled as we get accustomed to so much of it. On any given morning the front page of the *Times* should leave people in tears. Everything bad has already happened and will happen again. This is how the world is, we say.

But not this time. The focus is there and a gut reaction tells me that I'm to blame. In the last few days I've been surprised at how much even the mention of Mountbatten's name has affected me."

Weeks spent with Deirdre this past summer brought Mark to the realization that her entrance into his life was bringing him out of a period in which he had been abandoning people, discarding appetites and vanities, narrowing his interests and enthusiasms, closing off rooms in a once elaborate mansion. Unconsciously he had been reducing himself to a fraction of the man he once was. Even Raven Park took on a new look, with fresh flowers and greenery clipped daily to grace the hallways and living rooms on the ground floor.

When not campaigning for Peaceful Means Deirdre spent as much time as she could with him. To his astonishment he discovered that she was an excellent cook; daily he found new facets in her to love and admire. She picnicked with him, sailed with him, swam at Rosses Point with him, made love to him, prepared his favorite dishes for him, and massaged his back and neck at night until he fell asleep. Peaceful Means had brought her into contact with the headliners of the world, famous people whom she relished telling Mark about. Jimmy Carter had received her at the White House and she and Martha Quinlan had had tea with Mrs. Thatcher at 10 Downing Street. Valéry Giscard d'Estaing had complimented her on her fluency in French. Moreover her knowledge of French literature was impressive, and Mark was flattered to learn that she had read a fair sampling of his own books and had a more than passing knowledge of his father as an Abbey Player.

New insights into her character were constantly cropping up, and he loved this woman as he had never loved another. For a time he wondered what she found in him to love, but soon stopped that inner searching, afraid that the answer might be that what she loved really wasn't there. Irish women were passionate, he had been told, but nothing could match the revelation of the ardor of her lovemaking. He had been totally unprepared for the fire that flared when she gave herself to him for the first time. The voyage to the bed, born of and inflamed by more than mutual consent, had taken on the quality of a gallop, and he made love to her as if he would never see her again. This happened after he had begun to wonder if he were totally well, but all such thoughts vanished when overcome by a desperate erotic fever, completely subliminating any physical shortcomings. She was his only refuge and he buried himself in her, knowing that life, not death, lay in this particular act of love. She went with him blindly, climbing. He drew her after him as she shouted, "Please—oh Christ!" He hit the mark for her and for a blessed moment the whole world evaporated in a heavenly, prolonged spasm that left her weak and weeping.

Deirdre was thinking about that moment as she wheeled into the driveway to Raven Park. As she did so an unfamiliar automobile passed her on the way out. Two men, both strangers, were in the front seat. Peter Lindsay, who was driving, turned to say to his companion, "We got out just in time. That's Mrs. O'Brien."

Fereyes nodded. "Yes, I know. Now he's going to tell her about the hundred thousand pounds. He says he doesn't think we'll have to bail him out."

Despite mild misgivings over what he knew lay ahead when he told Deirdre about O'Farrell and COMMEND, their reunion was the occasion for that special joy that seizes lovers after a separation. They were back in the same small sitting room, which Mark had had filled with cut flowers to welcome Deirdre.

"Now, Mark darling, tell me all about San Francisco and what your friend Dr. Sanner told you. Your health comes first. I've been worried sick over you."

"You know he told me I needed bypass surgery. I told him that was okay by me, but that I wanted to see you again and was coming back to Ireland." All of which was true, but the emphasis had been elsewhere, so Mark added quickly, "I told him I'd be back in six weeks and that he could then cut and patch to his heart's content."

"That can't be the real reason, Mark; otherwise you would have stayed there. And I would have come to you—you know that. Now tell me the truth."

For an answer he handed her the clipping from the *San Francisco Chronicle* about MacKenzie's assassination. The minute she read it she knew it spelled trouble.

"What's this got to do with you?"

"I may have killed him," he said simply.

"From San Francisco?" Then came the terrifying thought. "COMMEND! Have you contributed again to COM-MEND? For the love of God, Mark, say no."

"I can't say no, Deirdre, because I have—under circumstances that I hope you'll understand."

"Understand?" she replied, angrily. "Try me."

"This is going to be difficult for you, Deirdre, as it is for me, but I ask particularly that you hear me through. To begin with let me say that occasionally an opportunity comes to a man at a time in his life when he sees, perhaps for the first time, how wrong he has been and how he can work to correct that wrong. Some men rise to the occasion and are successful in putting things right. Others shun the risk—my God! I'm talking like a character out of a book!—others shun the risk for their own selfish reasons and lose the opportunity to save not

2 2 1

only themselves but also people and places that they love. I've been presented with that opportunity—to help Ireland out of this nasty business." He hesitated, then said, "I'm going to take it."

"You're going to take the opportunity to save Ireland by supporting a bunch of terrorists? Tell me how." Deirdre's eyes were blazing.

He reached for her hands. She pulled them back. The wall between them was rising rapidly.

"Deirdre, stop talking and listen. Sit down. Be rational. I love you more than life itself but I've been asked to help put an end to all the violence. A lot has changed since we first met. On my honor, I'm telling the truth. Beyond that, and again on my honor, I can tell you no more—at least for the moment."

"It sounds to me like you're in this up to your neck. How much have you given these murderers?"

Mark hesitated, then said quietly, "A hundred thousand English pounds."

She exploded. "How can you do this to me? Who are you now—King Midas dispensing his gold? What do you expect to get out of this? An ambassadorship, no doubt, from the new Marxist People's Republic of Ireland!"

"God dammit, Deirdre, stop talking nonsense. You're not only totally wrong, you're insane. I'm not doing anything to help the IRA—quite the contrary."

"Again I ask—tell me how."

"I can't."

"'I can't,'" she mimicked, close to tears. "'I can't.' Just like that. Then what *can* you do, Mark? I'll tell you what you can do—you can bloody well say good-bye to me."

"Wait!" Mark grabbed both her arms. "There's an explanation for all this."

She pushed him away. "Don't touch me," she said, icily. "Leave me alone."

"Deirdre."

"Get out of my life. I'm sorry I ever knew you. I feel betrayed. I've given you not only my love, but my life as well. People have begun to talk about us. In Ireland affairs are not taken lightly. I'm a widow, you're divorced, and we're not married. Scandal I don't need. You've violated my trust, Mark. I could hate you for this, but God damn it, I love you—too much for my own good. But I can't see you again—ever. I love you more than I've ever loved any man, but I love Ireland more. Don't try to see me. Don't call. I've got to get over this. Good-bye."

She turned and ran through the library and across the gallery, Mark behind her. Sobbing, she stopped to say, "Why does it have to end like this?"

"It doesn't have to, Deirdre, and it won't. Please listen."

"Yes, it does. I never want to see you again."

She was out the front door, slamming it behind her, before he could react. He knew that further protest, at least for now, was useless.

Mark listened as the wheels of her car bit into the gravel of the driveway, taking her away. Given a chance, he knew he could get her back, but even as he thought about how, a stabbing pain and a shortness of breath hit him again. He walked slowly into the library to sink down on a sofa and take several deep breaths. Two minutes later he felt all right. He sat there, making his plans.

First he had to go to Dublin, but when this was over he and Deirdre would go to San Francisco together. Then, after Sanner had finished with him, he and Deirdre would be married—maybe at his mother's little church at Woodside. Suddenly, everything seemed all right.

"McCarthy, you bastard," he said to himself. "See what you've done? I'll get you for this."

ZURICH
KLOTEN AIRPORT
17 SEPTEMBER 1979

The boardroom of the Soviet Union's Wozchod Handelsbank does not conform precisely to what one might expect from the dictatorship of the proletariat. For reasons best associated with image, the financial and diplomatic minds of the Soviet hierarchy went all the way to Leningrad's Hermitage Museum to give the right touch to their showcase establishment on Zurich's Bahnhofstrasse. Four paintings, one by Goya and three by the Frenchman Nicolas Poussin, added an eye-popping element to a handsomely paneled room where luxurious furniture looked even better when viewed in the aura cast by the dozens of lights glittering from two eighteenth-century chandeliers. *First class,* observed Burdin as he looked around. *Nothing like this in Moscow.*

Seated around a highly polished mahogany table were four men—Burdin; Akim Chernyshev, a ranking official of the bank; Molnar Razani, representing the Libyan government; and Jacques Freiburg, whom Burdin was told was there on behalf of the banking consortium that ran the trucking facility used by all the major international banks for the physical transfer of large shipments of bullion.

Nine days earlier Burdin had endorsed, in the name of Nicholas G. Moran, Raven's draft on the Midland Bank for a hundred thousand pounds and turned it over to the KGB's Bern *rezident,* thus raising the ante to the amount demanded by Libya prior to the release of the arms shipment assembled in

Benghazi. Wire transfers from four different banks, in London, Leningrad, Budapest, and South Yemen, made up the total of four and a half million pounds sterling.

The preliminary paper work had been completed and the receipts that Razani would sign were in his hand as the group left the boardroom to go to the lower level where the bullion would once again be inspected, then packed in the container supplied by Associated Transfer.

"Is Freiburg or somebody from his group present whenever there's a big shipment of specie?" Burdin asked Chernyshev.

"From bank to bank, no," replied Chernyshev. "Out of the country, yes. We're a member of the combine and participate with the rest. There's always a third party present."

Ninety-three gleaming gold bars were stacked neatly in the middle of the bank's vault. After an initial count by Razani, two vault attendants, with gloved hands, quickly and expertly slipped each bar into a soft flannel sack of corresponding size, then placed it into the wooden container.

As the packing began Freiburg surreptitiously punched a stopwatch in an inside pocket. In less than a half hour the job had been completed, and the hinged top dropped, locked, and sealed. Razani signed in four different places, then the container and the pallet on which it rested were picked up by a forklift and wheeled to the waiting truck. Freiburg had watched with mounting satisfaction. *So far so good,* he thought. *Now it's up to Youssef.*

8:26 A.M.—Associated Transfer's truck TF87, powered by its new transmission, got off to a smooth and easy start as it pulled away from the loading dock in the rear of the bank's building on the Bahnhofstrasse. Its rear doors had been slammed shut and locked, steel locking pins in place. As an extra precaution Razani placed another seal, on which he had written his name, across the juncture of the two doors—a very tight fit. The run to Kloten International Airport would, under normal circumstances, take half an hour.

As it emerged from the alley that intersected with the Paradeplatz a Swiss bank guard, one of hundreds of that special coterie of Swiss nationals guarding Swiss banks of all nationalities, waved TF87 into the steady stream of traffic to work its way across the congested city to the highway leading to the airport. Falling in behind the truck was one of the Wozchod Handelsbank's commodious black Chaika sedans, the best that the Soviet automobile industry has to offer the world. Freiburg was in the back seat talking with Razani. Burdin was in the front seat, next to the driver, soaking up the sights of downtown Zurich on his first leisurely visit to Switzerland.

Inside the truck the sound of the locking of the rear doors triggered action that, had it been observed, would have to have been considered a theatrical triumph. As if from nothingness two murkily clad figures materialized from behind the false front interior wall. They wore skintight black stretch nylon ski suits, and their faces were similarly blackened. Each wore a miner's cap equipped with an electric light, and on their feet dark blue jogging shoes. They moved quickly but quietly.

Around the waist of each man were several lengths of nylon rope with metal snaps on the ends. Below the ropes each wore a leather belt like those worn by telephone linemen, to which was hooked a cordless electric drill, adaptable for use with various wrenches and screwdrivers. From one belt hung a small, hand-held vacuum cleaner, of German origin. An integral part of each belt was a holster containing a Czech 9-mm automatic, against the ultimate catastrophe. Out of sight, taped to each man's chest, was a wallet containing several thousand East German marks, as well as a forged East German passport bearing a name that, traced, would indicate association with the Baader-Meinhof gang.

2 2 6

8:28 A.M.—Reaching up under the pallet on which it rested, in less than a minute the two men had located the hidden springs that held the four sides of the crate to the bottom, on which the whole weight of the shipment rested. Neither spoke a word as they went about what they had rehearsed a hundred times. Using their nylon ropes and the metal handles bolted to both ends of the crate, they quickly suspended the now bottomless crate, its locked and sealed top intact, to four metal eyelets inconspicuously placed in the ceiling of the truck, snapping each measured and precut piece of rope into place. Then, with the top suspended above them and out of the way, noiselessly and with surprising speed they started transferring the bullion to the empty space under the bench on the left-hand side of the truck.

8:31 A.M.—In the Chaika limousine following the truck, Freiburg was in the midst of telling Razani of his impending departure for Brussels to take up a new position in a bank there when the truck turned into the Badenerstrasse, heading for the airport. He glanced at his watch. Right on time, he noted. Another three minutes and Sabrina should make her appearance.

8:33 A.M.—TF87 was moving along without incident. Inside, the orderly stack of bullion had been cut in half by its transfer to the space beneath the bench. It was hot and the men were sweating. One stopped momentarily to turn up the air-conditioning, which had an outlet in the false front wall where he had been concealed.

8:35 A.M.—Where the Altstetterstrasse crosses the Badenerstrasse an eastbound red sports car driven by a young girl tried to turn left into the Badenerstrasse. A delivery van from a delicatessen coming in the opposite direction hit it a glancing blow, crumpling the right fenders of both vehicles, smashing the headlight on the red sports car, and reducing its driver to tears. TF87, two vehicles away from the intersection, had to stop. In moments the traffic seemed hopelessly snarled.

2 2 7

Freiburg again glanced at his watch. Sabrina was right on time.

"A nuisance, Herr Razani," said Freiburg, "but you have nothing to worry about. Your plane is not going to leave without you. The police should be here soon to get us going, but if you'll excuse me for a moment I'll see if I can be of any help."

Freiburg trotted up to the red sports car, whose occupant was still sitting inside, dabbing her eyes with a handkerchief between efforts to light a cigarette.

"Are you all right, *liebchen?*" he asked.

"You tell that idiot driving the van that he was coming too goddamned fast. I didn't expect all this damage. And look at my stockings! My knee's bleeding and it hurts."

Freiburg, whose wire-rimmed glasses perched on a nose well suited to his even-featured face, patted her gently on the arm.

"Good show, Sabrina. It'll all be fixed, including the knee and the stockings. Stay where you are. When the police arrive, don't be in a hurry to move."

"Jacques, you're too much," Sabrina replied. "Promise that you'll tell me what this is all about and how it comes out."

"You have my word," replied Jacques, turning to return to the Chaika. Sabrina was one of the Mossad's consummate operators. She was half in love with Freiburg and hated the thought that he was leaving Switzerland.

8:45 A.M.—TF87 was whistled on its way, but inside the truck ten priceless minutes had been gained. The last of the bullion had disappeared under the bench and the alternate cargo from under the bench on the right was being put in its place.

8:59 A.M.—Kloten International Airport. The Chaika had now moved in front of the truck as the two-car convoy was stopped at the gate through which all outgoing shipments of bullion had to pass. Freiburg showed the guard the necessary documents. He checked them over, noting the signatures of the representatives of the Wozchod Handelsbank, entering the amount, time, and method of conveyance in his log book. From long experience he was familiar with the procedure. He waved them on.

9:00 A.M.—Inside the truck Youssef Shuhan, the team captain, checked the time. *May the God of Abraham be with us!* The stop at the gate had alerted him to the fact that he and David had no more than four minutes to complete the job— with not a telltale trace remaining to betray the deception. Otherwise he and his equally sweating teammate would have to hijack the truck and make a run for the Italian border. The whole operation would be blown, including Freiburg's cover. He was drenched with perspiration.

"Hurry, David. We'll make it. Only the last two bolts!"

The four sides and the top had been lowered back onto the substituted cargo, and the nylon ropes detached and hidden under the bench with the gold. Now the last and most important step was to replace the release springs with permanent lag bolts heavy enough to sustain the weight of the crate. Two of the four were in place and secure. Some drilling had been necessary to enlarge the holes from which the release springs had been extracted. A sprinkling of wood particles was easily visible on the floor of the truck.

9:01 A.M.—The truck started to move again. The two remaining bolts were in place.

"Tighten them up, David, for Christ's sake! The vacuum's behind you. Hand it to me!"

As David took up the head slack on the bolts with his electric wrench Youssef, working behind and around him, vacuumed up the last of the wood particles.

9:03 A.M.—Once more the truck stopped, this time at the air freight terminal. As it did so, Youssef closed the door on David's hiding place, scanned the floor of the truck once more, hung the vacuum cleaner back on his belt, checked the snaplock on the left-hand bench under which the purloined bullion was hidden, then stepped into his own hiding place, pulling the door closed behind him. As he heard the spring latch take hold he said softly to himself, "By Jesus, we did it!" It was exactly 9:05 A.M.

He had a lot to show for his student years in America. Cal Tech '75, physics, mathematics, metallurgy and architectural drawing, magna cum laude. But in other areas he had come up short. Christian blasphemy, B-minus.

Razani checked the seal that he had placed across the point where the rear doors met vertically. The doors were heavy and the seal unbroken. He had considered the seal superfluous when it had been suggested, but after the delay caused by the automobile accident he was glad it was there.

Razani had been uncomfortable in the presence of Freiburg. He recognized him as Jewish despite—or perhaps because of, he couldn't tell which—his cosmopolitan manner, his courtesy, and the air of self-confidence which seemed to cling to Swiss bankers. He was glad the ride was over.

As the driver was unlocking the doors, Freiburg was standing behind Razani, the picture of composure. Inwardly he was experiencing some turmoil. What if the doors opened and they were confronted with two black-clad, armed men who would attempt to seize the truck and use it as a getaway vehicle? It was an uncomfortable moment. A disinterested Burdin had wandered off.

The doors swung open. There stood the solitary crate waiting to be fork-lifted to the Libyan plane, seemingly untouched since leaving the Wozchod Handelsbank. Freiburg, his countenance unchanged but his relief palpable, eased up to the truck. No one else would have noticed, but on the floor were a few flecks of what appeared to be sawdust. To Freiburg they were the icing on the cake.

* * *

Twenty-five minutes later the bullion had been transferred to the Libyan plane. Razani had gone off to the airport bar for two fast whiskies before returning to Tripoli. He didn't know the plane crew well enough to risk bringing a bottle aboard. As Freiburg said good-bye to him, he knew Razani was in for a bad time. Libyan or not, he felt sorry for him— but only momentarily.

AT SEA
THE *NOVOSIBIRSK*
AND HMS *TAURUS*
14-17 SEPTEMBER 1979

THE *NOVOSIBIRSK*

"Increase speed to one-third."

Captain First Rank Anatoly Bereznoy put down his binoculars to look down from the bridge at the deck of the *Novosibirsk*. The waters of the eastern Mediterranean were choppy, driven by a brisk wind. With the ship's increased speed they began to lap over the submarine's spherical bow, then to flood the flat missile deck before breaking to port and starboard as they hit the base of the towering black sail. Captain Lieutenant Valeri Leontovich, the ship's navigator, whose computerlike mind was capable of a readout on the ship's location almost without instruments, repeated his captain's orders over the bridge telephone.

Ahead of his ship by two miles Bereznoy could see two of the three Soviet surface vessels that had accompanied the *Novosibirsk* through the Dardanelles. Astern he could see the receding outline of still another, a cruiser, sailing to the southeast. Atop the sail the cramped control station was already crowded by the presence of the captain, the navigator, and an ordinary seaman standing his first watch. But still another of the ship's complement was on his way up.

"So, my captain. We go to sea again to protect the *Rodina?*" It was Captain Second Rank Petr Yessenin, the *zampolit,* poking his head through the hatch while struggling to get his bulky frame up the ladder with all the awkwardness of a landlubber.

The nerve of the man. Bereznoy knew that this was Yessenin's maiden voyage, and his presumptuous attitude served only to heighten the already strained relationship that normally existed between those truly in command and any political officer.

Bereznoy chose to ignore him. They would soon dive— *that's one way to get the bastard off the bridge and out of my hair*—and Yessenin would be taken up with his duties overseeing the political climate aboard ship and the actions of the crew. Moreover Bereznoy had other things to think about than this loud-mouthed oaf who never allowed a person to forget who he was and what he represented.

Captain Bereznoy didn't like his mission and liked even less the thought that he would be taking instructions—even by indirection and in the limited degree that he recognized as necessary—from Viktor Soroshkin.

He didn't know Soroshkin but he knew about him. Who in the Soviet submarine service didn't? His feelings toward Soroshkin, for screwing up when he was in command of the *Admiral Razhnikov,* were nothing short of contemptuous. The incident off the South Carolina coast was a disgraceful performance for which Soroshkin deserved much greater punishment than he got. Captain Bereznoy also didn't like the idea of his ship being used as a cargo vessel. In its present condition it was useless for anything else, he had to admit, but he saw this assignment as degrading, not only to himself but to his crew and to his ship. And worst of all he knew that after loading the secret cargo at Benghazi he was going to have to carry Soroshkin with him on the rest of this highly irregular voyage, through the Strait of Gibraltar and up into waters off the Irish coast before returning to Sevastopol. He viewed this association with extreme distaste, hoping that Soroshkin would have the good grace to keep to himself. He wanted no guilt by association. Let Soroshkin spend his time talking with Yessenin. They deserved one another.

The *Novosibirsk* had left Sevastopol accompanied by the *Sverdlow*-class cruiser *Admiral Ushakov* and two *Munuchka*-class missile corvettes, the *Nikolayev* and the *Naporisty*. Skirting the Dodecanese Islands, the flotilla had passed between Cape Matapan, at the southernmost tip of Greece, and Crete, headed for mid-Mediterranean waters. Once there, in an area generally southeast of Malta, the *Nikolayev* and the *Naporisty* would cruise sufficiently far away from the Libyan coast to divert attention away from the *Novosibirsk*—should NATO forces be watching—as she maneuvered her way into the Gulf of Sidra and into the approaches to the harbor at Benghazi. The real reason for their presence, however, was to relay coded information from Soroshkin in Benghazi to the *Novosibirsk*. The *Naporisty* had been chosen for this delicate task and her electronic communications gear modified accordingly. Once submerged and committed the *Novosibirsk* was under orders to adhere to strict radio and other electronic silence. It could receive messages but could not send them.

After clearing the coast of Crete, the *Admiral Ushakov* had broken off from the flotilla and sailed for the coast of Israel. Long before she reached the outer limits of Israeli territorial waters her presence would be detected by Israeli radar, thus prompting her continued observation by Israeli Air Force planes. Which was exactly the diversion intended.

In a matter of minutes the chop became heavier and the

submarine began to roll. The movement was accentuated by their height above the deck, driving Yessenin below. *A still pond sailor, seasick at the first ripple.* Bereznoy shared the observation silently with Leontovich, who shook his head unsmilingly in agreement. Their unspoken contempt for the *zampolit* was contrary to all doctrinaire Soviet behavior.

"Control room, what is the sounding?" Bereznoy asked over the bridge telephone.

"One hundred and twenty meters below the keel, Comrade Captain."

"Increase speed to two-thirds, come left ten degrees." Bereznoy looked at Leontovich. "Signal the *Naporisty.*" He checked his watch. "Diving at 1624 hours. Exercise Sandstorm begins as scheduled."

In Leontovich's experienced hands the blinker light flashed the message in a matter of seconds. From her own bridge the *Naporisty* responded at once: "Confirmed. We transmit to Fleet HQ. Good luck."

"Prepare to dive." Bereznoy turned to the lookout and ordered him below. The young recruit moved toward the hatch, but only after a last lingering look at the sun, the shadows, and the sea, reluctant to return to the constrictions and confinement that awaited him at the foot of the ladder.

"Clear the bridge. Stand by for other assigned duties when you get below, Valeri." Leontovich nodded and dropped down the hatch, leaving the captain alone.

Through his binoculars Bereznoy once more scanned the horizon. To the southeast the *Admiral Ushakov* was little more than an indistinguishable blur, while the two missile corvettes ahead of him, accelerating their own speed as they broke off from their submerging companion, were kicking up wakes that increased the wave action on his own bow. To his left the late afternoon Mediterranean sun was momentarily obscured by thin, low-lying clouds, giving a wistful quality to the seascape. He thought about home and Lydia; he should be back with her within two weeks to resume his interrupted leave. Going to sea on the submarines that he loved was always exciting but always a little bit sad.

His mind raced ahead to where he would be taking his vessel after leaving Benghazi. The one aspect of this madcap mission that dispelled doubts of success was his instructions on the disposition of the cargo. There would be more on this from Soroshkin, but once he reached the rendezvous at fifty-four degrees twenty-eight minutes north latitude and eight degrees forty-five minutes west longitude—a point that he and Leontovich had plotted out as within fourteen miles of the coast of northern Ireland—and Soroshkin had identified the group that would receive and unload, he was to allow *three hours only* for unloading, beginning at 0001 hours on the day of the rendezvous. Any cargo on board after 0300 hours was to remain. Departure was not to be delayed under any circumstances—a safety measure to insure a predawn dive and the avoidance of detection by unfriendly eyes. *Well now! A clever man,* he mused, *could hamper the unloading process so that much of the cargo stayed aboard. After all, the arms were Soviet and could be used elsewhere.* What would be the effect of this on Yessenin? As far as he could determine the bastard had never commanded anything bigger than a harbor tug. If it would be a black mark against him, he'd see that his crew behaved like decrepit old men.

He slid down the ladder inside the sail and readied himself for the rest of the diving procedure. His thoughts about Yessenin cheered him and he felt better.

HMS *TAURUS*

Under a brilliant sun a southwest wind was blowing at eight knots, just enough to create gentle whitecaps on the sea's inky blue surface. On the bridge of HMS *Taurus* Captain Wiggins leaned back against the aft bulkhead, enjoying the day, the weather, and the sight and sounds of his ship plowing through the open seas. To his left his executive officer, Commander Geoffrey Castlewood, elbows resting on the forward coaming of the bridge shield, was sweeping the horizon through binoculars, and beyond him Bochenkev, arms folded and eyes shielded by dark sun glasses, looked inquiringly around. A surface run was a luxury not often experienced. The *Taurus* would soon dive and run submerged, but for now Wiggins was enjoying himself to the utmost. A half-dozen porpoises had adopted his boat, surfing on the bow wave. It was a toss-up who was having the more fun, the captain or his frolicking companions.

At the beginning of the forenoon watch the *Taurus*'s position had been read as forty-three degrees twenty-eight minutes north latitude and thirteen degrees fifty-six minutes west longitude, ninety nautical miles due west of Cape Finisterre. She was moving at thirty knots in a southeasterly direction to skirt Cape Saint Vincent, the southernmost tip of Portugal, before changing course for the Strait of Gibraltar. Since clearing the mouth of Saint George's Channel, between England and Ireland, her course had been almost due south, running under clear skies and in calm seas.

Despite some earlier second thoughts, Evelyn Wiggins's confidence in himself, his boat, his crew, and the successful accomplishment of his mission was high. The eight assorted men who comprised his unusual supercargo had at first been a major source of worry for him. A submariner's life is isolation, silence, and avoidance of detection twenty-four hours a day, and a crew—collectively—must act with unfailing grace under unrelieved pressure. But that worry had vanished. The eight mavericks, as they had immediately been termed, while at all times remaining directly under his command, were led by Bochenkev and responded willingly and quickly to instructions he gave them, in Russian. To the extent possible they were segregated in the crew's mess, moving wordlessly out when required and keeping to themselves. They spoke only Russian and talked to each other and no one else, ignoring the few questions put to them in English by the crew, as if they didn't understand.

It was weird, he had to admit. Seven pseudo-Russian sailors aboard the *Taurus!* When he left Dartmouth to enter the Royal Navy he never expected a cruise like this one—like having aboard the enigmatic Lieutenant Commander Bochenkev, a Russian-speaking British naval officer in charge of a group of outer space aliens, recruited on short notice but including two SAS men from the 22nd Regiment, to engage in a mission fraught with danger for them all. Or like Feodor Roguchin, a White Russian by birth, with his name changed to Roger Chinn Delafield as more compatible with his mother's second marriage to a benevolent stepfather, a British banker. He was amused at the subtlety of the metamorphosis of Roguchin to Roger Chinn, but otherwise had nothing but admiration for what he saw in the slightly built, naturalized Englishman, one who had the ideal physique for a submariner, including reactions that were lightning fast. Beyond that he knew that Roguchin—as he would refer to him in front of the others for the duration of this operation—would supervise the placement of the bogus sail planes on the sail, having played a big part in their fabrication at A-V's yards at Barrow. That aspect alone of this cruise would make Royal Navy history. He looked over the side of the sail to glance reassuringly at two large bolts protruding from its side, halfway down to the opposite side of the sail. What he saw brought back to him the fact that the daring coup that lay ahead had the full approval not only of Whitehall but of the Prime Minister herself. This and the scene at 10 Downing Street following Brigadier MacKenzie's assassination had been spelled out for him by no lesser person than the First Sea Lord. By the Lord Harry he and his motley crew would pull it off!

Three days earlier, when Bettelmans left Muhayshi's office to catch his flight to Rome, he had been gone less than a minute before Muhayshi opened his desk drawer to count his take. *Ten thousand Russian rubles!* He'd have no trouble exchanging them for rials or for pounds sterling or for dollars, depending on how he wished to spend this latest windfall. Not bad for a couple of telephone calls, for that's all it would take to accomplish what Bettelmans had asked.

He left a message for Petrovskiy to call him, then tried to get Soroshkin in Benghazi. An hour later he hadn't succeeded, which was no surprise as phone service between the two cities was unreliable at best, and at worst nonexistent. So he took his other option and sent a telegram.

CAPTAIN VIKTOR SOROSHKIN
HOTEL METROPOLE
BENGHAZI—STRAIGHT WIRE

NOTIFY YOUR PEOPLE AFLOAT TO SCHEDULE PICKUP FOR 0400 17 SEPTEMBER STOP LIGHTER TO PROCEED AS PLANNED FOR ARRIVAL 2200 16 SEPTEMBER AT RENDEZVOUS POINT STOP IN INTERIM PETROVSKIY WILL MAKE FINAL INVENTORY OF SHIPMENT ON LIGHTER AFTER REMOVAL OF GOODS FROM WAREHOUSE AND DEPARTURE FROM DOCKSIDE STOP CONFIRM UPON COMPLETION OF ARRANGEMENTS

MUHAYSHI
FINANCE MINISTER

Four hours later Soroshkin got the telegram. Bettelmans again—and his influence! However, it all fit with what he'd been told so he'd follow Muhayshi's instructions and transmit the message to Watchdog, the code word for the *Naporisty,* and keep the telegram as evidence that he was doing as he was told to do. If there was a screwup he'd pass it to Petrovskiy to sort out. Twenty minutes later he had fed a casette with a shortened version of the message into his shortwave transmitter and shot it off, at accelerated speed, to Watchdog.

CALABASH TO WATCHDOG SHIPMENT WILL NOT ARRIVE AT TRANSFER POINT UNTIL 0400 HOURS 17 SEPTEMBER DELAY UNAVOIDABLE CONFIRM PASSAGE TO PROWLER IMPERATIVE THAT LATTER COORDINATE MOVEMENT TO ARRIVE AT SAME HOUR

South of Malta, in choppy seas, the *Naporisty* cruised at a comfortable twelve knots. On her bridge a *michman* handed Soroshkin's coded message to her captain, who read it with interest. The *Nikolayev* was out of sight, having turned in an opposite direction, toward the Tunisian coast, in the realization that both vessels were under aerial observation by carrier-based aircraft from the U.S. Sixth Fleet. Wasting little time, the captain wrote out his message to Captain Bereznoy on the *Novosibirsk,* code name Prowler.

WATCHDOG TO PROWLER YOUR ETA AT TRANSFER POINT NOW SET FOR 0400 HOURS 17 SEPTEMBER IMPERATIVE YOU ARRIVE SAME TIME DRAGON FLIES ALL AROUND

"For immediate dispatch," he said to the waiting *michman.* Four minutes later it went out on the single shortwave band chosen for use in communicating with the *Novosibirsk.*

Soroshkin's squirt transmission had been aired at 2245 hours the same night following receipt. In addition to being picked up by the *Naporisty* it was also plucked out of the air by an alert National Security Agency listening station at the U.S. Air Force Base at Torrejon, Spain. NSA headquarters, Fort Meade, Maryland, had it within minutes as did the British at

Cheltenham. MI-5 and Captain Wiggins, aboard HMS *Taurus,* had it within an hour. In mid-morning Peter Lindsay took the word personally to Sir Alistair Widener, who hurried to 10 Downing Street to inform the prime minister. Everyone felt better.

HMS *TAURUS*

Delafield, as Roguchin, looked around him. He was in familiar territory, a place of solid metal and grated decks called Sherwood Forest in missile submarines in both the British and American navies. Despite their gray paint the missile tubes, protruding downward from their hatch openings, looked like the trunks of enormous trees, their bases just below the grates, embedded firmly in the vessel's keel. One tube had been completely removed before the *Taurus* left Faslane, for modification to accept the newer Trident missiles with which it would be armed. Its hatch would be the opening through which the contraband would be lowered for storage during the short run back to Gibraltar where unloading would take place.

In such familiar surroundings Delafield felt completely at home. The mavericks had just responded to a general quarters drill and the last of them, Pontriagyn, was just disappearing through a bulkhead door. In the event of real trouble their assigned area was here, away from any action.

As Delafield prepared to follow, a yeoman's mate appeared with a message for him.

"Captain Wiggins's compliments, sir. He'd like to see you in his quarters."

"Come in, Roger, and close the door." Captain Wiggins had sent for both Delafield and Bochenkev. The latter was already there. The CO's quarters were, as might be expected, the most commodious aboard, but still small. Wiggins occupied one of the two chairs in the cabin, Bochenkev the other. Delafield stood, his back to the closed door.

"The scenario's getting better by the moment," said Wiggins. "I can now tell you that we're going to have a defector on our hands, a Soviet naval officer called Soroshkin. Our intelligence people have been in personal contact with him, in Libya, as recently as three days ago. He's coming out willingly, so no problem there. But he has not been told that this is a British submarine, against the possibility that this operation could be blown. Obviously he couldn't reveal what he didn't know. So he will be pleasantly surprised to find himself aboard the *Taurus* rather than the *Novosibirsk*. The reassuring factor, however, will come—prior to the time when he comes aboard—when he is given a coded message indicating to him that he is not being betrayed. Roger, old son, you will deliver the message as quickly as you can get to him. Here it is." He handed him a card with the message typed on it. "You must translate the message into Russian and tell him verbally, as Soroshkin doesn't speak English. For Christ's sake don't lose it, or we'll all be in the soup."

Delafield looked at the card, then looked up and smiled. "I sense romance here. I'll take the greatest pleasure in playing Cupid. How do I know which one is Soroshkin?"

"The presumption is he'll be in uniform," replied Wiggins. "There'll probably be another Russian on the lighter, a man called Sergei Petrovskiy. Alexei, that's where you come in."

"As you wish, Captain Wiggins. I'm yours to command. I'm on active duty, you know."

"By Jove, so you are. I keep forgetting," said Wiggins. "Your assignment is to see that Petrovskiy does not get aboard this vessel—not even on deck. You'll have two SAS noncoms to assist you in this. Both will be armed with submachine guns, one on our deck close to any boarding facility, and one on the lighter. In case of trouble they're authorized to fire—at your command. Or in case of *real* trouble—at will. They know it. Now you know it. Let's pray to God that all goes well."

THE *NOVOSIBIRSK*

Off the coast of Libya, forty-one miles east northeast of Benghazi, the *Novosibirsk* lay submerged and motionless. Captain Bereznoy read the *Naporisty*'s signal with annoyance. The delay added a six-hour stretch to his waiting time, and he wanted to get this assignment over. He needed no reminder from *Naporisty* that surface elements of the U.S. Sixth Fleet were above him, so he had imposed maximum silence on his crew and forbidden all unnecessary movement inside the vessel. That never sat well, and especially at this time, as the *zampolit* was using the occasion for quiet, soporific lectures to selected crew members on the values of the work ethic in the Soviet state. Screw him! Moreover Leontovich was beating him badly at chess and he never liked to lose, under these or any other circumstances.

HMS *TAURUS*

"In less than two hours we will reach the rendezvous point off the breakwater at Benghazi, in water twelve fathoms, or seventy-two feet deep. I will be on the bridge and take the *Taurus* in. I will position the ship so that the bow faces northeast, ready for the quickest possible departure. The lighter will be there, stabilized by her tug. She will tie to us on our starboard side. As we now know, the lighter carries its own crane; otherwise the loading process would be extremely difficult. We cannot risk anchoring, so to hold our position against the wind and tide, the tug that has brought the lighter out will be made fast to our port side. Instructions to the tug will be given by Commander Bochenkev, relayed through the Arabic-speaking SAS man on deck. This is the one big chink in our armor, but since we cannot anchor, it is a factor we simply have to deal with. If it becomes necessary, we'll axe the hawsers to get loose for a fast getaway."

Captain Wiggins had assembled his crew—less the mess attendants and the communications, navigational, and engineering personnel—in the crew's mess for a final briefing.

"When the loading starts you Russian-speaking volunteers on deck will look to Commander Bochenkev, a commissioned officer in the Royal Navy, as your leader. This will come as a surprise to you, but it is true, I assure you. You will address him as captain. As second in command I am delegating the one whom you know as Feodor Roguchin. You will address him as captain also. I should tell you that Captain Roguchin, and I do not use the term lightly, has had as much to do with the building of this submarine—HMS *Taurus,* the ship that all of us love and call home—as any man alive. I'll let that sink in for a moment before telling you something of even greater importance."

The silence was pervasive. The only sounds were those of the ship itself. Not a man spoke. Some hardly dared breathe. All eyes were on Captain Wiggins.

"A Soviet naval officer—his name is Soroshkin but that's not important—will be on the lighter, in charge of the men on it," Wiggins continued. "It is anticipated that he will remain on the lighter until the loading is completed, when he will come aboard. Not only will he come aboard, but he will be leaving with us, of his own accord." Wiggins spoke clearly, accentuating his words. "He is a defector from the Soviet Union who has played a significant part in this operation."

Again there was a momentary silence as the full implications of Wiggins's words sank in on the stunned crew. Then cheers, and applause. Someone shouted, "Lord love a duck! Fantastic!"

Wiggins held up his hands for silence.

"Other than the Russian-speakers among us no one— *repeat, no one*—goes on deck unless ordered to do so. I will be in the free-flooding area of the sail, out of sight but in full command of the situation, able to communicate upward with Captains Bochenkev and Roguchin and downward with Commander Castlewood at the foot of the ladder. Two men from the Royal Marine detachment, armed and ready, will be with me in the sail. The other six will stand by with Commander Castlewood at the foot of the ladder, ready to move out at his command."

Once more there was silence, broken only by the beeping sounds of the electronic scanners at the navigator's desk.

"What questions do we have?" Wiggins looked around. A sense of excitement was endemic. He knew the crew was with him.

In reply there were only clenched fists, raised and pumped in approbation.

"Then," continued Wiggins, "in words attributed to Lord Nelson at the Battle of Trafalgar I will say 'England expects every man will do his duty.' God save the Queen!"

The unified response came back, voiced as one man, "God save the Queen!"

HMS *TAURUS*—BENGHAZI

"**W**ave him off, Corporal. Tell him who we are and that we're not going in."

Captain Wiggins, still on the bridge of the *Taurus,* was talking to Corporal Christopher Peacock, one of the Arab-speaking SAS men on board, who stood next to him.

The Benghazi pilot boat was alongside, with three men

aboard. In the glare of the searchlight held by Commander Bochenkev the small converted tugboat looked minuscule in comparison with the nuclear submarine, now running on the surface and throttled down to a bare four knots.

A few shouted sentences later Corporal Peacock turned back to report to the captain. "He says he knows that we're the *Novosibirsk* and that we're going to lay to off the mole. Apparently there's a medical officer on board, and he wants to know if anyone will be going ashore."

"Tell him no, thank him for his attention, and that we'll proceed accordingly."

"Aye-aye, sir."

Peacock was amused by his own use of navy parlance. The rebellious son of a professor of economics at the University of London, he had been born in Lebanon while his father was teaching at Beirut's American University. Arabic had been his first language. Now a life in the SAS was exactly his cup of tea, even the hard-time assignments in Northern Ireland. There was another exchange of shouted sentences and then, with a wave of the hand from one of its passengers, the pilot boat picked up speed and headed for the harbor.

"Okay, Corporal," said Wiggins, "and much obliged. Now I'll get you to go below and pass the word to Captain Roguchin that he's wanted on the bridge."

Another "aye-aye, sir" and Peacock was gone.

Suddenly, as if from nowhere, a Libyan Air Force reconnaissance plane was over them, coming in from the southwest at no more than five hundred feet. And just as suddenly the beam from the high intensity searchlight with which Bochenkev continued to pick up both port and starboard navigational buoys was relegated to insignificance by the brilliance of the flare dropped from the plane—bright enough for Captain Wiggins to make out the coastline tower on the high cliffs at Ra's Sidi Khuraybish to the east of Benghazi, as well as the minarets of the Siret Ben Gazi mosque in Benghazi itself.

"The beggars are taking pictures," said Wiggins, looking up. "Wave at 'em, Alexei. We're the friendly types, remember?"

Twenty minutes later the plane and its North Korean pilot were on the ground at its base at Okfa-Ben-Na'afi. Four minutes after that the videos had been processed. Lieutenant Colonel Rakshar Pooran, in charge of the photo interpretation group, looked at them carefully in projection. Then he called the Villa Lucia to report his conclusions to Qaddafi.

There were no preliminaries. Qaddafi wanted the information, and fast.

"Excellency," said Pooran, "we have fourteen very clear frames, taken from four hundred and eighty feet. When projected, the ship's profile and superstructure conform exactly to *Yankee*-class Soviet submarines. In short, we can say with assurance that the submarine at Benghazi is the *Novosibirsk*. Our photographs are good enough to show Soviet officers on her bridge, waving at our plane."

Pooran listened, then said, "Yes, Excellency. Thank you, Excellency. I will tell them. Good night, Excellency. *Allah akbar*."

Turning to his men, he said, "Our leader is pleased. We can all go home now. We are relieved from any further part in the alert."

"I think I see her," said Soroshkin. He was apprehensive, not knowing what to expect.

"I see nothing," countered Petrovskiy. "Your eyes must be better than mine. Point in her direction."

There was no longer any doubt about it—the *Novosibirsk* was approaching. Soroshkin could see her more plainly now, the elliptical shape of the leading edge of her sail, her sail planes, even the curving of the upper reaches of her hull. To Soroshkin's practiced eye she appeared to be at least half a mile away. Even as he looked, raising his hand to point in the direction of the approaching submarine, another flare exploded in the air, several hundred feet above her and somewhat closer to the waiting lighter and tug. Suddenly the whole area was lit by the white light of the slowly descending flare, held aloft by a small parachute that had spread itself automatically at the apogee of its arc.

Despite the apprehension that was enveloping him in direct proportion to the drop of the flare, it was a moment that Soroshkin never forgot. There was a surrealistic beauty about it, as if a sea serpent had surfaced, spitting fire in order to see. The running lights on the tug were enough to pinpoint its position, but there was nothing to indicate that the lighter was lashed to it. Using his flashlight, Soroshkin quickly blinked out the word HERE. An almost immediate answer was blinkered back from the sub's bridge atop the sail: DA. WE READ YOU. Soroshkin felt for his Czech automatic. Reassuringly it was there, hidden under his jacket.

The rhythmic beat of the sub's engines could now be plainly heard. All eyes on the lighter were watching as two floodlights appeared, fore and aft of the sail, directed downward. Soroshkin lifted the binoculars slung around his neck for a closer look. The sheer mass of a missile-bearing submarine is an awesome sight; this was no exception. Above the protruding sail planes, midway up the sail, he could see several men on the bridge. Others were on the deck, both fore and aft of the sail, responding to commands in Russian that he could hear across the water.

In the glare of the floodlights the full length of the submarine's deck could be seen by anyone. With his binoculars

Soroshkin focused in on the bow, then moved his sight line slowly to where the aft deck ceased. Quickly he repeated the process. Again, then once more. *Something was amiss!* An alarm bell rang. He had never before seen the *Novosibirsk,* but he knew when and where she had been laid down and the general details of her construction. His own vessel, the *Admiral Razhnikov,* was her sister ship. Despite Bettelmans's assurances a sense of panic, accompanied by a despair such as he had experienced in the months of his detention and trial, swept over him. But with no place to hide, all he could think about now was survival. He'd come this far and there was no turning back.

On the submarine, a hatch was opened and in minutes an inflatable dinghy had been launched, complete with outboard motor. Its ignition took hold with the first kick of the self-starter and the dinghy headed for the lighter. In it were Delafield and two SAS men, both armed with AK47s. In the background the massive sail of the submarine reached upward like the dorsal fin of some mammoth sea creature. The stagecraft of an Ibsen could have offered nothing better.

"**A**hoy, the lighter! Is Comrade Captain Soroshkin aboard?" shouted Delafield from twenty yards out.

"I'm here, comrade!" replied Soroshkin in a loud voice. "Come aboard here." He waved his flashlight to indicate where.

The dinghy eased alongside and Delafield scrambled aboard. Speaking in unaccented Russian, Delafield introduced himself. "I'm Feodor Roguchin, comrade, second in command." One of the SAS men—silent, alert, and ready—was by his side. The other stayed in the dinghy, making it fast, its motor throttled down but left running, ready for any miscue.

A Soviet navy watchcap covered Delafield's head. His

face wore blended applications of both brown and black camouflage paint. In blue denim fatigues from which all telltale identifying marks had been removed, there was nothing of any kind to indicate rank. The SAS men were similarly dressed, Soroshkin noted, and did not find it strange.

"You're right on time," he said, in greeting Delafield.

"*Da*. We're looking for a fast load and departure within two hours—certainly no more than three. We want out before the Americans get wind of us."

There were handshakes all around as Soroshkin introduced Petrovskiy. "He's from the embassy in Tripoli," Soroshkin explained, "here to complete a final inventory of the shipment. All was found to be in order."

"Our orders are to take you with us," said Delafield. "Is that correct?"

"That is correct, Comrade Captain." The SAS man was right behind them. Petrovskiy had gone off. "But before we go any further, I need answers to some questions."

"Such as?"

"Such as why do these two crewmen appear to me to be personal bodyguards for you—ready to shoot me or anybody else at any moment? They are armed with AK47s. AK47s are not standard equipment in the Soviet navy. Who are these men?"

"A good question, comrade. You are very observant. They are indeed armed with AK47s. But the men are *Vysotniki*, detailed to the *Novosibirsk* for this voyage only, to insure that no unruly Arab gets out of hand. All *Vysotniki* are armed with AK47s."

"A good question, you say, and I say a good enough answer. But I have another question."

"Which is?"

"Which is this. Who are you and what's going on? The submarine out there in the stream is not the *Novosibirsk*. On

Soviet boats the missile tubes come through the foredeck, not aft. Nor do I think the submarine is British—British boomers don't have sail planes."

Soroshkin was surprised at his confident tone, at the defiance of his mood. He had visions of a hijacking by the Israelis, or wilder still, by insurgent Arabs, possibly the PLO.

Delafield turned to the SAS man, who had understood everything Soroshkin said. A nod was sufficient. The metallic sound of the bolt of his AK47 going into the load and lock position sent a readily understood message. Petrovskiy was out of earshot.

"Viktor, we are getting off on the wrong foot." The use of Soroshkin's first name was a ploy designed to bring the conversation back to where Delafield wanted it. "Let's not talk about that for a moment. It's more important for you to know I have a message for you. I'm sure it'll put your mind at ease."

"I'm all ears, Comrade Captain. Your men can cut me down if that's your wish, but I'm no fool."

"I'm sure you're not, Viktor," Delafield said, quietly. "Now—here's the message. It is from Lyskya. Surely you remember Lyskya? She sends her love and says she is looking forward to seeing you again. I'm told that the message has a meaning that you alone will understand and that you should be pleased by it. If so, let's get down to work."

The change in Soroshkin's attitude was instantaneous, even visible. *Bettelmans hasn't let me down!* Overcome, he reached out to grasp both of Delafield's upper arms in friendship.

"Lyskya!" His face lit up like a Christmas tree. "A name that I thought I'd never hear again. Do you swear that this is the message?"

"I swear that this is the message."

"And it is from Lyskya?"

"It is from Lyskya."

"Nichevo! May I live to piss on Lenin's tomb! But tell me, Captain Roguchin, as one Russian to another, what are you doing on a boat that's not Russian? Are you a CIA agent? Surely you're not an Israeli? Israel has no boomers."

"Viktor, in a matter of hours all of these questions will be answered for you. Meanwhile we've got a job to do. Let's get along with it."

"You are right, Comrade Captain." Soroshkin's enthusiasm was palpable. "We go."

By 0115 hours on the morning of 17 September the loading was all but finished. Captain Wiggins, from his concealed position, never lost control, passing on what few instructions were necessary through Commander Bochenkev. Voroshilov and Pontriagyn were on deck, one on each side of the silo hatch, to guide the hoisted cargo routinely through the opening, then to relay instructions in Russian to Sanchez in Sherwood Forest below. Delafield, playing his role as Roguchin to the hilt, was on the lighter. With him was one of the SAS men who spoke both Russian and Arabic, to pass on verbal or hand signals to Selim, the gang boss of the Libyan stevedores, or to Abdullah, the crane operator. Toward the end of the load Voroshilov changed places with the other SAS man, who had been guarding the gangway.

Petrovskiy, cold, irritable, and impatient to return to shore, noticed the change when he came back from the rear of the lighter where he had gone to urinate. He would have liked to go aboard the submarine to wait out the loading process but had been told firmly that he was not allowed on board. Earlier he had complained to Delafield.

"I'm sorry, comrade, but there's really not room. As you've no doubt noticed, none of the crew has been allowed on deck except for the loading detail, as they need maximum space to maneuver. And that makes the areas below very crowded. We want to be long gone at first light. Why don't you go over and sit in the cabin of the tug?"

When Voroshilov took up his post at the top of the gangway he thought he'd try again. The answer was the same.

"Sorry, comrade, no one's allowed aboard." Voroshilov raised the AK47 to indicate he meant what he said.

Petrovskiy retreated to one of the remaining crates, one marked with an X, sat on it, and lit a cigarette. Beneath the camouflage paint on Voroshilov's face he thought he recognized familiar features.

He got up and went again to the gangway. Voroshilov immediately moved to block his way.

"Have a smoke, comrade? American cigarettes—the best." He held out the pack, looking at Voroshilov intently.

"No, comrade, but thank you anyhow. Now back off."

"May I not just look down through the hatch where the crates are going?" Petrovskiy was playing for time.

"You may not, comrade. Get back on the barge." Voroshilov pulled back the firing mechanism on the automatic weapon. It settled into place with an ominous click.

"As you say," replied Petrovskiy, turning to retreat. *That face*, he thought. *Where have I seen that face before?*

HMS *TAURUS*—OUTWARD BOUND

Captain Wiggins was back on his bridge. A fingernail moon was almost directly overhead, surrounded by the galaxy of stars so clearly visible on a cloudless night in the western Mediterranean. The lights of Benghazi's harbor were receding as HMS *Taurus,* her bogus sail planes jettisoned, headed northeast by east, bound for Gibraltar at near maximum surface speed. With Wiggins were Commander Castlewood, Roger Delafield, and Soroshkin, the latter clutching his encased shortwave transmitter. He and Delafield had been conversing in Russian. The last crate of the hijacked cargo had gone through the open missile hatch at 0150 hours.

"Captain Wiggins," said Delafield, "Captain Soroshkin says it's vital that he transmit a final message to the Soviet corvette *Naporisty,* his relay point for communication with the *Novosibirsk. Naporisty* is waiting to hear from him before telling the *Novosibirsk* to proceed to the rendezvous at Benghazi. He says the message will be short and that he'd better get to it fast. I'll listen while he puts it on tape for squirt transmission."

"By all means, Roger. We've got a good lead on them, and God knows we don't want to blow the operation now."

"Yes, sir. The signal's got to go out from here, as his transmitter is useless if we're submerged."

"Very good. Tell him to get with it, as we're going to dive momentarily."

Captain Wiggins looked up into the heavens, then turned to Geoffrey Castlewood.

"Look up there, Jimmy," he said, using the name given by custom to every XO in the Royal Navy's submarine service, "there's old Taurus sitting right in the middle of the Pleiades— a star that maybe rules our destiny. It watched over us, didn't it? What is it that we say every Guy Fawkes Day? 'Please to remember the fifth of November, gunpowder treason and plot'? God knows there's been enough plotting, and with the loot we've got aboard we could blow up hell. Old jolly Sir Roderick and Maggie ought to be pleased. Now let's get ourselves to dry country, old son, because we're going down to run for the Rock."

THE *NOVOSIBIRSK*

WATCHDOG TO PROWLER PROCEED TO OUTER MOLE RENDEZVOUS AT INSTRUCTED TIME STOP SIGNAL

At last. The word to move. Captain Bereznoy received his instructions with relief. The waiting had become a burden. He stood at the command station at the base of the periscope with his navigator at his elbow and a step away from the chart table. Losing no time, he called the control room on the intercom.

"Report sounding below the keel. Prepare to start engines." To a senior lieutenant he said, "Alert the crew to stand to."

There was a momentary delay, then the answer came back from the control room. "Thirty meters below the keel, comrade captain. Engines ready."

Bereznoy turned to face his navigator. "Valeri, take us in. We figured the course at ninety-six degrees south southeast of present position, but check it again to correct the drift of these last hours." Then back through the intercom: "Start engines."

"At once, Comrade Captain."

A pervasive rumble accompanied by gradually diminishing vibration was apparent as the submarine's nuclear power plant came to life. Five minutes later the *Novosibirsk,* her course plotted, was under way at one-third speed. At surface level, off the Benghazi harbor, Bereznoy could dispatch the signals requested by *Naporisty.* He was in a relaxed mood, disturbed only by a gnawing apprehension that Soroshkin would screw up the detail one more time. Most certainly his mood would have changed had he known that as he set his course for the Libyan coast, HMS *Taurus,* sixty miles northwest of his present position, with its makeshift cargo hold full of the contraband destined for the IRA, was running at maximum submerged speed for the harbor at Gibraltar.

THE HOTEL METROPOLE, BENGHAZI

When Petrovskiy finally got to bed in the room vacated by Soroshkin it was almost four in the morning but he had difficulty sleeping. That face. There was something hauntingly familiar about that face. But why should it bother him? After all, it was a typically Russian face belonging to a typically Russian seaman on a Russian submarine. Or was it? He rolled over and tried again to sleep. Nothing doing. The flaw in that rationale was that he had had little or no exposure to the Soviet navy, and consequently had little knowledge, personal or otherwise, of naval personnel. Moreover that face belonged to a person with more bearing, greater confidence, and more presence than one expected to find as an ordinary seaman on a Soviet submarine. The puzzle continued to haunt him.

Then, like Saul of Tarsus on the road to Damascus, he had a sudden revelation—less divine but no less compelling. As he thought it through he sat bolt upright in bed. He was sweating, but not from the heat.

In July he had gone to the Dublin Horse Show, a lodestone for those who ride, own, or simply love thoroughbred horses of sufficient quality to make it to this quintessential equine event. It is an unlikely place to find a KGB agent from a Russian peasant background, but in common with other Soviet embassy personnel he had been drawn to it by the presence of five singularly good Russian entries, all from the Krasnodar Agricultural and Horse Breeding Collective, the same source that had sent Zaryad to the Washington, D.C., International race at Laurel, in nearby Maryland, in 1956. The horse ran a very respectable second. Now in 1979 the Russians, with two excellent riders along—one a girl—were hoping to do as well or better at Dublin.

After watching one of the jumping classes, which he

2 5 5

found repetitious and boring, Petrovskiy had gone to the stabling area with the chief security officer at the embassy to talk with his visiting countrymen. What they found was an animated group surrounding the girl rider. She had taken a spectacular spill earlier in the day, but without serious injury. The security man suddenly grabbed Petrovskiy by the arm.

"Back off!" he said. "Go no further."

"What's the trouble?" replied Petrovskiy.

"The tall man—the one in the checkered cap. He's a defector. The bastard jumped ship on us some years ago. He's a horse trainer now, living in England. His name is Voroshilov."

As the security man was speaking, Voroshilov turned in their direction. Petrovskiy had a good look at him. He was the first Soviet defector he had ever seen, and he was curious. Why should a man like Voroshilov—or any true son of the *Rodina*—wish to leave it?

Now Voroshilov—that face—shows up on board the *Novosibirsk*. He hadn't the slightest doubt about it, but how could that be possible? Was he dreaming? Everybody on board, or at least those he had seen, was Russian. Something was terribly, terribly wrong.

He lay awake all the rest of the night, wondering and worrying. If he spilled his guts to the *rezident* in Tripoli he'd be stuck in this miserable country forever and he didn't want that. He decided to do nothing and say nothing until he could get back to Dublin and talk with his own *rezident*—and with Burdin, who seemed to have an answer for everything.

This apparent contradiction in reality was still uppermost in Petrovskiy's mind when he was seized and roughly handled by Qaddafi's security police the next afternoon at Tripoli's airport, en route back to Dublin. Despite his vigorous protests, a certain Major Dukhovar would have none of it. Somehow Petrovskiy knew that Voroshilov's presence on the submarine at Benghazi had something to do with his arrest—for he recognized that that's exactly what it was.

TRIPOLI
ALL THAT GLITTERS . . .
17 SEPTEMBER 1979

Wali Muhayshi, Qaddafi's Finance Minister, viewed the wooden crate containing the bullion with satisfaction. It had arrived that morning from Zurich via Libyan Air Force jet and had been brought, with little ceremony, into the boardroom of Libya's Central Bank by sweating porters who quickly disappeared, cutting and taking with them the two steel straps that had secured the crate. A wheeled dolly had been brought into the room to transfer the bullion into the bank's vaults. Molnar Razani, the lesser functionary who had accompanied the shipment to Libya, stood by, having once again checked the seal on the lock. It had not been tampered with. On the table beside him was the single typewritten sheet that he had brought with him listing the serial numbers of the shipped gold bars.

"Well, Razani, open it up. Let us see what we have here." The finance minister's breath was heavy with the smell of peppermint to cover the telltale aroma of scotch whiskey. In defiance of Qaddifi's strict Muslim tenets forbidding the possession or consumption of alcoholic beverages anywhere in Libya, even by foreigners, he consumed large quantities of scotch, a commodity that his position allowed him to smuggle in with relative ease.

With a confidence that soon turned to numbing shock,

Razani broke the seal, unlocked the top of the crate and flipped it open. At first glance all appeared to be in order. The top layer of the pseudobullion was of the proper size and shape, each bar in a soft but thickly woven cotton container used universally in such shipments to eliminate damage and loss of troy weight. As Razani slid the covering from the first bar he picked up, he couldn't believe his eyes. His heart skipped a beat. He looked more closely, scratching the bar with a fingernail. Lead—pure, unadulterated lead. He dropped it heavily on the table and picked up another. It, too, was lead, as was the next, and the next, and the next. Hysterically, with the bewildered Muyhayshi looking on, he ripped through the first two layers. All were the same. Then came another and more humiliating blow. The rest of the shipment was composed of ordinary building bricks, several of which were broken, with their severed pieces wedged into place to hold the layers from shifting.

Razani's hysteria had turned into a piteous wail. In panic he turned to Muhayshi, who merely shook his head. Razani slumped into a chair, his head buried in his arms on the boardroom table, the wailing interrupted by sobs, as if he were hyperventilating.

The Finance Minister was no less affected, but not to the point where he couldn't act—which he did, and fast. He rushed from the room, called to two of the armed guards in the bank's lobby, and ordered Razani's arrest. After the struggling Razani had been taken away, screaming his innocence, Muhayshi returned to the boardroom, locking the door behind him. Going into the adjoining bathroom he removed the top from the toilet tank and retrieved a pint bottle of scotch from its watery recesses, took a long drink, then returned to the table.

He picked up one of the spurious bars for a closer examination. On its top and all the others was indented the hammer and sickle of the Soviet Union. It was, he had to concede, a nice touch.

For a long time he sat, traumatized by the ghastliness of his position. Nor was he more able than Razani to hold back the tears. Finally he got up, dried his eyes, and finished off the scotch, purposely leaving the bottle on the table. Then he left the room, once again locking the door behind him. He called for his car, had his chauffeur drive him home, told his wife he wasn't feeling well, went upstairs and—after one more consoling drink of his favorite highland whiskey—blew his brains out.

By the next morning it was common knowledge that Muhayshi had committed suicide. Insiders laid his death to his known alcoholism, or to the fear of its discovery by Qaddafi. Muhayshi, however, knew that the messenger bearing bad news to his king would have his life ended, so he chose to do it himself. Better that way than to be slowly strangled to death by Major Faisal Dukhovar, Qaddafi's principal executioner who, from long practice, could prolong the agony to a full hour.

Razani was taken aloft in a Libyan Air Force plane, stripped of his clothes and other identification, and unceremoniously dumped out, stark naked, at twenty thousand feet over the Gulf of Sidra. The unfortunate Sergei Petrovskiy was being held incommunicado under heavy guard.

It is unclear precisely who made Qaddafi aware that he had been duped and humiliated by his enemies, but never had his close associates seen such a display of frustration and outright rage as accompanied Qaddafi's realization that he had been outwitted. The bullion had been stolen—that he knew. Gone, at least temporarily, was the hoard that he had planned to use as bribery for those who might pass on to him the secrets of the atom and the fabrication of the ultimate weapons of destruction. The arms were another matter. Were they in fact on their way to the Irish Republican Army or had they too been hijacked? The Soviets had come to the harbor at Benghazi on schedule and had departed on schedule, taking with them for delivery to the Irish the shipment of arms so carefully inventoried and packed. He had in front of him the manifest, countersigned by the Soviet captain. He did not understand. It was when he tried to fathom this mystery that his blood boiled and his rage became destructive. A Walther P-38 automatic lay in plain sight on his desk. Members of his personal staff as well as his house servants weren't sure that, once summoned, they would leave his presence alive.

Finally, as he often did when he felt that circumstances were closing in on him or that he was about to be overwhelmed by the frustrations and disappointments that somehow accompanied his seizure of power, Qaddafi retreated to the desert that had given him birth, the rolling seas of sand stretching from below Cyrenaica to the great oases of Tazerbo and Rebiana. Here were the ancestral lands of the nomadic Qadafodam tribe and here in his well-guarded camp this son of those same nomads faced east toward Mecca to spread the *madrushah*, his prayer rug, on the sand as the first light of *El Reiji*, the desert dawn, was breaking. Kneeling, he bowed three times, touching his forehead to the sand each time while saying the prescribed *sourais,* invoking the name of Allah and praying for divine guidance. Here this former student at Sandhurst shed any last vestige of assimilated western culture to drink once more from the wellsprings of his being. He had no doubt that his prayers would be answered and that he would be shown the way to erase the blot upon his honor and the shame inflicted upon his country by as yet unidentified enemies.

The day was fading into an orange and purple dusk as a helicopter brought Qaddafi back to an ornate villa eighteen miles southeast of Tripoli. Prior to 1971 it had been the quarters of the commanding general of the Wheelus U.S. Air Force Base. Now it served as Qaddafi's residence and as the headquarters of a worldwide terrorist network masterminded personally by him for the better part of a decade.

First he gave certain orders regarding Sergei Petrovskiy, the Soviet diplomat imprisoned in an upstairs room. Then into the night he labored over a letter to Leonid Brezhnev, the leader of the Soviet peoples—one whom he considered an ally. Had he been wrong? He would soon find out.

It was a remarkable letter—remarkable as much for its daring as for its guile. Qaddafi had been shamed by deceitful and cunning people. So be it. This son of the desert, anointed by Allah the supreme sovereign to stand out above all others, to perform God's work in the service of his and other oppressed people, was about to show that he could be deceitful and cunning in return, that he still might be the master of the game.

2nd Zeyher al Awal, in the 1357th year of the Hegira To His Excellency Leonid Brezhnev, the leader of the Soviet Peoples:

I greet you respectfully, as a friend and ally. May this message find you, thanks to Allah the All-Merciful, in good health and savoring the happiness of the peoples of your great nation.

My intelligence service, which I am proud to say has no peer anywhere in the world, including the decadent West, has reported to me that Israeli assassination squads have infiltrated my country, with Soviet personnel as their principal targets. Insh'Allah, they will soon be apprehended, but it is with a heavy heart that I must report to you that in an incident less than twenty-four hours old these enemies not only of your country but of mine were successful in shooting down Sergei Petrovskiy, a Soviet diplomat. His remains are currently en route to the embassy of the Union of Soviet Socialist Republics in Bern.

In consideration of the present hazard and to further protect your people, whom we Libyans value as friends against oppressors everywhere, I have issued instructions that they stay within the confines of the Soviet Embassy. Some were not happy with these arrangements and had to be escorted, under duress, to your embassy. But be assured, my most honored friend, that their safety is my most vital concern. Your embassy will be guarded day and night by Libya's bravest and finest troops under the command of Major Faisal Dukhovar, in whom I have implicit confidence. This situation will remain until the last of the Israeli dogs are removed from our midst, for not only have these Zionist conspirators succeeded in murdering a valiant ally but they have absconded as well with the hard-earned monies sent to us by the oppressed Irish peoples. I take pleasure at least in knowing that due to the Grace of Allah the arms destined for them are safely in the hands of our Soviet comrades, to be delivered as planned.

Also be assured, my most honored friend, that we revolutionary forces—the Libyans, the steadfast Syrians, and the Palestinian resistance—will continue to move forward to overthrow our enemies including those who, sinking into head-to-toe treason, have entered into the Camp David Agreement. I speak specifically of the traitors Anwar Sadat of Egypt and President Nimairy of the Sudan. We must escalate the peoples' liberation wars in Somalia, Namibia, Lebanon, Latin America, and Africa. And we must aid in forcing the British out of Northern Ireland.

In support of our joint efforts and in order that the *jihad* decreed by Allah the Almighty may go forward, I appeal to your sense of justice to replace, in double amount, the gold bullion that the Jewish infidels have taken from us by trickery. Evidence of this trickery is being sent with the remains of your comrade Sergei Petrovskiy.

We have jointly agreed that we wish to destroy the evil system that rules the once mighty British Empire, and I beg God's favor upon you for that noble aspiration. Upon the safe receipt by us of this replacement gold—which I will publicly announce—I am certain that the impression upon our enemies will be such that your people will once again be able to roam the streets of Tripoli feeling as safe as in their homeland. I have known both the *guebli,* the searing wind that rises in the desolate expanses of the Sahara, as well as the blessings of the winter rains that bring the flowering of the great oases of Kubla and Tevis. I pray that I may know the generosity of spirit and nobility of purpose that this communication solicits.

I await your reply, content in the knowledge that you will move in the direction to free all peoples—including your own.

Allah akbar—God is great. Let us not forget.

Muammar el-Qaddafi
Ruler of the Peoples of Libya

The letter was dispatched the next morning by courier. Had his Jewish enemies seen it they would have labeled it chutzpah of the most quintessential nature.

Leaving Tripoli that evening, bound for Zurich in a Libyan Air Force plane, was the same container in which the spurious bullion had arrived. Its contents, however, were somewhat different. It looked the same and weighed about as much, but this time its principal characteristic was a sickly, unpleasant odor.

BERN
THE SOVIET EMBASSY
19 SEPTEMBER 1979

Qaddafi's mischief men were back in Zurich. The Libyan Air Force C-15A had been cleared for landing at Kloten International Airport just prior to midnight. Deplaning were two Libyans, both traveling on diplomatic passports, who watched carefully as a large box was unloaded. As diplomatic baggage it was not subject to inspection. With equal care the two Libyans insured that it was reloaded aboard a small twin-engined charter that had taxied to within twenty yards of the Libyan freighter. Once the box was loaded, the two men also boarded. Within minutes the pilot had called the tower and received permission to take off in accordance with a flight plan filed earlier.

Thirty-five minutes later it had landed at Belpmoos Airport, four miles southeast of Bern. It was met by a Buick station wagon. The men, one of whom was Major Dukhovar, saw to it that the box was put in the back, then they too got in. Within another half hour the car, its passengers, and its cargo were at Bern's principal intersection, now deserted but dominated, night as well as day, by one of the world's most renowned clocks, the Zeitglockenturm, which not only strikes each of the twenty-four hours, but in doing so parades for the Bernese and tourists alike its wondrous mechanical figures. It was exactly 1:42 A.M. or, as marked by the world's military, 0142 hours.

Senior Sergeant Yuri Kostrytkin was one of the lucky ones. He had a permanent limp, the result of a hip fractured by shrapnel, but he was alive. He had been a member of the *Vysotniki,* the unconventional Soviet unit trained in special operations to be the equivalent of the U.S. Green Berets. In Afghanistan his team of specialists, despite their rigorous training, had been ambushed by the wily Afghan *mujahideen* in the mountains near Charikar, thirty miles north of Kabul. Capture would have meant torture, castration alive—or worse—and death, a fate from which they were spared by the timely arrival of a Soviet helicopter gunship.

So now, despite his slightly unbalanced gait, he found himself assigned as the senior noncommissioned officer among the guards at the Soviet Embassy in Bern. He was happy with this cushy job, especially since he had cozied up to one of the sous chefs in the kitchen, an East German girl from Leipzig, and was sleeping with her regularly. To the small guard detail, however, he was always a martinet and often a terror. None of them had been in combat and he was determined to ready them for it. In Afghanistan God speaks from the muzzle of a 73-mm recoilless gun, so by that same God, in whom he had only the most faltering belief, he'd whip them into shape!

In the guards' cramped day room he had just drained the last of his bitter Turkestan coffee and was on the point of inspecting the three guard posts giving line-of-sight protection to all but one side of the embassy compound. He wanted to see if his men were sufficiently alert in this next to last hour of the graveyard shift. It was at that moment that the bomb went off. Windows broke and the whole building shook. *Nichevo! What has happened?* Instinctively he looked at his watch—0304 hours. In his haste to reach the area where he judged the explosion to have occurred he upset the table where he had been sitting. He dashed for the side door leading out onto the Avenue Pays d'Enhaut.

A quiet street only one block long, it runs from the Marketstrasse to the Zahringenstrasse, on which the embassy faces. Its name is an anachronism in a city founded and populated mostly by German-speaking Swiss. As if to deny it recognition, a high wall punctuated only by a single door, used exclusively and infrequently by embassy personnel, stretches from one end of the block to the other. Behind it a windowed side of the embassy peers inquiringly, like a professorial face over a starched collar. By day parked cars line both sides of the short street, bumper to bumper, but after six in the evening the shoppers and the business people are gone.

Just prior to midnight a solitary figure had parked an old model Renault down the now deserted block, locked it, and departed. Underneath, taped to the transmission housing, was a sizable charge of gelignite packed in highly flammable magnesium, timed to go off in three hours. The blast was four minutes late, but it had the desired result. Windows fifty yards away were shattered, and the flames from the fiercely burning car spread to the linden trees above it, dropping burning branches behind the wall onto the embassy grounds. A secondary explosion of minor proportions, from a device placed under the back seat, went off seconds later. As it did so, no one noticed a Buick station wagon parked two blocks away pull from the curb and head in the direction of the embassy.

When Sergeant Kostrytkin reached the scene the two guards from the front of the embassy were already there, joined almost at once by one from the opposite side of the grounds. The heat was intense. Only when he realized that the explosion could have harmed no one except a casual passerby did Kostrytkin understand what had happened.

"Quick! Back to your posts!" he bellowed. "Sound the alarm!" Into his consciousness flashed never-to-be-forgotten images of gaunt-faced *mujahideen* bent on assassination.

As the guards raced back to their posts the station wagon, with French license plates, had dropped off its cargo and was disappearing into the darkness.

Inside the front forecourt, just short of the embassy steps, a box was found addressed to His Excellency Yevgenni Petrovich Shumilov, ambassador from the Union of Soviet Socialist Republics to the Republic of Switzerland. Sergeant Kostrytkin and his inexperienced embassy guards had been suckered.

It took a full two hours to determine that the box was not booby-trapped. The ambassador was present when it was opened. He looked, then looked again in disbelief. He saw the lifeless eyes of Sergei Petrovskiy, open and blank, looking back at him. Petrovskiy's head, cauterized at the neck to prevent further bleeding, was cradled neatly in a nest made for it with the spurious leaden bars. The ambassador gagged and reached for his handkerchief, then rushed for the nearest toilet. He made it just in time to avoid vomiting on the floor.

Three hours later, shaken, apprehensive, and still ill, the ambassador was on his way to Moscow with all that was left of the unfortunate Sergei Petrovskiy.

* * *

Nobody thought it unusual—least of all Jacques Freiburg, who heard about it in Strasbourg, where he had gone to visit his family before reporting to his new assignment in Brussels—that Associated Transfer's garage in Zurich had burned to the ground three days after Swiss newspapers carried the news of the suicide of the Libyan Finance Minister.

Newspaper accounts said that the fire started in a fuse box. The building, once a bakery, was known to be old and the interior wiring not up to code. Three of six steel-bodied trucks were rendered useless, especially the one numbered TF87, the interior fittings of which were completely destroyed. It had been parked next to two oil drums filled with motor oil, immediately below the fuse box. The fire soon spread to the drums, then to the truck. Its gasoline tank, which apparently was full, quickly exploded. The top of the tank had been left off, a fact totally obscured by the explosion.

The Mossad men had done their job well. They had been airborne for two hours, en route back to Tel Aviv, when the fire broke out, touched off by the overheated solenoid planted in the fuse box.

TRIPOLI
QADDAFI'S VILLA
19 SEPTEMBER 1979

When the full extent of Qaddafi's incomprehensible—some said suicidal—action was apparent, reaction was immediate. The Soviet hierarchy was shocked into a state of temporary paralysis, but not before a readiness alert had been issued to all Soviet armed forces. The Soviet ambassador to Libya was instructed to seek an immediate explanation from Qaddafi for behavior that the Soviet Union found "barbaric, repugnant, and uncivilized." The interview took place at the Villa Lucia. Major Dukhovar, his hands bloodied by Petrovskiy's execution, was present, as was the counselor from the Soviet Embassy, as interpreter. Qaddafi had his own, who said nothing.

It was a make or break situation for which the Soviet ambassador had had little time to prepare. When he came into the room, Qaddafi eyed him coldly. He had scarcely begun his inflamed protest when Qaddafi cut him off by handing him a copy of his letter to Brezhnev—and watched him read it like a cat watching an unwary bird, ready to spring. Before the ambassador had finished Qaddafi interrupted him again.

"Excellency, you will note that I informed your chairman that I was sending Comrade Petrovskiy's *remains* to Bern. I have done so. The Israeli dogs not only killed him but decapitated him as well. Then, with an arrogance that befits them, they threw his head over the wall into the gardens that surround this villa. His body has not been found. With respect, how can I send what I do not have?"

Does this murderous madman expect me to believe that this villa is so unguarded as to allow anyone within striking distance, particularly an Israeli assassination team? Preposterous! Close to speechless, he tried another angle.

"But delivery at three o'clock in the morning? Concurrently with a diversionary tactic to draw off the embassy guards?"

"We know nothing of any diversionary tactic," replied Qaddafi coolly. "Our men from the Libyan Peoples' Bureau in Bern who were charged with delivery—and who were instructed to see that it was done properly—were frightened away by the explosion. They will be punished."

"Three A.M., Your Excellency, seems a strange hour for such a delicate task."

"Your point is well taken, Comrade Ambassador. But we

Libyans are lacking in many resources known in your country. Embalming is one of them. We considered it vital that Comrade Petrovskiy's remains be delivered to you at the earliest possible moment."

"Nevertheless, Your Excellency, the Soviet Union views Libya's behavior in this matter as beyond belief—something the Americans might do. I am instructed to inform you that unless a full and complete investigation is launched by you immediately, and the guilty persons found and punished, the gravest consequences will follow. Furthermore, the Soviet Union demands an apology—at once."

"*You* demand an apology!" Qaddafi was almost screaming. "*You* demand an apology! Look at this!" He handed the ambassador one of the spurious bars. "Lead. Common, ordinary lead. You should recognize the hammer and sickle. Packed in a crate with pieces of brick. Must I remind you that the shipment came under lock and key—and sealed—from the Wozchod Handelsbank, the Soviet Union's own bank in Zurich? We have been embezzled out of bullion worth four and a half million British pounds. By whom, I ask? By the Russians, I say. And you have the audacity to come into my presence and demand an apology. If I were not a man of peace, I'd have half a mind to send you home in the same shape as your comrade Petrovskiy. There will be no apology."

"Your Excellency," replied the ambassador very quietly, hiding his mounting anger, "I have heard about the bullion—or lack of it. In fact not more than an hour ago I talked with Zurich and the managing director of the Wozchod Handelsbank. He assures me that he himself not only saw the bullion as it was being packed for shipment, but also saw it sealed by your man Razani—in the bank. Razani accompanied the shipment back to Tripoli. He was present when it was unpacked. Why is he not here? Where is your Finance Minister? There are rumors that he has committed suicide. Does this not suggest to you that somewhere along the way there was collusion, that some of your own people may be guilty of this theft?"

"I will have none of this, Comrade Ambassador," replied Qaddafi threateningly. "My people do not steal. If they do, I cut their hands off. I suggest that you go to Moscow and come back with an explanation regarding the gold. Now get out of here, but let us part in peace. Insh'Allah. God is Great."

MOSCOW
THE KREMLIN
20 SEPTEMBER 1979

Black clouds were forming over the onion spires of the Kremlin, matching the mood of the handful of Soviet leaders called together for an extraordinary meeting. A cold front was moving through Moscow and a dusting of powdery snow, the first intimation of the Russian winter still to come, swirled about the admiral's head as he got out of his black Chaika sedan to enter the guarded door off Gorki Street. His name was Gavrichev and he was the chief of Soviet naval intelligence. He was apprehensive, for although he had met innumerable times with the GRU, the Red Army's powerful intelligence apparatus, and with General Fedorov, the aging but still active hero of the siege of Stalingrad who had been rewarded with the mantle of Defence Minister, he had never before been included in such a high-level meeting.

Yuri Andropov had arrived ahead of him, as had General Fedorov and the Foreign Secretary, the latter accompanied by the Soviet ambassador to Libya. No others had been summoned. Leonid I. Brezhnev, First Secretary of the Communist

Central Committee and Chairman of the Politburo, had good reason to keep the meeting small.

There were few preliminaries. Brezhnev, stunned by Qaddafi's perfidy and enraged by the tone of a letter that he had expected to be obsequious rather than insolent, had the Soviet ambassador to Libya repeat the details of his interview with Qaddafi, first recounted to Brezhnev late the previous night. The others present had been briefed, but there had been no distribution of copies of Qaddafi's letter. Andropov, however, had seen the original.

Speaking from notes, the ambassador gave a factual account of the interview. When he had finished, Brezhnev, who seldom displayed any emotion, could contain himself no longer.

"That excrescence! That Arab turd!" He slammed the table with his fist. "Fedorov, hit them with everything we've got. Fire the missiles we have aboard our submarines on patrol in the Mediterranean. Incinerate those bastards from one end of Libya to the other. Turn the whole damn place into a sea of glass. Wipe them out. When we've finished I don't want so much as a single goat left alive between Egypt and Morocco."

It was a catharsis. He slumped back in his chair, looking again at Qaddafi's letter, held in hands that trembled slightly.

"Comrade Chairman," replied the Defence Minister, "if the threat were great, we could respond accordingly. But we are not threatened. This is a slap in the face of the *Rodina*, our motherland, and must be answered. But all-out war? No, Comrade Chairman, something else but not that." Memories of Stalingrad were fresh in his mind and he was sure enough of his ground to speak frankly. "If we attacked with nuclear weapons the turmoil in the Middle East would be such that the Israelis might counter, which means that the Americans would move, and we're not ready for that."

Andropov, whose grasp of the situation was undoubtedly greater than that of anybody else present, spoke up.

"Comrade Chairman, I too advise caution. We all know that Petrovskiy's death is Qaddafi's doing—to think otherwise is utter self-delusion. This business of a marauding group of Israelis wandering around Libya killing Soviets is totally unrealistic. But there are still many unanswered questions. We must proceed very carefully. Where is Soroshkin? Did Qaddafi kill him also? Qaddafi says he never received the bullion. Can we believe this, coming from a man who, for his own venal reasons, would stoop so low as to kill a member of the diplomatic corps of a friendly country? Who delayed the *Novosibirsk?* Where are the arms? Who loaded them aboard what submarine? We know that the crew who performed the actual loading were Russian—or at least spoke Russian—since we have located a Libyan dock worker who understands our language. He was on the lighter with the arms when it was towed out to open water to facilitate the loading. He swears that the captain and his crew all spoke Russian."

Andropov paused momentarily while he opened his briefcase. "I have here some photographs, received less than an hour ago. In my opinion they give us answers to some of these vexing questions."

Brezhnev looked at him with narrowed eyes. "Go on," he said.

"These photographs," continued Andropov, "were taken by high altitude satellite. They are of the British naval base at Gibraltar." He handed one to Brezhnev and one to General Fedorov. "Notice the submarine docked at the north mole, just south of the aircraft runway. Notice, too, that there are no sail planes off her sail. I'll return to this in a moment. She is nuclear-powered and missile-bearing. The chances of her being other than a UK boat are only one in a thousand. We know that this area was dredged to a minimum of ten fathoms and that improved cargo handling facilities were installed within the past year. Deep draft vessels can now be berthed there.

"Look closely at the submarine, comrades. There are two points of significance that I wish to make. One—the hatch covers for its Trident missiles are forward of the sail. Nothing unusual there, as this configuration is common to all UK and U.S. nuclear submarines. On the other hand our nuclear boats—particularly the *Novosibirsk*—carry their missiles *aft* of the sail. The same Libyan dock worker who told us that the loading crew at Benghazi all spoke Russian also informed us that the cargo was lowered into empty missile silos *forward* of the sail."

The silence was deafening.

"Comrade Chairman," Andropov continued, "there is another piece of evidence of even more significance. Here is another photograph, computer-enhanced and enlarged by a factor of twenty, then run through the cameras again to bring the image up even further. This shows a portion of the UK submarine's sail. Look closely. Even though it is blurred one can see two large bolts protruding from the side of the sail in the same relative position where a sail plane would be—if British *Resolution*-class submarines carried sail planes, which they do not."

"What are you saying, Andropov?" Brezhnev was impatient.

"I am saying, Comrade Chairman, that the British went into Benghazi with one of their own boats, probably HMS *Taurus,* made to resemble the *Novosibirsk* by the addition of fake sail planes, picked up the shipment, and got out. My belief that this is the case is strengthened by a report from our London *rezidentura* that the *Taurus* was at the Armstrong-Vickers yards at Barrow last week under tight security for modifications, the nature of which we have as yet been unable to determine."

There was a stunned silence. Admiral Gavrichev reached for a cigarette, unaware that smoking in Brezhnev's presence was forbidden.

"Put that thing out!" barked the Chairman. "We've got enough problems without all worrying about dying of emphysema!" Sheepishly the admiral complied. "My apologies, Comrade Chairman. I did not know." His voice shook. He was unaware not only of the rules but also of the fact that Brezhnev was suffering from the disease.

"Where is the *Novosibirsk* now?" asked Brezhnev.

"On her way back to Sevastopol, Comrade Chairman, to complete her refitting." Admiral Gavrichev, relieved to switch the subject, broke in with the answer.

"And her captain?"

"Anotoly Bereznoy, Comrade Chairman. A senior captain, a great Russian, and a thoroughly qualified officer."

"Is he trustworthy? How do we know he's not implicated?"

"He has had an unblemished record, Comrade Chairman, and was chosen to command such an important vessel only after most exhaustive screening. He will be detained, however, when the *Novosibirsk* docks, pending further investigation."

"What does he say about this disgraceful episode?"

"When the *Novosibirsk* arrived at the rendezvous point off Benghazi's outer mole he found no one there—no Libyans, no lighter and consequently no cargo, and no Soroshkin. Having surfaced and having received earlier permission to break radio silence once at that point, he called the corvette *Naporisty,* his communications link. *Naporisty* in turn, fearing treachery—and rightly so, as it now turns out—ordered him away from the area immediately."

"What about the *zampolit?* What are these men for if they can't detect treachery? Who might he be?" Brezhnev was burrowing in like a terrier after an animal gone to ground. He had the feeling that the true situation was eluding him, eluding all of them in fact, and he did not like it.

"All the *zampoliti* are chosen with the greatest care, Comrade Chairman. I'm sure you're aware of that. Petr Yessenin, a commander, is aboard the *Novosibirsk*—a first cruise for a very able man. Moreover, at this point we don't know that Captain Bereznoy is implicated. Whatever the case may be, I trust Yessenin."

"And at this point I don't trust anybody," replied Brezhnev. "Arrest the *zampolit* also."

This would never happen in the GRU, thought General Fedorov. He didn't particularly like Andropov, directing toward him some of the bias he felt against anybody who spoke English well. Gavrichev he considered an amiable idiot. He was smug in his enjoyment of the discomfort these two seemed to be laboring under.

"Now we come to Soroshkin." Brezhnev was relentless. "What about him?"

"Unknown, Comrade Chairman." Andropov was once again fielding the questions. "Qaddafi claims that Captain Soroshkin left on the submarine, but since we cannot say with certainty what submarine that was, who can say? For what it's worth I think Qaddafi's still holding him and will continue to do so until we pay to get him back—which we may have to do in order to determine what happened."

"And Petrovskiy?"

"It's possible, of course, that he may have sold us out to the British," said Kovalenko, the Foreign Secretary. "In which case I suspect that we would have dealt with him in very much the same way that Qaddafi did."

"Nonsense," retorted Andropov. "He was the KGB's man, not yours, even though under diplomatic cover. He's been under my personal supervision off and on for twenty years. He is, or was, ideologically sound and totally trustworthy. I'm much more inclined to suspect Nikolai Burdin, who's in London. He spent his formative years in Washington, where his father was posted. We've used Burdin's attributes to our own advantage but his emotional ties to the West sometimes appear to me to be too strong."

Brezhnev was not smiling when he said, "There's been a great deal of talk around here this morning about trust, a commodity that seems to be in short supply. I'm beginning to believe that nobody's totally trustworthy. Maybe not even you, Yuri. What about Burdin? Has he had a hand in this?"

"He has, Comrade Chairman," replied Andropov. "I'll send for him at once."

"Better still, apprehend him in London and bring him home under guard. Somebody must pay for this disgraceful business."

Andropov, who chose to think that he alone in the Politburo saw and dealt with the world as it really was, took charge. He was not one to shy away from seeking an advantage, and any intimation of untrustworthiness, even if said lightly, had to be expunged.

"Comrade Chairman, with your permission I will give you my considered opinion on this deplorable matter. Not only are we dealing with some unknown factors, but where the factors are known, the information has been given to us by a madman. Mad, perhaps, but shrewd in the manner of madmen. Qaddafi is cunning, a schemer, perhaps even demented. There is a saying in English: 'He may be a son of a bitch, but he's our son of a bitch.' So with Qaddafi. He's our son of a bitch. At this point we need him. The reality is that the Mediterranean is a half-Arab lake dominated, if not by the Arabs, then by a combination of NATO naval forces. Qaddafi understands this. One needs but to read his letter to you—which I have done, thanks to the confidence that you have placed in me and in the Committee for State Security—to realize that he is playing a game with us, a game in which he holds all the cards. No word of this has reached the outside world, nor is it likely to. Surely the British, if indeed they are responsible, will not release the story, nor will the Irish. They and Qaddafi have been humiliated enough. The Israelis are one of the unknown factors, although the Swiss banking affiliations of the Mossad will bear some investigation. And we cannot afford again the world's ridicule, such as happened when pictures of the *Admiral Razhnikov* foundering in the seas off the coast of South Carolina appeared in papers everywhere."

Admiral Gavrichev squirmed uneasily in his chair.

"Yuri, you're a very smart man." Brezhnev was looking at him intently. "But I sense that you're going to say something that I may not agree with. So get along with it. Tell us all how the Soviet Union, the mightiest force on earth, is going to deal with this dog's breakfast, this pig's ass who calls himself the ruler of Libya. If we're not going to destroy him I suppose you want us to kiss him." In a gesture of contempt the Chairman tossed Qaddafi's letter across the table in Andropov's direction.

Andropov picked up the letter and put it carefully aside.

"We cannot destroy him, Comrade Chairman—at least not yet," he replied. "He is too valuable to us as a pipeline to liberation movements all over the world. There is a segment of the black population of the United States that considers itself Muslim. He supports it—generously. The same is true for peoples everywhere who are trying to throw off the yoke of imperialism. So with the IRA. Why Qaddafi insisted upon being paid in this instance I do not know. Even dictators sometimes run out of money. But he serves our purposes, Comrade Chairman, so let's keep him on our side. Without kissing him, I might add."

Andropov shifted in his chair and looked around the conference table. He had an attentive audience. "Which brings us to the death of Petrovskiy," he continued, "and to Soroshkin and his whereabouts. I don't think we can get to the bottom of this without interrogating Soroshkin. I think Qaddafi is holding him for ransom—the double amount of bullion that he has had the colossal gall to ask us for. In my opinion that's negotiable. I say negotiate and get Soroshkin back. Another shipment of arms might accomplish this. It's worth a try.

"As to Petrovskiy's death and the thoroughly vicious method of returning what remained of him, we'll simply have to write that off as the maniacal actions of a very frustrated man."

Outside and overhead, the front that was bringing the unusual September snow to Moscow had thickened, turning mid-morning into dusk. Beyond the walls of the Kremlin lights were appearing and traffic was slowing in response to the snow, which had turned from flurries into a swirling curtain of white. In the steadily darkening room there was a long silence.

Brezhnev pushed a button on his desk, got up, then walked slowly across a magnificent antique Herez rug that dominated the room to look out of a window across the broad expanse of Red Square. Admiral Gavrichev was watching him closely. Capping a drawn and pallid face, Brezhnev's eyebrows looked to him like two overgrown black caterpillars facing off against one another, backs arched. Evidence of the Secretary's illness, an open secret in the upper echelons of the Moscow hierarchy and speculated upon by the world's press, was apparent in his shuffling gait. He seemed to have lost his punch. *His peasant origins are showing,* thought the admiral, who still harbored secret feelings of superiority—feelings that thirty years of bourgeois schooling and proletarian associations had failed to dispel. His father had been a Soviet naval officer before him, but beyond that his maternal great-grandmother had been not only English-born but the daughter of a peer as well. Since late childhood when he had discovered this background—one now certain to be considered shameful—he had been extremely careful that neither fact became known. His place in the *nomenklatura,* the privileged ones, was not all that unshakable, and he was not a man to take risks.

As Brezhnev, lost in contemplation, continued to gaze out the window a female attendant—a junior KGB officer, Andropov noted with satisfaction—entered unobtrusively to turn on the lights in the crystal chandelier and the matching wall sconces to dispel the sombre atmosphere pervasive in Brezhnev's handsome paneled office.

Turning away from the window, Brezhnev shuffled back to the table. He picked up Qaddafi's letter, then spoke directly to Admiral Gavrichev.

"You shouldn't smoke, Admiral. It's a lousy habit. I advise you to give it up. But in the meantime let me have your lighter." He held out his hand.

Gavrichev handed it over wordlessly. Brezhnev took the letter to the fireplace, held it over the logs laid there, then touched it with the lighter's flame. He watched as the letter was consumed, dropping the last shreds, still burning, on the logs. Then he turned again to the group at the table.

"The letter never existed, comrades. If any word of its *supposed* existence gets back to me, some or all of you in this room will answer to charges of subversion. Is that clear?"

There were murmurs and nods of affirmation.

"Yuri, since Petrovskiy was your man, you deal with Qaddafi for the return of Soroshkin. No offense to our diplomats," he gestured in the direction of the ambassador, "but you've got the muscle. Use it, but strike a hard bargain. No gold. Weapons or credits, but no gold. Remember, you owe me a lot of answers. Get them. And get the proper detention orders out at once—including Burdin. London and Washington are cesspools that corrupt a lot of good men. Bring Burdin back to Moscow—under arrest."

The meeting was over.

At the Soviet Embassy in London the *rezidentura* was alive with speculation. A telephone call from the Soviet Embassy in Dublin had triggered rumors of the wildest sort: Petrovskiy is overdue on his return from Libya. Word from the Embassy in Tripoli is that he has disappeared, as has Soroshkin. All Soviet Embassy personnel in Tripoli have been restricted to the Embassy grounds. Does Burdin know where Petrovskiy is?

When summoned, an alarmed Burdin, just back from Zurich, presented himself to the *rezident,* a veteran of some twenty years in the KGB named Tamorovich.

"What do you make of all this, comrade?" asked the *rezident.* "This has been your case as much as Petrovskiy's."

"I wish I knew, Comrade Tamorovich. I'm as baffled as any of us."

As he spoke a subordinate came into Tamorovich's office, unannounced, to hand him a decoded cable from Moscow. The *rezident* read it with growing concern. He looked up to say, "Bad news and growing worse. The gold has been stolen and the arms shipment is in unknown hands. I'm putting you in full charge of finding out what happened, Comrade Burdin. I suggest you start with your Irish friends. Go to Dublin at once, get all the information you can, and report back to me by this time tomorrow."

"Right away, comrade." Burdin's alarm was rapidly turning to panic.

* * *

The potential danger hit Burdin at once. The shipment hijacked, Soroshkin disappeared, the gold gone, and Petrovskiy in doubt. Somebody would have to pay, to be the scapegoat, and who better than he? No word of this on the outside and little chance that it would get there. Once the KGB, fulminating in its headquarters in Dzerzhinskiy Square, regained its composure, there would be immediate action, beginning with his recall. With no clear explanation of his part in the whole nightmarish mess except the unvarnished truth—which he felt certain would be rejected—he knew he was in deep trouble. At best he would be detained and at worst shot or jailed indefinitely in Lubyanka prison. A glance at his watch told him that it was eleven forty-five. In his wallet he counted sixty pounds. Two hundred more in his apartment, but he dared not go there. A summons to Moscow might be on the wire at this very moment. Flight—there was no other way. What was unthinkable yesterday had to be done today.

He unlocked the safe, took out his own and his Moran passport, and cleaned out the petty cash account—another forty-two pounds. He also took out a shoulder holster and a Czech .75 automatic, a favorite with KGB hit squads and an item that on this assignment he had never carried before. He saw to his satisfaction that, in place under his coat, it was virtually undetectable. Quickly he wrote two notes, one for his secretary who had already left for lunch, saying that he had gone to Dublin—God, he'd miss the sight of those pretty breasts! Who knows? A couple more dinners out and maybe he could have bedded her down—and another, of two short paragraphs that he corrected several times with inserts and scratchovers. He sealed it, put it in his inside pocket, and then, as nonchalantly as possible, made his way to the street. He knew that once he was missed, the KGB would make every effort to find him, watching all exits from London. For once he viewed with satisfaction the crowding of the streets that came with lunchtime. Not a moment to lose.

At Berkeley Square he hailed a cab for Euston Station. An hour and five apprehensive minutes later, twenty of which were spent in a locked stall in the men's toilet, pervasive with the smell of urine, sometimes with his feet off the floor, he was on a moving train, headed for Shrewsbury. He breathed a little easier.

But not for long. At Wolverhampton, apprehensive and racked by uncertainty, he got off. By late afternoon he had checked into an out-of-the-way bed and breakfast place for a two-day stay. It was a fatal mistake.

"Jesus H. Christ! Look at this!"

Frank Hergenroeder, the CIA's London station chief, burst into Peter Collins's office, note and envelope in hand. Collins, second in command at the London station, was reading the day's cable take, a procedure that required at least an hour, often more. He took the note from Hergenroeder's outthrust hand. It was handwritten on plain white paper. Collins quickly noted the hastily made corrections.

"Mr. Hergenroeder," it began, "I write in great haste as I face arrest and am choosing to run rather than risk imprisonment and possibly death. I am a career officer in the KGB whose name may be familiar to you, as yours is to me. I must leave London at once. As you read this I'm on my way out of the city. I dared not phone you as your line may be bugged. I'm on my way to Shrewsbury where I'll hope to put up at the Lion Hotel, as Nicholas G. Moran. I seek political asylum in the United States and am willing to cooperate fully, as I have information of importance to the West. To get out of England alive—perhaps through your Mildenhall Air Base—I'll need your help. Don't appear until I contact you again, as you may run squarely into the security people from my own embassy.

"No time for more, but I will add that your last assignment was in Washington. Prior to that, Vienna. You were born in Milwaukee and speak fluent German. Your assistant Peter Collins is the son of General Gatewood Collins, a former deputy director for plans, CIA. Who else would know these things? Offered in truth, with the enclosure as my bond. Believe me, I am in desperate need. Nikolai Burdin."

"God almighty!" exclaimed Collins. "Where did this come from? And what's the enclosure?"

"The enclosure is the clincher—or so it would seem." And Hergenroeder handed him Burdin's Soviet passport—genuine in every respect.

"It was on my desk when I returned from lunch—addressed to me. Beyond that I don't know where it came from. I just this minute opened it. Here's the envelope."

Collins took the envelope. It was marked PERSONAL—URGENT. OPEN AT ONCE. "Did you have security vet this? It could have blown up, you know."

"It had to go through the scanner at the front desk. Other than that, no. It was light and pliable—no wires. Something told me it was okay."

"I know Burdin. I've seen him around—Novosty cover. God damn, he knows plenty about us. Until I learned otherwise, I thought he was an American. He certainly writes like one. Do you suppose this is on the up-and-up?"

"We're sure as hell going to find out. Send a facsimile through to Washington and get Jake on the scrambler."

A secretary appeared at the door. "Elsie," said Hergenroeder, "where did this come from?"

"The message center sent it up. It was left for you at the front desk by a taxi driver—logged in at twelve twenty-two."

"Okay. Tell Jim Adkins I want to see him right away." Adkins was the station's security chief. "And tell him to bring with him anything he's got on Nikolai Burdin of the Novosty Press Agency. Got it?"

"Got it." The girl disappeared.

In a major miscalculation Burdin figured that the KGB's reaction time would be faster than it turned out to be. Brezhnev's instructions to detain him didn't reach London until two full days after Burdin's hurried departure from the city. When the instructions finally hit the desk of the London *rezident* he was dumbfounded. Burdin to be placed under arrest? But orders were orders and he acted quickly. First he called Dublin to alert his opposite number in the Soviet Embassy there, then sent for the *rezidentura*'s security people.

"Where's Comrade Burdin?" The KGB security man stood menacingly over Burdin's secretary. His name was Igor Makushkin, a six-foot, hundred and ninety pounder whose facial scars hid a once disabling hare lip.

"He left for Dublin the day before yesterday," she replied, handing him the note Burdin had left for her.

He scanned it quickly, then thrust it into an inside pocket.

"You have access to his safe? If so, open it."

Olga Ustimenko, the bosomy secretary whom Burdin had viewed with covetous eyes, was nervous. Something was obviously wrong but she didn't know what. The security man's attitude frightened her. It was a far cry from Burdin's seductive politeness. *Perhaps I should have gone away with him for a weekend when he asked me,* she thought. It took her longer than usual to open the safe, but on the third try it yielded to her touch.

"What's usually kept in here?" Makushkin asked.

"Papers with a low security classification, petty cash, passports—and Comrade Burdin's gun."

He pulled out the petty cash drawer. It was empty—and there was neither gun nor passport. The scenario was off to a bad start. He turned to her quickly.

"Where does Comrade Burdin live?"

"One forty-two Westmoreland Street, in Knightsbridge. Flat C."

Just as quickly, he wrote it down. Since Burdin didn't live in the embassy compound, there would be a key to his flat in the security office, as required by regulations.

"Stay here," he said to Olga. "Don't leave until you are told you may do so." His worry was becoming acute, as reflected by his hasty departure and by the unceremonious slamming of the door as he hurried away.

In a London district known for its high rents, Burdin had found an affordable flat, one large room supplemented by a combination kitchen and bath on the fourth floor of a building without an elevator. It was sparsely furnished, so Igor and a second security man were able to search it thoroughly in little time. In a clip on the table that Burdin used also as a desk they found a significant clue, one which sent them racing back to the *rezidentura* to further interrogate Olga.

"What's this?" demanded Igor, the senior of the two interrogating officers. He thrust a pamphlet into her now unsteady hands. It was a threefold color advertisement on slick paper, typical of those put out by dozens of inns and small hotels from one end of England to the other. This one called attention to the glories of the cuisine and lodgings at the Lion Hotel in Shrewsbury. More to the point, on the margin of one page, next to an inviting picture of a double bed complete with folded down comforter was written in Burdin's handwriting, "Olga would like this."

"I never went. I swear it!" cried the now genuinely distressed Olga. "I've been out to dinner with him, twice, and he did ask me to go to Shrewsbury with him, saying we could use a passport other than his own, but I never did. I swear it. You've got to believe me!" She was now crying hysterically, wiping her eyes with a handkerchief.

"Shrewsbury? Why Shrewsbury? Why not Brighton or Cambridge? That's where most Englishmen go to do their screwing." Igor could speak English and read the newspapers.

"I don't know. I really don't know. He talked a lot about the Iron Bridge Country, which is close. He travels a lot and has been all over England. I've never been outside of London, but he said he wanted to take me there, that it was a pretty little town with an interesting square. He's been there more than once. You've got to believe me. I don't want to get into any trouble."

"More than once? That means he'll probably go back. What's the country of origin of his other passport, and in whose name was it issued?"

"It's a U.S. passport, issued in the name of Nicholas G. Moran."

Igor looked at her more closely. He couldn't remember seeing her before but she had a lot of appeal, her temporarily red nose and weepy eyes to the contrary.

"Cheer up, ninochka. We believe you. And anytime you're lonely, let me know. I'll take you somewhere myself." He patted her on the head, then turned to his companion.

"Come on, Vadim. We're going to Shrewsbury. I have a feeling we're going to find Comrade Burdin at the Lion Hotel."

An answer to Hergenroeder's urgent facsimile transmission to CIA headquarters at Langley was back within the hour.

TO: COS/LONDON
FROM: DCI/WASH/CAREY
REFERENCE: YOUR FAX SAME DATE
PRIORITY: IMMEDIATE
NO: 71495/18 SEPTEMBER

MOVE FAST. DON'T LET HIM GET AWAY. ADVISE AC-
TION TAKEN AND RESULTS. FOR EXTRAORDINARY
EXPENSE CHARGE DCI SPECIAL FUNDS VOUCHER 14
OL/CK. END OF SIGNAL. SIGNED CAREY DDO

The authorization to use the DCI's special funds, a sure
indication that the Director of Central Intelligence had been
briefed, and that such authorization came straight from the
top, was reassuring.

By mid-morning the following day several calls to the
Lion Hotel, placed from phone boxes not in the area around
the CIA station, confirmed for Hergenroeder that a Mr. Moran
had indeed called to inquire about rooms but without specify-
ing an arrival date.

One more day went by. A frustrated Hergenroeder, pon-
dering his next move, was on the point of talking with Langley
on the secure line when the call came. Within seconds he knew
that it had to be Burdin.

"You know where I am. I don't think anybody's after
me, so it's safe to meet. At six tonight I'll be at the Old Post
Office, a pub on Milk Street, just off the town square, to the
right of the statue of Clive of India. If we miss connections,
I'll be at the bandstand in the Quarry, a park along the river.
Don't fail me." The short conversation was over and Burdin
was off the line.

A U.S. Air Force helicopter was available, even on short
notice, but that option had been quickly discarded as giving

the two CIA officers too much visibility. Going by train was ruled out as too unreliable, so Hergenroeder and Adkins took off in Adkins's 1977 Chevrolet station wagon, shipped all the way from Honolulu when Adkins got posted to the London station after a three-year stint in Hawaii. It had a left-hand drive, but driving on England's keep-to-the-left roads was not a problem to Adkins and they arrived in Shrewsbury just at dusk, minutes before the two KGB men.

They parked on a side street and at ten after six sauntered into the Old Post Office, looking and acting like two Americans coming in for a predinner drink. On the drive up Adkins had given Hergenroeder a full briefing on the contents of the station's file on Burdin, including his surprising educational background at Washington's Sidwell Friends School and the University of Maryland. A picture of him taken surreptitiously on a London street completed the file.

From a side table they nursed two pints of ale while scanning the other people in the pub. In a matter of minutes it was obvious that Burdin was not there. Among the couples present, the men were too old, too English, or laughing too loudly to contain the man they sought, and none of the eight single men fit the bill.

"Check the hotel, Jim. I'll stand watch here," said Frank. The Lion Hotel was just around the corner, facing the town square and its imposing statue of Clive of India.

In less than five minutes an agitated Adkins was back. He sat down before saying quietly to Hergenroeder, "Frank, I think we're in big trouble."

"What's the problem?"

"Burdin—or Moran—is not at the hotel, although he's expected. He called to say he'd been delayed, but that if anybody inquired for him, to say that he'd be in by ten o'clock."

"So?"

"We're not the first to inquire for him. Two other guys,

described as big, burly, and foreign, were there just before me, asking for Moran. And they did ask for Moran, not Burdin."

Hergenroeder's face sagged. The implications were obvious. "Jesus! What now? We'd better get to the bandstand in the Quarry in a hurry."

"Not so fast. Let's think this one through. They may have spotted me—and now you and me together."

"True enough. If those guys are from the Sov Embassy, we'd lead them straight to Burdin. On the other hand, maybe we've been had, and all of this is a setup."

"No way, Frank. For what purpose would this be a setup? We've got his passport, remember? Burdin's genuinely running, and we've got to find him. I say go straight to the local police and count on the Brits to keep any fracas that erupts out of the press."

The two Russians had entered Shrewsbury on the same road from London as Hergenroeder and Adkins, and had followed the same traffic pattern once inside the city limits. Shrewsbury is relatively small, and all of its arterial streets lead to the town square. Looking for the Lion Hotel and a parking place for their Morris sedan, they had been drawn to the same side street where Adkins had parked his Chevrolet station wagon. They too parked, then headed for the Lion.

Suddenly Makushkin stopped, putting his hand on the arm of his companion.

"Look at that," he said, pointing to Adkins's station wagon. "A left-hand drive. Americans. I think we're on target."

A long-time enforcement officer for the KGB, he was called on periodically for assignment to Department V— *Mokrie Dela,* or "Wet Affairs"—the assassination arm of the KGB. On this trip he was ready for anything. He looked more closely at the front, then the back of the station wagon. On the rear bumper was a sticker that, while not bearing any outwardly recognizable letters or symbols, allowed Adkins to park in the U.S. Embassy compound.

"We *are* on target," he said, straightening up. "Burdin's not only checking out, he may be trying to defect to the Yanks. Let's go."

Hergenroeder and Adkins got up to leave. Suddenly the front door of the Old Post Office was pushed open and Burdin walked in. His appearance was that of a badly shaken man. He hurried over to them.

"Thank God you're still here," he said, thrusting out his hand. "I'm Nick Burdin. You're Frank Hergenroeder, aren't you?"

"Call me Tony," replied Hergenroeder. "This is Sam." He motioned to Adkins.

"Frank or Tony, Sam or whatever, they've found me—and will kill me if they can. Please—help me get out. You've got all kinds of assets in this country—use them. I can be invaluable to your side." Burdin's eyes were pleading.

Hergenroeder looked at him closely. Here was a man who looked, dressed, and talked like a well-placed East Coast college professor or a Wall Street banker, but who was in fact an agent of the KGB. But he was Burdin all right. The face matched the picture on his Soviet passport.

"Welcome to the free world," said Hergenroeder. "But our first order of business is to get the hell out of here. We'll talk later. Have they seen you? And how many of them are there?"

"As far as I know, two. Both security men from our embassy. There may be more, but I don't think they've seen me. I saw them from the hotel men's room, while they were inquiring at the front desk. Then they left. One of them is Igor

Makushkin, who would kill you or me or all three of us with the same emotional impact that he would get from swatting a fly. He's a Department V man—a known assassin and very dangerous. Not many in our service know this, but I do. We were together once before, in Paris. You may remember that Adolphe Fleuriot, of the Sûreté, was gunned down on a crowded street. Makushkin shot him on the Rue de la Tour. Just walked away."

"Okay. Let's get moving. If we can make it to our car we'll take you to the local police. You'll be safe there, and so will we. And you should know that we are clear with Langley on this."

"No!" Burdin's reply was almost explosive. "No police. That will mean nothing but an endless diplomatic hassle, with me ending up back in Moscow. I'll go to Lubyanka and will never be heard from again. I implore you—take me to your embassy or to a safe house and then get me out of the country."

"This is no time to talk about such matters, Mr. Burdin. You're going to be okay, but first of all we've got to get out of this pub and hopefully out of Shrewsbury. Sam, see if anyone's lurking around the front door. No, scratch that. We'll do better making a quick exit through the rear. We're heading for the kitchen. Follow me."

Igor and Vadim hurried to their car, knowing that they would need it and certain that a watch on the Chevrolet station wagon would pay off. They were right.

Minutes later Hergenroeder and Jim Adkins came around the corner, with Burdin between them. In the pub he had opened his coat enough for them to see his Czech automatic and had told them he would use it.

"So far so good," said Adkins. "No ominous types in sight."

He couldn't see Igor and Vadim in their car on the opposite side of the street, facing in the same direction, watching intently, and ready to respond to any move made by the trio. From the trunk of their sedan Igor had retrieved two weapons, one a Czech automatic identical to the one Burdin was carrying, but this one equipped with a silencer, and the other a Kalashnikov semiautomatic rifle.

"What triggered this, Mr. Burdin?" asked Hergenroeder as they approached the station wagon. "Have you been threatened by your people? Maybe compromised by a blown operation?"

"More likely the latter," answered Burdin, "although the full extent of the failure isn't yet known—at least by me. And can't you call me something besides Mr. Burdin? I'm uncomfortable enough without having to answer to that."

"Okay. What do your friends call you?"

"Nikky."

"Okay, Nikky. Here we are. Get in the back seat and lie flat until we clear town. London's out and since you've vetoed the police—and I can understand that—we'll head for the English Bridge and a safehouse in East Anglia not too far from Mildenhall."

The Chevrolet pulled away from the curb. Vadim let Adkins get a slight lead on him, then eased the Morris out into the street, allowing one car to get between him and the now accelerating station wagon. It was dark enough to use headlights, but Vadim left his off. As Adkins turned left toward the English Bridge the intervening car turned right. Vadim followed Adkins, unnoticed.

In the Chevrolet, Hergenroeder was half turned in the front seat, his attention focused to the rear while also keeping an eye on Burdin, prone on the rear seat.

"Surrendering your Soviet passport to us is what brought us here, Nikky. Either you wanted out badly or this is the goddamnedest mousetrap I've ever heard of. Either way we're committed to seeing what happens. You've got another passport, obviously. Where and what is it?"

For an answer Burdin reached into his inside coat pocket and handed his bogus U.S. passport to Frank, who flipped through it hurriedly.

"Looks pretty damn good. Nicholas G. Moran. Protestant, age thirty-six. Born Washington, D.C. Why Washington, Nikky?"

"I went to school there, as I'm sure you know. I know the city well. Hell, I'm a Redskins fan."

The main road out of Shrewsbury bears to the right after crossing the English Bridge, headed for Wellington and Birmingham. There was still enough traffic to keep Adkins from making a run for it. Vadim, lights still off, was a discreet hundred yards to the rear. Once again he had allowed another vehicle, a plumber's van with a load of pipe in its side racks, to come between him and the station wagon.

Hergenroeder was still thumbing through the passport.

"Lot of Republic of Ireland entrance and exit cachets here, Nikky. Want to tell us why?"

"I've been one of two case officers on a big op involving a shipment of arms, primarily of Soviet origin, from Libya to the IRA. It blew."

"Who blew it—the Brits?"

"I don't know. Somebody intercepted the shipment. Moreover, there was a big payoff in Zurich, by the IRA to the Libyans, and in gold yet. I know that for a fact because I was there. The other case officer, Sergei Petrovskiy from our Dublin station, is missing—from Libya. Personally I think he's dead. And the gold is gone. Qaddafi says he never got it. I think he's a garden variety son of a bitch, as you do, I'm sure. Furthermore I think he's got the gold, wants to keep it, and killed Petrovskiy in the biggest cover-up since your Watergate." Burdin's initial shock at the discovery that he had been followed was subsiding. "Either one of you two guys got a cigarette?"

"I'm a nonsmoker," replied Frank. "I've given up the minor vices to concentrate on whiskey and my three girlfriends, namely my wife and two daughters. Sam, give me one of your cigarettes for our guest here."

Adkins made no reply, his attention distracted by the sudden appearance of a pair of headlights where there had been none. They were still on the outskirts of Shrewsbury but the road ahead was clear. He accelerated. So did the headlights following him, making no effort to shorten the intervening space.

"I don't want to appear paranoid, but I think we've got company. Look behind us, Frank. You'll see." Pseudonyms had been forgotten.

One look was sufficient. "Son of a bitch!" he exclaimed. "You're right. Give it the foot and we'll see what happens."

Burdin, from his prone position, sat up. "If it's Igor he'll soon take some sort of violent action to stop us. I'm not going to take this lying down."

They were approaching a rotary traffic circle. "I know this road," continued Burdin. "The second turnoff to the left goes to Stafford and Stoke-on-Trent. Take it. We might shake them off. The road to London is beyond."

The Chevrolet went into the rotary at close to sixty miles an hour, tires screeching. In the Morris, Vadim followed, closing up. Adkins waited until the last moment to make his turn, hoping to throw his pursuers off. The station wagon nearly went over on its right side, but Adkins staved off disaster by turning right, running off the road into a graveled area, then back again into the road. He poured on the speed. Burdin crawled over the back seat into the flat space beyond.

"They're heading in the direction of Mildenhall Air

Base," Vadim said. "They're going to fly him back out of the country—any unauthorized flight, avoiding customs and immigration procedures."

"No, they're not," replied Igor, grimly. "Get a little closer."

"Are they still there?" shouted Adkins.

"Yeah," replied Burdin. "Put the back window down." He'd taken his gun out of its holster. "Just a little."

Adkins pressed the electronic control on the dash. The chilly air of a Shropshire dusk was sucked into the speeding station wagon. As the window went down, Igor, leaning out the side of the Morris, got off two shots with his silenced automatic, *pit-too, pit-oo,* aiming for the tires. He missed, but one bullet hit the back of the careening Chevrolet just below the rear window.

"Jesus! The game's getting rough!" exclaimed Hergenroeder. "Turn off anyplace where you see people."

"No!" Burdin heard that. "They'll kill me! They've got diplomatic immunity. We've got to run for it!" Then in an apparent contradiction he said, "Close the window all the way. And slow down."

Burdin was holding his gun at the top of the open window. As the reinforced glass panel rose it pressed the barrel of the gun against the top of the window frame, bracing it in a steady position but leaving enough room for Burdin to aim and fire.

"Slower, slower. They're coming up on us. I need another five yards." Burdin was now on both knees, the top of his head pressing against the inside of the roof.

Suddenly the pursuing Soviets were no more than twenty yards behind. Burdin squeezed off a shot. There was a receding sound of shattered glass and one headlight disappeared.

"Bingo!" Hergenroeder said. "Turn it on, Jim. We'll shake the bastards yet."

Behind them Vadim flipped his headlights from low beam to high. "Shit," he said. "If they do that again, we're out of business."

Both cars were going at top speed. "No one puts Igor out of business," replied Igor. "Close up."

The road was good by English standards, now gently twisting and turning through a sparsely settled rural area. The single lanes of macadam, divided by the yellow line, were broad enough to extend well under any roadside trees. Shoulder-high gorse hedges lined roadside meadows, locking in sheep and cattle.

"Hang on!" Adkins looked at his speedometer. Seventy-five plus. A single headlight in the rear was close and getting closer.

Igor leaned out of the left-hand front window, ignoring two more shots from Burdin, who was still aiming for the remaining headlight. With the stubby AK47 aimed over the hood of the Morris, he pulled the trigger. The gun's report was more like the vomiting of a drunken sailor than the blast of an assassin's weapon.

The pervasive assault, spewing up hundreds of bullets, did what single shots hadn't been able to accomplish. Both rear tires on the Chevrolet blew out with loud and angry snarls. One came completely off its rim, steel against the hard-surfaced road, setting off sparks like a Chinese pinwheel. Adkins, braking, saw ahead a five-bar gate leading from the road into adjacent grazing land.

"Time to dismount!" he shouted. "Take cover behind the hedges!" Turning sharply, he slammed into the gate, crumpling it as the station wagon faltered and died.

"Everybody out on this side!" cried Hergenroeder. "How much ammo you got, Nikky? We're going to need it."

"Two in the gun and another clip in my pocket—ten shots." It was now completely dark.

"Christ! The back window won't go down." Adkins had

pushed the control button on the dash. "They must have shot it out. Out the side, Nikky!"

In his anxiety to escape Burdin scrambled over the rear seat. The side door was open and he sprang out. Disaster. His left foot hit a rock and his ankle turned almost ninety degrees. He didn't lose his footing but screamed, half in pain and half in an agonizing realization of what had happened. He turned and leaned against the side of the station wagon, automatic in hand.

Frank and Jim rushed to help him, grabbing him on either side. Without warning Burdin shook them off and stuck his gun directly in Frank's face.

"Back off!" He was distraught. "Get away from me—both of you! Otherwise I'll kill you. And that'll sound right to Igor, because I'll say you were trying to kidnap me."

"Nikky, for Christ's sake, we're trying to help you," Frank was shouting, trying to pull Burdin at the same time. "Don't you understand? We gotta get the fuck outta here. Come on!"

"Don't hassle me, Hergenroeder. For the last time, I'm staying. I can't walk and you can't carry me. Get moving. And take your lackey with you."

Frank could feel the tip of the automatic, warmed by firing, right under the end of his nose. The tone of Nikky's voice told him he'd better move off. Adkins had listened in astonishment.

"As you wish, but you're committing suicide. Jim and I will try to cover you any way we can. Your firepower can't match theirs. You don't want to surrender?"

"Never! You've done your best. If I go, they go with me."

Frank and Jim crouched and ran behind the hedge. Burdin hobbled to a point behind the hood of the station wagon—and waited.

The Morris came to a screeching halt ten yards short of

the demolished gate and the all but abandoned Chevrolet. Igor heard the shouting but couldn't make out the words. Then an eery silence, broken only by the sound of a mooing cow and indistinct running footsteps.

In a house on the opposite side of the road, just beyond the gate and hidden in the trees, a lone and anxious woman opened her front door to listen.

Cautiously Igor eased out of the door of the sedan, its one headlight still on. He had the AK47 with him. Vadim stayed behind the wheel.

Burdin, standing on one foot to ease the pain in his ankle, took careful aim and fired. The report from his gun and the sound of shattering glass broke the stillness as the beam from the headlight disappeared. Quickly Igor ducked behind the car as Vadim got out on the far side to join him, the silenced automatic at the ready.

Inside the house the woman hurried to the telephone. She had closed and locked the door behind her, unobserved.

Hergenroeder and Adkins were prone on the ground, head to head under a hedgerow some distance from the gate.

"The stupid bastard totally misunderstood you," whispered Jim. "What did he think we were going to do—hogtie him and turn him over to the local police? He's going to die."

"No, he understood all right—and maybe he is going to die. He's weighed the consequences and just wants to do this his way. But we can't stop now. We gotta get around behind them. Follow me. We're coming up on the next corner of the field and some cows. Watch out for them."

They took off again in the darkness, running silently along the hedgerows. The cows, frightened by the moving figures, created a minor thundering noise as they moved away.

There was the sound of more shattering glass as a burst from the AK47 stitched the side of the station wagon. In the darkness Burdin could just make out Igor's blurred form relinquishing a fraction of his cover, ready to fire again. Burdin

2 9 8

forced him back with another round. Igor tried another approach.

"Can you hear me, Nikky? We're here to help you escape from the Americans. We know they're trying to kidnap you. We're shooting at them, not you."

"Go to hell, Igor," shouted Burdin. "You'll have to kill me first. And my fire is meant for you in particular." He fired again. Igor could feel its impact on the rear fender of the Morris. *Inches more and that traitor would have had me!*

Cursing, he went to his coat pocket, pulling out a fragmentation grenade. Made in the shape of an oblong minicamera but twice as heavy, it was covered with black pebbled plastic, enhancing its deceptive appearance. It was the latest of the sophisticated devices available to KGB hit squads.

In Brompton Wadley, a village six miles away, those late at the supper table looked up, their attention diverted by the wailing siren of a police van as it roared away from the station.

Igor found the release pin and pulled it, keeping his finger on the delay mechanism—five seconds to explosion. Then, from long practice and in a motion similar to a softball pitcher throwing an easy one to a sure strikeout, he lobbed it over the end of the hedge to land squarely behind the station wagon. As Igor finished his pitch Burdin fired again, this time with deadly accuracy. Igor, hit full in the face, went down without a sound, dead by the time he hit the ground.

Burdin's stand was too late. A dozen fragments of the exploding grenade caught him squarely in the back, two penetrating his lungs and one the back of his head just above the neckline. He was unconscious when Frank and Jim reached him, his jacket drenched in blood. They had rushed back at the first sound of the police siren, fearful of what they would find. They were trying desperately to save him when the police van roared up, an ambulance right behind. Vadim had bailed out, leaving behind the Czech automatic with its telltale silencer.

Without regaining consciousness Burdin died in the hospital in Shrewbury just before midnight. A Metropolitan Police helicopter, with Fereyes aboard, flew up from London to pick up Hergenroeder and Adkins. Fereyes had looked at the Moran passport with professional interest.

"Done by the Sovs, no doubt, but the IRA has a significant capability for this kind of mischief. This opens a lot of doors. TESS will want a closer look at this and so will we. You'll do that for us, won't you? Meanwhile don't worry about this night's fun and games getting into the press. I've read the riot act to the local constabulary, and Lord Macomber, who controls two of London's most unruly tabloids, has a son, Bertie, who's gay and who was mixed up in some very sordid business. I kept the lid on that, so he owes me one. You'll be needed as material witnesses at the coroner's inquest, but otherwise we're not going to detain you. Just don't leave England for a few days."

The flight back was short. Ahead, with little or no sleep, lay immediate sessions with the U.S. Ambassador to Britain, Kingman Brewster, and with MI-5 and MI-6.

PART THREE

THE
RENDEZVOUS

"**L**adies and gentlemen, I give you Ireland's newest patron saint—Deirdre O'Brien! She has heard the right voices." Jerry Fitt, the Irish member of Britain's Parliament from West Belfast, had to stand on a chair to make himself heard over the hubbub. In response glasses were raised from one end of the room to the other and cries of "Hear! Hear!" and "To Deirdre!" echoed back.

It was noon in Belfast and the morning papers had carried the often rumored but now confirmed news that Martha Quinlan and Deirdre O'Brien were co-winners of the Nobel Peace Prize in recognition of the founding of Peaceful Means. At the Crown, Belfast's famous watering hole, a jubilant crowd of well-wishers was in a festive mood. Beer and ale were flowing freely and noisily, courtesy of the Bass Brewery, which ran the Crown as a proprietary outlet, always mindful of the restrictions placed upon it by the National Trust in designating the Crown as a monument to be preserved. In one of the "snugs," as its well-publicized cubicles were called, sat a radiant Deirdre O'Brien, surrounded by men and women associated with the movement. At the bar Belfast's mayor was deep in conversation with Austin Currie, another moderate political activist and ardent supporter.

A favorite gathering place for generations of Irish writers, actors, and personalities, and mercifully spared by the bombers who haphazardly make life in Belfast a trial, the

Crown stands on Great Victoria Street, one of the city's busiest, opposite the Forum, a major tourist hotel. Its stained glass windows would do a cathedral proud, and its marble walls and mosaic floors will stand comparison with the elegance of the best of the excavations at Pompeii. Where the marble stops, carved gargoyles and intricate woodwork set off handsome mahogany panels, each bearing mottoes, mostly in Latin, which give the place an air of a museum as much as a place of public accommodation.

Peter Lindsay had left London for Belfast on an early morning flight, learning of the award from the London *Times,* and then only after reaching Heathrow. *That might make my task a little easier,* he thought. It was his first time back as a civilian, and as the taxi took him to the center of town old familiar landmarks crowded in on him. At the Forum Hotel, he inquired about the cheering and chanting crowd outside the Crown.

"It's Mrs. O'Brien in there, governor, our own wee lassie. She just won the Nobel Peace Prize, she and her friend Martha Quinlan. Yes, sir, lots of the green stuff for 'em, as well as an acknowledgment that they speak for the vast majority of us. That should make the Provos sit up and take notice."

As he crossed Great Victoria Street he spotted Tom Fenton, chief European correspondent for CBS, with an attendant cameraman readying a spot for American television audiences. Outside the Crown the ever-increasing crowd was chanting, "We want Deirdre! Peaceful Means!" endlessly, when Deirdre herself came through the double doors. There was an immediate roar of approbation and wild applause. A pickup truck parked in front became a speaker's platform, with Deirdre lifted up by willing hands. Despite her smiles, Lindsay thought she looked pale. Seeing familiar faces in the cheering crowd, she waved greetings and threw kisses in acknowledgment. Then, holding up her hands for silence, she began to speak.

"Thank you, you lovely men and women of Ireland, for your support and for this moment. Along with the pride that I feel on this unforgettable occasion—an occasion that should be celebrated by all Irishmen, Catholic or Protestant, those here in the North or those in Eire, those of any and all persuasions, rich or poor—I must pay tribute to Martha Quinlan, who cannot be here today as she is in Saint Mary's Hospital with appendicitis. I talked with her late last night when we were notified of this honor and will see her, God willing, this afternoon. I ask all of you to remember her in your prayers and to let her know, by whatever means, of your love and pride in what she has done. Believe me, without her Peaceful Means would never have become the force for peace that all of us have been working so hard to make it."

She stopped for a moment to wipe away incipient tears from eyes that glistened.

"I accept this honor not only for Martha and myself, but also on behalf of all Irish men and women of good will—everywhere. Jerry Fitt says I hear voices. Perhaps—but let me tell you that there are voices that I do not hear. I speak of the voices of intolerance and bigotry—unreason, the voice of the mob. Within a mile of where we stand is Catholic West Belfast. It is the breeding ground for the terrorists who carry the banner of the Provisional Wing of the Irish Republican Army, as well as for the terrorism that is being escalated—rhetorically as well as actually—into a religious war. The continuing hopelessness and hatred of the Provos is there to be exploited by twisted elders and outsiders of both persuasions, who really do want confrontation between Catholics and Protestants, the English and the Irish, between the gods and men of democracy and those of authoritarianism. Those evil men, whether or not they are parts of governments, are succeeding brilliantly in using a few frightened and dispossessed young men to escalate what should be a relatively minor regional political grievance into a kind of world war without armies. All of us praise the resolve of the Israelis, but what has been its result? The diffusion of terror? No—the PLO now seeks out its targets on a worldwide basis. Our interest is to minimize the escalation of carnage, to isolate the terrorists and those who send them arms and money.

"Hear us, Mrs. Thatcher! Tell the Protestants you want no more of discrimination in schooling and employment. Hear us, the Ulster Defense Force! Catching the guilty and punishing them is the best revenge, but random revenge is another word for terrorism. Hear us, you Irish-Americans who support the IRA with guns and money. The strategy of the manipulators is to provoke more confrontation, more death, more hatred. Here in Northern Ireland we kill people on both sides, each invoking Christ's name, with almost no one daring to utter the assertion of brotherhood. We are all brothers. Forgive. Forget. Live. Heal the sick—not the sick in body, but those who are sick in mind. Forgive! Forget! Live and let live! Peaceful Means is the only way."

The shouting and applause that had magically disappeared when Deirdre's clear well-modulated voice rang out to summon its attention once more came roaring back from the crowd, now growing with each passing moment. Lindsay, pushing his way toward the truck, wondered how he could have the private conversation with her that had brought him from London. Stopping to reach into his pocket, he was able to write a few legible words on a page torn from his notebook, then continued to jostle his way toward her.

She was leaning over the side of the truck, clasping the hands of well-wishers, as he succeeded in reaching her. In one of hers she took his outstretched hand while with the other she took that of an ancient Irish woman whose wrinkled face was framed by a cotton kerchief knotted under her chin. Fleetingly

Deirdre's almost violet eyes looked down at Lindsay's up-turned face. To gain her full attention Lindsay held on to her hand. Puzzled, she looked back at him.

"Please take this, Mrs. O'Brien. It's important." He held out the note. She said nothing, but continued to look at him as she took the folded piece of paper.

"I'll be at the Crown," he managed to say. "I have something for you."

Inside the Crown the crowd was thinning out. Choosing the bar as the least conspicuous place, Lindsay ordered an ale and succeeded in toying with it for the ten minutes that passed before Deirdre reentered, accompanied by two young men, self-appointed bodyguards from the group of moderates that normally surrounded the leadership of Peaceful Means. They went into one of the snugs and sat down. A moment later one of the young men approached Lindsay.

"You look like a decent sort. You want to see Mrs. O'Brien?"

"Yes, I do. Please tell her my name is Peter Lindsay and that I wish to speak with her privately."

He came back with the word. "Over here, please."

Deirdre was seated at the ample table inside. "Thank you, Jimmy," she said. "You and Sean wait outside. Please sit down, Mr. Lindsay. Then if you don't mind you might explain your note." She put it on the table in front of him. On it was written, "Mark Raven. Important information."

"Who are you, Mr. Lindsay?"

"I'm a British civil servant, Mrs. O'Brien. I said I had something for you. Here it is." He handed her a photoprint of the bank draft, cleared through the Bank of England, which returned to Raven the £100,000 passed to Nicholas Moran.

It took her a moment to realize its significance. She

looked at it unknowingly until she could make out the signature. *Ian MacKenzie! Dead at the hands of the IRA! But payable to Mark Raven!* She looked up at Lindsay, who nodded his head slightly.

"I—I think I understand what you're trying to tell me, but what is Mark's connection with all of this?" A sudden dread seized her. "He's not dead, is he? Oh, my God!" She reached across the table to seize Peter's hand, her eyes brimming with tears.

"No, Mrs. O'Brien, he's not dead, and we have no reason to think that anything's going to happen to him. I'm going to answer your question fully, but before I do let me tell you that without Mark Raven's help, including a contribution to COMMEND of proportions that I'm sure you know about, the just accomplished seizure by British authorities of the biggest shipment of arms ever bound for the IRA would have been impossible."

"My God! What have I done!" she blurted out. She felt as if she might be losing control. "I'm sorry, Mr. Lindsay. You wouldn't know what I'm talking about. Please continue."

Choosing his words carefully, Lindsay gave her the whole story, starting with the first conversation with Mark at Buck's Club on the day of the Mountbatten funeral, the revelation that British intelligence—no mention of TESS by name or inference, or of his or Brigadier MacKenzie's part in it—was aware of the arms shipment and had the means to stop it, but only if the IRA had money enough to pay for it, and that Raven was the likeliest source of the shortfall.

"He made it very clear, Mrs. O'Brien, that he had given you his word that he would make no further contributions to COMMEND. We were able to persuade him otherwise—that without his help a carefully orchestrated operation *against* the IRA would never take place. What you have here is proof of the fact that the funds were the Crown's, not his, and that his motives were wholly in line with your own. Brigadier Mac-

Kenzie promised him faithfully that he would make it plain to you that he was acting only as a conduit for the Crown's funds. Now MacKenzie's gone, and I'm here in his stead. I've sworn to catch the man who murdered him. I was here in Ulster with the Queen's Own Cameronians for fourteen months and have seen men—innocent men, civilians on both sides—blown to bits by bombs planted by the IRA, but nothing has angered me as much as MacKenzie's senseless murder."

"Do you know who did it?"

"Yes, we do—proof positive. We're after him and we're going to get him."

"Can you identify him for me?"

"No, Mrs. O'Brien, I cannot. Moreover, if people thought you knew, your life wouldn't be worth tuppence. Don't talk about this, even after we bring Mark Raven back to you, safe and sound. If you wish, you may have the photoprint."

"Bring him back? Where is he now? Are you telling me he's not at Raven Park?"

"I doubt it. More than likely he's in Dublin. Wherever he is, he's after the same quarry."

"You make this sound like a foxhunt. He's not a well man, Mr. Lindsay—do you know that? He's been told to have coronary bypass surgery."

"He told us that, Mrs. O'Brien, but he was not to be deterred."

"Oh, my God! Then I've got to find him—I simply must. I've been so wrong. I had reason enough to find him before you showed up, but now it's imperative." She was distraught and beginning to show it. Since that tearful retreat from Mark at Raven Park she had thought about nothing else, missing him, wanting him. She had gone to the phone a half dozen times—*why doesn't* he *call* me?—but pride and a feeling of having been betrayed kept her from dialing the one number that would bring her back into contact with the one voice she yearned to hear. "I don't know what to do, which way to turn. Tell me what to do, Mr. Lindsay. I can't ask Mark, so I'll ask you."

"Stay out of it, Mrs. O'Brien. You've just had one of the great honors of our time paid you. Savor it. Continue to use your influence to arouse the conscience of the rightful thinkers in Ulster and Eire. Don't risk your own life by exposing yourself unduly to elements that would be relieved if you were dead. But if you really feel that you must be in contact with your friend, you should get in touch with a man called Tim Costello. He runs a pub called the Corkscrew, in Leeson Street, in the Ballymurphy district. He's not a Provo, but they trust him. It's just possible that he can help you locate him."

It seemed a tenuous lead, but better than none. She thought a moment, then said, "You've got Eton or Winchester or Rugby written all over you, adding to the considerable risk you put yourself under by coming here. Why did you do it?"

"Actually it's Winchester, and in this part of town, little risk." He didn't tell her that two years ago and less than two hundred yards away he had almost lost a leg to a hand grenade. "It's really very simple, Mrs. O'Brien. You see, a promise is a promise, especially one made by my late chief, Brigadier MacKenzie. But now that you know the truth about Mr. Raven's action, and his motives, I feel that I've done my duty."

"You're an honorable man, Mr. Lindsay, and thank God I can now believe Mark is, too." She was calmer now—more in control. Pointing to the mahogany panel at a point just over the table, she said, "See these two little holes? They've been plugged and polished, but if you look carefully you can see them. There used to be a little ivory plaque where the holes are, marking this as the snug in which James Mason, the British movie actor, met his theatrical death as the mortally wounded gunman in the film *Odd Man Out*. All too true in these parts, Mr. Lindsay, all too true. But so many tourists wanted to sit and be photographed in this snug that they'd sit in no other, so the plaque came down. But do you know what, Mr. Lindsay—or may I call you Peter?"

"Please do, Mrs. O'Brien. That would be fine."

"You know what, Peter? I think I'm going to call the scenario that we've just acted out 'Odd Man In.' You've done something for me that could change my life. Mark Raven's no longer odd, and he's no longer out. I thank you from the bottom of my heart."

She reached across the table to take his hand in hers again. "Not only are you honorable, Peter, but you're not bad to look at, either. So now get along with you. Go back to London and to that certain someone who loves you while I look for mine." They got up to leave. Standing, Peter put out his hand. She took it, but pulled him toward her to kiss him on the cheek.

"God bless you, Mrs. O'Brien," he said. "I have the feeling He will." He looked once more into those searching eyes, then turned and walked away.

The two companions who had accompanied her came up.

"A friend of a friend," she said. "A friend of an *old* friend. Thanks for standing by. Now I'll have a cab, if you don't mind. I have an errand to do."

"Leeson Street? Should you be going there, me lady?" the cab driver asked as she settled in the back seat.

"You heard me, old man. I'm as Catholic as the Pope. Just take me there." He shrugged and they drove off.

She had known instinctively that Lindsay was from British intelligence and knew as much as could be expected from anyone from that side. But there was so much he didn't know, plus a lot she didn't want him or random others to know—principally that Dr. Malone, at Saint Ursula's Hospital, genuinely shocked but no less friendly, two days ago had confirmed that she was pregnant. And now the revelation that Mark—on whom she had wrongfully turned her back, whom she loved as she had never loved before—the father of her unborn child, was fighting for the same ends as she was, whatever the means. He would have to know about the child, and in order for that to happen, she would have to talk with this man Costello. If the Provos trusted him, could she? They were crossing the Shankill Road, a Protestant stronghold, headed for Leeson Street and the Catholic section as she wondered what lay ahead.

ON THE BEACH IN ISRAEL, JUST SOUTH OF ELIAT

It was one of those cloudless days in the eastern Mediterranean, hot and humid. The lack of any sort of breeze encouraged scores of pesky, green-headed flies to bite as sailors unloaded cargo from an Israeli LST, beached for that purpose just south of the Israeli naval base at Eliat. Several hundred yards away a group of children were splashing happily in the water, oblivious to the flies and to the activity that had brought important Israeli government figures to the scene.

Two days earlier the LST had picked up its cargo at the British naval base at Gibraltar. As the last of the crates was brought ashore General Hofi, top man in the Mossad, said to his companion, "Well, Saul, you pulled it off. Congratulations. When do you return to London?"

"As soon as you turn me loose, General," replied Ben-Udris. "I want to wrap up the operation with Sir Alistair Widener. Britain's receipt for the bullion is all that's lacking."

"Send it to me, or better still, bring it back personally. I'll want to talk with you about your next assignment. Maybe Cairo, or more likely, back here as a regional chief in headquarters. Your talents are wasted in London. Moreover the KGB will be watching you like a hawk after this one."

Ben-Udris smiled. "Now that they've got their own *Riddle of the Sands* they can look all they want. But the answer lies not in the Baltic but in the Gulf of Sidra. They'll never figure that out."

DUBLIN—BELFAST
AND A DESIGNATED HITTER
19 SEPTEMBER 1979

O'Farrell was worried—and with good reason. He was lame, paranoid, and almost stony broke. The taxi ride from Shannon had stripped him of all but eleven of his remaining Irish pounds. He had put up in a cheap hotel on Upper Dorset Street and now had to face the fact that surely he was a hunted man, with only his own resources to get him out of a jam. And he wanted out, badly, just as he wanted the approval, expressed or otherwise, of his peers in the 2nd Provisional Brigade for blowing away MacKenzie. He'd tell them about it—he wasn't afraid to do that—but he'd tell them when he damn well felt like it, and in his own way.

For the better part of six days he had stayed in or on his bed with the daily newspapers or glued to the television set, his only connections with the outside world, while his ankle got slowly better. He had subsisted on tea, biscuits, fish and chips, and an occasional steak and kidney pie, until a terse note with his morning tea stated that his bill needed prompt payment. Until then, no more room service.

Okay. He had to go sometime, and today would be the day. First the phone calls, there being no phone in his room. Seven o'clock. Too early. He shaved and dressed, then with the help of his crutches went out looking for a proper breakfast. An early morning fog, thin but not unusual in Dublin in September, blanketed the city. By the time he reached Marlborough Street and Saint Mary's Catholic Pro-Cathedral the sun was breaking through the mist. It was ten minutes to eight and the church bells were ringing, announcing early morning communion for the faithful. He was hungry, but put aside any thoughts of food when an elderly man, walking haltingly with a heavy cane, attracted his attention. He watched him with growing interest, correctly judging him to be an American visitor. Several minutes after the man had entered the church, O'Farrell followed him in.

From the narthex he could see that the old man had settled in a pew close to the rear, his head bowed in prayer. O'Farrell looked around him. The narthex was empty. Behind him was what appeared to be a closet door. Opening it, all he saw inside were a number of cartons and boxes stuffed with papers that were yellowing with age, and a bell rope—used just moments before—dropping from a hole in the ceiling. The narthex was still empty. Quickly he stashed his crutches in one corner and shoved several of the boxes against them, putting one on top of another until only the tops of the crutches were visible.

He closed the door quietly and limped into the church, sitting directly behind the old man, two pews back. The organist was playing softly as the priest entered the church to begin the service. Including O'Farrell there were only nine people, mostly elderly women, in attendance.

During the short service O'Farrell remained seated or on his knees, using every opportunity to cover his face with his hands. When the time came for the few communicants to go to the chancel, the old man left his cane in the pew. Moving as noiselessly as possible, O'Farrell started up the aisle also. With several steps he reached the pew with the cane, took it, turned, and left the church.

"Thanks, old man," he said to himself as he reached the street, "but I need the cane more than you do."

In Northern Ireland the weather was a match for Nolan O'Rourke's mood. He was waiting on the northwest corner of Roden Street and the Donegall Road. Rain was falling by the bucketful. Summoned by the Chief of Staff of the IRA—a first for O'Rourke—he looked anxiously at each passing car to see if it was the one he had been told to expect. Then suddenly the car was there. A face appeared through a lowered window.

"Get in, Nolan. In the back." It was a command, not a request.

He got in, his raincoat dripping puddles on the seat and floor. Next to him was a youngish man in a cap and a turtleneck sweater with droopy eyes and a full lip, like the American movie star Sylvester Stallone.

"See if he's wired, Shamus. Sorry, O'Rourke," said the man in the front seat, whom O'Rourke judged to be the Chief of Staff, "but we don't need informers or anyone else like your man O'Farrell. He's an idiot, that one, totally untrustworthy, and you've got to get rid of him."

O'Rourke got a thorough frisking by his back seat companion, who then said, "He's clean, Mr. T."

Uneasy, O'Rourke didn't like what he was hearing, but said nothing as the man in the front seat turned to address him. The broad face, seen elsewhere, would have been identified immediately as belonging to an Irishman. Ruddy complexion, intense blue eyes, sharp features topped by iron gray, crinkly hair. It was an intelligent face, but willful, and given an intellectual aspect by Tiernan's choice—a lawyer's choice—of wire-rimmed eyeglasses. It was not at all what O'Rourke expected.

"Nolan," he said, "this is about the arms shipment, the

3 1 5

operation that we call Sealift Two. You may have heard it called that yourself. Something is very wrong. There were two people that I was to hear from, but neither has checked in. One is the man you know as Moran and the other is the emissary of a powerful friend who's been helpful to us." He saw no reason to mention Petrovskiy by name. "This is ominous. Sealift Two may have been blown. Which means that we can't count on delivery when we expected it, and maybe not at all. Your man O'Farrell, Nolan, is to blame. I *know* he killed MacKenzie, triggering events that I don't understand. He was seen close to Abbotswood the day MacKenzie got his." Tiernan was becoming agitated. "Who else but O'Farrell? He's a traitor, O'Rourke, maybe one that's been in touch with the crazies in the Irish National Liberation Army. But we—you and me and your boys in the 2nd Brigade—are going to take care of him. He's in Dublin—we know that. He's already checked in and out of Kelley's garage, and when he comes back you're to take him by the hand and lead him right to where we want him."

"And where do we want him, Mr. Tiernan?"

"Right at Mullaghmore, Nolan, in plenty of time for you to deliver him to the submarine—to ride away from all of his troubles."

"I don't follow you. You just finished telling me that the delivery won't take place."

"Come off it, Nolan. What are you, a schoolboy? Get him in a boat, get him away from Mullaghmore, then give him what he deserves. It's taken us a year and a half to raise the money for arms enough to blow the stinkin' Brits away for good, then that trigger-happy American cowboy spoils it all by killing MacKenzie. If he hadn't done that we'd be home free and you and your lads in the 2nd Brigade would have all the arms you need to set things right. I don't care how you do it, with help or alone, but he's not to come back from that boat ride."

"You want him done in?" O'Rourke bit his lip. The situation was getting blacker by the minute.

"O'Rourke, you're a mind reader." Tiernan said it gently, but the sarcasm was there. "What else would I mean? And who can I trust more than the man who did such a fine job in getting Inishmurray ready for the shipment? I want him off, and you and your lads can do it. And what better place to bury him than under the rocks at Inishmurray?"

"So that's why I'm here? That's asking a lot." Already O'Rourke was wondering how he could shake off the assignment.

"Yes," replied Tiernan, "it is. But if you want to stay healthy, it would be well for everybody concerned if you did what you've been told. We started this together and we'll finish it together. This is the first time we've talked, you and I, and if you've learned anything we won't have to talk again—for a long time. Do you understand?"

"I understand." O'Rourke wanted to stay healthy; in particular he wanted to be able to walk for the rest of his life. Kneecapping he did not need.

The car had been cruising in the Crumlin Road area of West Belfast, away from the town center, and was now approaching Woodvale Park. A Saracen stood at the park's main entrance, just yards away from a sandbagged communications outpost used by patrolling British troops.

"You'd better get out here, Nolan, before Maggie's boys see you." Tiernan spoke in a more conciliatory manner. "There's just one more thing to remember. Mind you, have your boys at Inishmurray as originally planned. If O'Farrell were to learn otherwise, the jig would be up, and we wouldn't want that, would we?"

They let him out at the edge of the park. He was a shaken man, but orders were orders. At least he could use Fitzsimmons, his second in command, and even Costello to help him over this hump. He headed for the Ballymurphy area and the Corkscrew, via the Springfield Road.

Up river from the O'Connell Street Bridge, across the Liffey from the Guinness Brewery but almost in its shadow, is Frank Kelley's Garage—Maintenance & Repairs, All Makes and Models. It is also the dispatching point and safe harbor for Colleen's Taxi Service, six sedans of indeterminate age that mostly run but seldom all at once. Colleen was long since gone, married for the second time to Frank's brother and moved to County Antrim, but the name and the business lingered on. It was not only a useful supplement to Frank's repair business but also served as a focal point for certain elements in the IRA, and its vehicles and its telephone a communications center for messages from Northern Ireland and transportation for those who needed it.

After wolfing down an omelet, kippers, and toast, O'Farrell made his way to Kelley's. He could walk better with the cane than with the now abandoned crutches, and was beginning to feel better about himself on all counts.

He had worked out what he would do. *Renée—there's the answer!* He had his Ambrose passport and a credit card to match it, but it was too risky to use, except as a last resort.

"What brings you here?" Frank was surprised to see him. A dour and taciturn man, he wasn't much given to words. He'd been a prizefighter in earlier days, but not good enough to make it pay. After minor brushes with the law he'd settled in to making a reasonable living as an auto mechanic. In addition he served as a reliable pipeline for the higher echelons in the IRA in Belfast. "What's the matter with your foot?"

"A dog bit me." For once the truth sounded like evasiveness. "I need a few pounds, Frank, and a taxi. Can you fix me up? I also want to call Belfast."

"Is this going to be a free ride or are you paying?"

3 1 8

"I'm paying, out of the money you're going to lend me. The cab and I'll be back shortly."

"Okay, but if that's the case I'll pay the driver myself. Easier and cheaper all around. Use my office phone."

O'Farrell tried to reach Costello at the Corkscrew but he was out until late afternoon. "Okay, but have him call Ajax as soon as he comes in, at the usual Dublin number."

Within minutes after O'Farrell left, Frank Kelley also called Belfast.

"The one who calls himself Ajax was here," he said, "limping and on a cane. Hit me up for a few quid, which I gave him, like you said."

He listened, then replied, "It'll be done."

"Come back and see us again, Mr. Ambrose. I'm glad your leg is better." The hotel clerk took O'Farrell's money with relief. He knew him to be an American, but contrary to all past experience, had him tagged as a deadbeat.

"I'm going up to get my stuff out of the room. While I'm doing that, would you please call the airport to see which line flies to Brussels and when the next flight leaves?"

"Certainly, Mr. Ambrose."

Fifteen minutes later he was back to turn in his key. Colleen's taxi had waited.

"It'll be Air Caledonia, Mr. Ambrose, and there's a flight to Brussels at twelve-oh-six."

O'Farrell made a great business of looking at his watch. "By God, if I hurry I think I can make it! Thank you very much—and this is for your trouble." He tossed the clerk a pound note and hurried out to the waiting taxi.

Smoke—a little was always needed, deception to throw off those who might be coming after him.

"Take me to the main post office," he told the driver. In Ireland the telephone system as well as the postal service is a function of the government. He thought his best chances of contacting Renée quickly would be from there.

In the main concourse was the all-Ireland telephone information center.

"The number, please for the post office at Swinford, in County Mayo."

In moments he had it. Going to a bank of phones opposite, he placed the call. Busy. Fretfully he waited, then tried again. This time he got through.

"I'm trying to reach a Renée Koulatsos. I have only a general delivery address for her, at the Swinford post office. Can you tell me, please, if there's any mail there for her?"

There was a moment's hesitation before a female voice asked, "Who's speaking, please?"

"A friend."

"I'm sorry, sir. I cannot give you that information. It's against postal regulations."

"Well, can I leave a message there for her?"

"Again, I'm sorry sir. That too is against postal regulations. There would be no postage on it."

"Aw, come on! You can certainly do this. It's important, and the message is short. I'll send you a pound note the minute I hang up the phone."

"Well, I—" There was another hesitation. "I shouldn't be doing this." The postmistress knew Renée, and knew she was in the neighborhood. She was amused by her, and from very limited horizons fantasized about her life, envying her apparent freedom. "What's the message?"

"Just say 'Please call Mike in Dublin at 42-94401 as soon as possible.'"

"Very well. I will do this. I will write the note, put it in an envelope and put the proper postage on it. But please send me twenty pence. My name is Megan."

"Megan, you're a sweetheart. You've got it. Maybe I'll bring it to you myself."

* * *

Despite the considerable comforts of the Shelbourne Hotel Mark felt as if he were a prisoner. He had been there for four days, holed up in his room, alternately reading and writing, awaiting word from Lindsay. The temptation to try to reach Deirdre was overwhelming, and never more so than after banner headlines in the morning papers had trumpeted the news that she and Martha Quinlan were the recipients of the Nobel Peace Prize. But he knew that to do so would jeopardize his one chance to clear himself not only with her but in his own conscience.

Maybe it was that news, coupled with his frustrations, that brought on another period of shortness of breath, forcing him to lie on the bed to regain his normal breathing cycle.

He had been there perhaps ten minutes when there was a knock on the door. He opened it to recognize one of Lindsay's men, casually dressed in corduroy slacks and a pullover sweater.

"We're getting a handle on the situation, Mr. Raven," he said, after he had come in and sat down. "I've just spoken with Major Lindsay, from Belfast. Here in Dublin Kelley's garage, in the North Ring area, is known to be a focal point for IRA men in the city. We've had it staked out from a room across the Liffey. For whatever reason, O'Farrell has been there, and now his own men are intent on getting him out of here and to the same rendezvous where we want him. We don't yet know the reason for that, but we're working on it. In any event, Major Lindsay now wants you to go home to await further word from him. He knows the game's not over, and said to tell you that he'll get back to you shortly."

"Well," said Mark, "at least we're getting some movement. You tell Major Lindsay I'm still in his corner, ready and anxious to do whatever he wants—that I'm retreating to Raven Park only for strategic purposes, to regroup and to be close to the action. Can you remember that?"

"I certainly can, Mr. Raven. Major Lindsay will be reassured. I know I'm speaking for him when I say that all of us appreciate what you're doing."

When the MI-5 man left, Mark picked up a yellow foolscap pad on which he had been writing, crossed out several paragraphs, quickly rewrote them, then wrote several more. The news that the Provos themselves were trying to get O'Farrell to Mullaghmore put a whole new perspective on the tale that was taking form in his mind. *Suppose I die before I can finish it? Get it to Owen Newcombe right away.*

In another twenty minutes Mark had thrown the few clothes he had brought with him into his overnight bag, ready to take off for Raven Park. Last to be packed was a Colt .45 automatic, the only thing he could consciously remember stealing in his life. He simply took it with him when he was mustered out of the army at the Presidio at the end of World War II. The last man he had killed with it was a German captain, an engineer in the Das Reich Division, as he stood on the river bank at Garonne, supervising the repair of a pontoon bridge that Mark and his maquis had blown up. He remembered the look of utter surprise on the German's face as he stood up from his concealed position and coolly pulled the trigger.

"Maybe one more time, old friend," said Mark, half aloud, patting the weapon. "That is, if I live that long. But this time for love."

On his way out he stopped at the concierge's desk with an envelope addressed to Newcombe in New York. He paid the concierge for air mail postage, stressing that he wanted it dispatched at once. In it were the paragraphs he had just written, plus character notes as well as an outline of the novel he had discussed earlier with Newcombe on his way back to Ireland from San Francisco. He thought again about its title, *The Tides of Sligo*. It had a good sound to it—and it fit the bill.

Kelley was out driving a cab himself when O'Farrell got back to the garage. He was in Kelley's cramped and cluttered office, fishing around in his pockets for the number of the Corkscrew, when the phone rang. To his surprise it was Costello.

"All bloody hell's broke loose here, mate, and O'Rourke is pissed to the armpits with you. He thinks you did Mac-Kenzie in—and not knowing where you've been all this time hasn't helped either. I'm talking from a box, so you can speak freely. Mike, if you come to the north you're a dead one, as the Brits will lift you at the border, on suspicion if nothing else—and you know what that means. But what's trouble for one is trouble for all, so Nolan and the boys are going to see you right. He wants me to tell you that your only way out of the mess you're in is to get to Mullaghmore and get out of Ireland on the vessel that's delivering the goods. Nolan can arrange that, and get you up to Mullaghmore as well. Frank Fitzsimmons is on his way down now to bring you back in time to get on the boat, a submarine actually, and—"

"Wait a minute! Did you say submarine? What kind of submarine?"

"Your guess is as good as mine, mate, but for my money I'd say it'll be a Russky—or am I saying something out of turn?"

My God! A submarine, and a Russian one at that! Well, life is full of surprises. I can buy some time that way, and somehow get back to Northern Ireland when things quiet down. I'd better go for it. But why this sudden display of concern?

"I don't know anything about any submarine, Tim, but if that's the way O'Rourke wants it, that's the way it has to be. When am I supposed to be at Mullaghmore?"

"Fitz'll tell you. He had all the details. But don't worry.

We're going to see you right. O'Rourke and the lads from the 2nd Brigade will have a ring around the town. We're going to see you right, all right. You can count on it. Nobody's going to get through but you and Raven—if he shows up."

"Raven? Why Raven?"

"Well, we keep hearing that the Brits are going to ask for his extradition as an accessory to murder—something to do with his support. He may want out if the Garda goes after him. They'll go after you too, if the Brits get wise and ask them to."

"Holy Christ! Will you be there?"

"That I can't say. I'm waiting for word from O'Rourke as to where he wants me."

"What about Fitszimmons? When's he coming?"

"He should be there by nightfall. He'll get you to Mullaghmore. He'll have a few pounds for you, too, if you'll be needin' 'em. I'm moving along now, Mike, so keep an eye out for Fitz and we'll be lookin' for you soon."

O'Farrell hung up in a state of indecision. He had to stay out of sight for a while, that much was certain, but he was relieved to learn that even in the face of the incurred wrath of the leaders of the 2nd Brigade resulting from his freewheeling foray into political murder, they were going to try to get him out of Ireland. He was smart enough to know that his freedom meant theirs also, so until something better came along he'd pay atttention to O'Rourke and his scheme. He'd talk more with Fitzsimmons when he showed up. God, he'd like to hear from Renée! He could hide out with her indefinitely!

At four-fifteen that afternoon a nondescript Opel sedan driven by Tomas Koulatsos, Renée's uncle, stopped in front of the Swinford post office. A cracked windshield was but one manifestation that the car had seen better days.

Renée got out and went into the small whitewashed

building. Inside, Megan's dog, a beige ball of uncertain origin who had been napping on the cool, uneven brick floor, looked up to flap his tail several times in an affectionate greeting. Megan, who had seen Renée coming, went to the general delivery box to look over the half-dozen letters awaiting pickup. As Renée approached the window Megan said to her shyly, "Today I have something for you. A man called here this morning and left a message. I have written it out."

Renée tore it open eagerly. She seldom got any mail and had really come to see if her Uncle Tomas, the acknowledged leader of the small family group that traveled together, had anything awaiting him. She read it twice before she realized who it was from. Then with mounting excitement she thrust it down the front of her blouse. "Thank you, miss," she said to Megan. "It's a nice note."

"It's such a wee note. I hope you understand it."

"I understand it, miss. You nice lady. Tomorrow or the next day I come back and tell your fortune. Real nice—for free."

She went out to report to Uncle Tomas that he had no mail, thinking fast about where the closest telephone box would be so she could call Mike O'Farrell in private to tell him where she could be found.

Fitzsimmons had arrived a little after 4:00 P.M. He and O'Farrell were talking out on the cement apron leading from the street to the single petrol pump.

"O'Rourke is furious, and that's no blarney. He'll take your hide off—verbally anyway. I'm not asking any questions so don't give me any answers, but he's convinced you blew away MacKenzie—something about a map that he thinks he must have dropped at the Corkscrew. I know too that O'Rourke has been told by Mr. Big to get you out of Ireland. I'm here to take you to a hideaway we've rigged for you in the country near Dromahair. You'll be nice and cozy and nobody's going to be lookin' for you there. It's to the east of Sligo Town and no more than an hour from Mullaghmore. You'll be with Tom Mahoney and his wife and as snug as a bug in a rug. Wee Eddie and his boat will be waiting for you at the dock at Mullaghmore at three on the morning of the twentieth."

"I assume that you came with a gun, the same one that I've seen in this car before?"

"Yes, in the same place—and it's loaded." Right away Fitzsimmons regretted responding to any query about guns.

"Frank, I want you to let me have that gun. I'm naked. How do I know what I'm walking into? I need the heat. Give it to me. I'm not going without it."

Fitzsimmons was in a spot. "If he's got no gun, don't give him one," was O'Rourke's last admonition. "It's going to be a bad enough scene without him cutting loose on us."

"Mike, you don't need it. Leave it where it is. Nobody's going to be around but Nolan and his boys. We're going to get you out of Ireland safe and sound."

"Gimme the gun, Frank. Let me carry it. You'll get it back when I get on the boat." O'Farrell walked over to the car as if he were going to take it by force.

"No!" Fitzsimmons's reply was vigorous. "And what happened to that cannon you've been known to carry? It seems to me you always had it when necessary. Or did some customs or immigration type relieve you of it?"

The rebuke, coupled with lingering suspicions, stoked the fires of O'Farrell's noted short fuse. He was just about to go for the gun when a mechanic appeared in the doorway, wiping the grease off his hands.

"Mr. O'Farrell, there's a call for you. In the office."

He limped to the phone, heavy cane in hand. When he picked up the receiver he could hardly believe his luck. Renée's voice, faint but audible over the rural lines, was coming through to him.

3 2 6

"Renée! Hey, good-lookin'! I want to come to see you
. . . yeah . . . yeah . . . Oh, I dunno. Maybe a couple of days."
He listened, then said, "Just a minute while I get something to write with." He listened again, then said, "Yeah, right
away. Take care. I'll see you as soon as I can get there." He
hung up in a perceptibly changed mood, but with the same
purpose in mind.

When he went out again Fitzsimmons was standing at the
curb, smoking.

"When is it I'm supposed to be at Mullaghmore?"

"At three on the morning of the twentieth," replied
Fitzsimmons. "Now you're being reasonable."

"At three on the twentieth," repeated O'Farrell. "Tell
O'Rourke I'll be there."

Wordlessly he moved around behind Fitzsimmons, grabbing him around the neck with his left arm, effectively yoking
him. With his right hand he twisted Fitzsimmons's right arm
up and behind his back. Fitzsimmons was older than O'Farrell,
thirty pounds lighter, and no match for the younger man's
strength. He cried out in pain.

"Christ almighty, O'Farrell, what the hell are you
doing!"

"I'm taking the gun, Fitz, and the car too. Where are the
keys?"

"Left-hand coat pocket." He had a hard time getting the
words out.

"Kneel down—then hand them to me. If you don't I'll
lay your head open with my shillelagh."

"You're a fookin' madman, O'Farrell. What am I supposed to do? Walk back to Belfast?"

"Maybe—I don't give a shit. I've got other things on my
mind. Kelley'll send you home. I'll see you at Mullaghmore."

He grabbed the keys from Fitzsimmons's outstretched
hand and was in the car and away before Fitzsimmons could
get to his feet. When he did so he shook his fist in the direction

3 2 7

O'Farrell had taken and shouted, "You're a goddam loon, O'Farrell, a goddam loon! You'll get yours!" Then he rushed into Kelley's office to call O'Rourke.

Ten miles outside of Dublin, having assured himself that no one was in hot pursuit, O'Farrell stopped to take stock. Plenty of petrol—okay on that score. But the next check gave rise to more suspicions. Pushing the front seat on the passenger side forward on its hinges, he loosened the floor mat and pried up a square segment cut into the floorboard. Underneath, a shallow box had been welded to the frame, the usual depository for a Webbley .38-caliber automatic.

Empty! Christ, no heat! Fitzsimmons had been lying to him, but why? In the trunk he found what he thought was the answer, and he didn't like that either. Jammed behind the spare tire, wrapped in a blanket, was a standard U.S. issue M-16 semiautomatic rifle. He knew it well, having fired countless thousands of rounds from an identical one in Vietnam. Next to it, similarly wrapped, were two magazines of lead-cored 7.62-mm bullets, sheathed in copper—impact killer stuff. No time to investigate further, as the cops might be right behind him. He doubted it, but common sense told him to press on.

In the glove compartment he found a road map of Ireland. O'Farrell knew pretty well where he was going, as his destination was just off the N5 motorway after he reached Swinford. He had made some notes but he could remember Renée's instructions. "Come to the lay-by on the west side of the road from Swinford to Kiltimagh. It'll be about half a mile beyond the church on the same side of the road. Come after dark. Leave your car by the church and walk the rest of the way. I'll be waiting in my caravan—the red and white one."

He pulled out of the picnic area where he had stopped and headed northwest.

BELFAST
THE CORKSCREW
19 SEPTEMBER 1979

Distances in Belfast are measured not by miles but by attitudes. When Deirdre's taxi left the Shankill Road to turn south on Mayo Street she rode for no more than five minutes before she arrived at the Corkscrew, on Leeson Street, deep in the heart of the Ballymurphy district, one of West Belfast's poorer sections and a Catholic stronghold. The difference between this area and the relative prosperity of Great Victoria Street was apparent on every side. The streets were littered with debris and broken glass. There was not a tree, a patch of greenery, or a flower pot in sight—just a monochromatic expanse of cement running between tiny red brick houses. Coal smoke came from squat chimneys, a few with television antennae reaching skyward like grasping hands. On one whitewashed wall the graffiti read: GOD MADE THE CATHOLICS AND THE ARMALITE MADE THEM EQUAL. Men doing nothing gathered in small groups on the sidewalks while young children played in the streets in relative freedom from traffic that was largely nonexistent.

At the intersection of Leeson Street and Sullivan's Alley the Corkscrew was a fading monument to better times. Across a large front window, half shrouded on the inside by a dark green curtain hanging from a brass rail stretched from one side to the other, the words THE CORKSCREW BAR AND GRILL were written in a once gilt scroll. Time had obliterated much of the gilt but enough remained for it to be legible.

3 2 9

Deirdre pushed open one of the frosted glass doors and walked in. A long mirrored bar was to her right. On the wall to her left were framed pictures of Patrick Pearse and Eamon de Valera, alongside the Proclamation of Irish Independence of 1916.

Irishmen and Irishwomen: In the name of God and of the dead generations from which she receives her old tradition of nationhood, Ireland, through us, summons her children to the flag and strikes for her freedom . . .

Beyond that was a poster with the glaring headline WANTED FOR MURDER crowning an almost life-sized picture of the face of a scowling Mrs. Thatcher. Under her picture, in lesser but still readable type, was the plea: "Remember our brothers who are fighting and dying for freedom, and who are unjustly imprisoned at Long Kesh. Contribute to the Committee to End Oppression in Northern Ireland."

The subdued conversation among three middle-aged men in old suit jackets and baggy trousers who had been drinking stout at the bar when Deirdre came in stopped suddenly as they looked at her with suspicion. A young boy who had been sweeping up the sawdust on the floor disappeared through a door at the far end of the room, leaving Deirdre awkwardly alone in the filtered light coming through the front window. The atmosphere, if solidified, would have taken on the form of an iconoclast's raised fist.

The far door opened and the boy reappeared, followed by Costello.

"Mr. Costello?" inquired Deirdre.

"I'm Tim Costello, Mrs. O'Brien, at your service. What brings you to the Corkscrew?"

"You know me, Mr. Costello? I'm flattered."

"Call me Tim, please, Mrs. O'Brien. After this morning, you on the telly and all, who in Belfast wouldn't? What can I do for you? Sit over here and we'll have a pint."

"Thank you very much, but not right now. I do want to talk with you, however. I need your help. Can we talk privately? It won't take long."

"Certainly. Let's go to me car. That should be private enough, then I can be takin' you home at the same time. It's not well for you to be here, Mrs. O'Brien."

"Why not? I'm a Catholic, as I'm sure you are. And this is a Catholic bar, is it not?"

Costello smiled. "That it is, Mrs. O'Brien. But we've got some strange ones that come in—a loose cannon every now and then. The lads there at the bar, they're all right except they've got no jobs. If they see someone from the Shankill or strangers who look like trouble, they'll have a wee word with them. Yourself, now, anybody can see that you're not huntin' for trouble so they didn't trouble you. They'll ask me, though, why you come, and I'm going to tell 'em you came on Jerry Fitt's say-so, lookin' to have a word with the wee small boys who do the fightin'. Jobs for 'em, Mrs. O'Brien—you can see to that—or else everybody who's standin' on corners now will be going around pulling triggers."

Outside, Costello again asked the question: "What can I do for you, Mrs. O'Brien? Not trying to hurry you but today the world has caught up with you, acknowledging what so many in Northern Ireland have thought for a long time—that you and Martha Quinlan are ladies worth listenin' to. On this day of all days why aren't you off with your friends, celebrating? What has brought you to a scruffy bar in West Belfast, asking for me?"

"I've celebrated enough, Tim. Why should I call you Tim? I scarcely know you."

"You should call me Tim because I want to be your friend. If I had my way there'd be no fighting. Now tell me—what's the problem?"

"Mr. Costello—Tim—I *have* to find a man called Mark Raven. You know him? Yes—I'm told that you do. I don't know where he is. He's been gone from my life for a matter of days, but it seems like years. We quarreled, *I* quarreled over an issue that I considered so controversial, so vital to me, that I turned my back on him. I've just found out how wrong I was. But that's not the important part. The important part is that I've also found out that he may be actively hunting for a man—a Provo for all I know—who's very dangerous, and who may want to do him harm, even kill him. I think both of them are in Dublin. My information is that you would know, and can help me find Mark."

They were walking slowly toward Costello's car, parked in the lot in back of the pub. The air of self-assurance that normally enveloped her had evaporated. She seemed close to tears. She needed reassurance, and hoped desperately that this total stranger, who was trusted by the Provos, could help her. Where was the calm and steadying voice that would tell her that everything would be all right? If she let Mark be destroyed she would be destroying herself, for she had given herself to him so completely that life could never be the same again.

"Just who is it, Mrs. O'Brien, that your friend Mr. Raven is looking for?"

"I don't know. That's what makes it all the more frustrating. Do you know?"

"Maybe I do and maybe I don't," replied Costello. *The loose cannon—O'Farrell!* "But I'm going to help you all I can. I'll be going south meself. If I can locate Mr. Raven, what must I tell him?"

"Will you take me with you?"

"No, no, Mrs. O'Brien. In the shenanigans that may happen, it'll be no place for a lady, especially you. But I'll be your courier, and I think I can find him."

"Thank God—and thank you, Tim. I don't know who or what you really are, but I trust you. I have to. Now—please tell Mark that I misjudged him terribly, that I now understand about the money, and that I love him all the more for what he

3 3 2

has done." She took a deep breath. "And tell him to come back to me, because we're going to have a baby."

Contrary to what she had expected, Costello's face expanded into a broad smile. "Grand news, Mrs. O'Brien, grand news." His whole expression seemed to twinkle. "Now ain't that somethin'! I'll tell him that right away—and not forgettin' your other messages either."

"I'll be so grateful to you, Tim. Tell Mark to call me at once." They had arrived at Tim's old car. "You can drop me at Saint Mary's Hospital. One more thing—don't let anything happen to Mark. I just don't know what I would do without him."

Costello looked at Deirdre, seeing in her vestiges of old loyalties, old lost horizons. As she waited for him to open the door, he patted her reassuringly on her arm.

"I promise to do my best, Mrs. O'Brien. Hop in."

FARNBOROUGH, ENGLAND—THE FOLLOWING DAY

"I don't suppose, Mr. Ben-Udris, that you'd like to reveal to Her Majesty's government just exactly how the Mossad was able to relieve the Libyans of such a handsome haul of bullion? I haven't read of any gunplay involving you fellows, and other than the suicide of the Libyan finance minister—they say he was an alcoholic—the news out of Tripoli has been remarkably dull."

Sir Alistair Widener and Saul Ben-Udris were sitting off to themselves in the VIP lounge at the Royal Air Force Base at Farnborough, twenty miles from London. Across the room Peter Lindsay and two representatives of the Bank of England were talking with Group Captain Whittlesey, the base commander.

Ben-Udris chuckled. "Well, not 'just exactly,' Sir Alistair. You know what some misinformed people say about us Jews—'Everything they touch turns to gold.' Let's just say it was the Midas touch. But what about the arms? It seems to us that you lifted that whole shipment with monumental ease."

"It wasn't that easy, Mr. Ben-Udris, and we had plenty of help. You know how these things go." Sir Alistair had every reason to believe that the secrets of Operation Pleiades would remain secure. All of the voluntary participants except Commander Bochenkev had been released and flown home from Gibraltar after having been sworn to secrecy. Petrovskiy's death had been confirmed through intelligence sources, and Soroshkin had been whisked away to a safe house in Scotland for exhaustive debriefing by naval intelligence under Captain Jeremy Lewis. "Peter tells me you're leaving London."

"That's true, Sir Alistair, at the end of the month. I'll be in Tel Aviv for a while. General Hofi seems to think I'll fit in there."

Moments later the cargo plane that they had all been expecting landed with its cargo of bullion, picked up from an airport near the Italian side of Lake Lugano. On board, in addition to the RAF flight crew, were the two Mossad men who had successfully spirited the bullion out of Switzerland.

In half an hour the Bank of England representatives had tallied the gold and Ben-Udris had his requested receipt. As he and his two recently arrived companions were leaving to return to London, Sir Alistair went over to have a last word.

"It's certain you're going farther up the ladder, Mr. Ben-Udris. May all of your operations be as successful as this one. What has that fertile mind of yours conjured up for the future?"

The Israeli's smile was enigmatic as he replied, "Two things, Sir Alistair. First, I'd like to take Ilyich Ramirez-Sanchez, the world's most audacious terrorist—the one whom we all know as Carlos—alive, and secondly, to collar the man who's pressing him hard for top honors in that slimy world, Abu Nidal."

"Amen to that, my dear fellow," said Sir Alistair. "If you need a little British folderol in your efforts, let us know. Good luck."

Wallace Spenser-Smith, Britain's chief of mission at its embassy in Washington and MI-6's ranking intelligence officer in the United States, was making his instructions very clear. He was talking to Commander Richard Fordyce, Royal Navy, currently on a six months' tour of duty at the Electric Boat Division of the General Dynamics Corporation at Groton, Connecticut, a principal builder of nuclear submarines for the United States Navy. Certain components that end up in British nuclear submarines are also built there. On short notice Fordyce had been summoned to Washington by the British naval attaché, Captain Roger Pendleton, who was also sitting in on the meeting held in Spenser-Smith's office.

"A Dr. Stefan Nagy, a British subject and Cambridge professor," said Spenser-Smith, "is being retained by the Royal Navy to work closely as a consultant with Mr. John Richmond, the managing engineer at the Armstrong-Vickers Shipbuilding Group's yard at Barrow-in-Furness. When Nagy arrives at Groton tomorrow, meet him at the train, accord him all possible courtesy, introduce him to all of the available brass, and show him around. But don't let him out of your sight, even if he wants to take a leak. Be very cordial, but also be sure that he sees *nothing* of a classified nature, written or visual. Take him to lunch, show him tender loving care, then *escort* him back to New York. Be seen with him publicly as much as possible, especially at the airport when you put him on the plane back to London. If he's of a mind, give him high tea in the Palm Court at the Plaza, or dinner at Twenty-One. Be a chum, or look like one. You'll be in uniform, of course. Then back to Groton with you. Incidentally the pitch is that he was in New York on other business and came to Electric Boat at the suggestion of A-V. I'm told he will not ask a lot of questions."

"That's it?" said Fordyce.

"That's it," replied Spenser-Smith. "Short and sweet. 'Give my regards to Broadway' and to wherever else that song mentions."

As Commander Fordyce left, Spenser-Smith turned to the naval attaché. "Sorry, Rog, to usurp your prerogatives, but I was ordered to pass on these somewhat abrupt instructions personally."

"No sweat, old son. Happy to oblige. I don't suppose you want to tell me what this is all about?"

"Believe me, chum, you'd be the first to know if I knew myself. But I'm totally in the dark. I'm going on a short trip to London a week from tomorrow, so maybe I'll learn something. If it's passable info—as it probably won't be, you know how these things are—I'll clue you in."

It was a euphoric Dmitri who reported to the KGB's London *rezident* that Dr. Nagy was now to be a consultant to the Armstrong-Vickers Shipbuilding Group, working closely with the top people at A-V's yard at Barrow. The Soviets would at last penetrate a long-time prime target. Furthermore Dmitri could also report that Nagy had been in the United States, presumably to further cement A-V's ties to Electric Boat, and that he had been observed in the company of the Royal Navy's procurement man at that installation, thus—according to Dmitri's reasoning—doubling Nagy's value, as Nagy would, in time, have access to information from Electric Boat as well.

A month after Roger Delafield returned from Operation Pleiades he began feeding Nagy flawed information, close enough to the mark to allay suspicion, but incorporating carefully contrived technical irregularities. In due course Nagy, still at Cambridge but stripped of his other consultancies, passed this information along to his new KGB control, an enigmatic man known to him only as Igor, Dmitri having been promoted and transferred to Mexico City. Sometimes the information was not strictly technical but of a more general nature, information that British Intelligence knew would become public knowledge in a matter of days. Known in the trade as OBE (overtaken by events) info, it was of no great significance but calculated to give Nagy the appearance of having prior knowledge of and access to vital classified information.

In all cases his reports were received with mounting gratification, with much of the technical information being incorporated into Soviet submarine design. It was not until a year later, when fires broke out on two Soviet nuclear-powered submarines cruising in almost identical areas in the Sea of Japan—fires that might well have resulted in meltdowns in the reactors—that Soviet nuclear engineers began to question the value of their purloined material and to reassess what they had once eagerly embraced. In true Soviet fashion, however, the word never got back to the KGB and Nagy continued with his subtle disinformation, collecting between twenty and twenty-five thousand pounds yearly from the KGB, sums turned over to the Royal Navy Relief Fund.

KILTIMAGH—COUNTY MAYO
TINKER TERRITORY
19 SEPTEMBER 1979

Two hours after he left Dublin O'Farrell had cleared Longford, a notorious traffic bottleneck where three main highways converge, had crossed the Shannon, and was approaching Strokestown on the N5 motorway. It was eight-thirty and the long twilight of a September evening was just giving way to darkness.

He switched on his lights. *Another hour,* he thought, *and I should be at the church.* As he settled back in the driver's seat, a glance in his rearview mirror revealed a set of headlights closing up on him despite his speed of better than seventy miles an hour. He accelerated, and after a moment was relieved to see that he was holding his distance.

Then—trouble. At close to eighty miles an hour he cleared the brow of a hill to find himself almost on top of a string of cars trailing a slow-moving flatbed truck carrying an oversized mobile home. Flashing lights and a sign: CAUTION—WIDE LOAD, were enough to slow down all but those who had reason to believe they might be pursued.

Cursing to himself, O'Farrell made his move. If the cops were behind him he'd have to get through Strokestown before this lumbering mass held everybody up. Swinging wide to the right and with no idea of what might be approaching from the opposite direction he passed the six cars that were trailing the truck with the wide load, and was just getting by the flatbed itself when he saw that a car was coming straight at him in the right-hand lane. With a super human effort he was just able

3 3 8

to squeeze back into the left-hand lane between the big flat-bed and its lead pickup truck with its corresponding sign CAUTION—WIDE LOAD, to warn those approaching from the opposite direction. His speed was such, however, that he hit the rear of the pickup with sufficient force to smash its taillight and to leave the rear license plate dangling by a single screw.

The driver of the pickup pulled off the road on the left, expecting O'Farrell to do likewise. O'Farrell, however, now all the more concerned to put as much distance between himself and anyone coming after him, and neither knowing or caring whether or not he had damaged his own car, sped off into Strokestown. *Screw 'em all! Nobody knows where I'm headed anyway!*

Which was true, but two irate truck drivers had not only a good description of the car he was driving but the license plate number as well.

A basic tenet of Gypsy culture is to keep themselves apart from whatever society they live in. In Ireland and England they are called tinkers, and by convention and choice try to live outside the legal system as well. Most people think Gypsies will steal just about anything that's not nailed down, including cattle and horses. As a result they are a minority group not welcome for long in any one place. Many stay in Ireland, roaming the countryside to feed off Irish rural society, where a large number of farmers and small tradespeople provide a constituency to give them a living from mending pots and pans or making wooden spoons and bowls, or telling fortunes.

Renée's Uncle Tomas and her cousin Lucasci had become reasonably skilled ironworkers, traveling with a portable forge in the back of a battered pickup truck. In the winter months Tomas would move his motley entourage to the southern counties of Wexford, Waterford, or Cork, where some farmers would even allow him to shoe a remaining plowhorse. In the summer and fall, however, he liked the northern counties of the Republic, where extra pounds could be made smuggling pigs into Northern Ireland. Sometimes caught, he never went to jail, suffering only the loss of his contraband. The lay-by at Kiltimagh was a favorite camping ground, remote enough so that it was usually a fortnight, even a month, before the Garda had had enough of the Gypsies to tell Tomas to take his traveling family group and get the hell along.

When O'Farrell reached Swinford it was totally dark. Confident now that he was not being followed, he had lessened his speed, and only after turning off the N5 did he stop to assess any damage to the car he had hijacked from Fitzsimmons. A crumpled fender was the extent of it. He pressed on, looking for the church.

In the high beam of his headlights he soon picked it up, on the right-hand side of the road. A graceful red brick structure, it was surrounded by a matching brick wall. A graveled parking area separated the front of the church from the road. O'Farrell pulled in with a sigh of relief, cut his lights, got out, urinated, then had a look around. Aided by a flashlight he discovered that like many other churches in Ireland, this one had a burial ground to one side, inside the brick wall. Away from the parking area, but affording ready access to the graveyard, was a lych-gate, a peak-roofed structure about ten feet long, to allow pallbearers a place to set a coffin on the ground, under cover, while awaiting the arrival of the priest.

The lych-gate fascinated him. He had seen one before, but never examined it close up. With his flashlight he looked it all over, from top to bottom, ignorant of its purpose. He found that there was a flat wooden ceiling under the pitched roof, open at both ends, creating a space about eight inches high hidden by horizontal boards. Standing on a side railing, he looked inside. Two empty beer bottles and pigeon droppings were all that he saw.

He went to the car's trunk, got the M-16 and the ammunition clips, and stashed them away over the ceiling in the lych-gate, wrapped in the same blanket in which he had found them.

His ankle felt so much better that he left the purloined cane in the car, locked it, and took off on foot for the lay-by, half a mile down the road. *What made me hide the rifle? I don't know, but it was the smart thing to do.* He felt invincible. It was a dangerous feeling.

O'Rourke listened with astonishment and dismay as Fitzsimmons told him what had happened.

"The bloody bastard's crazy, Nolan, and that's for sure. Here you're offerin' him a way out of certain big trouble, and what does he do? He fookin' near breaks me arm, grabs me keys, and is off quicker'n you can say Sweet Molly Malone. I hope he gets lost and drives over the Cliffs of Moher."

"No, we don't want that, Frank. It's important that O'Farrell gets to Mullaghmore—and that he shows up when he's supposed to." Fitzsimmons had not been told of the death sentence imposed on O'Farrell by the IRA's Chief of Staff. "Where's the M-16 we were sending to Mahoney?"

"Locked in the trunk of the car."

"Sweet Jesus! He'll find it for sure, and that'll compound our troubles. What did you say he said about being there—Mullaghmore, I mean."

"He said to tell you he'd be there—at three A.M. on the twentieth, for sure."

"Can you add anything to that? Did he say *anything* that might indicate where he was going?"

"Nary a word, Nolan. I don't know what your interest in O'Farrell is, but if I never see him again it'll be soon enough.

An' I'm coming back on the train. I got no car and I'm fookin' fair fed up with answering to those snotty Brits at Belcoo."

It was a worried O'Rourke who hung up. What if O'Farrell didn't show up at Mullaghmore? He'd have Wee Eddie and his boat there just in case, but if O'Farrell was a no-show, he'd have to answer to Tiernan. He shuddered to think of the consequences.

The road from Swinford to Kiltimagh is a secondary one, paved, with only a few gentle changes in elevation and a single long curve between the church and the village. The area is one of small farms and cottages, and agriculture the principal means of support. Kiltimagh is a village not big enough to support a post office, but there is a grocery store and a bakery, plus the predictable pub, the Whistling Pig, more commonly referred to as O'Neill's. Tinkers not welcome.

O'Farrell had no trouble seeing, even in the absence of a moon, as the night was clear and the stars out. Occasionally he switched on his flashlight, principally to see what was on either side of the road, as it occurred to him that he might have to make his way back to the church in the dark as well, and cover was an essential element, as any ex-Marine was well aware.

A hundred yards before he reached his goal he knew he was coming up on the lay-by. This particular one was something of an anachronism—one of the few found anywhere in Ireland on a secondary road. Until the early 1930s it had been part of an imposing entrance to a great house belonging to an Irish industrialist, wiped out in the Great Depression. His ruin was complete when a disastrous fire gutted the house. Over the years the front gates had been vandalized and disappeared but the graveled expanse remained, now casually paved to serve the touring public.

O'Farrell could see a cluster of caravans parked in a semicircle, covered-wagon style. There was a dim light shining through a small window on the closest one. He brushed it with his flashlight. It was painted a bright red, with white trim, the only one in these colors. *Hot damn! There's my girl!* A child's toy lay on the ground, and he was careful to avoid it. Moving quietly he went to the door and gently knocked.

Renée had been sitting on the bed, waiting for him. At his knock she got up at once and went to the door, having seen the beam of his flashlight as it passed over the window. She was dressed in a pair of blue satin pajamas, a late acquisition from Texarkana, Texas, and her jet black curly hair was swept back and held in place by a tortoise-shell and rhinestone barrette. The ever-present gold earrings were there, moving as she turned her head. A single strand of imitation pearls hung around her neck. She had prepared herself carefully for Mike. A radio was playing softly, tuned to a station in Sligo.

The full warmth of her greeting was not apparent until after she had opened the door and pulled him inside, finger on lips to denote silence. Before he could say anything she had embraced him with a long and lingering kiss, then pulled him down beside her as she once again sat on the bed.

"Mikey, mon," she said, "welcome to my little home. But you must be quiet. My uncle would raise hell with me, beat me too, perhaps, if he knew *gazhe* were here. He doesn't trust outsiders." She was calling him Mikey, not Mickey. He liked that.

He looked around him. A kerosene lamp, its rays dimmed by a rose-colored silk shade from which hung gold-threaded tassels, was clamped to a small built-in table. Designed for no more than two people to live and travel in comfortably, the caravan was equipped with electric lights operative only when hooked up to a common source at a campsite. The lay-by had no such source. In the pinkish rays of the lamp O'Farrell could make out two Kewpie dolls sitting on a shelf, their blue eyes staring at him from rosy-cheeked faces in expressions of eternal surprise, arms and legs spread wide apart, fugitives from some long-forgotten carnival midway. A plastic vase filled with dried flowers was on another shelf.

On one of the brown-stained veneer walls a dart board sprouting four darts hung next to an unlikely crucifix, a gift from Sister Teresa, one of the two Sisters of Charity—eager for a convert—who had been indispensable to Renée in helping her to get first a birth certificate and then her passport. The bed—another could emerge from the small plastic-covered settee in the cramped living area—was covered with a knitted spread in a red and yellow pattern against a black background. On it were two garish, fringed pillows, one with a picture of Blackpool's big Ferris wheel on it and the other displaying two crested Malay cockatoos in all of their unbelievably wild colors. A Mickey Mouse clock, yellow gloved hands pointing to the hour, hung on another wall, its monotonous ticking adding another quality to an already unusual scene. On the small two-burner stove an incense burner, just extinguished, gave off the sweet smell of sandalwood. Despite Renée's obvious appeal, the atmosphere was decidedly kitsch.

"So this is the way Gypsies live?" said Mike. "Renée, honey, count me in. I don't know if I'm ever going to leave."

He leaned toward her to kiss her again. As he did so she lay back on the bed, pulling him over on top of her. In the distance a dog barked and at Castlebar, the county seat fifteen miles away by road, the Garda was stirring.

LONDON—LATE EVENING

Bloody fucking hell! And shit thrown in for good measure! All the planning and all the scheming gone out the window! Now—how to find O'Farrell, how to get him to Mullaghmore? What if the Garda gets in the act?

Lindsay's obscenities were of the mind only as he sat

with Sir Alistair and Chief Superintendent Detective Fereyes to contemplate the next move in the battle of wits between the two opposing forces. The table on which the jigsaw puzzle was being assembled had been kicked and the pieces were in disarray. O'Rourke's knowledge had soon become O'Ryan's knowledge and word of O'Farrell's unexpected bolt had been passed speedily to Whitehall.

Lindsay was alarmed. He blamed himself for having been too sanguine in believing that TESS could count on the Provos to themselves deliver O'Farrell to the rendezvous point.

"We've got to get to Raven—right away," he said. "I'm not at all certain that O'Farrell, who's almost schizophrenic in my view, hasn't taken off after Raven—object, murder. On the other hand O'Farrell may buy our story that Raven is wanted as an accomplice, and for reasons unknown contact him for help in getting to Mullaghmore. One reason he may do this would be because of distrust of what O'Rourke has been telling him. It's a slim reed, but it's the only game in town."

Fereyes, steel trap mind poised, agreed.

"You're right, Major Lindsay. Who's left in Dublin of your group sent there to back up Raven before you sent him back to Raven Park?"

"Only Summers. Good with his fists, but otherwise unarmed."

"That's enough. Call Raven now, then send Summers up to Raven Park. His presence alone may be enough to halt any mischief. For appearances' sake he can be just a friend on a short visit."

With nods all around, Lindsay picked up the phone.

"I'll inform Whitelaw at once," said Sir Alistair. "He has explicit instructions from the PM to keep her fully informed, hourly if the situation changes—as it surely has. This is a change of major proportions."

* * *

In addition to their mutual attraction, tacitly acknowledged seven months earlier on that flight from Heathrow to Shannon, Renée and O'Farrell had brought great expectations to this next meeting. Seduction, uninhibited and classy at the same time, is a rare commodity, and O'Farrell had once been its lucky recipient. He had had many women in his life, but none more unforgettable than Gabrielle, a solitary remnant of the glory days of French colonialism in Vietnam. Trying to sustain herself and the memories of pre-Dien Bien Phu days by running a gift shop on the Rue Toutant, the older, wiser and lonelier woman had stumbled across the good-looking American soldier while he was in Saigon on leave. His animal magnetism had attracted her at once and she made him her own. Her image stayed with him and O'Farrell was unconsciously seeking her when he found Renée. *Hell, Renée's a French name, isn't it?*

In the preceeding February Renée was bringing back to rural Ireland lasting memories of the great American southwest. Then all of a sudden there she was, sitting on a plane next to and talking with a good-looking *gazhe* who seemed to like her—and he kissed her good-bye. She fantasized about that, and about him, dreaming of roaming around the great expanses of the U.S.A. with him. He would be driving one of those big mobile homes—land yachts, really, the ninety-thousand-dollar kind—with two or three kids in the commodious living quarters.

They lay on the bed, embracing. O'Farrell's hand was under her pajama top, stroking her bare back, as he kissed her lips and eyelids, holding her close to him. Renée, after gently extricating herself, swung one leg over him to sit on him, astride his hips. Then, with a kind of ceremonial deliberation, she took off the pearl necklace and her earrings and loosened her hair. She unbuttoned the top of her pajamas and let it drop to the floor. She had nothing on underneath. She shook her

3 4 6

head until her hair fell around her face. O'Farrell, aflame with desire, reached up to caress her breasts and to pull her down to kiss her again. Tiny, inarticulate sounds of pleasure were coming from her as she moved to one side and started to remove O'Farrell's clothes. She was a natural and spontaneous toucher and used her hands to advantage, arousing him all the more in the process. When she had finished she slid out of the bottom of her pajamas and stood by the side of the bed. In the pink glow of the tasseled lamp she was inexplicably beautiful.

"You like me, Mikey?"

"You're gorgeous, Renée. Do I like you? Yes, I like you. In fact, I'm nuts about you. I'd like to stay here with you for a long, long time."

It was just what she wanted to hear. She lay down next to him again. "Maybe we go back to America together? I won't be a Gypsy anymore. And I'll be real nice to you." *Nice* was a favorite word with her, overworked and with far deeper meaning than in its ordinary use.

The suggestion was lost on O'Farrell. Her mouth was too inviting to be wasted in conversation. She responded passionately as his open mouth was pressed to hers and her fingers tightened on his back as, legs apart, she guided him to her.

"Come to me, Mikey, mon. I've waited for you for a long time, too. Come to me. I'm ready."

As he thrust himself into her she started to laugh, but then the laugh became a soft moan. Her legs began to tremble and she tightened up all over. She sucked in her breath, held it, then let it out in short spurts. And again. And again. She rose against him, hooking her heels behind his hips.

The tempo increased. Unable to restrain herself, Renée moved her hips up and down, faster and faster, totally absorbed in her own pleasure. It built and built until she felt utterly possessed by the rapture of the moment. She wrapped her legs around his waist and abandoned herself to ecstasy as the fire streaked down her nerves to envelop her whole body as she came. She could not talk and her breath seemed to be caught in her throat, then suddenly it burst out all at once.

They were quiet for a long time. Renée felt warm, as if she were glowing. When their breathing subsided, she could hear the dog barking in the distance. O'Farrell was heavy on top of her, but she did not want him to move . . . she liked his weight and the faint tang of perspiration from his skin, whiter than hers. From time to time he moved his head to brush his lips against her cheek.

She stirred and he rolled off her, onto his back. Leaning over him she glided one of her shallow, unfrightening breasts into his waiting mouth. Her fingertips began to play lightly around his lips, quick little butterfly touches, and then move down to his chest and stomach. She saw him start to grow hard and erect again. She touched him there, then leaned over with her cheek next to his, her black hair cascading over them both, to whisper, "Mikey, mon, you remind me of a unicorn—a beautiful unicorn. Last time was for me. This time for you. I make you feel nice—real nice, Gypsy style. Wait."

She arose and went to the two-burner stove. A moment later she returned to slide him quickly into her mouth. Her mouth was hot, filled with warm water.

He gasped, overcome by almost unbearable pleasure as she moved her mouth up and down. "Oh, Jesus!" he cried out, seizing her head to hold her to him. The voluptuous spouting seemed not to come from within his own body but was a tide pouring through him, drenching them both, like an all-enveloping flood. He arched his back as his head thrashed from side to side, involuntarily in paroxysms of uncontrollable rapture.

Garda officers Tom Shanahan and Dermot McSwain pulled away from the police station just before 10 P.M. With four other members of Ireland's national police force they comprised the total complement assigned to County Mayo's Castlebar station, responsible for law and order in one of Ireland's poorer and less populated counties. This night's territorial assignment lay in the easternpart of the county, one that was divided into two almost equal parts by Loch Mask on the south and Loch Conn on the north. They would cruise from Castlebar to Ballinrobe, then to Claremorris and into Balla. Custom dictated tea from the thermos at that point, then on to Kiltimagh and Swinford. Left at Swinford to Foxford, then to Strade, Bellavary, and back to Castlebar, arriving about 5:00 A.M. Alternate routes on alternate days. Write the report, then off to home, breakfast, and bed—barring unforeseen incidents along the way.

At 10:30 P.M. the incessant chatter on the radio ceased as the hourly broadcast to all stations and squad cars came on the air from the main northern barracks at Roscommon. Shanahan, notepad and pencil at the ready, listened as the usual litany of things, people, and events to be watched for began: a fire at Kilkelly—not on their route tonight; two traffic accidents, one serious, on the N5; a bridge out at Ballyhaunis, and trees down due to local heavy rains. Loose cattle at Hollymount. More inconsequential stuff, most of it off their beat. Then came the APA—the all points alert. "Hit-and-run accident east of Strokestown. Offending vehicle is dark blue four-door Ford Cortina sedan, license number 32-152, headed northwest on N five. If sighted, stop and apprehend. Report location of interception. Over."

"Well, there's one number we can play bingo with," said Shanahan, writing it down. "Maybe he'll look in on us."

"Not bloody likely, that one. The plates, Tom, were issued in Northern Ireland—look at the first two numbers. For my money Mr. Accident headed for the border, especially since there's no mention of personal injury. The word will be there before he is, but the chances are he doesn't know that, so he'll get nabbed regardless of where he tries to cross."

The village next to Balla is Kiltimagh. As the squad car approached the lay-by a short distance beyond the village going in the direction of Swinford, McSwain slowed down and switched on the car's spotlight, adjustable from the inside.

"Fookin' tinkers," he said, "look at the mess they make. I'd like to run 'em all in. They've been in this bloody lay-by long enough, keepin' everybody else out. Tomorrow we'll find a good enough reason to move 'em out of here—and out of County Mayo if I have my way."

The squad car had stopped opposite the lay-by, a traffic infraction of which McSwain would never be guilty in daylight hours. He moved the beam of the spotlight from one end of the cluster of vehicles to the other several times. Next to Tomas's pickup truck were two old passenger cars. Beyond them were the caravans, four including Renée's red and white one—the newest of the lot. Laundry hung on a line between two of them. A bag of charcoal, its contents spilling out, lay on the ground beside a wheeled grill. Next to it was a chicken coop with three live chickens in it and next to that another from which the pink eyes of a child's pet rabbits shone back at the Garda men. Then two aluminum beach chairs, one broken and leaning forward precariously on two legs only. A tricycle lay on its side, surrounded by candy bar wrappers and empty soft drink cans.

In Renée's caravan O'Farrell stirred uneasily as Renée, totally nude, left the bed to look furtively out of a small window covered by a venetian blind of thin metal slats. *God, what a build!* thought O'Farrell. *And what a lover! I'm going to have to stick around for some more of this.*

Renée stood and watched until the spotlight was turned off and the car moved on.

"It's the Garda," she whispered as she came back to bed, "but they've gone along."

"Which way did they go?"

"Toward the church, and Swinford."

3 5 0

"Jesus! They'll find my car." *Thank God I stashed that rifle away!*

"What difference will that make, sweet mon?" Renée snuggled up closer to him.

"Maybe none—maybe a lot. We'll have to wait and see."

At the edge of the church parking area McSwain stopped the car again and switched on the spotlight. The rear of Fitzsimmons's car was facing the road, its rear license plate in plain view. In the spotlight's beam Shanahan recognized the number at once.

"Well, I'm a monkey's uncle!" he exclaimed. "There's the car on the APA. Let's have a look."

Guns drawn, the two officers advanced on the car. Minutes later they had access, had looked in the glove compartment and the trunk, had noted the crumpled left fender—the clincher—and had radioed the Roscommon barracks that the APA had had its effect and that the car had been located in the parking area at the Church of Saint Barnabas, Kiltimagh. No sign of driver anywhere. Instructions: Drive or tow it to the Garda station at Castlebar.

A half hour later O'Farrell, alert to the danger arising from the discovery of the car, was just about to leave Renée to find his way back to the church through the fields when the squad car returned, lights flashing and Fitzsimmons's car in tow, on its way to the Castlebar station.

Christ almighty! Marooned! thought O'Farrell, peering through the slatted blinds of Renée's darkened van. *What now? The bastards will be back, sure as hell, looking for the driver. I gotta get outa here!*

TOWARD MULLAGHMORE
THE WHISTLEBLOWER
20 SEPTEMBER 1979

LA FLÈCHE, EURE-ET-LOIR, FRANCE
—MIDNIGHT, 24 MAY 1945

The roofless grain mill, damaged by artillery fire, stood next to an arched stone bridge beneath which the body of a dead German soldier had been given shallow burial by Captain Mark Raven and two of his maquisards *of the* Armes Secrete. *In the game of silence he had been dispatched several hours before by a knife thrust to the stomach, after Mark had effectively yoked him from behind. He had been part of a German night patrol searching for the French irregulars who were successfully throwing roadblocks in the way of the 2nd Panzer Division, Das Reich, on its tortuous way to Normandy.*

The ground floor windows and door of the mill appeared intact, a good enough place for Mark and his men to seek a few hours' rest. Inside, grain dust and the smell of it was pervasive—pleasantly so, in marked contrast to the destruction all around them. Mark dropped his knapsack to the floor, sat down, and leaned back against the wall, bone tired and weary to the point of exhaustion. After an hourly watch schedule had been set up with Louis Broussard, a baker from Toulon, and with Jacques Giraud, a one-eyed ex-convict from Marseilles who gloried in killing Germans, he dropped off to sleep, his head on his knapsack and his radio by his side. In moments— it seemed no longer—Baker Street was calling BLUE BOY, his code name, with new instructions.

3 5 2

* * *

Awake, Mark reached over to retrieve his radio, to pull himself out of a deep sleep and try to comprehend the message. He looked around him. The dream, the mill, and Louis and Jacques were all gone. He was at Raven Park. Instead of reaching for his radio at La Fleche he was reaching for his ringing bedside phone. The voice was accented and unfamiliar but the gist of the message came through urgently, loud and clear. He listened carefully, wrote down what he had been told, then said, "I'll be there," and hung up. Moments later he had called Lindsay, left a message, and was called back as he was throwing on his clothes.

"Peter, this looks like what we've been waiting for. I've just had a call from a woman who identified herself as a Gypsy named Renée. She says she has O'Farrell in her caravan at Kiltimagh in County Mayo. That's about forty miles from here. O'Farrell is stranded—no way of getting to Mullaghmore and time's running out on him. She can't take him there or get anybody in her band of brothers to take him, because to do so would expose her to ostracism and probably to a helluva beating. She had walked to a phone box to call me, as O'Farrell is afraid that Garda's looking for him. He wants me to come get him and take him to the docks in Mullaghmore."

Lindsay interrupted with a question. "Did she say why the Garda's hunting for him?"

"No, she didn't," answered Mark. "She may not know herself."

Raven listened again to Lindsay's further questions. "Yes, I know exactly where it is. I can get there in an hour. I'm on my way."

He put down the phone and hurried to the kitchen to brew a cup of tea. While waiting for the pot to boil, his incipient trouble hit him again—this time a sharp pain in the upper part of his left chest, radiating down his arm. It worried him, but he laid it to his sudden awakening. By the time he had finished his tea it had moderated. He picked up his .45 automatic, tucked it in his belt under his sweater, and was off.

Hiding out with a tinker woman! thought Lindsay. Clever bastard! Why the hell is the Garda after him? We'd better coordinate with Belfast, quick. But not until Sir Alistair gets the word.

"Remember," said Sir Alistair, after listening to Lindsay's report, "the PM is not interested in a wild scene and a dead outlaw. She wants O'Farrell delivered intact—to stand trial in Britain, not Dublin. When he killed MacKenzie, O'Farrell not only twisted the tail of the lioness, he wounded her as well. And the PM is no wounded lioness to fool with."

"Sir Alistair," replied Peter, "an hour ago we didn't know where our man was. Now he's back in our sights—and the rest of the pieces are in place. Tell Mrs. Thatcher she can count on us."

"Can Raven do all this?" asked Sir Alistair. "After all he's no spring chicken."

"Granted, Sir Alistair, but he's a man with a mission. He'll deliver."

"Did you get him?" Renée had just returned to the caravan. O'Farrell was dressed and ready to go. "If not, I'm taking off on my own." He was thinking about the hidden M-16, with which he could hijack another vehicle.

"Yes, I got him," said Renée breathlessly. "He said he's coming right away—and knows where we are."

"That's my girl," replied O'Farrell, "you're a sweetheart. Renée, I'm going to miss the hell out of you. When I get to where I'm going I'll send for you, and we'll have some more good times together."

3 5 4

"Why are you running, sweet mon? You very nice mon, but you're on the lam. Tell me why."

"This and that." Despite his best efforts at nonchalance O'Farrell's anxiety was beginning to show. "I was speeding, coming up here from Dublin, and I hit another car. I didn't stop because I was anxious to see you, honey. That's all."

Renée sighed with relief. "I'm glad. I was afraid maybe you kill somebody. Gypsies always moving. But you come back to me. We make love again, sweet mon. You do that real nice."

"Baby, you're the best. I'll be back—I promise."

He kissed her and settled down to wait for Mark Raven and his ride out of Ireland.

In Belfast Nolan O'Rourke—the commander, no less, of the 2nd Provisional Brigade, the Irish Republican Army— made a decision that would bring him kneecapping and worse if anyone discovered what he had done. He called the Garda to blow the whistle on Mike O'Farrell.

He made no attempt to disguise his voice. He had never talked with the Garda before and never expected to again. He would tell no one that he had reported Fitzsimmons's car as stolen, and obviously didn't give his own name in making the report. He did say, however, that the man who he *thought* had taken the car was armed and dangerous and would be heading for Mullaghmore from the south.

Ever since his session with the top hierarchy of the Provos on yesterday's rain-swept morning he had been in anguish over his instructions to kill—there was no other word for it—O'Farrell. It was a strange reaction for a man who would instruct his boys to mine a road, hoping to kill or maim all of the occupants of a British personnel carrier, or to firebomb a known Protestant pub, but he wanted no part of internecine murder, principally because he realized that it could backfire and that he himself could be gunned down in a hail of vengeful bullets. So steer O'Farrell into the hands of the Garda, hope that they would discover enough about him to put him away for good, then make it plain to the Provo chief of staff that O'Farrell had brought it all on himself by hijacking Fitzsimmons's car. And if O'Farrell succeeded in keeping the rendezvous at Mullaghmore, he'd deal with that later.

The Garda officer who took the call at the Collooney barracks made no mention of the fact that the car had been found, but got a full description of O'Farrell. O'Rourke left the phone box feeling that he had at least taken the first step in getting himself off the hook.

As he knifed through the predawn darkness on his way to Kiltimagh Mark's thoughts again returned to Deirdre. Tomorrow would be the day, without fail. Tomorrow he would call her, win, lose or draw. Tomorrow he would be rid of his obligation to bring down the terrorists responsible for MacKenzie's death, would have atoned for his past transgressions made in the name of charity, and could take up again a normal existence. But this time with the goal of restoring himself to grace with Deirdre and getting rid of this increasingly troublesome business of shortness of breath. He'd keep his promise to Charlie Sanner and let his old friend cut and patch to his heart's content. Deirdre had never been to San Francisco and he was looking forward to introducing her to the city of his youth.

He was a fast driver, the roads were deserted, and before he knew it he had almost missed the N17 turnoff at Charlestown to take him to Kilkelly and on down to Kiltimagh. Under his sweater he could feel the reassuring bulge of his automatic pistol. "He's a rough one," Lindsay had said, "But once you reach Mullaghmore O'Farrell will be up against as good as he can dish out."

When Mark pulled into the lay-by the door of Renée's caravan was opened before he could knock. O'Farrell was ready to go.

"This is Renée, my little Gypsy friend," he said by way of introduction. With a ready smile she stuck out her hand.

"Pleased to meetcha, Mr. Raven. Middle of the night no time to call anyone but my sweet mon here, he need you."

"You saw how quickly I came, Renée," replied Mark, looking around. He was breathing with some difficulty but taking everything in. "That means I was glad to. This is a very nice van. All the comforts of home. How does the stove work?"

"It's home for me. Where I go, home goes. Stove works on kerosene—converted from propane by my Uncle Tomas. Kerosene cheap and always available."

"Do you have any excess?" asked Mark.

"Sure. Five-gallon can."

"May I buy it from you?"

"You nice mon. Treat my sweet mon nice. I give it to you."

"Raven, what the hell do you want with five gallons of kerosene?" demanded O'Farrell. "We gotta get the hell outta here. Let's go."

"Never mind—I want it. Renée, you're not to give it to me. I'll buy it from you. Here." He took out his wallet and gave her a ten-pound note.

"You like that girl, don't you, Mike?" Mark had noted the near tearful farewell on Renée's part as they drove off. The atmosphere between himself and O'Farrell was not all that it could be and Mark welcomed the opportunity to talk—or to have Mike talk. He wasn't looking forward to too many questions and certainly not to supplying the answers.

"Yeah. She's a good kid. When I get back to Belfast I'm gonna have her come up. She's Irish, you know, despite being a Gypsy. Born in Cork. I didn't believe it until she showed me her passport."

"I'll be damned. Seems nice enough, and certainly very pretty. But tell me, Mike, why is it so important for you to get to Mullaghmore?" Mark eyed him quizzically, probing.

"I'm to meet Nolan O'Rourke there, and some of his boys." Then he almost blew it, almost blurted out information about his scheduled rendezvous with the submarine that would be delivering the arms, but caught himself, just in time. "I'm going to get a ride back to Belfast in a boat," he managed to say, "around the northern tip of Ireland. No confrontation with the police that way."

"You're telling me that you couldn't just drive across the border? That the Garda's hunting for you?" said Mark.

"It seems that way. Frank Fitzsimmons was going to drive me back up from Dublin, but I took his car—borrowed it, really—so I could get to see Renée. She's a real good kid. I met her on a plane about six months ago. I guess Fitz got edgy and reported the car stolen. Hell, he shouldn't have done that."

Noting where they were, O'Farrell continued by saying, "There's a church just up here on the left. I want to stop there to pick up a semiautomatic rifle and some ammo that, thank God, I had sense enough to stash away there before the police picked up the car."

"You stashed a rifle and some ammo in a church?" Mark was genuinely surprised. "Wasn't it locked?"

"Well, not *in* the church, but outside, over a sort of covered gate leading to the graveyard."

"That's called a lych-gate. Lots of them around these parts—and in England as well."

"Pull in here," said Mike, as they reached the church parking lot. "I hope to Christ the rifle's still there. I won't be but a minute. Leave your lights on so I can see." In moments he was back, rifle and the two ammo jackets in hand.

"Well, I didn't expect anything like this," observed Mark, "but with your rifle and my automatic—and the kerosene—we're well equipped for any opposition."

"What in the name of God is the kerosene for?" replied Mike. "I'm curious as hell. Is it for some sort of gambit you learned in France?"

"You got it, Mike. Maybe we're not going to need it, but it's a great little weapon in a pinch. Get in. We've got a lot of ground to cover—and damn little time to do it."

When O'Rourke left Belfast for Mullaghmore he had planned well, having studied several maps of all the known approaches to that small village to more effectively deploy his forces. He would infiltrate his two contingents of Provos into the Republic by dividing them into two groups—three men in one group and two plus himself in the other—and by taking different routes south. One team would take the long way around and enter at Lifford, in County Donegal, from Strabane, the crossing where the least provocative questioning normally took place. These three, led by a brute of a youth sometimes called the Boston Strangler—primarily because of an often expressed desire to go there to live, and secondarily as a tribute to his capacity for mayhem—would travel in a borrowed pickup truck. O'Rourke had with him the other two, and would cross at Belcoo-Blacklion. The first group would come down the main coast road from Ballyshannon and approach Mullaghmore from the north, while he and his companions would come up from the south—and nobody would have to go through Sligo Town. O'Rourke didn't know where Costello was, having decided he didn't need him anyhow—in fact didn't want him around if O'Farrell made it through the trap that he hoped he had set for him with the Garda.

The Boston Strangler and his lads would be posted just south of Tullaghan, close to the turnoff to Mullaghmore but north of it, while he would position the two other Provos—after they had delivered him to dockside—in his car at Cliffony, just south of the single road leading into Mullaghmore, thus making it impossible for anyone to enter the seaside village unobserved by one or the other of the two groups.

And then there was Wee Eddie. He would have the *Ballintra Lassie* ready to haul them out to Inishmurray, ignorant of the fact that there would be no offshore rendezvous and that he was, in essence, playing the part of the ferryman on the River Styx. But on this trip he would be carrying not the souls of the dead but at least one man whose immortal soul would soon be ready for such a journey, if other men were successful in taking his life—which was the name of the game they were playing.

AT SEA
THE *NOVOSIBIRSK* AGAIN?
THEN A VOICE FROM KOREA
20 SEPTEMBER 1979

A wide-ranging cormorant moved its wings in an effortless rise from the glassy surface of a cheerless gray sea. Drops of water fell from its legs and underbelly as it flew to the west in long sweeping curves, clear of the delicate furrow made by the periscope of the approaching submarine. Less than a foot of a mirrored tube was all that showed above the water.

Below, inside the control room of HMS *Taurus,* Commander Castlewood swung the periscope full circle. To the east the craggy Irish coast, scarcely visible, loomed as a blackened, irregular shape in the dawning hours. The *Taurus* seemed to be quite alone in the cold gray waters of the North Atlantic—but she was not.

Some twenty miles off the northwest coast of Ireland, within sight of the island of Inishmurray, two Soviet fishing trawlers, the *Petri* and the *Vashtilora,* with enough sophisticated electronic equipment aboard to make them effective in their primary role as spy ships, were cruising at reduced speeds half a mile from one another. The emerging day was windless, a rare phenomenon in these latitudes, and an overcast sky would preclude any sunrise.

From a point due east of the two vessels they were under the close scrutiny of British radar, operating from a mobile van parked on Tappaghan Mountain, the highest point in Northern Ireland's County Tyrone, butting up against the Republic's County Donegal, which overlooks the Atlantic Ocean and Sligo Bay. From that strategic installation open lines were being maintained by the Royal Signal Corps to Whitehall and to the temporary staging area of C Squadron, the 2nd Royal Parachute Battalion, alerted and on line for the last phase of Operation Pleiades.

Two hours earlier, at 0304 hours, the *Petri* had acquired a reading on its QR-6 undersea sonarscope of a submarine approaching from the south. Alerted, the *Vashtilora* picked it up also, the two vessels remaining in visual communication with each other by blinker signal.

Captain Wiggins was at the second periscope.

"Well, Jesus bloody Christ," he said to Castlewood, "what do you know? We're here! But we've got company—two unknowns. My God, who the hell are they? Not the

Irish—they're not supposed to be around. This is going to take some doing."

He picked up the Tannoy microphone. "Stand by to surface," he broadcast. "Report main vents. Main blowers, get ready."

A boatswain's mate undid the hatch clips on the lower sail hatch, then stood back to allow Captain Wiggins to go up.

A minute later the first lieutenant reported, "Ready to surface, sir."

From the bottom of the tower Wiggins called back to his XO, "Jimmy, take her up."

"Aye-aye, sir," responded Castlewood. "Boats, let her come up. Blow one, three, and five main ballast."

"Forty feet, sir. Thirty-five, thirty . . ." The ballast pumps hummed softly, running water from aft to forward to compensate for the change in the angle of ascent as the *Taurus* came up.

"Fifteen . . . on the surface. Pressure in the boat, sir."

At the top of the ladder Wiggins unlatched the last remaining hatch clip. He tucked his binoculars firmly into his duffel coat as the boatswain's mate on the ladder below him grabbed his ankles. With the hatch released, the bottled-up air from below roared past him, lifting the skirts of his coat up to his waist.

The hatch fell open and Captain Wiggins stepped out onto the dripping sail bridge.

On the bridge of the *Petri* her captain, alternately cursing the semidarkness and looking in the direction of the submarine through his binoculars, was approached by his radio operator. The submarine had surfaced at 0541 hours a thousand yards to the southwest.

"We have a signal from the as yet unidentified submarine, Captain—an international codebook request for identification, with a reply by semaphore."

The captain pondered. *Probably a British sub, maybe American. We'll reply, but stay in the area to see what's going on.* He dismissed the radio operator and sent for a crewman to respond.

"Tell the submarine who we are. Transmit in Russian. We'll see what happens."

From the bridge the signal went back. "We are the *Petri* and the *Vashtilora,* Soviet trawlers out of Murmansk. We are bound for home after fishing off Iceland. Reciprocal iden requested."

Several minutes went by. Then, to the intense surprise of the *Petri*'s captain, when the blinkered reply was made, it too was in Russian.

"Greetings, comrades, from the people's *Novosibirsk,* Captain First Rank Bereznoy commanding. You are a welcome sight but you are to leave the area immediately. Our presence here is part of a mission for the *Rodina.* Acknowledge."

With little hesitation an answer came back from the *Petri.* Her captain had served in the Soviet navy and knew the power vested in any of the Soviet armed forces. On the bridge of the *Vashtilora* the whole interchange was being monitored.

"Understood, *Novosibirsk.* Greetings to our brothers who serve on the frontiers of our defensive wall. We depart."

Ten minutes later the two trawlers were heading to the northwest under increasing speed.

Aboard HMS *Taurus* Captain Wiggins called down from the sail bridge to Commander Bochenkev, who had been operating the portable blinker light on the deck below.

"Well done, Alexei. What did you tell them?"

"I was a little rusty with this stuff, Captain, but I identified us as the *Novosibirsk*. I told them we were on a mission for Mother Russia and to get the hell out of here."

"Good man. The signal couldn't have been intercepted by anybody else, so we're safe. Now we wait."

In the radar van the movement of the trawlers away from the targeted sight zone was duly noted. The lessening tension was palpable, as it was in Whitehall where the operation was being monitored as if it were a major naval encounter.

As Costello pulled into Mullaghmore midnight had come and gone and the bungalowed terraces, holiday chalets, and caravans drifting down the steep hillside fronting Sligo Bay were asleep. He drove past the principal village parking area overlooking the harbor, then turned inland at the end of the line of houses, inns, and pubs that faced the water, leaving his car parked out of sight but well placed for a quick getaway. He walked back to the stone steps leading down to the massive stone dock, built to withstand the heavy seas that sometimes penetrated the breakwater. A solitary street lamp cast an inadequate light over a scene in which he appeared to be the only actor. The prevailing sound was that of old automobile tires, used as buffers by the boatmen, rubbing against the dock as the boats they protected rose and fell with the lapping tide. No sign of O'Rourke or any of his lads, nor any sign of Wee Eddie and the *Ballintra Lassie*.

He seized the opportunity for a quick reconnaissance. He had spent the previous afternoon studying admiralty charts of Mullaghmore's harbor and its approaches as well as a detailed sketch of the principal stone dock and two ancillary but smaller wooden docks. There was no moon, but with a flashlight he found the dockmaster's office and next to it, as he expected to, a storage shed. By long-standing custom it was for the use of all of the lobstermen and fishermen who docked their boats in the harbor. As he was looking inside he heard a car pull into the graveled parking area. Over the sound of the running motor he could hear voices, then the vehicle was driven away.

In moments a solitary figure, flashlight in hand, started down the stone steps. Costello could hear a half-muffled obscenity as a step was almost missed. The figure advanced.

"Wee Eddie?" It was O'Rourke.

"No, Nolan," replied Costello, "It's Tim. Tim Costello—at your service."

"Christ almighty, Tim, how did you get here? Sure as hell I didn't expect to see you." He didn't add that he might not have wanted to see him.

"I'll answer your question like you've asked it, Nolan—I drove down. But I don't think that's what you want to know. What you want to know is *why* I'm here."

O'Rourke was angry, but his anger was tempered by relief. Costello was not only his friend, but a contemporary as well. The lads—well, the lads would do his bidding because they knew he spoke for the leadership, but he couldn't talk with them the way he could talk with Fitz and Costello. Most of 'em were still wet behind the ears.

"Yeah, Tim, why are you here?" He was hoping for a good answer and he got it.

"O'Farrell—where's O'Farrell?" Costello was leading with his left, looking for a knockout punch. "Nobody's seen or heard from him. He's a loose cannon, Nolan, dangerous as all hell. Then you and your boys all of a sudden pay a surprise, concentrated visit to the south, and I smell trouble. I think maybe he's putting the heft on you. Over what, I don't know, but I'll tell you what I think. I think he killed Brigadier MacKenzie."

"Jesus Christ, Tim, who told you that?"

"Is it true?"

"As God is my witness, I don't know, but Tiernan thinks so. He's pissed to the gills with him and sent me here to do him in."

"Are you going to do it?"

"What choice have I got? It's him or me. I'm working on Tiernan's direct orders. He means what he says, you know that."

"I've never met or even seen the man—and not often heard his name."

"He'll shoot me or his mother or anybody else in the name of Ireland. Just for your information, the Garda's set up a roadblock right out of town. I'm praying to God they pick O'Farrell up, then I'll be off the hook."

"And if they don't, and he shows up here?"

"I'll have to kill him—offshore, in the boat or on Inishmurray."

There was an awkward silence. Costello had sparred enough. This time he led from the floor. An uppercup should take him out.

"I'll do it for you. You're right—O'Farrell's not to be trusted. I never liked the bloody bastard anyhow. I'll do it for you. Gimme your gun."

O'Rourke looked at Costello in amazement. "Tim, I can't believe this of you. You're a smart one, I'll say that for you, but this is a side of your nature I've never seen before. What's in it for you?"

"What's in it for me? I'll tell you. What I want is to run the 2nd Provo Brigade. I'm fookin' fair fed up with runnin' that goddam pub. You let me take care of O'Farrell and you have my word that I'll do just that. You run the Corkscrew— we'll work out the details later. Fitzsimmons can't run the bridgade. He's over the hill—so are you if the truth be known. Let me do it. I've got a lot of ideas, all good for Ireland. But right now we've got to put you out of business, so you'll have

3 6 6

somethin' that will hold up with Tiernan. Tell him I was drunk, tell him anything. Tell him I wanted to dispatch O'Farrell myself to show that I've got the stuff to run the bridgade. I'll answer to him gladly."

Suddenly O'Rourke realized that Costello was serious. His mind raced through the alternatives. Fitz would raise hell, but screw him. All else seemed to fit. Almost unconsciously he nodded his head. Costello knew all the lads. Why not?

"Well, Tim—okay. You're sure now?"

"Sure I'm sure. Come with me." He led the somewhat dazed O'Rourke into the storage shed. Inside he propped up his flashlight on a shelf so that its beam lit a portion of the floor.

"Sit down."

Obediently O'Rourke sat down on the oil-soaked planks between two drums of diesel fuel. All around him were the accoutrements of the sea, shelves full of cans and bottles of paints and lubricants, some years old, pieces of rope in various lengths and sizes, a torn oilskin slicker hanging forlornly from an oversized nail, pitch, tar, and kerosene, a usable wrench or two, a piece of a brass binnacle, and a solitary red-shaded lantern. Costello moved one of the drums to make more room for O'Rourke, then went to his pocket, coming out with a three-inch roll of medicinal adhesive tape—the kind holdup men carry to plaster over a victim's mouth during a bank heist.

"Hold still," said Costello. "Take off your shoes and socks."

Quickly and expertly he taped O'Rourke's bare ankles together so that they were securely bound. Then with a handy length of rope he tied O'Rourke's wrists together behind his back, tight enough so that to loosen them was impossible.

"Okay, Nolan, now comes the tough part. You'll be able to breathe, but no sound—not even a wee one—can you make. Necessary for the act that Tiernan is going to hear all about."

3 6 7

O'Rourke nodded, then asked, "You've told nobody else about this, have you now, Tim?" If he had any lingering doubts they came too late.

As Costello was about to gag him he answered, "Not a soul, man, not a soul. Easy now, Nolan. Here we go."

He stuffed a handkerchef from O'Rourke's pocket into his mouth, then closed it off with layers of tape, going all the way around his neck. When he was finished he stood back to inspect his handiwork, then pushed O'Rourke, who was still in a sitting position, to the floor. Satisfied with what he saw, Costello stood over him, the Roman gladiator waiting to hear from the chanting crowd in the Colosseum whether or not to kill his adversary. Then came the chilling words.

"You never were much for a fight, were you, Nolan? And that goes for November of 1950, when we had to fight our way out of Korea. I'll lay it out for you, just in case you've forgotten. The Duke of Wellington's Regiment, you and me, at the Chosin Reservoir. Christ, was it ever cold! The Duke of Wellington's Regiment and thousands of bloody fookin' Chinese. I got hit, I did, and Captain MacKenzie, God rest his soul, came to get me. You were to cover us, but you didn't. But somehow we all got out alive, thanks to Captain MacKenzie, who saved me fookin' life—something I've never forgotten. Middle age is a great disguise, and you never knew, did you? Somebody will find you here, but just remember—what goes around, comes around. Think about it, ex-Corporal O'Rourke. I've made some promises in me life, and I've just made one to you. O'Farrell ain't coming back from that boat ride and you can count on it. Ta-ta, brigade commander. Love and kisses from me and Captain MacKenzie."

Outside the first evidence of the breaking day was just appearing in a sky reluctant to let it in. To be sure that O'Rourke couldn't straighten up Costello eased the two heavy drums of diesel fuel closer to his upper body, wedging him into virtual immobility. As he left he threw a kiss to O'Rourke—

forcefully silenced and now paralyzed by what he had just heard. Sick with apprehension, the prone and bound man knew that the physical jam in which he found himself was nothing in comparison to what he faced when and if somebody turned him loose.

In the glare of the car's headlights the man appeared to be drunk, possessed by demons, wandering in the middle of the road. He wore suspenders over a turtleneck sweater to hold up his oversized trousers, and a mop of unruly black hair appeared in wild disarray beneath a battered derby hat. As Raven's car approached he assumed a gunman's stance, sans weapon.

"It's Mulligan," said O'Farrell. "Always the clown. He wants us to stop."

Raven pulled over. Sean Mulligan, twenty-four and six months out of Long Kesh prison, came to the driver's side of Raven's Jaguar sedan.

"The hat, Sean," said O'Farrell, leaning forward to talk around Mark. "Where'd that silly-looking hat come from? You look like something at the county fair. You know my friend Mr. Raven, here?"

"How do, Mr. Raven. I took it off me old man. It looks better on me than him, even when he's sober. Listen, there's bad news ahead—two Garda officers in a squad car, on the road into Mullaghmore, about half a mile beyond where you turn off. They're parked in the middle of the road and stoppin' everybody goin' in."

"How far into Mullaghmore from where they're stopping traffic?" asked Mark.

"Four, maybe five miles."

"Is the road wide enough to get by—even with their car parked in it?"

"Yeah, but they're armed, and would fookin' well love to have reason enough to come at us."

Mark looked up the road to where O'Rourke's car was parked. "Who's with you?" he asked.

"Paddy McGarvey—helluva wheel man, best in the business. Drive anything, anywhere, even a Saracen. We took one from the Brits, you know, last month at Norton's Cross Roads."

"I heard," said Mark. "Please get your friend."

When McGarvey arrived O'Farrell asked the two Provos, "You bring any heat with you?"

"Not me," said McGarvey. "I'm a driver, not a gun toter."

Mulligan looked uncomfortable. "O'Rourke told us to come empty-handed," he said, "but that ain't my style. I never go anywhere without my security blanket, so I'm packin' a solitary hand grenade hidden in me lunch pail. O'Rourke didn't know."

"Very good," observed Mark, who had been listening intently and planning strategy. "This is what we're going to do. The objective—the *only* objective—is to get O'Farrell to the dock. The Garda's looking for him, so we've got to get by them—and we can do it. Do what I tell you and we'll make it hands down, and you lads can get the hell out of here scot-free. And there's to be *no,* repeat, *no* bloodshed. Does everybody understand that? Okay—now listen up."

At the roadblock two Garda officers leaned against the front of their parked sedan, its shortwave receiver tuned to the transmitter at the Collooney barracks. Its volume was turned up high enough for its signal to be heard over their random conversation, but what they were hearing mostly was the crackling static that filled the recurring silences, effectively eliminated whenever transmission came on. Atop the sedan, amber and blue lights bracketing a white one circled endlessly, a sure sign of a police vehicle. The officers were alert, expecting at worst the possible apprehension of a car thief who might be armed—not the firestorm that was about to burst around them.

Two hundred yards short of where the Garda squad car was parked, just around a bend in the road, Raven stopped his car and turned to O'Farrell.

"Okay—now we execute. Stay on this side of the road; I'll stay on the right. I'll fire three times. When you hear the third shot, fire two sustained bursts from your rifle, toward the ground and away from the road. And remember, keep going until you're about twenty yards beyond the police car—and stay low."

"You're telling an ex-Marine how to take cover? Get lost, Raven."

"And you get moving. We're late now."

"I'm on my way." O'Farrell got out, rifle in hand. In seconds he was lost in the shadows and hedges that lined the road.

Mark turned his car sharply to the right and drove it across the road. In front of him, down a steep incline, was an outcropping of rock, waist high, and behind that a wooded copse running parallel to the road and separated from it by a barbed wire fence. He cut his motor, reached into the back for the can of kerosene, then went down the slope to the rock. In less than a minute he had doused the rock and the surrounding weeds and bushes with half of the contents of the five-gallon can. He returned to the car, positioned it on the incline so that it was headed directly for the rock, held in place by the hand brake. He sloshed the remains of the kerosene all over the inside and outside of the car, being sure that some of it covered the area around the fuel tank, after he had taken its cap off. He took out his .45 automatic, released its safety, then did the same with the hand brake on the car.

Slamming the front door, Mark gave the car a shove, sending it careening down the slope. It hit the outcropping squarely on just as he fired the first of his three shots, aiming directly at the fuel tank. The heat of the bullet did the trick.

WHOMP! The erupting fireball rose thirty feet in the air. Mark could feel the scorching heat as he skirted the inferno to crawl under the barbed wire fence and into the woods. Twice more he fired. From across the road, in the direction of Mullaghmore, the sound of semiautomatic gunfire in two staccato bursts erupted to violate the normal quiet of a September dawn in rural Ireland. Mark almost expected to see German SS troops come pouring down the road to reinforce the action.

Silently he left the sight of the raging fire and moved toward Mullaghmore.

Two hundred yards away the Garda was brought to maximum attention by the erupting gunfire, the explosion, and a flaming sky that looked like a reflection of hell.

"Mother Machree! What the fook is goin' on?"

"God knows, Jerry, but we gotta find out. Get in!"

"No! If ever I saw an ambush, this is one! Call the station, then we'll walk it up—nice n'easy. Leave the car here."

A minute later the report had been made. With guns drawn the officers moved cautiously in the direction of the wrecked and flaming car.

Using roadside hedges to full advantage, O'Farrell had worked his way past the Garda sedan with no risk of detection, easily running the last twenty yards as Jerry and his partner were headed in the opposite direction. No sign of Raven on the opposite side of the road. He judged it had been no more than two minutes since he had fired the second of the two bursts from his M-16. He felt the barrel. It was somewhere between warm and hot.

As the Garda got closer to the raging fire it was apparent that a major accident had occurred—cause unknown. They broke into a run, forgetting the gunfire, concerned with the possibility that someone might be in the burning wreckage. Fed by flammable liquids and the interior fittings of the car, the wreck and the area around it were burning fiercely as the two men reached the limits imposed by the intense heat.

"Jesus Christ!" exclaimed Jerry. "Anyone in there's a goner."

"You're bloody right, Jerry," his companion shouted, to make himself heard over the roar of the fire. "We'll have to wait until it burns itself out. Homicide, sure as hell!" He was thinking of the gunfire.

As they moved to the far side of the blaze for a better look, a car passed on the road above and behind them, lights off and unnoticed. McGarvey was the driver and Mulligan his passenger.

Another minute passed. O'Farrell was getting nervous. He could see a car coming from the direction of the blaze. It had to be McGarvey and Mulligan. Then he heard his name called.

"Mike—over here." The strained voice was Raven's. "I need a hand."

He crossed the road. Raven was leaning heavily on a sign reading MULLAGHMORE—3 MILES.

"My God, Mark, that car you just torched must have cost thirty grand," O'Farrell said. "I like your style, but why are you doing all this? I don't get it. You in trouble? What seems to be the matter?"

Before Mark could answer another violent explosion and more flames erupted to further disturb the early morning hours. Mulligan had pulled the pin on his grenade and tossed it into the open window of the Garda sedan as he and McGarvey passed. It disintegrated as if it had been a child's toy.

"I'm doing this for love—of Ireland," Mark was finally able to say. "To hell with the car—I need a new one anyhow." He looked down the road. "Here come the others. We've got to get going." He held out his hand for help.

What am I doing—getting a lift from a guy I'm trying to set up! What did Judas Iscariot do—kiss Jesus before betraying him? Whoa, Raven, back up. Your name's not Screwtape! There's no betrayal here. I'm just trying to bring a murderer to justice, to prove to Deirdre that I'm not a murderer myself. I wonder if I'm going to die? If I get out of this I'd better get back to San Francisco and Charlie Sanner—soon.

Despite the early morning chill Mark had broken into a cold sweat. The heart attack had hit him as he was moving in a crouching position in the woods past the Garda squad car. It had literally knocked him off his feet. Dropping to his hands and knees, he remained that way, gulping for air, trying to rid himself of the excruciating pain, which he first felt in the middle of his back. After a few gulps it seemed to lessen somewhat, but then came a numbness in his jaw as well as renewed pain down his left arm. More gulps, more pain. When he got to his feet he was lightheaded and had to call on every ounce of strength he could muster to get him to the roadside sign where O'Farrell found him.

McGarvey pulled up and stopped.

"How'd I do, Mr. Raven?" asked Mulligan. "Looked good to me."

"No time for that, Sean," said O'Farrell. "The guy's hurting. Give me a hand." Raven was leaning on O'Farrell, with his arm around his neck.

Hurriedly they got Raven into the car and headed for Mullaghmore as the two Garda officers raced back to what had once been their squad car.

INISHMURRAY
THE RENDEZVOUS
20 SEPTEMBER 1979

To an alert Costello the two widely separated noises that broke the early morning stillness shrouding Mullaghmore's stone-flanked harbor seemed almost simultaneous. From a distance came the ominous sound of an explosion, then another, punctuated by gunfire. It had to come from the road leading into the village. When silence returned, he was straining to hear what might follow when the welcome sound of a diesel-powered boat, out of sight but surely approaching the box-shaped breakwater, infiltrated his consciousness. *Wee Eddie! Thank God!*

He started down the planked pier toward the opening to the bay when a car pulled into the parking lot. There were voices, concerned voices, overly loud, then someone called O'Rourke's name. He turned and hurried back to the steps.

In the parking lot O'Farrell and Sean Mulligan got Raven out of the car. He was still sweating but the pain had lessened. He knew he was in trouble, but didn't know the extent of it. O'Farrell was holding him on one side and Sean Mulligan on the other. At the top of the steps they stopped.

" 'And how can man die better than facing fearful odds,' " said Mark to no one in particular, " 'For the ashes of his fathers, and the temples of his gods?' "

"What's that supposed to mean?" O'Farrell was puzzled. Mulligan acted as if he had heard nothing.

"That's poetry I once quoted in some book or other. It's by Macauley. It means we've got to get you to the boat, Mike. The boat's the important thing. We must be almost there."

3 7 5

"Right at the foot of the steps, Mr. Raven." It was Costello. "Tim Costello here. Glad to make your acquaintance. You're almost there. What's the trouble?" He was sure he knew and was afraid of the answer.

"We had a shoot-out at the O.K. Corral," replied O'Farrell. "Raven got us through it. No one's hurt, but I think the guy's had a heart attack. He says if he can get to the boat and stretch out he'll be okay. What the hell are you doing here, Tim? And where's O'Rourke?"

"He decided to go to the island with the unloadin' gang. I'm here in his place. You spooked Fitz so much he decided to stay home."

"What are we going to do with Raven? He says he wants to come with us, but the guy's in real bad shape."

"We're gonna take him with us. The Garda's gonna be swarmin' all over this place in no time, with maybe a bit of shootin'—at us, if we don't get the hell out of here. If we left him here they'd give him no mind, except perhaps to arrest him. No, he's better off with us. The sub's gotta have docs on it, and they can do for him."

Costello looked at Mulligan carrying the M-16 in his free hand. "You and your buddy better take off," he said. "Go up to the other end of town. You'll find my car there—a black Cortina sedan. Lie low until the cops come down to the quay, then you can slip away. And take the semi with you. You may need it." He handed Mulligan his keys.

Raven, who had been slipping in and out of consciousness, had heard most of the conversation. "Tim," he was able to say, "stuck in my belt is a Colt .45. Take it." Then as a mumbled afterthought, "Two shots left."

Before Costello had a chance to respond O'Farrell had reached around and taken the automatic.

"I got it, Mark," he said. Then to Costello, "Tim, you and I'll get him on the boat. Sean, you and McGarvey beat it."

Bloody hell! thought Costello. *I get rid of one gun and O'Farrell gets another! How am I goin' to handle this?*

Two minutes later Costello and O'Farrell had helped Mark to the bottom of the steps. He could walk but it was heavy going.

"Stop here a minute, Mike," said Costello, "I've got somethin' to tell you."

"Okay, but you'd better make it fast." O'Farrell was looking for the Garda any minute. After the bombing of the squad car, they might even come in by chopper. What he heard blew his mind.

"Eddie McKenna—Wee Eddie—is a snitch. That baby-faced bastard's been shootin' his mouth off to the cops."

"Go to hell! You sure?"

"Sure I'm sure. Otherwise how come they were waitin' for you on the road in?"

"Son of a bitch! I'll blow him away!"

"No. Let me handle it. You do that and you'll be in big trouble with O'Rourke and the Man. He likes to give the orders, you know. I've got a better idea."

"Which is?"

"Leave it to me—and keep your mouth shut."

"Mr. Raven, can you hear me? Do you understand what I'm sayin'?" Costello was leaning over Mark, who was stretched out on what was left of a thin mattress on the stern deck of the *Ballintra Lassie,* covered by an equally thin blanket. The fore cabin from which these remnants had been taken had long since been given over to Eddie McKenna's principal livelihood as a lobsterman.

Mark's voice sounded stronger as he raised his head and answered, "Yes, I can hear you. I take it we're on the boat and headed out. That's good. Is there any liquor on board? I'd like to have a drink."

"Wee Eddie?" The question was passed to McKenna, who—by nodding and pointing in the direction of the cabin—passed it to O'Farrell.

"In a boot in the port locker, Mike. A bottle of Jameson's. Be a good lad and get it, will you? I've got to adjust the bow light."

The lockers were at the far end of the cabin. *I'll have a slug myself,* thought O'Farrell as he rummaged around for the bottle. *I need it just as much as Raven.*

Costello watched as O'Farrell disappeared into the cabin, flashlight in hand. He lowered his voice and, fighting the competition of a noisy engine, seized the chance to tell Mark about Deirdre.

"I'm glad you're feelin' better, Mr. Raven, and what I'm about to tell you should make you feel better still. Mrs. O'Brien came to see me at the Corkscrew—yes, she did, that lovely lady. Right now I'm actin' as her messenger, because she asked me to tell you all this. She knows about the money. We talked for a long time. She knows about the money and says she made a terrible mistake in misjudgin' you. 'Tell him I love him,' she said, and 'I'm waitin' for him back at Raven Park.' She's havin' a baby, Mr. Raven—yours. She sent me here to be sure you knew. You can't die on me, Mr. Raven—I promised her I wouldn't let it happen. She says the three of you can build a better Ireland."

Mark was sitting up, leaning back against the cabin bulkhead. No longer sweating, he felt cold as he groped for understanding. *Thank God,* he thought. *Thank God! Lindsay must have come through—and just in time.* Then it dawned on him that Costello had said something about a baby. His mind had been so focused on forgiveness that he almost missed it.

"What about a baby, Tim? What did Mrs. O'Brien say?"

"She's havin' one, Mr. Raven—yours, and she's very happy about it. Ain't that grand? Here's O'Farrell with the whiskey. I'll join you to toast the happy occasion."

Even in his weakened condition Mark's spirits soared. But now Deirdre needed him more than he needed her. She was unprotected and vulnerable to scandal. He'd have to get back to her on the double. He tried to get up but fell back, exhausted.

"That's wonderful news, Tim," he managed to say, "and I'm grateful to you for coming to tell me. When we get ashore, I'll get you to drive me back to Raven Park."

You ain't going ashore, Raven, or any place else! O'Farrell, flashlight out and with bottle in hand, had come back within earshot. There was something in that interplay, some hint that rekindled the fires of suspicion that had been smouldering for a long time. "She knows about the money . . . She knows about the money and says she made a terrible mistake in misjudging you." The words kept echoing through his mind. All at once their true meaning hit him like a rock. *Peaceful Means was feeding money through Mark to the Provos. Purpose—to get rid of him, O'Farrell! Talk about hypocrisy!* Any doubts in O'Farrell's mind as to the truth of his conclusion disappeared as Costello acted to reduce the odds against him.

Costello was at the wheel as Wee Eddie returned from adjusting the bow light. As he stepped down to the stern deck Costello saw his chance. *Two against one. That'll never do.* They were opposite the slab-sided rocks at Bishops Point, over the lobster pots where the *Shadow V* had exploded, killing Lord Mountbatten.

Wee Eddie was standing close to the port gunwhale, no higher than his knee.

"Can you swim, Wee Eddie?" asked Costello offhandedly.

"Enough. Why do you ask?"

"I've often heard that men who make their livin' from the sea seldom know how. So if you really can swim, show us!"

Wee Eddie McKenna went overboard without another word as Costello pushed him—hard. Taken entirely by surprise, he was fifteen feet behind the slowly moving boat as Costello called out to him.

"You can make it, Eddie! I hope the water's not too cold. Strike out for the buoy if you think you're goin' under."

Wee Eddie was still sputtering and speechless as Costello gave the boat more power. The diesel cleared its throat and rumbled into action as the *Ballintra Lassie* sped toward Inishmurray. Seconds later there was a howl of outrage as McKenna took Costello's advice and headed for the buoy.

"See what I mean, Mike?" said Costello. "Just as easy to give him a bath as to fill him full of lead. And if he opens his mouth any further O'Rourke and that other man in Belfast will break his leg—literally."

"Yeah, I see what you mean," replied O'Farrell. His mood had turned ugly and he had Mark's automatic in his hand. "But I'm not buying your line of bullshit any longer. I see it all now."

He turned to face Mark, still sitting on the deck leaning against the bulkhead, then spoke directly to him, eyes ablaze with anger.

"I took MacKenzie out and now it's your turn. I know what you've been doing, you and that O'Brien woman—plotting against the Provos. The plan is to get you out of Ireland before you're lifted as an accessory to murder, isn't it? And then get rid of me before I can blow the whistle on you. Moreover we think you've been talking to Scotland Yard. Chief Superintendent Fereyes was seen leaving that fancy club of yours the night of Mountbatten's funeral. MacKenzie and his gimpy assistant, that horse's ass Lindsay, were there too. What were you doing? Cutting a deal about the arms, or laying some kind of trap? But it didn't work, did it, Mark? Remember I once told you, 'Once in, never out'? It's a bloody fucking shame you couldn't remember that. Now we've got enough muscle to blow the whole goddam British army out of Northern Ireland. A hundred thousand pounds you gave us, so we could bring in the arms that are offshore now. The great writer of best sellers financing the IRA! How's that going to sound when it hits the papers? Should I thank you again for this generous gesture? Maybe so, Mr. Raven, but I'm going to kill you instead. No wonder you torched a car that cost a bundle—you didn't expect to come back, did you? So now, lover boy, you're going to get yours."

Costello was thinking fast. *O'Farrell, the bugger, must have heard me!* Things were unraveling, right and left. Two bullets left in Mark's automatic. He had to get it back from O'Farrell—for Brigadier MacKenzie, murdered by the man in front of him. But better still for Deirdre O'Brien, who daily spoke her mind, flinging defiance in the teeth of the IRA, to keep his promise to her that nothing would happen to Mark.

"You shouldn't have killed MacKenzie, laddie, you shouldn't have done it. Now you're in the soup, and you're goin' to the Scrubs." He shouted, for effect as much as to make himself heard.

"Like hell I am. You crazy?" was O'Farrell's retort. "I'm going to Moscow. I'm going on the Russian sub that's bringing in the arms—but not before I blow away this son of a bitch." He waved the gun in the direction of Mark.

"No, Lee," replied Costello, "you're not. I've given my word to the wee lassie, Mrs. O'Brien, that no harm's to come to him, but speaking of Moscow, I fancy you'll be better off there than back in Belfast. Nolan O'Rourke and the other lads in the 2nd Brigade are very upset with you."

"Lee?" O'Farrell caught his breath. "Why did you call me Lee?" He was trying to be calm.

"Liam Francis McCarthy, called Lee for short. Born in Queens, New York City, 17 June 1950." Costello was looking right at him. "And I'd put that gun down if I were you. Thrown out of college for takin' drugs. Former pro football player—was it the Los Angeles Rams? Vietnam veteran, then active in COMMEND in New York. Wanted for murder in Rhode Island—"

"God damn you, Costello. What are you, a bloody informer? I'll kill you too."

Distracted, O'Farrell had taken his eyes off Mark and had turned to face Costello. As he did so consciousness momentarily surfaced in Mark. The chill in the predawn air made him shiver as his eyes slowly opened. There was no emotion, no anger in him now, only a kind of subliminal awareness that he had to get O'Farrell to the submarine. Old buried instincts took over. His strength seemed to flow again and he rose to his feet, his movements dreamlike and lethargic. It was as if an old dancer, his legs gone, had been called out for a brief nostalgic cameo as a reminder of another age.

He could hear the sound of the sea and once again he was back in enemy territory. He wondered if he had buried his parachute and how far he was from the coast. But he had to get moving. He'd contact his maquis and before nightfall another bridge would have been blown, more trees felled across roads, and more Nazi throats slit. But the fog—strange, he had never seen it before in this area. An indistinct figure loomed in front of him and he raised his hand, half in defense, half in greeting.

Then suddenly—clarity. The figure was O'Farrell, pointing a gun at Costello. In a reflex action and with his last ounce of strength Mark kicked O'Farrell squarely in the crotch, his foot coming up between O'Farrell's legs. The blow landed just where it should have. Screaming with pain, O'Farrell stumbled, almost going overboard. He turned and fired at Mark, point-blank.

With Mark reality had faded as quickly as it had arrived, and voices from his childhood came tumbling through what consciousness he had left. *Hosanna in excelsis! Benedictus qui venit in nomine Domini!* Then once more the pain, worse than before, searing and pervasive. He clutched his chest and tried to call out to Costello, but there was no breath, no voice. Once more he tried—this time to Deirdre. And then he began spinning abruptly into space, into darkness and then into light, and everything grew silent.

An infinitesimal fraction of a second later O'Farrell's bullet tore into his heart, severing the aorta from its muscle complex at the top of the juncture of the right and left ventricles. Mark's body fell to its knees, then forward. Mark had felt nothing; he had lost consciousness and death had taken him a millisecond before, a massive heart attack brought on by the stress and exertion of the last few hours. To those who saw him die, however, the evidence was clear. O'Farrell had shot him. The findings of an autopsy were the same; the bullet had blown away any evidence of an occlusion. The verdict—murder.

As the sound of O'Farrell's blast faded Costello looked up to see that the submarine was less than two hundred yards away, its sail a black monolith, a protuberance from the body of a sea serpent, against which the waters of Sligo Bay were beginning to lap from the freshening wind. From the top of the sail a rifleman with a telescopic sight attached to his weapon was aiming in his direction. Next to him stood someone with a loudhailer in his hand. From the lee side of the submarine, fore and aft, rubber dinghies appeared, four men in each.

The bloody bastard's got one shot left! Heading straight for the black tower ahead of him, Costello gave the engine full throttle, then thrust the *Ballintra Lassie* into a violent turn to starboard. With the control of the boat in his hands he knew he had a more effective weapon than O'Farrell's remaining single shot. The boat's quick acceleration and its abrupt change of direction threw O'Farrell to the deck. He fell toward Costello, almost on top of Mark, dropping the gun in front of him. Costello grabbed it, then kicked O'Farrell as hard as he could in the jaw, snapping his head back.

"So one murder's not enough for you," said Costello, raising the gun. "Stand back or I'll put a hole in you that you'll not soon forget."

O'Farrell had struggled to his feet, unsteady but threatening. His breath was coming in shudders and his hands were beginning to shake convulsively. The pain in his groin was intense.

"Not bloody likely you won't!" O'Farrell's eyes were full of hatred. "You haven't got the guts. That's why you pushed Wee Eddie overboard—you couldn't bring yourself to kill him. I'm coming at you, you goddam turncoat."

The PM wants him alive, not dead! Lindsay's words were uppermost in Costello's mind as he aimed and fired. He wanted to hit him in the right shoulder but caught him in the arm instead, shattering his elbow. O'Farrell could take only one more step before he dropped, contorted with pain. Costello looked at the automatic. It was empty, the slide locked back on a dry clip. *And a good thing too. Otherwise I'd be tempted to shoot the son of a bitch again.*

Atop the sail on HMS *Taurus* Captain Wiggins cursed. What now? With a hand-held radio he signaled the chopper.

"*Taurus* to AF-5. Troopers, prepare to drop on the boat. Three men aboard instead of the two expected. Somebody's shooting. Two men appear to be down. Situation unclear. Approach with extreme caution. Over."

Instantly the answer crackled back. "Roger that, *Taurus.* We execute. Over."

Each word was an effort but despite the pain O'Farrell was able to say, "Costello, you miserable shit, the Russians will deal with you, and if they don't O'Rourke will. You goddam pig shit Irishman, I hate all of you!"

"Lee," said Costello, calmly, "I'd be real offended if I didn't know that you're as Irish as Paddy's pig yourself, maybe more so. For what's more Irish than O'Farrell? What else but McCarthy, particularly when it's for real? Where'd your people come from before they got tainted with all that Yankee money? But I've got some news for you. There aren't any Russians and there isn't any Russian submarine. What you see here is courtesy of the British navy and my guess is that you're goin' to get a real warm welcome aboard." Costello had cut the motor and the *Ballintra Lassie* was drifting aimlessly.

As he spoke there was a thump as one of the paratroopers, encased top to bottom in a wet suit, hit the foredeck. With perfect timing he had flipped the release mechanism on his parachute, which billowed over the side. His boyish face was at odds with the rest of his equipment, particularly the Uzi with which he covered Costello and the two inert forms that confronted him. Almost at once there was a splash to port as another paratrooper hit the water, close enough to grab the side of the boat as he went in.

"Stand easy, mate," said Costello to the trooper who had him covered. "Don't get itchy fingers. All the shootin's over. Here." He held out the automatic. "This one's empty and there ain't another gun on board."

Minutes later Costello had restarted the motor and had brought the *Ballintra Lassie* close to the concave side of HMS *Taurus,* where it was held by temporary lines.

Captain Wiggins was on the slatted deck, down from the sail bridge. "What have we here?" he asked. He was not pleased by what he saw.

"One dead, captain," replied Costello, "and one for Wormwood Scrubs. Both Yanks—the former an honorable gentleman and the latter a bloody murderer." He staggered slightly as the boat rocked, caught his breath, then looked down at both inert forms. "If I had me druthers, I'd make it the other way around."

"And who might you be?"

"I might be Leonid Brezhnev, but no such good luck. What you see is what you get, with some Provo mischief thrown in." His manner embraced the jocular familiarity used by those whose lives skirt the edges of danger. "No disrespect, Captain, none at all. I'm Tim Costello, Her Majesty's faithful subject and an agent runner for MI-5. Timothy Tribett Costello, comin' in from the cold and goin' home to Blighty, as me old man was fond of sayin'. You got a hot cuppa on this floatin' bathtub? But begorrah, I haven't yet said the magic word, have I? How does Pleiades strike you?"

The words, so unexpected, came just as Captain Wiggins was motioning to two of his own crewmen to go to O'Farrell's aid. Sullen and dispirited, O'Farrell continued to clutch his right elbow with his left hand, crimson and sticky from his own blood, crying out in pain as the two sailors struggled to get him to his feet. The veins in his neck showed as clearly as the last strands of spaghetti on a plate, and in his frantic, bulging eyes was the glint of fear. It was a long time coming, but all at once, O'Farrell knew. *Christ! These are the Brits! They've got me!* Then came the cry, a banshee's wail of frustration and defeat.

"**A**ttention all hands, this is the captain. We are under orders to return to HMS *Neptune* at maximum safe speed. Our course will be east by northeast to the North Channel, then into the Irish Sea. Transit time will be twenty-two hours, and depth will be restricted to two hundred feet. Liberty orders will be issued upon arrival. I am going to recommend the ship's company for a unit citation, and there will be individual citations as well. Special rations in the mess, beginning on the next watch. Prepare for maneuvering. That is all."

The base chaplain at HMS *Neptune* had radioed instructions as to the proper prayers to read over Mark's body. In accordance with navy custom it had been sewn in canvas and covered with the Union Jack, then put in cold storage. McCarthy was in the brig under guard after pain killers had been administered, his wound dressed, and a temporary splint put on his arm.

While Wiggins was trying to keep ahead of the signals pouring into the communications center and to prepare himself, Castlewood, and Bochenkev for the swarm of officials—naval, legal, intelligence, and police—with which HMS *Taurus* would be met upon its arrival, a yeoman interrupted him with a priority message. He read it in silence, then hurried to the wardroom where he found Costello watching a video replay of *Star Trek*.

"Mr. Costello," he said, "a priority signal has just come through from fleet headquarters, relayed from Whitehall. It tells us that a suspected IRA man called O'Rourke was found by the Garda in a storage shed, bound and gagged. While they were releasing him he tried to make a run for it and was shot and killed. The signal specified that you be told. You are also requested to reply at once as to the whereabouts and security of a man whose code name is O'Ryan."

Sweet Jesus! With this unexpected news it all came together for Costello, the data registering in his mind like numbers in a computer. Fitzsimmons sidelined by O'Farrell, and Wee Eddie saved from possible harm at the hands of O'Farrell only by his own intervention! And now O'Rourke had bought it at the hands of the Garda. Mark Raven gone too, murdered in plain sight of the British. He could never go back to Belfast—McCarthy in prison would see to that, although McCarthy knew him only as Costello—but otherwise he was safe, and with him the secrets of his double life. Moreover the speed with which this latest news had reached the British made it crystal clear that MI-5 had a backup man—or woman, how was he to know?—on the scene. *That MacKenzie! That tough old Scot was reaching out from beyond the grave.* For the first time since the frozen hell of Korea he felt that his debt was paid in full. He looked up at Captain Wiggins.

"Beggin' your pardon, Captain," he said, "no disrespect but I need a little sustenance. Forgive me while I take care of that need, then I'll be answerin' your questions." He shoved the tea cup on the table in the direction of the mess attendant standing by with a teapot. "I'll be havin' another cuppa, mate, if you have a wee drop left."

Wiggins waited while Costello took a sip, savored it, and put the cup down. Then he settled back in his chair, and raising the cup as if in a toast, said, "My compliments on the tea, Captain. Now, sir, if you please, tell 'em O'Ryan is here—here and secure. In from the cold he is, thanks be to Jay-sus. In from the cold and gettin' warmer all the time, thanks to this lovely ship and to this lovely cuppa tea."

He smiled, then moved the cup and its steaming contents to his lips for another warming draft.

It was close to dusk as the car emerged from the woods, moving speedily up the lane to the graveled forecourt. It stopped at the foot of the shallow stairs leading up to the front terrace of what was now the Raven Park School. Peter Lindsay and three young children, two boys and a girl, got out. They had been fishing.

One of the boys was eight years old and black-haired. His name was Michael Raven and he looked for all the world like a young Spaniard. The other boy was a red-headed nine-year-old, an orphaned Protestant. The girl, eleven, was the child of a widowed Catholic mother whose husband had been killed in a Protestant ambush in Londonderry two years earlier.

To all outward appearances Raven Park and its surrounding acres had not changed much in the years since Mark Raven's death. A rugby football field laid out on the left of the road was used intermittently by the children in the school to play that and other games. There were in fact other changes, but they were at the back of the house itself, out of sight as one approached it. The most radical was a two-story frame addition containing eighteen bedrooms, nine to a floor, with communal bathrooms on each, to house the orphaned children or those from the poorer families of Northern Ireland whom Deirdre and her small coterie of devoted teachers recruited for at least two years of a free education. She had founded the school with her inheritance of much of Mark's estate and the continuing royalties from his books. Almost equally divided between

Catholic and Protestant families, the children were exposed not only to first-class schooling but, more importantly, they were immersed in an atmosphere calculated to teach respect for the views of the others and how to live with them in harmony.

Tim Costello, who had become a jack-of-all-trades maintenance man, general all-around friend to the children, and butler whenever there were guests, came down the steps to help them unload their gear. Three trout, none less than two and a half pounds, were held up in childish glee.

"Beggin' yer pardon, Major," said Tim, "but Mrs. Lindsay sends compliments, and she'd like to see you on the double. And if you're askin', I'd say the wee lass seemed to be in a high state of excitement."

When Peter entered Deirdre's office, once Mark's study, she got up from her desk to greet him, her face reflecting her anticipation of telling him her news.

"Peter darling! How did it go?"

"Three lovely rainbow trout—one each for Michael, Sean, and Nellie. I got skunked."

"I'm surprised. You're usually top rod. You must have been paying a lot of attention to the kids."

"I was—but that's as much fun as catching fish. Out of the generosity of our hearts, we are contributing them to everybody else for breakfast. I told Tim to turn them over to the cook. What's up?"

"You'll never guess, so I'll tell you. I've had two calls while you were out, the first from Dr. Charles Sanner, Mark's old friend from San Francisco. He was in Dublin when he called, but was leaving shortly to drive up here. Like you and Michael he's mad on the subject of fishing, so you two can take him in tow. But more important, he is anxious to meet Michael and wants to see the school. He was Mark's closest friend as well as his doctor, and in a sense blames himself for

Mark's death." Deirdre stopped, shook her head as if in disbelief, then continued. "We've got to get him over that.

"The second call—and this one nearly bowled me over—was from a man named Owen Newcombe in New York. He was Mark's literary agent. I've known about him for years, but never talked with him before. It seems that the day before Mark died he sent Newcombe some pretty sketchy notes, but accompanied by a complete outline, of a new novel that Mark called *The Tides of Sligo*. Newcombe was very keen on it, but did nothing due to Mark's death. Now it seems that one of Newcombe's good contacts in Hollywood called to ask him if he had any kind of a script on Ireland and the current troubles. Newcombe said yes but he'd have to call him back. To make a long story short the Hollywood chap said if it were Mark's and if he could advertise it as such, he'd take it in any form, for two hundred and fifty thousand dollars. Under the terms of Mark's will, the outline and all the notes are my property—hence the call from Newcombe. But that's not all. He's dispatched the outline and all the related material to me by express mail and wants us to write the ending, as he's fearful of what Hollywood scriptwriters will do to it. Newcombe says it's largely autobiographical, written almost as if Mark had a premonition of his own death."

"My God!" Peter exclaimed. "What a story! If it's done properly, and you can do it, it could be bigger than any of Mark's other novels."

"But do I want to do it?" answered Deirdre. "If so, you'll have to help me. You of all people know more about Mark's last days than anyone else."

Both were silent as they pondered the implications of Newcombe's suggestion.

"Do I want to do it?" she repeated. "My life with Mark, though incomplete, was very happy, and I want to do what would make him happy. Dear Lord, how I wish he could have known Michael! Perhaps he does, as I often feel his presence here strongly. Michael's only eight, but even at this early stage—no pun intended, Peter—he's told me he wants to be an actor. He's very aware of his inheritance, including the fact that he's named for his grandfather." She smiled in contemplation, then continued. "You know, I think he'll be a good one."

Deirdre went to the window and looked down, as if trying to see Michael. There were voices below—Tim and the children still talking. As she turned back, a car was just entering the far side of the front woods. Peter hugged her. She kissed him, then looked up again into the sensitive face of this warm, strong, and affectionate man.

"Once widowed and twice bereaved." she said, "I couldn't survive if I were to be left alone again. Every day of my life I thank God that you're out of the service completely, and that you're here with me and Michael. The Provos would have gone after you next, Peter, no doubt about it. Michael adores you, and like all boys he needs a father's guiding hand. He can have no absolute memories of his real father other than what we both can tell him and what he can read, which heaven knows is enough. I often catch him looking at the photograph of Prince Charles and Mrs. Thatcher and myself taken after the memorial service for Mark at the Guards' Chapel. You arranged that, Peter, and now I have you to bolster my life, full time. How can I have been so lucky?"

"Luck, like love, is blind, Deirdre. But how about my luck? In retrospect, I know I fell in love with you that day at the Crown when I came to tell you why and how Mark made that last contribution to COMMEND."

They looked at each other for a long moment. Her once beautiful hair was graying now, and she was heavier than she had been. But her eyes were still the same, large and violet and remarkably beautiful. Those eyes looked back at him now and they both were very still, remembering.

Until Michael burst into the room, bubbling with excitement. "Hey, guys!" he shouted. "A man named Dr. Charles Sanner has just arrived. He's downstairs. Says he was a friend of my father's and that he's come to Ireland to fish. Isn't that neat? Come on down and meet him." And with that he was gone.

Hand in hand they followed him, the spell unbroken.